Black Wings & STOLEN THINGS

USA TODAY BESTSELLING AUTHOR

KAYLEIGH KING

Cover Design: Cat Imb at TRC DESIGNS

Copy Editing: Rumi Khan

Paperback ISBN: 979-8-9863360-6-0

*For the ones who understand how
Persephone could fall in love with Hades.*

"I WOULD WRECK YOU, RUIN YOU COMPLETELY... SIMPLY BY SHOWING YOU THE RIGHT WAY TO BE PROPERLY LOVED."

-DirtySweetPoetry

BLURB

I've been called a lot of names.
Depraved. Monster. *Unhinged.*

I never thought I'd see the day someone called me *husband.*
Me? Have a wife? It's a terrible idea all around, but once I saw
her, there wasn't a chance in hell I was walking away.

Rionach Moran. The Irish mob's very own princess. So pretty
and poised, you'd never guess there's fire burning in her veins.
She keeps it hidden behind her reserved mask, but I can see it.

I see her.

My obsession was instant and all consuming. When her father
tried to marry her off to my enemy, I knew I had to act fast.

They think I've stolen my bride, but I know I've freed her.

A NOTE FROM THE AUTHOR

Black Wings & Stolen Things is a dark forced marriage romance. Due to the graphic and explicit adult content, it is recommended for readers who are 18+. If you would like a to check out the full list of TW/CW, you can find them on my website.

https://bit.ly/Kayleighkingtriggerwarninglist

Emeric Banes first made an appearance in **Golden Wings & Pretty Things**. Which was originally part of the Bully God Anthology (release date 2.22.22), and then was later released on its own on 5.27.22. In both books, there are very *loose* themes of Greek Mythology.

IMPORTANT: Emeric wants you to know he doesn't apologize and he definitely doesn't grovel.

·PLAYLIST

Listen Here: https://spoti.fi/3vTA1mY

If I Had A Heart – Fever Ray
From Persephone – Kiki Rockwell
Woman – Emmit Fenn
Take Me to Church - MILCK
Blood Sport – Sleep Token
Euclid – Sleep Token
Rain – Sleep Token
Fantasies – Llynks
House of the Rising Sun – Lauren O'Connell
Purify – Roniit
Seven Devils – Florence + The Machine
Night - Zola Jesus
Freak of Nature - BROODS (ft. Tove Lo)

PROLOGUE

EMERIC

New Year's Eve

I've been called a lot of different things in my time.

Insane. Cruel. Calculating. Monster. Depraved. Sociopath. Or my personal favorite, *unhinged*. All accurate to some degree. Never have I considered '*stalker*' to be an appropriate moniker for myself. That's largely due to the fact that my attention span is historically shorter than my temper and my tolerance for other human beings is basically nonexistent. Neither of those attributes create the right... *disposition* for a stalker.

And yet here I am.

I've followed her through the quiet hallways of the historic New York hotel and up to the roof with a silence and patience I don't recognize in myself. My normal course of action would be far less discreet. While I would just *loathe* to come across like a cocky asshole, I'm all but clapping myself on the back at the astonishing level of restraint I'm showing. Nova isn't going to believe this when I tell him. He'll probably think I'm fucking lying. Or *ill*.

She has no idea that I'm trailing behind her or that she's caught and held my attention for the past hour. It's no fault of her own that she's ensnared me for the night. It's not as if she went out of her way to prance around and draw eyes to her. No, unlike many of the empty-headed socialites and pompous cunts loitering around this so-called charity event, the auburn beauty that's currently slipping through the unlocked roof access door didn't so much as look in my direction all night. She walked amongst the partygoers like an apparition, keeping to the shadows and corners of the room.

It wasn't the well-practiced empty expression on her face or the way she tries to make herself seem smaller in an effort to remain unnoticeable that initially caught my gaze. It was the fire that burns in her jade-colored eyes that she doesn't hide but for some reason everyone seems oblivious to. That fire—*spark*—tells me her docile and passive persona is nothing but a façade. A ruse to make herself invisible amongst a room full of unbashful, attention-seeking whores.

Everyone else around us wants to be the center of attention, but she doesn't. And I want to know why she tries to make herself seem inconsequential when, with one look at her, I knew she could set the world aflame if given the opportunity.

She already has the fire inside her. She just needs someone to give her the gasoline so she can really blaze.

The good news for her is I've always had a proclivity for fire. It's gotten me in *and* out of trouble more times than I can count. Being burned has never scared me either. If anything, the dancing flames excite me, and I'd bet my bank account this girl would feel the same way.

This isn't the first time she's caught my eye. The first time I watched her was years ago when she was barely a legal adult, and back then the flames I'm currently fixating on were missing from her.

It was at a political fundraiser and her parents had been there trying to schmooze their way into the governor's pocket. Their daughter had stood beside them, conversing with some of the most powerful people in the city with surprising ease. So pretty and poised. I was impressed with her ability to hold her own, but what kept my attention lingering on her was the way the perfect mask fell and the light in her eyes dimmed when she turned away from the group. How she'd peeked over her shoulder at her parents, as if she were silently begging them to acknowledge her. To just *look* once at her before she left. I watched, waiting for them to do just that, but they never did.

Tonight, nearly six years later, she's grown up and the longing on her face has been replaced with that well-rehearsed emptiness. What's changed in these past years for her to try and mold herself into something she's clearly not?

She is still oblivious to the fact that I'm following behind her. Part of me is angry she's not paying better attention to her surroundings. This insensible behavior is making her vulnerable. Doesn't she know there are monsters lurking around every corner in this town? And that the most volatile monster is currently hunting her as if she's his prey?

It's probably for the best that she doesn't know I'm here. I don't want to spook her before I've fully had a chance to take her in. The reputation I've cultivated for myself isn't one made of sunshine and rainbows, but of carnage and darkness. If she knew I was following behind her, I'm sure the fear that would seep from her pores would be suffocating, albeit *delicious*. Sane people with a strong desire to continue breathing go out of their way to stay off my radar. They know my temperament can change on a dime and without warning. Sometimes I have no idea how I'm going to react to a situation, but that's okay. I like to keep even myself on my toes. It makes life *exciting*.

Like now, I have no idea how I'm going to react once I finally have her cornered. Will I taunt her for a moment and then let her go? Perhaps I'll sink my teeth into her creamy flesh and allow myself a small taste before setting her free. One thing I know for a fact is that keeping her isn't an option. I don't keep my toys. Never have. I use them and break them, releasing them when I inevitably grow bored.

My hand slips between the metal door and the frame before it can slam shut behind her. I wait a beat before opening it again and stepping outside. It's windier up here, eighteen stories from the ground. The frigid winter New York air cuts through my three-piece black suit and chills me to the bone. She has to be freezing wearing nothing but that dark green silk dress. The thin straps leave her arms completely bare and the slit on the side that goes up to her mid-thigh leaves her long leg exposed.

My guess is that she's simply up here stealing a moment for herself away from her family.

Her family.

The thought of them has a smirk growing on my face. The Irish Moran clan. The name once held power. People respected them. But that was well over a decade ago and before I took over my family's empire. I'll admit, when I first started out, I made a show of destroying my competitors. All these years later, it's still one of my preferred hobbies. I've found it's just not as fun doing this job if people aren't pissed or shooting at you. In this world, if no one is trying to kill you, you're just doing it *wrong*.

After her grandfather kicked the bucket, her dad, Niall, donned the Irish crown. The unimpressive man is a walking joke. It's become one of my favorite pastimes to toy with him.

He's an easy target and the way his pudgy face turns red when he's angry makes me smile. The fear and control his family once had has slipped under his reign, and now they're getting sloppy and, quite frankly, desperate with their dealings. Niall is still clinging to whatever status he has left. Showing up at events like this one tonight is his desperate attempt to prove his family is still relevant. It's cute... in a pathetic kind of way.

Sticking to the shadows, I round the corner of the roof and stop dead in my tracks.

All my assumptions of what she could be doing up here go out the window when I notice her discarded heels on the gravel-covered ground and see her pulling herself up onto the roof's parapet wall. My heart seizes in my chest. It's a sensation I'm not accustomed to and one I don't quite understand, but something about watching her stand with surprising grace on the brick railing eighteen stories in the air has the organ constricting.

Did I follow her up here only to watch her fall?

My foot lifts off the ground to go to her, to stop her from doing something irreversible, but I freeze in place when the most breath-taking smile spreads across her face.

Arms spread wide at her sides and her face tilted up, Rionach Moran grins at the dark cloudy sky above her as if she's embracing an old friend. In this moment, I can't think of a single thing more alluring than the sight of her standing there, a curtain of dark red hair blowing around her shoulders and back.

Anyone else looming up this high would be shivering with fear, but she's coming alive. And suddenly I get it. I understand what she's doing up here. She didn't come here to end it all, to snuff out that fire simmering inside her. She came up here to let it blaze, to let the inferno free.

I recognize the look on her face as she holds her arms at her sides and tiptoes across the wall, her eyes looking over the edge, glancing at the earth many stories below her feet. It's a look I've felt grow across my face many times.

It's one of pure freedom.

People would call her crazy for standing up here like this, for finding pleasure in the danger, but I *get* it. I understand it— understand what she's *craving*. There's an addictive kind of freedom that comes when you give in to the fear. An intoxicating rush.

And then I know. I know what I'm meant to do with her. I know what she is to me. I've never been more sure of anything in my entire life.

She isn't a toy for me to break. She isn't a toy at all. She is so much more than that.

Rionach Moran's soul matches mine in a way she doesn't yet understand. How could she? These little stolen moments of danger are all she's been given her entire life. Her wildfire has been snuffed out by a family who doesn't *see* her. They refuse to. But I see her. I see the potential of everything she could be if simply given the chance.

Around us, the sky illuminates with fireworks, the city below celebrating the new year. They shine around her, outlining her lithe silhouette as she teeters on the edge. They reflect in her jade eyes as she looks at them with wonderment.

Don't worry, princess, you'll be free from that cage soon enough.

Rionach doesn't know it yet, but I'm going to steal her and she's going to be *mine*.

ONE
RIONACH

I WAS fifteen when I came to terms with the fact that I was never going to be the center of anyone's attention.

Second born *and* a girl.

Those are both traits that are deemed *undesirable* in my family's eyes. My parents' priority will always be my brother. He's the heir to the Moran family empire and their goddamn golden child. There isn't a single thing that Tiernan can do wrong. Doesn't matter what vile thing he does or says, my parents' rose-colored glasses will stay firmly in place when it comes to their deranged man-child of a son. I don't even want to talk about my mother's twisted relationship with him. If she could figure out a way to put him back into her womb, I'm pretty sure she'd do it. It's gross and makes family holidays fucking weird.

And then there's... *me*.

I got used to the blank look in my parents' eyes when they stared at me. More often than not, it felt more like they were staring straight *through* me rather than *at* me. As if I wasn't there at all.

For a long time, I fought hard for their attention. The twinge of pain in my chest from those blank stares caused me to act out. My infamous rebellious phase was short-lived and ended in disaster, but at the time I didn't care what kind of attention I was getting. Good or bad, attention was attention, and that's all I craved from them.

Looking back at my behavior, I'm embarrassed by my desperation. You shouldn't have to demand—beg for—attention from the people who are supposed to love you the most. It was a tough pill to swallow as a teenager, but as I've aged, the pain has faded and my *fuck you* attitude has grown.

I stopped begging for attention from my family—from *everyone*—and found a way to be okay with their bland stares and general disinterest in me. Like an actress playing a role, I can shift seamlessly into the silent, well-behaved mobster daughter. What they see is a pleasant smile but, in my mind, I'm flipping them all off and pounding against the invisible steel bars that imprison me in this life.

The true version of myself, the one who enjoys standing a little too close to train tracks and feels most alive in a room full of chaos is something I keep tucked away. Safely out of everyone's grasps. That side is for me and me alone. Even if there was someone who I could be myself with, I don't think I could ever trust them enough to not try and destroy that side of me. Or destroy that sacred wild part of my soul.

I'd be lying if I said protecting that piece of me wasn't a lonely task, but sometimes it's better to be lonely than to lose yourself completely.

These days, I've found ways to use everyone's indifference against them. It's become a game of sorts for me. *What can I get away with when no one is looking?* When you make yourself appear small, people assume you're not a threat. When you're not a threat, people don't pay attention to you, and when they don't pay attention to you, you can move around a room like a ghost.

When you're a ghost, you can get away with all kinds of shit.

The circles my family run in aren't exactly made up of the most *moral* people. Money and blood go hand in hand in this world. Their squeaky-clean exteriors and practiced *Colgate* smiles hide the absolute hellscape that makes up New York's most affluent families. Don't let the political fundraisers and charity events like this one tonight fool you. This is a ballroom full of mobsters, crooks, and liars. I'd even wager that the political figures mulling about are just as—if not more—corrupt as the organized crime leaders they're rubbing elbows with.

There isn't a single person here who wouldn't put a bullet in their grandmother's head if it meant they'd become a couple million dollars richer. It's been done too. You know how I know that? Because months ago, at an event just like this one, the governor's own wife had one too many glasses of champagne and basically admitted to doing just that so they could get her inheritance money. The women who stood around her giggled and waved her off as if she'd just told them the funniest story before casually moving on to the next tidbit of juicy gossip. *What the fuck, right?*

While the men are out running their family's empire, the women are sitting back and spilling secrets like it's their job. Add in some free-flowing alcohol and then their overfilled lips really start moving.

And I'm there, silent and unseen, but overhearing all kinds of sordid tales.

I hear secrets similar to this all the time when I play my game. Like a collector, I store them all safely away in my head. I truthfully have no intention of ever repeating them to anyone, but there's something about knowing I could take down some of the most important people in the city with a single email that makes my blood hum with excitement and power. After all, knowledge *is* power, and power is the only currency people give a damn about in this world.

Knowing I hold this kind of power over these people almost gives me the same feeling I get when I stand on roof railings and stare down at the yellow taxies a dozen stories below. *Almost.* Nothing can really compete with the adrenaline rush that runs through my veins when I'm faced with real danger—when I experience true fear.

Fear.

For most people, it has them sweating and shaking where they stand. The good ole fight-or-flight response kicks in, and their bodies go into self-preservation autopilot. They're going to face whatever is in front of them, or they're going to run for the hills so fast they leave burn marks in their wake. They'll pick the path with the highest chance of safety because who in their right mind would seek out danger?

Me.

I'm the girl who searches for danger like an addict looking for a fix. While fear shuts everyone else down, it makes me feel *alive*. My body fills with intoxicating adrenaline and my soul ignites. And it's those fast and fleeting moments when I feel like I can truly breathe. When I don't have to don my mask and pretend I'm the innocent Irish mob princess.

The waiter nods his head as I lift my third flute of champagne of the night off his tray. He appears to be having just about as much fun here as I am. Which means he would probably prefer to be *anywhere* else but here. A dentist appointment, a trip to the DMV, *a funeral...* all preferable over this charade.

Turning my back toward the rest of the room and conversing people, I stare at the wall decorated with framed pictures of the hotel throughout the years. Three mouthfuls later, my glass is empty, and the alcohol in my bloodstream is well on its way to making this night more tolerable.

I made it an hour at tonight's charity event before I weaved between the ostentatious partygoers and fled to the elevator. It lifted me to the eighteenth floor and the closer I got to the roof exit, the calmer I became. The weight on my chest lessoned and the second I slipped off my painful four-inch stilettos and climbed onto the roof's ledge, I took in my first real breath of the night.

Standing there with the biting cold against my skin and sky alive with the New Year's fireworks, I was free. Free to just be... *me* and to *breathe*. But it was a fleeting feeling, one I could only cling to for a moment before I had to climb down and reenter the festivities here in the brightly lit ballroom. It was only a matter of time before one of my father's goons realized I was gone and alerted him. After all, the people who are on my parents' payroll are the only ones who would have noticed I was missing, not my actual parents.

Which is ironic, seeing as for the entire car ride into the city, my parents droned on and on about being on our best behavior tonight and that we were to continue to uphold the appearance of the *"perfect"* family.

It's a joke, honestly, and I'm fighting a genuine grin at the thought of it when my mother's willowy frame appears at my side. With her is a shorter blonde woman who looks familiar, but I can't quite place her.

Mom's boney, cold hand lands on my shoulder, giving me a little squeeze, and her red-painted lips pull upward. Observers would probably look at this as a woman greeting her daughter with a comforting gesture. Imogen Moran is a lot of things—a skilled actress being at the top of that list—but *comforting* isn't one of them. The grip on my upper arm isn't a greeting, it's a warning. *Play your part, Rionach.*

My spine goes stiff and the rehearsed pleasant smile slips into place as I lock eyes with the unknown woman. Her hair has been bleached within an inch of its life and is slicked back into a low bun I can only describe as *severe*. My guess is she's around my mother's age, give or take a few years, but like the rest of the women in this room, she's against aging gracefully. She's clearly had a face lift at some point. The untouched skin of her neck gives that away, just like it gives away her true age. The lines that decorate the skin around her pursed lips are the only "flaw" I can spot on her face. My guess is she's been a smoker for most of her life. We all have a vice. Hers is nicotine and mine is dangling dangerously close to the roof's edge, so I'm not entirely in a position to judge.

She's pretty, but just like my mom, she can't hide the coldness in her eyes as she reaches her hand toward me in greeting.

"You remember Polina Koslov, don't you, Rionach?" Mom asks, her Irish accent strong as ever. She takes the empty glass from my hand and silently passes it to a waiter walking past our chummy little trio.

Nope. "Of course, I do." I shake Polina's hand and return her smile. "Your dress is lovely, Polina." The black-and-gold embroidered mess looks like a figure-hugging tablecloth, but what do I know about fashion?

Her cool blue gaze scans me from head to toe, no doubt searching for any imperfections. That's what women in these social circles do. They need things to talk about at their next get-togethers, after all.

"You as well, dear. Green is really your color."

I'm a pale Irish woman with dark auburn hair. Of course green is my color.

Releasing her hand, I run both my palms down the front of

12

my formfitting silk dress, trying to subtlety smooth out any of the wrinkles I may have gotten while up on the roof. I should really start picking dresses with more forgiving fabrics if I'm going to keep up with my escapades.

"Thank you, Polina."

Thank God Mom jumps back in before I have to talk about clothes any longer.

"Polina is Bogdan's mother. He was at the event this fall at the Aquarium—you know, the one for the charity for pediatric cancer... or was it for the homeless? I just can't keep these things straight. I swear, we're dressing up and writing checks every month." Polina joins in as they both laugh at Mom's tasteless joke. Meanwhile, I'm over here fighting for my life trying to not roll my eyes. "I do believe you danced with Bogdan then, Rionach. Tall. Blond. The one with the scar..." Realizing her mistake, Mom's words die out as her fake smile tightens. "*Charming*. He was very charming."

Nice recovery, Imogen. 2/5 stars.

Polina's perfect face tightens at Mom's slipup, but she doesn't acknowledge it further.

"Yes. My boy seemed to be very taken with you." Sharp, red-painted nails reach for me as her fingers twist a strand of my hair around them. My molars grind as I force myself to stand still. *Jesus, who is this lady?* This whole interaction feels weird. "He spoke so fondly of this hair of yours. Which was interesting, seeing as he's always shown a proclivity for blondes, but now that I'm seeing you up close, I find myself understanding his fascination."

I didn't remember who the hell Bogdan was until Mom mentioned the scar. *Scar* is a kind word for what cuts through the young Russian's face. He looks like he was mauled by a wild animal. It runs from his hairline to his collarbone, slicing right through his left eye. I'm truly not sure how he still has an eye there, never mind be able to see anything with it. The morbid curiosity side of me wanted to know what happened to him, but my self-preservation side, which has historically not been very vocal, screamed at me to keep my mouth shut.

It wasn't just the scar that was... off-putting. Everything about that man was off. The unwavering intensity in his gaze when he looked at me while leading me around the dance floor made the hair on the back of my neck stand on end. Dangerous things are attractive to me, they're like sinful little treats that feed my soul, but nothing was alluring about that man. The alarm bells were wailing. *Loudly.*

His mother's weird-ass demeanor is making me think his entire family is like that. Which is concerning, and begs the question: what the fuck is my mother doing with her, and why is she bringing up Bogdan *now?*

"How... flattering." *I mean, come on, what else am I supposed to say to that shit?* Keeping my soft smile firmly in place, I reach for her hand and take it between both of mine. The sharp edges of her diamond tennis bracelet scrape across my fingertips as I do. "He was a lovely dance partner, especially since I can't dance to save my life. Without him leading us, I'm positive I would have tripped over my own feet and landed on the floor. He probably saved me from embarrassing myself."

"Taking the lead," Polina muses, while something I can't place flashes in her cold eyes. "Yes, that does sound like him."

I glance briefly at my mom before squeezing Polina's hand once again. "I'm so sorry, but I'm afraid I need to go find the ladies' room. My couple glasses of champagne have caught up with me. It was lovely seeing you again, Polina."

There's no doubt in my mind I'll get a tongue-lashing from my mom on the drive home for leaving, but Mrs. Koslov is giving off 'the witch from *Hansel and Gretel*' vibes, and I don't know how to speak with her. Which is a rare challenge for me because, like I said, I've honed the perfect-daughter persona. I can talk to a senator about his plans and in the next breath, I can navigate a conversation with one of the criminals that run with my father. It takes a lot to stump me, and Polina Koslov has done just that.

Nodding my head at both women, I turn gracefully in my stilettos and make my way across the boisterous ballroom. It takes everything in me to fight against the triumphant upturn of my lips when my fingers tighten around my consolation prize.

They say diamonds are a girl's best friend, but I find I enjoy them so much more when they're stolen.

I have no use for a diamond tennis bracelet, and I have zero intentions of keeping it for myself. The thrill of simply taking it was all I wanted. Before you get any ideas, I'm not a kleptomaniac. I don't have a compulsive need to steal from people. Much like my trip to the rooftop earlier tonight, I just enjoy the adrenaline rush. Plus, I pawn everything I acquire and donate every dime to charities. People like Polina and my mother use these charity events to help their own images. They don't give a single fuck about the cause. By donating the money from my stolen goods to them, it makes me believe I'm evening the cosmic score in a way.

Is that sound reasoning? I don't know, you tell me.

Polina doesn't know it yet, but she'll technically be donating twice to tonight's charity group after I send them the funds I get for the bracelet I subtly hide in my cleavage.

I get my adrenaline rush and people in need get a little extra help.

It's a win-win for everyone... well, maybe not for Polina, but I think she'll be okay.

TWO
RIONACH

"O'Malley went to grab the car, sir," my father's head of security, Brayden, tells us as we wait for the attendant at the coat check. Similarly to Mom, Bray moved here from the motherland and his accent is just as thick as it was twenty years ago when he first stepped foot in America. "It should only be a few more minutes. I'm going to wait by the door. I'll come gather you when he pulls up."

Like my father, he has a stockier build. Unlike my father, he doesn't have a gut. His hair is shaved close to his head and the red beard that gives away his Irish heritage is longer but still well groomed. Although he's not a very vocal man and I can count on one hand how many times I've seen him smile, he's always been kind to me. Honestly, if I were ever in a bind and needed help, he's the one I'd call. My parents would be my last resort, and my brother... well, I would literally have to be dying to call that man and even then, dying may be the better alternative. Owing Tiernan a debt of any kind is the last thing I want.

My father barely acknowledges Bray as he leaves us, he's too busy muttering about something with Tiernan. I somehow managed to avoid both of them tonight and after my run-in with Polina, I never spoke to Mom again. That doesn't mean I didn't hear her. Her fake-as-hell laughter tends to echo.

All in all, tonight could have been worse. It was boring as hell but I wasn't trapped in any more awkward conversations and my father didn't try to introduce me to any potential future husbands.

Yeah... *husbands*.

I've never been naïve to what my future is going to be. As the daughter, I was never going to be groomed to take over the business like Tiernan has been. If anything, they go out of their way to keep me blind to that side of our family. That doesn't mean I don't have a tendency to eavesdrop. What can I say? Our house is older, and the air vents carry more voices than actual heat.

My only worth in this world I've been raised in is my last name and my womb. Both things that will be auctioned off to the highest bidder when the time comes. And that time is fast approaching. At twenty-four years old, I'm already considered old in some people's eyes. Most prefer to marry their girls off by eighteen. My mistake years ago granted me a few extra years of singlehood, but it's only a matter of time before they find a made man willing to overlook my *flaw*.

If it weren't for my mother's parents, I'm sure I would have been married off the day after I turned eighteen, but they insisted that I attend college before that happened. My grandfather is the boss back in Ireland and I'm fairly certain my father is scared of his in-laws. Every day I was at NYU, I sent a silent thank-you to my grandparents for stepping in and gifting me that small taste of independence.

Those short few years are the only true taste I'm going to be granted. After I'm married off, I'll trade in my innocent-mobster-daughter persona for a well-behaved-mobster-housewife one. If I don't want to bring shame upon my family and my husband, they'll expect me to fall pregnant within the first year of marriage.

Domesticity is a lot of women's dream; the picket fences, golden retrievers, and minivans full of giggling children the ultimate end goal.

It sounds like another cage to me.

The girl gives me a quick nod when she hands over my long black coat before disappearing back between the racks of other outerwear. I've barely turned away from her when the wool fabric is yanked from my fingers.

"I got it." Tiernan gives me his signature grin, the one that portrays something more sinister than genuine happiness, as he holds the coat out for me to easily slip into.

"I'm more than capable of putting on my own coat."

His brown eyes, the same color as our father's, darken and the corners of his mouth pull tighter. "I know, but I wanted to help."

I stare at him a second longer, debating if it's really worth fighting him on this before giving in and turning my back to him. You know how they tell you, you should never turn your back to a mountain lion? This feels similar to that.

I've seen firsthand what happens when he gets his claws in his prey, and it's not pretty. On more than one occasion, I've woken up from nightmares of that night. The night all my suspicions about my brother were confirmed in a very bloody way.

My body aches at the effort it takes to remain still and it's a true test of my willpower to not flinch when I feel his warm fingers trail against the skin of my neck. I stop breathing altogether when he gathers the long strands of my trapped hair and pulls it free from my collar.

His hands press into the top of my shoulders and his breath tickles my ear when he murmurs, "There you go."

"Thank you," I grind out, stepping forward two steps once his hands are off my body.

Tiernan wasn't always bad at respecting my personal space. Most of my childhood, it was a miracle if he even spoke to me. Something happened when I turned thirteen, though. Suddenly I couldn't be in a room with him without him finding some reason to touch me. Similar to the one a moment ago, they've all been seemingly innocent touches.

While my parents act like I'm invisible and don't look at me, Tiernan's calculating gaze is locked on me more often than I'd prefer. The dark look has sent chills down my spine for over a decade. He hasn't done anything to me that could be considered a problem, but everything in me tells me that he's thought about it... that it's only a matter of time before the voices in his mind win.

"Mom said she introduced you to the Koslov woman."

He shoves his hands into the pockets of his coat like he's trying to make himself appear casual. Something he's failing miserably at. It doesn't matter how he stands, the crazy radiating from him is practically tangible.

"She did," I nod, unsure where this is going, but I'm even more suspicious about the odd interaction with Polina earlier. Something is definitely going on and I don't enjoy being in the dark.

"What did you think of her?"

Oh yeah, I'm not falling into that trap, so I lie. "I spoke to her for only a moment, Tiernan. It wouldn't be fair of me to create an opinion on someone based on a passing conversation." My head cocks. "Don't you agree?"

I'm saved from having to continue this conversation when Bray shows back up and motions to my father for all of us to follow him to the exit. Loitering back a couple steps, I wait for Tiernan to walk ahead of me so I can continue to maintain the distance I'd established between us.

With my head down and eyes locked on the shiny marble floors of the hotel lobby, I silently follow behind them all. I've taken no more than five steps when I feel the hair on the back of my neck stand on end and my scalp tingle in awareness. It's a different sensation than the usual one I get when Tiernan is leering. It still sets my alarm bells off, telling me something dangerous is lurking within the crowd, but it's not the same kind of danger that my brother emanates. It's the kind of danger I relish... the kind I go out of my way to find. To be sure it isn't coming from him, I lift my gaze to my brother's back, but it never finds him because someone else is standing directly in my path.

One look at his alarmingly symmetrical face and I'm stuck frozen in place, the air sucked violently out of my lungs. His wavy hair is black, the kind of black that doesn't reflect light but absorbs it, and his eyes are the color of the sky when a thunderstorm is rolling in. Like bottled lightning, I swear there are glints of silver flashing within those orbs every time he blinks. The energy around his tall frame is just as magnetic and alive as the storm in his eyes. The air surrounding him is crackling with a wickedness that, if I were normal, I'm sure would scare me away.

I think we've already established I'm not normal and that I don't run away from fear, but toward it. Even to my detriment.

I know who he is. *Of course*, I know who he is. The entirety of New York knows who this man is, and if for some reason they don't, they know his name. His name is almost more notorious than he is. It's a name I've heard my father curse more often than I can count. It's whispered in fear across the city and beyond, and looking at him now, I have no doubt it's moaned just as often.

Emeric Banes is the human embodiment of sin itself.

Between parted lips, I suck in my first shuddering breath since being trapped in his crosshairs. Like a predator, his head cocks to the side as he leisurely examines me. My skin warms with the trail his eyes make. With my long coat on, I'm basically fully clothed, and yet he makes me feel as if I'm standing here naked.

The Banes family makes the other organized crime families look like amateurs. Like they're nothing more than hobby criminals. And that's all thanks to Emeric and his ruthlessness. He took what his ancestors made and built it into something more. His family's influence expands far past this city, and it's said they're even pulling strings in the government now. That's something that will never be confirmed, but with one look at this man now, I know it's true. Unadulterated power seeps from Emeric Banes's pores and I'm all but choking on it as I greedily breathe it in. There is no doubt in my mind his power has successfully slithered its way to Washington.

This isn't the first time I've been in the same room as him. No, like us, Banes is a frequent flyer at events similar to this one. No doubt trying to keep up the upstanding citizen façade like the rest of the crime families here. Through the years, I've caught glimpses of the infamous man before me, but never have I had the opportunity—the privilege—to inspect him as I am now.

Tall, dark, and oh-so fucking dangerous.

I should break this spell and walk away. If the red soles of my Louboutins would unglue themselves from the floor, I'd do just that... well, I think I would. My brain may be short-circuiting right now.

As if he can read my mind, the corner of Emeric's mouth

curls into a smirk and I swear my heart momentarily stops. *Wicked.* That's the only way to describe that smirk. It's a look that promises something I haven't yet figured out but somehow, I know it'd be my kind of fun. A type of fun I'd be an idiot to indulge in.

His dark brow lifts as if he's daring me to do something. Your guess is as good as mine about what that could be. There's a litany of things someone like Emeric could want from me and I'm not in a position to give him anything—no matter how tempting. I learned my lesson when I was eighteen about the consequences of allowing men to come near me. If I think hard enough about it, I can still feel the sting of my mother's palm against my cheek after they found me in that hotel room.

When my eyes narrow at him in challenge, his smirk only grows.

Trouble. Trouble. Trouble.

His Italian leather shoe lifts from the ground like he's decided if I'm not going to come to him, he's coming to me.

His other foot never gets the chance to move because a thunderous voice cuts through the constant droning of the patrons around us and echoes off the marble of the lobby.

"*Banes!*"

The sudden sound is loud and abrupt enough that it has everyone halting and the *Emeric Banes* spell I've fallen under breaking.

You know in movies when something terrible happens and everything starts to move in slow motion? I didn't think that was something that could happen in real life, but as a man emerges from the crowd with a dark hood pulled over his head and he lifts his arm, the silver gun in his hand gleaming, time slows to a crawl.

The screams of the people around me sound like they're miles away and I barely feel their bodies bump into mine as

23

they try to flee from the gunman. I should probably be following their lead by running, just like I *should* be feeling what they're feeling—that sickly nauseating kind of terror when faced with the possibility of death. But I'm not scared.

Just like *he's* not scared.

The cunning gleam in Emeric's eyes never falters. Not when he turns his head to meet the man head-on and not when the man pulls the trigger. He barely even blinks when a giant tattooed wall of muscle slams himself into the gunman's smaller frame and takes him to marble floor at the same time the gunshot pierces through the air.

The two men crumble to the ground at Emeric's feet with a violent thud.

Like a rubber band snapping, time returns to its normal pace. It's utter and complete chaos around me and my ears are now ringing from the gun going off less than ten feet from me. People are still shoving past me, but I'm a rock in a river, refusing to move from the spot I've been glued to for these long minutes.

Blood seeps from between Emeric's fingers as he presses them into the wound at his left shoulder. If the tattooed beast of a man hadn't jumped in when he had, Banes would probably be dead on the ground, his blood staining the shiny pristine floors.

Despite the gunshot wound in his shoulder, he's still the picture of calm as he gives orders to the tattooed man. By the look of respect on his face, I'm guessing his savior is part of his security detail. Whatever Emeric commanded the guy has him pulling the assailant off the ground and violently yanking him toward the exit. No doubt cops are on their way here as we speak, and there's not a chance in hell someone like Emeric Banes is going to allow the NYPD to deal with his attempted assassin. My guess is that guy doesn't last the night and will inevitably die by Banes's own hands.

Emeric watches them leave before turning his attention back to me. This time it's his turn to narrow his eyes, but he's not challenging me. No, he's looking at me like I'm something he's trying to figure out, as if I'm a puzzle he doesn't understand.

A figure in a dark suit steps in front of me, blocking my view of the most dangerous man in New York, and a hand clasps my shoulder.

"Rionach!" Brayden's bearded face is suddenly level with mine and concerned dark green eyes scan me wildly. When I don't immediately answer my father's head of security, he tries again, this time yelling my nickname loud enough to cut through the ringing in my ears. "Rio! Goddammit! Answer me. Are you okay?"

Blinking slowly once more, I shift my eyes to meet Brayden's.

My shoulders shrug under his tight hold. "Jesus, Bray, you don't have to yell. I'm fine. Why wouldn't I be? I obviously wasn't the target." I gesture casually behind him. "They already got the guy out of the building. Honestly, the whole thing was anticlimactic, but who knew a hooded gunman is all it'd take to make one of these fucking events more exciting." I give him a rare, genuine smile. "We should keep that in mind for the next one they decide to parade me around at. Could be a quick and easy way to leave early."

The long exhale that comes out of him as he shakes his head at me only makes me smile harder.

"I swear to God, you're going to be the reason I retire early."

Bray is probably the only person in my household I don't

have to watch what I say around. He knows the soft-spoken and innocent persona is nothing more than a mask.

"That's a dirty lie and you know it," I wave him off. "You'd miss me."

His only response is an unamused grunt as his arm comes around my shoulders and he ushers me toward the exit. With his wide frame out of my way, I instantly seek out the captivating man from before, but the only evidence that he was truly ever in this room with me are the bright red drops of blood on the white floors.

"Fucking Banes..." Bray growls as we pass the bloodstain.

I can't stop myself from asking, "Why would someone be dumb enough to try and kill him during a public event?"

The real question is, why would someone be dumb enough to try and kill him, period? You don't come after a man like Emeric unless you're one thousand percent certain you're going to be successful in killing him, because if he can still get up when you're done with him, you're going to wish you were dead.

"The path to the top doesn't come without making a few enemies, and if there's anything Emeric Banes does best... it's making enemies."

THREE
EMERIC

By the time I'd removed his fourth finger, my attempted assailant had lost consciousness.

Like a total pussy.

I was raised to endure an immeasurable amount of physical pain and psychological torment without making so much as a peep. Apparently, this weakling wasn't afforded the same training because the screams that had ripped from his throat when I first brought the tip of my knife's blade to his thumb were deafening. And embarrassing.

When the tears started falling down the Italian mafia capo's face, my earlier assumption that he had balls of steel went out the window. I'd been giving Rocco the benefit of the doubt before that. If someone is going to come after me and actually fire their fucking gun, I've got to assume they have some serious gumption. I'd be lying if I said I hadn't felt a morsel of respect for the man when I first entered this room. To not only attempt to kill me, but to do it publicly? I'd been impressed. But then he started boohooing like a baby and I was

27

proven wrong about the size of his balls. He isn't brave. He's an idiot driven by his anger and a foolish plan to *even the score.*

Whatever the fuck that means.

Apparently when I burned down Rocco's family restaurant, he made some silly vow to his ailing father that he would get revenge for what they lost. That's the rambling, tear- and snot-filled story I got before he went and ruined all my fun by passing out. It's just not as satisfying to dismember someone when they're unconscious. It sucks all the fun out of it.

What he forgot to mention when he was sobbing and blowing snot bubbles was the fact that he and his family had been warned—multiple times—what would happen to their precious restaurant if they didn't cease the operation they were running in the cellar. I went to Rocco's boss first, Cosimo, but the head of the Italian syndicate didn't heed my warning. Then we went directly to the source and they still thought they could run underage girls in their underground prostitution ring in *my* city. They want to profit off flesh? Fine. They can go forth and get their cocks wet however they want, but they better leave children the hell out of it.

I'm not known for giving people multiple chances, but for this man I did, and to thank me for my generosity, he put a fucking bullet in my shoulder.

Ungrateful prick.

"Your silence is making me itchy, Nova," I finally address the head-to-toe tattooed lumberjack of a man who's been wordlessly leaning against the metal door for the better part of an hour. He crawled out of some godforsaken mountain town in bumfuck nowhere Alaska, and somehow made it all the way to me here in New York. He's my second-in-command and one of the few people I trust. If I didn't think he'd punch me in the mouth for saying so, I'd go as far as to say he's my friend. "Is there something I can help you with?"

Behind me, he shifts on his booted feet as he sighs. I have no idea when he changed out of the suit he'd been forced to wear to the charity event last night, all I know is I'm still wearing mine and it's going straight in the trash when I'm finished here. Even if I could get the blood out of the white button-down, there's no fixing the goddamn bullet hole in the left arm.

"I'm just wondering when you're going to be done with your art project so I can look at that shoulder. Need to know if I need to call in the good doctor to take a look at it. You probably need antibiotics too."

"It was a through-and-through, a flesh wound," I grumble, picking up one of the ten fingers sitting on the table in front of me.

The only reason Rocco's bullet didn't do any serious damage is because Nova was being more vigilant than I was. While I'd been distracted by an ethereal redhead, Nova had been watching the crowd. I can't remember the last time I'd made a mistake like this one.

The fact that I managed to walk away with only a flesh wound is the reason I only cut off his fingers. If it'd been worse, I would have cut off something more... substantial, like his head, and sent *that* to Cosimo. By limiting it to only his fingers, the capo can still have an open casket at his funeral. I'm sure his family will appreciate that.

By my count, this is the second act of generosity I've shown this man.

Nova's footsteps echo in the mostly empty room made of steel and concrete as he moves closer to where I work.

"Jesus Christ, Banes."

To his credit, he doesn't sound surprised by what he's seeing, rather just resigned. Like he's sick of my shit and after putting up with me for the past fifteen years, I can't say I blame him. We've been through a lot since my older brother Astor abandoned ship and left the family empire in my safe and oh-so gentle hands. Nova has been the only person to stay by my side through it all and help as I've grown the business and made it into something my father could have only dreamed of achieving. I don't want to give that fuckface any credit for what I've built, but I'll admit a lot of what I've accomplished is due to the spite I have for that man. Resentment is a wonderful motivator, if you know how to harness it.

"What? Too much?"

"Is that an Edible Arrangements bouquet?"

I examine the bouquet made of fresh fruit, chocolate-dipped strawberries, and fingers in front of me. "Yeah, but I wouldn't recommend actually eating it. I think it became a lot less edible about five fingers ago." Each of Rocco's digits have been stuck on wooden skewers and arranged within the fruit. It looks very artistic, if I do say so myself.

His tattooed hand, which is covered in roses and all kinds of other unsentimental bullshit, lifts to his face as he pinches the bridge of his nose. "What are you going to do? Send that to Cosimo?"

"Yes." When he doesn't respond, I look away from the severed thumb I'd just placed between a piece of pineapple and cantaloupe. "What? Do you think I should send a mini muffin basket instead?"

Eyes, the same color as the frozen lakes from where he was born, narrow before he releases a long breath. "What are you going to do with him? Send the fingers and let Rocco return home once you're done playing with him? Or will the rest of his body be arriving in some other colorful fashion?"

With the last finger placed, I turn from the table and face where Rocco is bound in the lone chair. His body is slumped pitifully in the seat, head lolled all the way back and his mouth gaping like he's doing his best impression of a bottom feeder fish.

"What kind of message would I be sending if I allowed the man who put a bullet in me to live?"

I hold my bloodied hand out to my second-in-command, a silent order he knows well. Nova removes his Glock from the waistband of his worn jeans and hands it to me. Not a second later, I return the favor to Rocco by putting a bullet between his closed eyes.

The gunshot pierces through the air of the cavernous room, reminding me of the reverberating sound of Rocco's gun going off in the hotel lobby eight hours ago. I'm fairly certain the screams that came from New York's high society were louder than the actual gunshot. They all cried and ran for their lives, scurrying around the elegant space like fleeing sheep.

All but one, that is.

Rionach.

She hadn't even flinched. The unwavering bravery I'd seen up on that roof remained steadfast as the chaos erupted around her. For the second time in a short period, I'd found myself completely enamored by the Irish princess. She's so unlike the other women who run in those privileged and pampered circles.

Before Rocco's utterly and completely rude interruption, when we'd locked eyes, she hadn't shielded away from me. Where most have the good sense to avert their gaze, Rionach had unabashedly continued to study me.

Unwavering and unafraid.

I've grown accustomed to the look of fear and uncertainty in people's faces when they look upon me. It was almost jarring to find both absent from Rionach's stunning face. She was simply intrigued by me, a feeling I can confidently say is mutual.

My obsession with the princess was fast and all-consuming. I want to know everything about her, from what makes her feel alive and her heart race to what makes that smile of hers grace her face. The one she gave the sky as it erupted with fireworks all around her, I crave to have that smile directed at me. *And only me.*

I'm a man who gets what he wants, and I want her. *Need her.*

"Have someone put the body on ice. We'll deliver it in a week or so. I want the Italians to think we're going to deliver him back piece by piece. Let them panic for a bit," I tell Nova, returning his gun to him. "Put in a call to the twins and get this place cleaned up. I want it so clean it sparkles."

The identical blond men make up my favorite cleanup crew. They can make any gruesome scene look brand spankin' new in an alarming short amount of time. With my proclivity for making messes, it's good to have them on my payroll.

Nova nods his beard-covered chin toward the basket behind me. "And that? When are we delivering your masterpiece?"

"Now." My entire body braces itself as I slowly begin to remove the sports coat and white button-down from my torso. Seeing as it's been hours since the bullet ripped through my flesh, blood has dried around the wound, creating a scab that tears open again once the stained fabric is pulled away. Despite the searing pain and the fresh blood now dripping down my bicep, I don't make a sound. Don't flinch. The last time I reacted outwardly to pain, I was fifteen. "I want Cosimo to know where his capo is as soon as possible. Pick some men to leave it at his estate's front gates and when you're done with that, I have something else I need from you."

"Besides calling the good doctor?"

"I told you it's a flesh wound. Just need you to put a couple stitches in it and I'll be as good as new." I wave him off, but he doesn't look convinced. "I need you to find out everything you can on Rionach Moran."

My favorite thing about Nova? He knows me well enough to discern when and when not to push for more information. His brow furrows and eyes narrow, but he doesn't ask the obvious question hanging between us. What the hell am I going to do with the Irish princess?

"Anything specific you want to know?" he simply asks instead.

"Everything."

I want to know every-fucking-thing about the woman I'm going to call mine.

FOUR
RIONACH

"Riona," my grandmother, Maeve, says from her spot across the large dining room table from me, pulling my attention away from the drop of condensation on my water glass that I've been busy tracking.

Riona... I can't stand that nickname. It's a name that's been reserved solely for my maternal grandmother and my mom. Mom used to use it a lot more often when I was younger, but something changed the older I got. The name started to sound and feel like the rest of her motherly endearment. Fake. Just another show she's putting on to keep up appearances.

"Yes, Nan?"

"I heard you had quite the scare last month at a gala. Your mother tells me there was an attempted assassination and you were close to where the gun went off. That had to be unnerving for you."

Nan takes a sip of the whiskey in her tumbler, the singular ice cube clinking against the glass. The woman is Irish through and through. You'll never see her drink anything but authentic Irish whiskey. She's tough as nails too. My grandfather will never admit that his bride is as involved in his empire as she is. Allowing women to be part of the business is borderline unheard of in our world. Producing the next era of made men is our job. The fact that she didn't sit at home and only raise babies makes my respect for my grandmother grow. I just can't wrap my head around how things went so wrong with her daughter.

The effort it takes to not look at my mother with wariness is astounding. There is not a chance in hell she shared this information with her mother because she was worried about my safety. Now, if Tiernan had been caught in the line of fire that night, this would be an entirely different conversation.

I'm not about to admit I was never scared that night and I'm definitely not going to lie and say I was. Painting myself as a damsel has never been my favorite activity to partake in.

"I don't think I was ever in any real danger," I tell her instead. "Brayden was there, and he got me out of the building quickly. I heard everyone made it out alive, too. Which is good."

My father scoffs loudly from his seat at the head of the table. His round face is redder than usual due to the amount of whiskey he's guzzled. He tries to keep up with his in-laws, but even after all these years married to Mom, he's yet to accept that they can drink him under the table without breaking a sweat.

It's pathetic.

"I can't believe that fool *missed*. He was *right* there. A trained poodle could have made that shot," Dad grumbles, taking another swig from his nearly empty glass. "It would have been a favor to everyone—to this city—if he'd been killed. A dead Banes is the only good Banes."

Okay, so apparently, it's not, in fact, good that no one died. Noted.

Dad's reaction to Emeric walking away from that hotel lobby isn't surprising. No, I'd be more shocked if he weren't pouting like he is now. I don't have proof, just a few snippets of overheard words shared between my father and his men—but from the sounds of it, dear old Dad has tried to take out Banes on more than one occasion. Emphasis on tried. If Niall Moran isn't a match for his sixty-five-year-old mother-in-law, he certainly isn't a match for Emeric fucking Banes.

"I agree." Tiernan's fist pounds into the table next to my half-eaten plate, making the glasses and silverware noisily clang. "One of these days, we're going to get the upper hand and make him look like a fool."

Trapping my amused scoff in my throat, I suck my teeth and fix my attention back on the condensation on my water glass. They're ridiculous thinking they can turn the tables and make Emeric look foolish.

Like a vulture, Banes has been picking at my family's slowly deteriorating corpse for fifteen years. He's leisurely and methodically taking us apart and he won't be happy until there's nothing but bones left. He's doing the same to other crime families—his other competitors—and I'd be lying if I said that didn't make me smile.

Dad and Tiernan are fighting to stay in the game, to keep the business afloat, but it's only a matter of time before the Moran clan sinks. Dad doesn't have anything left to fight Emeric with. If he decides to make a move against him, his only options would be equal parts stupid and desperate. Neither bodes well for a good outcome.

My grandfather, the infamous Tadhg Kelly, *hmphs*. "Sounds to me like the man takes after his father. Clever, cruel, and knows what the fuck he's doing." I don't miss the pointed look Grandpa sends my father and I highly doubt anyone else at this table did either. "Ambrose Banes was a force back in the day, but he never came close to accomplishing what his son has."

"You sound almost impressed with the idiot, Pop," Tiernan sneers as his arm rests on the top of my chair. I instantly regret wearing this thin-strapped black dress when his fingers lightly trail the bare skin of my shoulder. Like a piece of stone, I freeze in my seat and grit my teeth. Pushing his hand away would only cause a scene and despite his inappropriate behavior, I'd still be the one at fault.

"I am." My grandfather simply shrugs his broad shoulders. At sixty-seven years old, I would wager he's in better shape than my dad. "He's the youngest son of Ambrose. He was never supposed to be made king, but he was, and he's not only taken on the weight of that responsibility, he's thrived. The time to do something about him and his growing power was a decade ago when you stood a chance against him. When he was nothing more than a cocky *boy*, no one did, and now you're facing the consequences of your cowardice."

Dad's face is so red now, it's basically purple. "You could have sent assistance. Helped us fight this war against him."

If Pop is bothered by my dad's accusatory tone, he doesn't show it. His composure borders on shatterproof. It's a trait I admire and try my best to emulate when I'm stuck wearing my passive mask.

My mother's parents don't travel to the States very often. I think it's been two years since I've seen them in person. They can't take the time away from their own business. The Kelly clan are the largest arms dealers in the homeland and in the UK. Nearly thirty years ago when the Moran name carried the same weight here in the States, my grandfathers bartered a deal, and thus Imogen Kelly became Imogen Moran.

"I offered, but as I remember, *you* declined. Wanted to be a man and take care of your family yourself. I found that commendable at the time, but had I known that your family—the family I allowed my only daughter to marry into—would be a crumbling laughingstock a decade later, I would have rethought your answer and insisted you accept my charity. Might have rethought a lot of things if I knew then what I know now."

If I hadn't already been resting my chin on my palm, I'm pretty sure my jaw would have hit the table with the same force that Tiernan's fist did.

This is it... this is the moment my father's face is going to pop like a grape.

Before Dad or, worse, Tiernan, has the opportunity to come up with a retort, my mother is cutting in.

"Rionach, why don't you go get the dessert from the kitchen? Oh, and some clean plates." Mom pushes her chin-length red hair, the same color as mine, behind one ear as she smiles tightly at everyone at the table. "It's apple cake. I asked the chef to make it as it's Tiernan's favorite."

Of course it is.

For once, I'm happy to be dismissed. The air at this table is anything but comfy and I'm all but chomping at the bit to be free of Tiernan's touches. He'd started twisting a strand of my hair around his finger a moment ago, and the act makes me want to shear the long strands from my scalp.

To my surprise, Nan also stands when I jump from my seat. "I'll help you, dear."

Before she can catch herself, Mom's eyes turn into slits at her mother. The taut expression lasts only a moment before her fake-as-hell smile slips back into place. "Lovely idea, Mother."

Nan pats her daughter's shoulder as she rounds the table to follow me into the kitchen. It's a move my mother does often to me, but when Nan does it, it's a genuine display of affection, not a farce.

When the kitchen's swinging door closes behind us, I let out a subtle breath and try to steady myself. Visits from my grandparents never go smoothly, but I don't think they've ever been as tense as they are now. And it's all because of *him*.

Nan is quiet while she gathers up fresh forks and I grab the plates from the other side of the kitchen.

Her silence only lasts a moment, though.

"Have they found you a husband yet?"

Without my permission, my mask slips from my face. My only saving grace is the fact that my back is currently to her.

"I don't know," I answer, awkwardly clearing my throat. "They don't tell me these things. All I know is that they're definitely looking for one. Dad introduced me to a couple different men in the past year. I'm assuming they're on his short list."

The thought makes my dinner churn in my stomach.

She makes a *hmm* noise. "Did you find any of them up to your standards?"

My filter fails me and I speak before carefully thinking over my words. "I wasn't aware my opinion was *needed* let alone *mattered* in this situation." *Or any situation.* Realizing my mistake, I drop the plates on the granite countertop and turn to face my grandmother. "I'm sorry. That wasn't polite."

"I find that honest words are rarely polite." To my delight, there isn't any disappointment in her face. Only... understanding? That's an expression I'm not often awarded. "You don't have to tell me how your marriage isn't fair to you. Silly young girls all dream of marrying for love, but women like us have to marry for advantage. Our unions are business transactions and that can be a very somber thought, but you must remember, my dear girl, that we all have roles to play. The men make the money and build the empire, and we birth the next generation that will rule that empire. It's a balance we must all abide by."

I want to kick and scream, but all I do is simply nod. "I understand."

I don't understand. I never will. How anyone can look at their child and marry them off to men, most of whom are wholly inappropriate matches for young women, I'll never understand. That's their baby... *their blood.* It's disgusting and sad.

"Your options may be a tad bit more limited than most girls in your situation, seeing as you're older than most and you're no longer..." she trails off, knowing I know what she's talking about.

A virgin. Pure. Innocent.

I'm no longer a virgin and that is a turn-off for a lot of made men. The fact that they won't be the first to make their young brides bleed makes their nose upturn in disgust. To them, I'm now used goods. Dirty.

My lack of a hymen is the only reason I'm not married off yet, but it's only a matter of time before my father finds someone willing to look past my impurity.

Giving up my virginity didn't come without a price. It's something I'm still paying for six years later and something I dream about just as often. During those sleepless nights, the sound of the young man's head hitting glass echoes in my head, taunting me.

FIVE
EMERIC

Saturdays at Tartarus are always packed from wall to wall and alive with music and gyrating bodies. Originally, when I converted the old bank into a club, I thought it would be a good business to run my empire's dirty money through. On paper, the club is above board and is just another one of New York's top nightclubs. I pay accountants and bookkeepers out the ass to make sure that it stays that way. My own nephew, Callan, is currently putting his fancy private school education and forensic accounting degree to work by keeping our accounts looking squeaky clean.

Of course, my club is anything but clean. It's full of depravity and salacious acts. Most of said acts take place in the secret basement level. That level is where the real fun happens. Where I'd usually be spending my night, but since my attention and cock were ensnared by a certain princess a month ago, I haven't stepped foot in the basement.

Haven't so much as looked at another woman. The only action my poor lonely dick is getting these days is from my own fist, and let me tell you, sad shower hand jobs just don't hit the spot like a tight pussy does. The problem is, there's only one pussy I'm interested in having and I'm still biding my time before I finally make my move.

I wonder how Niall will react to me taking his daughter. Will he be angry because I've yet again humiliated the man, or because he genuinely cares about what happens to his child? My money is on the former.

For the past fifteen years, I've been watching Niall Moran's empire slowly crumble. It's been an entertaining and satisfying sight to behold. Watching all my competitors try and fail to contend with me has been one of my greatest joys. My climb to the top was bloody and difficult, but worth it. I'm now untouchable and sitting pretty on my throne.

Instead of spending my weekends in the basement level like I usually do, I'm locked away in my office. Something I've found myself doing a lot over the past four weeks. I'm surprised I'm not having withdrawals from the debauchery that takes place down there. The knowledge that I have something more satisfying coming has kept me at ease. For her, the wait will be worth it.

I stare at the four walls of my office and sigh. By normal standards, it's a nice office. Really fucking nice. Three walls have been painted black and are decorated in the black-and-white macabre artwork I've picked up over the years. The fourth wall is almost entirely made up of large arched windows. They're original to the bank's architecture. The building itself dates back to the 1780s, and when I bought it a decade ago, I made sure to keep many of its original details.

When my older brother, Astor, decided the organized crime life wasn't for him and abdicated his position as boss of the family, I didn't quite realize how much of my time would be spent sitting in this very office. I spend too much of my days sitting at this desk, talking to illiterate cocksuckers on the phone. Or worse, schmoozing politicians so they'll keep the law off my dick when I need them to. You know, quid pro quo or whatever.

If I'm chained to this room for too long without getting my hands bloody, I'll start to get bored, and it's never a good thing when I'm bored. That's when I get into trouble or someone ends up dead... sometimes both. I'm like a puppy. Without proper enrichment, I start to destroy things.

Nova knocks once on the closed door before he pushes into the room.

"If I don't get out of this office, I'm going to lose my mind."

"I think it's safe to say that's already happened, boss."

"*Ha.* Hilarious," I lean back in my chair and steeple my hands over my solid abdomen. "Are you sure there's nothing that needs my attention tonight? I need something to liven shit up around here."

Nova sits his brick shithouse of a body into one of the leather wingback chairs across from my desk and passes me the iPad in his tattooed hand. "Then you're in luck. There's someone here that wants to speak to you."

I look down at the screen, at the black-and-white security footage from a room I know well. It's the same room that Rocco and many just like Rocco took their final breaths in. It too is located on the basement level.

See, I told you all the fun happens down there.

A man in a dark hooded sweatshirt sits in the lone metal chair. His arms are crossed against his chest and his long legs are stretched out in front of him. Unlike many of the other unfortunate souls that find themselves in that room, the man is calm.

Between the camera angle and the hood, I can't make out his face. "Who is it?"

Nova runs a hand over his light brown beard. "When I saw

him on the cameras standing at the back entrance, I sent two of the boys to go grab him. He came here unarmed. I asked him what he was doing here, but he said he'd only speak with you. No idea what he's thinking showing up here. His people will be madder than hell if they find out."

I'm already standing from my desk and heading toward the door before he finishes talking. Having no idea how this is going to go, I wisely leave my black jacket over the back of my chair. There's no reason to ruin yet *another* suit if I don't have to, right?

———

"NOT MANY ARE brave enough to seek me out, let alone ask to privately speak with me," I tell the hooded man as I enter the soundproof room. He doesn't flinch or faulter as his head lifts and his eyes meet mine. I know this man. Not personally, but I know who employs him and that's enough information for me to know that he should not be here. "Well, shit... I did not see this one coming. You are a brave one. You do know that you're risking your fucking neck by being here, correct?"

"Yes," he answers simply with a single nod.

I let out a low whistle as I lean against the concrete cinder block wall. My ankles cross while I continue to take in the man before me. "Your owner will be beyond pissed if he finds out you're off your leash, which tells me whatever you have to tell me will be worth my time." My hands motion for him to start speaking. "Well, come on then, don't leave me in suspense for too long. Edging has never been my kink."

He pushes the hood off his buzzed head. "They've found her a husband."

And he's lost me. "Found *who* a husband?"

"Rionach."

46

This has me standing from my spot against the wall, my spine snapping straight and my hands balling into tight fists. Usually, I'm better at keeping my reactions to a minimum. Letting your enemy know how you feel about a situation puts you at an immediate disadvantage. It's best to keep them guessing. By my physical reaction to hearing her name, I've already shown my hand.

I force my body to relax, for my hands to fall limply at my sides. "And you're bringing me this information because?"

"Because I watched the security tapes from the charity gala, Banes. I saw you up on that roof with her and I saw how you looked at her in the lobby before the Italian moved in on you."

A protective surge rushes through me at the thought that someone else could have seen those tapes. That they could have seen my princess up on the roof, letting herself burn for those short, stolen moments.

Still keeping that air of false calm around me, my shoulders shrug. Soon everyone will know that Rionach Moran is *mine*, but not yet. Not until the time is right. This information, if it's true, is certainly going to be adjusting my current timetable, though.

"I still don't see how her being married off has anything to do with me." *It has everything to do with me.*

"Niall has chosen Bogdan Koslov as her groom." He shifts in his chair, the first sign of nerves since I walked in here. Normally, seeing my enemy anxious would make me grin, but the name Koslov has sucked the air out of my lungs and turned my vision a bloody shade of red. "I remember rumors from a while back that you have history with the Koslov family."

History is putting it mildly. Igor Koslov, Bogdan's father, was an associate and friend of my father's. For most of my childhood, Igor was an unwanted and permanent fixture in my life. At the age of twelve, he started to play an even more prominent role in my life. That ended when I turned fifteen. A lot ended when I turned fifteen. Those three years with him construct memories I prefer to keep locked deep inside my twisted mind.

But I'm not about to tell this man that. Only Astor knows the full truth about my time with Igor, and I want to keep it that way. "I know who Igor is, yes," is the only confirmation I grant.

"Then you know why she can't marry Bogdan. He..." The man's head shakes, visibly unnerved. "Bogdan makes Igor look like a bloody saint. The things he's done to people—to *women*. I saw the pictures of the dead prostitute who angered him. He *skinned* her. Some think she was alive when he did it. Rionach cannot be wed to that man."

It's not a secret that Bogdan Koslov is one sick puppy. The skinned prostitute is just the icing on that fucked-up cake. Nothing about his behavior is a surprise to me given who he was raised by. The kid never stood a chance against Igor's influence. The fact that Niall Moran is willing to marry his only daughter off to that family shows how little he cares about his child.

"What is Niall getting in exchange for the union?"

"Money. A lot of money and an alliance. Both the Koslovs and Morans have been struggling to remain in power ever since..." he trails off, giving me a look.

"Since I've started tearing down their empires," I finish for him.

He nods. "They think by forming an alliance they will be able to help each other reestablish their ranks."

I would have lost a lot of money if I'd ever bet on whether the Irish and Russian syndicates would team up. That's a pairing I never saw coming.

"Why are you telling me this?"

His jaw, which is mostly covered by a well-groomed beard, twitches as he ponders his answer. "I care about the lass."

My brows knit together. "You care about her? What? You've got a schoolyard crush on the girl?"

He actually seems offended I would say such a thing. "What? No, I don't have a... crush. Jesus Christ." His hand scrubs his face. "No one in that fucking house gives a single shite about that girl. This engagement proves that. *Someone* needs to care. *Someone* needs to save her from this, and if that person has to be me, then to hell with the consequences."

Green eyes, the color of freshly cut grass, meet mine and I swear I can see pleading in those depths. I examine his face, really taking in all his features like somehow, they will give me the answer as to why he's willing to risk his neck for the girl. I refocus on his eyes after a moment. That green color... *interesting.*

Feeling a bit more clarity about this man's motives, I return to my spot against the wall. "If you want to save her, why would you come to me? Safety and I don't typically play well together."

He leans forward, resting his elbows on his knees. "As I said, I saw the security footage. More importantly, I saw *your* face. How you looked at Rionach... have you ever looked at a woman like that?"

No. I haven't. "So, what? You think I should just steal her away?" He doesn't need to know I'm already planning on doing just that. "You think she'd be safer with *me*?"

A solemn, almost resigned look crosses his face. It's as if he can't believe he's really here asking me this himself. "You don't mutilate women."

He's right. I don't. There're not many lines I won't skip happily across, but that's one of them. I even stopped dealing in

49

flesh when I took over the business. My father's preferred method of income was trafficking women. I think he favored it because he enjoyed sampling the merchandise.

"You're the lesser of two evils. At least with you, I know she'll live because no one fucks with a Banes."

Brayden Kennedy doesn't know how fucking true those words are. My last name will be a bulletproof vest wrapped tightly around her. Once mine, she'll be untouchable.

SIX

RIONACH

"This isn't a good idea." Ophelia's hand flexes around mine with nerves as we weave farther into the dimly lit club. The only source of light comes from the purple strobes bouncing off the walls and the masquerade mask-wearing patrons. "We shouldn't be here. *You* definitely shouldn't be here."

My friend is right. This might be the second dumbest thing I've ever done, and *that's* saying something given my penchant for reckless behavior.

When Ophelia mentioned one of her students at the pole dancing studio she teaches at gave her a couple tickets to tonight's exclusive event, I basically browbeat her into going. She fought me at first, arguing it wasn't a good idea for us to attend given who the host of the event is.

What she still doesn't know is that the host is the very reason I am adamant about being here tonight.

I just want to see him again—to bask in that chaotic energy of his and absorb it into my own hungry soul. To charge my empty battery. The short time we'd spent staring at each other in that hotel lobby last month had fed the empty pit in my chest better than anything else I've ever tried. Standing on roof ledges or train tracks don't come close to the dangerous essence that surrounds Emeric Banes. They dull in comparison to him. Which is *troubling,* to say the least.

"It's fine, Lia," I lie through my ass.

If I get caught here and word gets back to my father, I'm beyond screwed. Not only will he be pissed at me, but he'll also be pissed at Brayden, since it's his security detail I slipped past two hours ago. The last thing I want is for Bray to take the brunt of my dad's fury.

The irony that my parents would give a shit if I snuck out isn't lost on me seeing as in reality, I'm just another pawn for them to move around their board. It all comes back to the fact that their image would be affected if their daughter got caught in enemy territory. I mean, what would it say about Niall and Imogen Moran if they couldn't control their own daughter? Insert eye roll here.

It's not very often I sneak out through my bedroom window. I try my best to limit my adventures for when I'm truly desperate—for when my skin is so unbearably tight it feels like I'm suffocating or the empty space beneath my sternum mirrors an endless cavernous pit. The sensation is comparable to hunger pains, only more intense. Painful on a soul-deep level, not physical.

There's been times I swear Brayden knows I've left the estate's iron gates. He's good at his job. Excellent, even. I have to give him endless props for willingly being at my father and brother's mercy. Bray is too good of a man to be their bitch, but what do I know? I'm just the docile daughter.

Whether Brayden knows I slip away or not, it's never come up and I'm not about to broach the subject unless I have too. If we're both pretending like I think we are, then it's best to just keep at it.

"It's not *fine*, Rio," Lia huffs. "If you get caught, which of our bodies do you think your father will put in the Hudson River? *Mine*, because I'm the idiot that brought your ass here."

"Relax. He's not even in the city. Tiernan called him from New Jersey about something this morning and he left literal skid marks on the driveway when he went to meet my brother." From the cursing that came from Dad's office and echoed through the air vents, whatever Tiernan's gotten up to in Jersey isn't good. *At all.* My brother must have really stepped in it this time because the golden child *does not* get cussed out or scolded like he was this morning. It's basically an unprecedented event, but a very refreshing change in pace nonetheless.

We come to a tight cluster of masked people blocking the arched hallway leading to the other side of the club. Not bothering to be polite and say excuse me, I push through them, forcing them to get out of our way. My hold tightens on Ophelia as I drag her through the group. Once through, I look back at her. Her pretty face is partially hidden by the white lace masquerade mask she wears, but even in the dim lights I can see the worry in her dark almond-shaped eyes.

"It's not just your dad I'm worried about." Lia pulls on my hand, forcing me to stop in my quest to find the bar. "You know whose party this is—whose club this is. Your family and his aren't on good terms. What if he sees you here and doesn't let you go? What if he sees this as an opportunity to use you as a bargaining chip?"

The yearly masquerade party at Tartarus is almost as infamous as the club's owner. I've never attended before, but I've heard stories about the kinds of things that happen at this event. Having been here for five whole minutes, I'm starting to think those stories were nothing but fiction. Which is more than disappointing, to say the least.

When I was at NYU and students talked about this party, they told tales that were so explicit, they'd make most people blush. I half expected to walk into this building and find people fucking against walls and running trains on women on the bartop, but so far, I've seen nothing more than some sloppy make-out sessions. Tartarus appears to be just another upscale New York nightclub. While I had no intentions of partaking in such activities, I was still curious.

"If Emeric Banes tries to take me as a bargaining chip, he's not as smart as people say. I can't think of a single thing my parents would be eager to give up in order to get me back." *Now, if Tiernan's life was the one on the line?* They'd trade me like I was nothing more than a lone penny they found on the ground to get him back. "Either way, we're not here to cause trouble. We're just here to have a few drinks and dance. Just some harmless fun."

Lia adjusts the black feather mask that covers my eyes. "Harmless fun," she repeats. "You can pretend all you want, Rio, but there's nothing harmless about you, and we both know it."

I give her my best appalled face and hold a hand to my bare chest. The strapless tight black dress leaves little to the imagination. I figured if I were already risking my neck, I might as well go big or go home with my outfit. This dress has sat at the very back of my closet for nearly two years. It was an impulse buy on one of my rare shopping trips with Lia. It makes me feel hot. Powerful, even.

"I don't have the slightest clue what you mean by that," I tell her, my voice sickly sweet. "I am always on my best behavior." Ophelia knows I push against the boundaries that have been shackled around me, but she doesn't know just how hard I push.

I met Lia in my second year at NYU. She worked harder than anyone else in the classes we shared, putting my moderately good grades to shame every time. Her studious habits weren't what originally drew me to her. It was the way she'd managed to live on the edges of the world I was brought up in without being fully pulled in. Her family, the Argents, were at the forefront of textile manufacturing for years. During that time, her parents mingled with the same CEOs and politicians as my family. They attended the same kinds of galas and since her father is currently sitting in prison, I think it's safe to say her family occasionally dipped their toes into the less savory side of things.

That lifestyle all changed when she was nineteen and her family's company went bankrupt. After that, Ophelia Argent became another scholarship student with a single mom.

She was raised close enough to my world to know the players, which means she knows what the Moran name means. She knows *who* I am. I don't have to lie and say that my dad's in importing and exporting and dabbles in real estate. I also never had to try and come up with an explanation for the men dressed in suits who drove me around in blacked-out SUVs. She just... understood. She never pries for information and avoids bringing up my family in general. Lia's a friend I can simply *exist* with.

"Yeah, sure," she rolls her eyes mockingly before taking my hand back in hers and leading me in the opposite direction to where I was headed before. "The bar is this way."

Glad one of us knows their way around here...

"I didn't know you'd been here before," I raise my voice so she can hear me over the heavy bass music.

"Yeah..." The look she sends me over her shoulder is one I can't quite decipher. "A few times."

───────

"I'LL BE RIGHT BACK," Lia leans in close so I can hear her. Two drinks in and almost an hour of dancing has relaxed my friend. She's still on alert, but she seems to be finally enjoying herself. "Don't go far. This place is like a maze."

Leaning against the ornate wrought iron bar, I wave the glass in my hands at her. "I'm not going anywhere. I don't need some idiot bumping into me on the dance floor and making me spill. Having gin-soaked clothes is not on my agenda for the night."

She glances behind her at someone, but I can't pinpoint who she's looking at in the commotion of masked patrons. Between continuing her education and getting her master's degree at NYU and the pole dancing classes she teaches, Lia is a busy person with a full contact list. We rarely avoid running into someone she knows when we're out.

Nodding her head, she gives my shoulder a squeeze. "Are you sure? I'll be quick."

I wave her off, perfectly content with where I am.

Curious, I follow her curtain of blue-black hair through the crowd, hoping to see who she's meeting, but I lose her in the crowd within twenty seconds.

With my back and elbows resting on the bartop and my drink dangling from my fingertips, I take a second to slowly examine the rest of the club and its guests. If he's really here, it will be almost impossible to find him out of a crowd, especially if he too is wearing a mask. Won't it? It's not like I'll be able to pick him out solely by the storm-like presence, right?

I take in the club as I continue my hunt. The building is old and historic, but any updates made to the space have kept the integrity of the architecture. The main floor is mostly one vast room. Along the outskirts of the space, marble archways lead to smaller, more intimate spaces. I'm assuming that's where people go when they want a little bit more *privacy*. The top floor, which is strictly off-limits, appears to be one big circular balcony that wraps around the entire room. Tonight, heavy black curtains have been pulled over the carved marble railings, but I can all but imagine Emeric standing up there staring down at the partygoers like he's their god. A king on his throne reigning over his subjects.

"I like your mask." A voice to my left cuts me out of my thoughts.

Turning to look at the man who now stands at my left, I find myself instantly underwhelmed and disappointed. In every sense of the word, he's handsome, but he gives off golden retriever and "missionary is my favorite and I leave my socks on" vibes. *Ugh.*

"Thanks," I tell him politely.

He smiles at me like he's won something. "It's very 'angel of death'."

I shrug my shoulder. "I'm afraid there isn't a deeper meaning here. It's just a black mask with feathers."

"Yeah," he rubs the back of his neck, "I didn't put much time into my costume either."

This has me fighting back a grin. "Really?" I question, eyes taking in the white plastic that hides half his face. The Phantom of the Opera at a masquerade party, how original. "Are you sure? It looks like you put a lot of effort into that."

The smile drops from his face, and his lips slightly gape. It takes him about five seconds too long to figure it out. "You're fucking with me."

Not being able to stop myself, I choke on a laugh. "Nothing

gets past you, does it?" Knowing this exchange isn't going the way either of us wants it to, I cut it off before he can continue with his failing attempt to pick me up. "I'll see you around, Phantom."

"Who? That's not my name."

Jesus. "Oh my God," I whisper under my breath as I abandon my drink on the bar and weave my way back onto the dance floor.

Sorry, Lia, I lied about staying put.

I'm halfway across the room when I feel it. When I feel *him.* I was so painfully wrong thinking I wouldn't be able to find him in a crowd. Every hair on my body stands on end when I turn in a slow circle and scan the balcony above me.

There.

There you are.

I imagined him standing above the club like a king or god, but with the dark red medieval horned mask that covers the top half of his face, he doesn't look like either of those things. He looks like the devil looking over the condemned souls of Hell.

Suddenly the club seems perfectly named. *Tartarus.* A realm of the underworld. The very place in mythology where the Greek gods imprisoned their enemies.

A delicious and addictive rush of adrenaline thunders through my bloodstream as I stare up at him. While I can't see his eyes from here, I can feel them. All over my body. Like small intimate caresses. Does he know who I am? Does he recognize me like I do him?

His tanned hands are wrapped around the intricately carved banister and his shoulders seem tighter. The composed demeanor from the hotel lobby is gone. From here, I can sense how wired he is, and I think I like this version of him more. The wildness and unpredictability appeal to that thrill-seeking demon who resides in my soul.

I don't know how many songs play as we continue our intense staring contest, but at one point, his head turns ever so slightly. It's as if he's silently asking me, *"What are you going to do next? Are you going to come to me?"*

A smirk pulling at my lips, I shake my head once. My answer is just as clear as his unspoken question, *"If you want me, come and get me."* I'm not going to him simply because he called. He'll have to find me himself.

I lied when I tried to tell myself all I wanted was to see Emeric. Turns out, I do want to dance tonight and, luckily for me, he's precisely the kind of danger I want to dance with. I want to feel its chaotic melody hum in my ears and vibrate my ribs.

With one last look at his tall frame, I turn away from him and melt into the shadows.

SEVEN
EMERIC

"Banes," a voice comes from my office doorway. I don't have to look up because there is only one fool brave enough to come in here without fucking knocking first.

Not yet bothering to glance at Nova, I continue to examine the security footage in front of me. It's grainy, but there's no denying what I'm seeing. That cocky fucker and his band of merry idiots really thought they could waltz into my warehouse without being seen? My lips curl when he looks right into the hidden camera. He cut the power to the building, thinking it would disarm the state-of-the-art security system I have in place. *As if I'd make it that fucking simple.*

Little does he know I want people like him to believe it's *that easy.* I want them to feel confident and believe they're getting away with stealing from me because after they do, I get to play. And after being on my best behavior for more than a month, I'm ready to let loose.

Like a rodent, this fool has fallen right into my trap.

"What can I do for you, Nova?" I ask, still examining the footage playing on my laptop. Crate after crate of *my* merchandise is carried out of my warehouse and loaded onto trucks. None of them have license plates. Another pointless tactic this fucker thought would help him get away with this. "Better be important, because something's just come up on our schedule."

My men who are stationed close to the building called me when the power was cut. They were ready to move in and put a stop to this blatant thievery, but I called them off when I saw who was behind this. It'll be so much more fun for everyone if we let them believe they're smarter than us. *Than me.* I'm not worried about the loss in profits. I'll be more than compensated for my troubles. On top of retaining the money for the stolen weapons, I'll be putting an additional interest on their debt owed to me. It'll be my favorite form of payment to date.

I couldn't have planned this better myself if I'd tried. Sometimes shit just falls into place and I fucking love it when that happens. These cocky assholes don't know it yet, but they've just made it that much easier for me to claim what is already mine.

"What's going on?" Nova asks, coming to a stop in front of my desk.

I spin the laptop so he can watch. "Half a million dollars' worth of guns and ammunition are being stolen from my warehouse."

My second-in-command looks between the screen and my face. "And this is making you grin like a sociopath, because...?"

"Because I'm really going to enjoy having them in my debt." I turn the laptop back toward me and rewind to the moment the leader of this shit show comes into frame.

Nova's eyebrows rise to his hairline when I face the screen toward him again. He lets out a low whistle and his head shakes in disbelief. "They're not this stupid, surely."

"Apparently they are."

"This makes what I came here to tell you a little bit more...

interesting." He hands over the iPad that seems to permanently live in his hand. "One of the boys working the party clocked her when she arrived at Tartarus. I had them watch her for a while before I came here. She doesn't have any security with her." This makes something in my chest tighten. Her family's lack of care when it comes to their daughter is astounding.

In the middle of my club—my territory—my princess dances amongst the other masked patrons. For the past decade, the annual masquerade party at Tartarus has been a yearly staple but never in those ten years have I felt more inclined to attend than I do now.

"She came with a friend." At my narrowed eyes, he quickly adds, "A *female* friend."

While the idea of ripping the hands off any other male who dares touch her is more than appealing, that's not how I want to spend my night. Not anymore. Not after seeing her in that tight-as-sin black dress and feathered mask. I'd planned to keep my distance from her until I could finally make her mine—officially—but my restraint is only so strong.

"You're right, Nova. This is *interesting*." Standing from my desk, I rebutton my designer black suit jacket and grab the leather devil mask that one of my assistants had left for me this morning. At the time, I hadn't planned on donning it since I had no intentions of attending this year's party, but plans have changed. "Shall we go see what the princess wants?"

———

SHE SENSED me the second my eyes found her in the bustling crowd.

The ride from my office to Tartarus was less than fifteen minutes. Nova had pouted in the front passenger seat of the black Escalade since I refused to return his precious iPad so I could continue to watch her on the security feed. When Rionach had brushed off the co-ed's lazy attempt to seduce her, I hadn't bothered fighting my approving smile. *Good girl.*

By the time I slipped through the club's back entrance and up the stairs that lead to the top floor of the building, she'd abandoned her spot against the bar and had started to weave back through the sweaty bodies on the dance floor.

I knew the second she felt me. Her spine snapped straight, and her shoulders stiffened. The fact that she innately knew it was me made something primal inside of me purr with satisfaction. It also answered the question that had been rattling around my head. Why was she here to begin with?

She came here for *me.*

My princess searched me out.

Head cocked, I wait for her to decide what she wants to do. This one time, I'm letting her set our course. After this, I won't be so... compliant. I'm curious to see what she decides, that's the only reason I'm willing to let her momentarily take the lead. Once I get my hands on her, the dominant beast that resides just under the surface of my skin will take charge. From there, she will be forced to play my game. Though, I get the feeling my games are precisely the kind she aches to partake in.

The smirk that pulls at her mouth all but makes me growl aloud, but it's the way she has the audacity to turn her back to me and walk away that has blood rushing to my cock. The unmistakable and blatant dare for me to chase her is like dropping blood in shark-infested waters. With that taunt, she's turned this into a game of prey versus predator.

She has no idea what she's just ignited.

That smirk tells me she isn't afraid to get burned.

You want to see how long you can play with fire, princess? Okay, let's play.

EIGHT
EMERIC

THEY HAVE no idea it's me under this devil mask, and yet, the partygoers are still quick to get the hell out of my way as I prowl through the main floor of the club after my little deer. It's as if something instinctive warns them that if they don't step aside, they're going to become my next bloody art project. All it'd take to make that happen is one nod at one of my men lurking amongst the crowd. Without fuss or fanfare, they'd have them detained in my concrete room and held there until I was feeling *crafty*.

In the strobe of a purple light, my eyes catch a glimpse of her feathered mask. Knowing I'm closing in on her, Rionach looks over one narrow shoulder at me, the same taunting smirk that sat on her pretty lips moments ago remains firmly in place, beckoning me to her.

She's trouble and I *like* it.

The woman from the events and fundraisers isn't here tonight. Gone is the placating smile and docile demeanor. The same Rionach that stood on the roof ledge is here and blazing with intoxicating boldness. How she's able to keep this side of herself so tightly restrained, I'll never understand. It must be akin to slowly killing a piece of herself.

I don't make it five more steps in her direction before she's ducking between groups of inebriated and euphoric people. They're all chasing their own highs tonight, just as I am. While theirs is booze and thin lines of white powder in the bathrooms, mine is a little minx who doesn't yet comprehend who she's fucking with.

She thinks she can outsmart and outrun me, but I know this place better than anyone. I designed the fucking thing. Every nook and cranny, I know. *There's nowhere to hide, my love.* She can run all she likes, but I'll be getting my hands on that creamy skin soon enough.

Darting down one of the arched marble hallways, I cut her off just as she tries to skirt around the corner. She doesn't realize that I've caught up to her until it's too late. My hands wrap around her upper arms, and I whirl her around, slamming her spine into the marble wall.

I've tried every drug under the sun, I've tasted the most expensive liquors... all that pales in comparison to what it feels like to have Rionach Moran in my hands.

Her breath rushes out of her lungs from the harsh impact, and I'm so close to her I can feel the air dance across my lips. Big round green eyes with flecks of gold dancing around the pupils stare up at me in surprise. And as they do, the people and the heavy bass music melts away until all that's left is *her*.

Spilled alcohol, stale cigarettes, and sweat usually permeate the air of the club, but all of that is gone. Rionach doesn't wear sweet-smelling perfume like most women I've been around. She smells spicy and musky. Inhaling deep, I take in the tobacco, cinnamon, and citrus scent that clings to her skin. *Yes... this is better than heroin.*

"What now, princess?" I question, face close to hers so she

can hear me over the obnoxious dance music. It takes all my willpower to not bury my face in her neck. "You all but begged me to chase you. I've caught you. You're trapped until I say otherwise, so what do we do next?"

Her breasts heave within the confines of her tight black dress with each of her labored breaths. She might hide it well, but that brazen attitude of hers is always close to the surface. It flares in her eyes like green flames as she bites out, "I don't beg."

Unable to stop myself or ignore the need to touch more of her, my hand releases one of her arms. Starting just below the ear that has a handful of different studs and hoops in it, I trace my fingertip down her neck.

"They all say that, Rionach," I tell her darkly. "Doesn't quite matter the situation. One way or another, the people around me always end up begging. Some beg for their lives or the lives of their loved ones. They beg me to stop the pain while others beg me to keep touching them. Pain or pleasure, I'm capable of either, but in the end, they're begging me for it. And you, my sweet siren, will be no different." The way her pulse jumps against the tip of my finger has a smirk forming on my lips. "What part of that excites you more? The idea of pleasure or *pain*?"

There's no fear in her eyes as she stares up at me. It's a sight I haven't seen in years. My actions and reputation have rightfully made people fearful of me, but not her. No, the only thing reflected in those big eyes is excitement and lust.

I bite back a groan as my cock continues to throb. She's exquisite and all these fuckers have been blind to it. Their loss is about to become my gain.

Not backing down or shying away, she lifts her chin boldly. "I'm not really picky." The next thing she says seals her fate. Whatever chance there was of me walking away from her tonight turns into ash at our feet. "Do your worst."

The hand I was using to trace her heartbeat wraps around her throat, applying just enough pressure to make it obvious who's in control here. Dipping my head lower so I can speak directly into her ear, I whisper, "You're going to regret saying that."

Breathing harder, her head shakes. "So far, I'm confident in my decision."

I drag my nose down her cheek, inhaling another lungful of that scent I'm quickly becoming addicted to. "We'll see."

Without warning or preamble, I release her throat and take hold of her slender fingers in a vise-like grip. Her shorter legs have to take twice as many steps as I pull her down the corridor to the guard and keypad-protected door beside him. Very few people in New York are aware of what resides below Tartarus. Those who do know have paid a hefty sum to partake in the pleasures that dwell there.

One story down is where the true underworld is.

My man spots me headed his way and opens the doors before I need to ask. Swiftly, I drag her through to where the elevator made of glass waits for us. She doesn't hesitate or ask questions, a move I can't decide is brave or stupid. *Recklessly fearless, this one.*

Rionach stands steadfast and silent beside me, her fingers still entwined with mine. She doesn't shake or tremble as we descend into the red illuminated abyss. It's not until the doors open and she's fully confronted with where we are does she make a sound.

A single, barely audible gasp.

Considering what she's currently looking at, it's impressive that's all she lets slip.

Like the main floor, this level is also made of marble. Large, decorative chandeliers hang from the tall arched ceilings. The light bulbs in them are red, casting a red-and-pink hue on everything and everyone. Long white curtains drape down, creating alcoves for patrons to lounge in. A fully stocked bar takes up much of the left wall, bottles sitting on glass shelves that are twenty feet tall.

But the decor and architecture of the space aren't what has Rionach gasping.

It's the people wearing studded collars while their backs are being blown out on the leather chaise lounges, and the naked women with ball gags in their mouths dancing on raised platforms. It's the Wall Street boys sitting at the bar, getting their cocks sucked while they drink old fashions. It's the men and women moaning and writhing in ecstasy. Some of them still wear masks from the party upstairs, but with or without them, their anonymity will remain preserved regardless.

Nothing is off-limits here, and nobody is fucking shy.

"What is this place?" she whispers to me as we step out of the elevator and into the fog of corruption.

"Heaven," is my only answer. If such a place truly existed, this would be mine. A room with no rules. Just pure, unadulterated debauchery.

Her head turns and I can feel her eyes on me as if she's trying to figure me out. She must find her answer because after a minute, her attention returns to the illicit sights surrounding us. Without a word, she wanders away with an air of curiosity around her. Just this once, I allow her fingers to slip from mine as I follow behind her. Letting her go is something I don't think will come easy for me in the future.

While she takes everything in, I watch her, waiting for the moment she decides this is all too much for her young soul to take. Twelve years longer than her I've been on this earth. There isn't much I haven't experienced, but for her, this is all brand new. I enjoy watching it through her eyes. It brings back a layer of excitement I've been missing for quite some time.

She comes to a stop in front of a wall made of glass. Behind it, a blonde woman sits in a swing with her legs spread wide, her pussy on full display to anyone passing by. A man kneels before her, devouring her like a fucking animal.

Rionach looks back at me, eyes wide behind her feathered mask. "Can they see us?"

My head nods. "That's the point. They want people to watch them get fucked. It adds to their pleasure, and that is the very reason people come here. This is a place where they can give in to every desire and craving without shame or consequence."

She asks nothing else, just turns back to watch the woman grind against the man's face. While her attention is consumed by them, I fixate on the way Rionach's fingers rhythmically trace along her plump bottom lip. My dick stirs at the thought of those very lips wrapping around it. Any other woman I would have taken by now, but something about her has me slowing down and taking a moment to just... take her in.

It's been nearly a month and a half since I've been this close to her, and I'm making up for lost time. Time that is limited. The second we stepped foot off the elevator, our clock started. While I want nothing more than to take her home and keep her locked in my room until I've had my fill, we simply don't have that luxury right now.

Her breath hitches and her teeth sink into the very lip I've been fantasizing about as the woman behind the glass comes with a dramatic scream. I know the man who's on his knees for her, there's no way in hell he actually made her make that sound.

In a move I wasn't expecting, Rionach whirls to face me. "Is that why you brought me here? To simply give in to a craving you have?"

This has me chuckling. "Love, I could have given in to my

craving at any time in the past month and a half. Your father's men aren't exactly what I'd call vigilant. That big oak tree outside your bedroom window would have been a breeze to climb up. I could have been in your bedroom and between your thighs before you could have so much as made one of those breathy gasps of yours." *My new favorite sound.* Telling her about the tree outside her window lets her know just how closely I've kept my eye on her. I want her to know that it doesn't matter where she is, she's never too far out of my grasp. "Forty-one nights have passed since New Year's Eve. I could have chosen any one of those nights and had you right then and there. Fuck, I'd be lying if I said the thought didn't cross my mind."

Something about my words has a spark igniting in her jade eyes. "What would you have done if I'd said no?"

I take a tendril of softly curled hair and rub the smooth strands between my fingertips. "Can you honestly tell me you would have said no?"

"That's not an answer."

"Neither was yours." I drop the piece of hair and let the honesty of my obsession drip from my lips. "I would have done it anyway. I would have stopped at nothing to taste you."

Most women—women concerned for their safety—would have taken a confession like that and run straight to the closest police department, but Rionach doesn't run. The only thing that moves are her pupils as they dilate.

Something resembling shame flashes across her face. "You shouldn't say that kind of thing to me, and I..." Her words trail off and her teeth sink into her bottom lip.

My hand collars her throat, giving a slight squeeze when her gaze flicks away from me. "Eyes on me, love. And you, what?"

"And I shouldn't *like* it." Her confession is a barely audible rush of words, and beneath the edges of her feathered mask, her cheeks grow a delectable shade of pink. "I shouldn't like how you make me... feel."

"And how do I make you feel, princess."

"Afraid."

"You like being scared?"

With my hand still necklacing her throat, her nod is restricted.

I already put that together when I witnessed her little jaunt to the roof, but I like hearing her admit it. "Is it the adrenaline rush you like? Or is it the idea of giving yourself over completely to the fear." My head dips and my lips skim the edge of her pierced ear. "The lack of control, perhaps?"

The shame is back with her softly spoken, "Yes."

"Don't." My order comes out like a whip's crack. "Don't you fucking dare. You get turned on by fear? Own it." Hand tightening on her throat, I give her a little taste of what she's craving. "Look around you. There isn't a single person here ashamed of what they're doing. That's the beauty of this place. They're simply taking their pleasure. So. Own. Yours."

Her hand wraps around my wrist, but she doesn't try to shove me away or interfere with the control I currently have on her ability to breathe. No, her thin fingers grasp my skin tighter, encouraging me.

I lean down once more to whisper in her ear, "You and I both know I can give you what you want. What your body fucking craves."

Her entire body shivers as my tongue traces her jawline. When I pull back to look at her, her eyes are basically black. The jade green is only a sliver on the very edge of her irises. Her breath is now coming in ragged pants, but the shame is diminished.

I know the second she's decided to play my game. The smirk from before graces her lips once more.

"I didn't come here for a fucking tour, Emeric." The raspy sound of my name on her tongue is sweet music to my ears. A noise so intoxicating it has my restraint all but snapping. "Get on with it, or go away so I can find someone who will."

For a second, I think she's testing me, seeing how far she can push me before I snap, but the wicked way she stares up at me is the only clue I need to know that isn't actually the case. She *wants* me to snap. She wants me to lose control.

That's my girl.

The look vanishes when my hold on her throat tightens to the point I'm cutting off her oxygen.

"You should know something about me, Rionach. I don't allow people who steal from me to keep their hands. If you let someone else in this place touch you, I'm going to keep their hands as fucking trophies. I'll display them on my fireplace mantel with pride," I warn, not at all exaggerating. "So, I ask you, do you really feel like putting another person's life in jeopardy like that?"

Of course she doesn't answer. She physically can't. She gasps for air, but I don't let up. Instead, I make her walk backward toward the impressive structure in the middle of the room that resembles a birdcage. It's at least fifteen feet tall, and the bars are unyielding, made of perfectly twisted iron. I've strung many willing victims up using these sturdy bars, leaving some of them there longer than I ought to. Once a *guest* is inside, they're locked in until their captor says so.

And I'm *always* the captor.

Inside is a circular mattress with maroon silk sheets and various black pillows that are cleaned and changed out after each guest by the staff down here. I'm a heathen and a proud menace to society, but I refuse to fuck on sheets soaked in another man's cum. The line has to be drawn somewhere.

My free hand fishes for the key I'd placed in my jacket pocket before leaving my office. I wasn't sure we'd end up in the cage, but I was optimistic. With the door open, I waste no time twisting her around and pushing her inside. Falling to the mattress on her hands and knees, Rionach's entire body heaves as she sucks in the precious air I'd deprived from her.

Everything with this woman has been a surprise, and it's no different when she looks over her shoulder at me with a fucking smile splitting her stunning face.

Trouble, trouble, trouble.

Her hand reaches for her mask, but I *tsk* before she can remove it from her face.

"Leave it," I snap as I remove my black jacket and dark gray button-down. I don't need one of the onlookers in here recognizing her and word getting back to her family. No, I want Niall Moran to find out I've marked and claimed his princess on my terms.

She watches me over her shoulder, and while she does, I wonder if the scars littering my skin are visible to her in this lighting. I didn't build up my family's empire like I have by making *friends*. No, I've made enemies, and my enemies like guns and knives. The blood I've willingly spilled has strengthened the foundation of my business. It's a price I'm more than willing to pay to be on top.

Her skin is smooth and burning hot beneath my fingertips as I run them up her bare thighs. It's not until her eyes flutter closed in soft serenity do I remind her who she's currently locked up with. My hands dip beneath the hem of her dress and wrap around the elastic of her thin thong. With one harsh yank, the scrap of cotton shreds off her body.

She gasps, eyes flying open just in time to watch me deeply

74

inhale the scent clinging to the fabric. The musky scent goes right to my cock, and it strains painfully against the confines of my pants.

Tucking them in my pocket for safekeeping, I tell her, "I would gag you with these, but I want the sounds I force out of you to drown out everyone and everything in this fucking place. Let them hear how good I make you feel." Taking hold of the hem of her short black dress, I shove it up her body, exposing every stunning inch of her to me. "I want to know if you taste as good as you smell, princess."

NINE

RIONACH

One second I'm on my hands and knees, the next my world is spinning at a speed my brain can't keep up with. My back has barely collided with the silk sheets when his lips close over my clit. And just like that, my world is spinning again, but this time for a completely different reason.

My spine bows and my neck hurts from the force in which I throw my head back in a silent gasp. Emeric's arms hook around my thighs, his unyielding muscles forcing me to keep them open for him so he can lick and bite at my pussy with unrestricted access.

At the first long swipe of his tongue through my slick center, I realize the two other men—boys, really—who've touched me had no idea what they were doing. With each passing second the miniscule amount of sexual pleasure I've had before Emeric instantly become a lackluster and distant memory.

I'm going to savor each and every one of these stolen moments with Banes. After tonight, I know something like this can never happen again. The fact that I've allowed it to go this far already… the last and only man to actually fuck me didn't walk away alive. While I highly doubt my father can take on Banes and *live*, it's still unbelievably foolish of me to rock the boat like I am. Right now, I'm struggling to care what the aftermath of this will look like. I know it's selfish of me, but I just want to let go and live. For these few stolen moments, I want to *live*.

I'll deal with the consequences if or when they come.

The fact that there are patrons standing just ten feet away from us, watching as he devours me, only adds fuel to the fire. The adrenaline is shooting through every inch of me like fucking lightning, waking up a side of me I didn't even know existed.

I don't know when he took it off or where it ended up, but I'm thankful his horned mask has disappeared as I sink my fingers into his black hair that is just long enough to curl around his ears and the nape of his neck. After he'd been shot, the dark strands had fallen into his face. I remember thinking that the unruly look only added to that dark presence of his.

I can't keep still when his tongue pushes inside of me. I twist and writhe, my body gliding easily against the silk sheets. It's as if I can't decide if I'm trying to escape his relentless attack on my pussy or if I'm searching for a more delectable pressure. Maybe both.

The growl that comes from deep in his chest vibrates against my clit and has my eyes rolling back in my head.

"Stay fucking still."

"No." My response is immediate, like a knee-jerk reaction.

This has him stopping and lifting his head between my thighs. "No?"

The part of me that seeks out fear whispers darkly, *Stand your ground. Let's see what he'll do.*

"I can move as I fucking please," I grit out. "And you can't stop me."

His teeth sink into the sensitive skin of my inner thigh. The clear warning makes me jump. "You don't think I can make you do exactly what I want when I fucking want?"

That is precisely what I crave for him to do. I want him to try and make me his whore. I want him angry. I want to fight him until I'm not sure if he's going to fuck me or kill me. That's the line I want to carefully tiptoe until he's made me come so hard my vision goes white and all I can feel is him.

"No, because I won't just lie here like a thing to be used by you. I'll fight you."

This has the storms that reside in his eyes growing violent and his eyebrows rising in challenge. "Is that so?" His arms unhook from around my thighs, and he slowly rises to sit on his heels. "Okay, love, show me what you got. Fight me."

It's like a gun being fired at the start of a race. Adrenaline going into overdrive, my foot rears back before shoving into the middle of his chest. The blow causes him to fall to his ass and while he's off-kilter, I take the opportunity to scurry away.

We both know this is nothing more than a game. We're locked in a cage that is no more than ten feet wide. Even if I really wanted to flee, there's nowhere for me to go. He's going to catch me and I'm going to fucking like it when he does, but that doesn't mean I can't make him work for it.

The snarl that comes from him is one of rage and the sound of it goes right to my throbbing core. He lunges at me, his fingers trying to wrap around one of my limbs, but all of my thrashing means he's only able to grab my dress. When I pull away from his grip, the thin fabric rips and falls away from my body. Completely bare since the dress's style required that I go braless, I backpedal away from the man most of New York is terrified of.

It's not that I don't understand their fear, it's just that at this moment I can't seem to give a fuck. His dangerous aura exhilarates me.

I'm sure psychiatric professionals would have a field day trying to figure that one out. It'd go something like this: *"So you got locked in a cage with the most dangerous man in the city and instead of complying, you basically poked him with a stick just to see what would happen? And you thought this was a wise decision because...?"*

"I dunno. For the plot?"

I make it several feet before his hand ensnares my ankle and I'm harshly pulled back. My hands try to reach for something to hold on to so I can better fight back, but my bare skin against the silk is working against me.

My leg flies out to kick him again. This time it's futile. He's expecting it and his hand captures my other ankle.

Emeric pulls me across the bed on my stomach, and once I'm close enough, he uses the weight of his larger frame to pin my legs beneath him. With nothing for my hands to grab, my struggling attempt to free myself is laughable at best. At least, it's funny until the unmistakable sound of his zipper lowering fills my ears.

Just like that, all the humor leaves my body, and in its place, I'm flooded by a wave of immense need. His big hands grip my hips and pull them back so my exposed ass is once again perfectly on display for him.

Through the eye holes of my now crooked mask, I watch as more heads begin to turn in our direction. It's as if they're watching a film and have finally gotten to the exciting part, and I couldn't agree more.

Time slows to a crawl. It feels like it's been minutes since he's trapped me, but I know it's only been mere seconds.

Emeric's hand smooths down my spine as he growls, "What? Is that all you got?"

This taunt sends another wave of combativeness through me, and just as I begin to battle his hold again, the head of his cock slicing inside of me in one harsh, unforgiving thrust has all the newfound fight leaving me in one choked breath.

Emeric gets his wish.

The cry that comes from my lips echoes loudly above any of the other noises in this place, drawing even more eyes our way. The multiplying stares makes my skin grow hot while my body trembles as it tries to adjust to his intrusion.

"Where's your fight now, princess?" he snarls as a hand wraps around the messy strands of my long hair. My scalp pricks when he yanks my head violently back, and a hiss escapes through my clenched teeth. "Or do you not want to fight now that you've gotten what you want? Me balls deep in your greedy cunt."

To really drive his point home, his hips snap back until only his tip remains before thrusting so deep, I feel him against my cervix. It's a unique kind of pain that I can't say I hate.

"You wanted this too," I manage to pant. Never in my life have I felt so full, so completely taken by someone. There is no doubt that this night will have a lasting effect on me. Whether a good or bad one is yet to be decided.

"You're fucking right I did."

One hand on my hip and the other twisted in my auburn hair, Emeric pounds relentlessly into me. I take everything he gives me happily and ravenously, throwing my hips back to meet his when I need it harder. *Rougher.*

The thought that I'll feel him when I move for days to come is one I'll embrace with open arms. The bruises he's leaving on my fair skin as we speak will be battle scars, proof that I laid with the devil and made it out alive. Never in my years of fear-seeking have I come close to finding something that makes me feel as alive as I do right now with Emeric inside my pussy. All those reckless things pale in comparison and seem like child's play now. For the rest of my days, I will be searching for the same kind of high he creates within me.

Friction builds in my core and the sound of the club around us dissipates as a rushing sound replaces it. My fingers dig into the slick fabric below me as my limbs begin to shake.

His hand leaves my hair and becomes a necklace around my throat. The knowledge that he holds my life in his hands has my pussy fluttering, and the warm fuzzy feeling as my oxygen continues to be restricted adds to the storm building in my core.

"Give in to me, Rionach." His words wash over me and with them come waves of sheer bliss.

TEN
RIONACH

I HAD no expectations for how our night together would end, but Emeric offering me his button-down and ushering me out of the birdcage not even a minute after he came on my lower back was the last thing I anticipated.

He didn't say a word to me, just led me by my upper arm to the glass elevator and kissed me on the forehead before pushing the button for the main floor. He stood on the other side of the glass door, stormy eyes watching me as I was lifted away from him. I'm not sure which sensation I focused on more during the short ride up. The lingering feeling of his lips on my skin, or his cum dripping down my ass cheek.

At the time, I was too dazed and confused to feel anything but those two emotions, but after this past week, I'm pissed. Not necessarily at him, but at myself for letting myself get hooked on something that was never going to be more than a one-time thing. I was right when I guessed that everything after Emeric was going to be dull. Colorless. *Lifeless.*

Since that night, I've teetered on balconies and stood

dangerously close to the ledge in the subway as the train barreled toward the platform, but nothing makes the adrenaline rush in my veins like it did when Emeric Banes touched me.

He used me and I used him, and I'm angry that I still want more. Like a virus, he's worked himself under my skin and into my bloodstream.

There's a knock at my closed bedroom door. The person behind it doesn't wait for an answer before it opens. My brother steps into my bedroom—my sanctuary—and just like that, my day is ruined. After graduating college, I was forced to move out of my rented apartment near campus and back home to my parents' New York estate. It's my childhood home and yet I have very few warm and fuzzy memories within these four walls. Coming back here meant giving up my indolence and privacy. It also meant being thrust back into Tiernan's direct path.

Through the vanity mirror in front of me, I flick my eyes to him before continuing to do my morning skincare routine. After his impromptu trip to New Jersey last week, he's had an extra pep in his step and to say it's concerning is an understatement. The gleam in his brown eyes doesn't exactly bring me comfort. It does quite the opposite. It's the same look a rabid dog gets when it finds something yummy to sink its teeth into. The little voice in my head tells me to run, but the logical side of me knows that would only excite him further.

He leans against my doorframe, his beefy arms crossing in front of his wide chest. He's not what I'd call buff. Big-boned is a term people use, right? That's how I'd describe my brother. Big-boned and big-headed.

"You're too pretty to be married off to one of *them*," he finally says after another tense moment of examining me.

My fingers freeze in their task of rubbing in my moisturizer.

"One of them?" I repeat. "I'm not sure what you mean by that, Tiernan." I also don't think my looks have anything to do with my impending arranged nuptials. Pretty sure that's my uterus's fault, but I digress.

"*Them.* The Italians, Albanians, Serbians, or even the goddamn Russians. The ones who aren't our blood. The non-Irish. They don't deserve you. Father is making a mistake selling you off to them like you're fucking chattel." The gleam in his eyes fades as it's replaced with something darker. "Marrying outside our heritage is what's weakened our bloodline."

Arguing with him would be a mistake of epic proportions, even if I want to demand what the hell he's rambling about. He sounds like one of the conspiracy theorists screaming their nonsense on street corners in the city. I found them amusing, but I find Tiernan worrisome.

"It's out of my hands. It always has been." I keep my tone neutral to avoid provoking him further. "You know this. Dad will marry me to the person that best helps strengthen the family."

It's a task to force myself to not look away from where his eyes hold mine in the mirror. How is it that I can face Emeric Banes without flinching, but my own brother has all kinds of alarm bells going off?

He releases a long breath through his nose with such force, I swear he momentarily resembles a pissed-off cartoon bull. "He's making a mistake."

"I'm not the one to have this conversation with."

In a move I find truly out of character for my brother, he nods his head once and seemingly moves on from this current topic. "Dad and I have to go into the city. We'll be gone until tomorrow afternoon, I think. We have a couple meetings we have to attend."

Not sure why you're letting me know, dude. I'm not the

keeper of your schedule and it's not like you're going to be missed.

He walks across my room, further tainting my space with his crazy vibes, and puts his hands on my shoulders. Bending, he keeps his eyes on mine through the mirror as he kisses the top of my head. I want to growl and scratch at him like a feral animal until he learns to stop touching me, but instead all I do is sit pretty in my seat. *Like I always do.*

"See you tomorrow, little sister." He pauses like he's waiting for me to say something back. When I don't, his entire round face tightens. "Aren't you going to tell me to be safe?"

Don't make him mad, Rio. It's not worth it.

"Please be careful, Tiernan," I tell him in my well-practiced and disgustingly placating voice. "Mom would be absolutely devastated if something happened to her boy."

I don't feel like I can breathe until my door closes behind him. Sitting frozen in my seat, my fingers like a vise around the bottle of moisturizer, I wait for my heartbeat to return to its normal rhythm.

"IS THE TABLE SET?" my mother asks behind me, her three-inch heels clicking against the tiled floor of the great room.

She refuses to wear anything else, even when she's home. *A lady doesn't wear flats, Rionach.* Well, *this* lady is wearing her favorite pair of black boots today and she's pleased as punch about it.

I keep my back to her as I continue to look out the large paned window. The backyard of my parents' Upstate New York home is covered in a fresh blanket of snow. There isn't a footprint or a single sign of life out there. A fitting visual for the coldness that wraps around this house and its tenants.

"Yes. I put it all out a little while ago," I answer, still not looking in her direction.

She'd left the expensive china and crystal with the gold accents out for me, a silent instruction to make the dining room table all pretty for today's family lunch.

"Good."

There's the telltale sound of glasses clinking together as she adjusts and *fixes* my work, because like everything else, nothing I do will ever be to her standards.

"I want everything ready and perfect for when they get home. Your father called, said your poor brother hasn't slept since he left yesterday. He'll be exhausted and famished when he gets here."

If my eyes rolled any harder in their sockets, they would fall out of my face. "Well, we definitely wouldn't want that. Should I make him a cheese and meat platter, perhaps have a glass of sparkling water waiting for him?"

She's so oblivious to everything when it comes to me that she fails to pick up on my obvious sarcasm. "Would you? I'm sure he'd really appreciate it."

I could argue this or even flat-out laugh at the absurdity of it, but instead I decide to not waste my time or breath. With my teeth biting down on my tongue to keep it quiet and my hands balled into tight fists, I leave the cold woman to fuss over her dining table.

But I don't escape more than five feet away from her when the windows I'd just been in front of explode and glass rains down on me in little sharp pieces. That adrenaline I've been searching in vain for barrels into me as my mother's shrill screams fill my ears.

In slow motion, I watch as men wearing head-to-toe black come through the now open windows. Their faces are hidden by black masks and there's a gun in each of their hands. My first guess is the government has finally caught up with my father and they're coming for him, but that theory is put to bed when one of them wickedly laughs at my mom's fear.

Nope, definitely not the government.

This is the doing of someone *much* more sinister. This thought has my skin prickling—not in fear, but from something else entirely.

My mom tries to run, but she's wearing those damn shoes and doesn't stand a chance against the gun-wielding men. Like a football player taking down his opponent, the laughing intruder tackles her to the ground. This causes the screams to grow even more irritating and high pitched.

When one of them moves in my direction with their handgun pointed at my chest, I stand perfectly still and raise my hands. There's no way I'm about to dash off screaming like a banshee like my mother just did. That was embarrassing for both of us to watch.

My brow quirks at the mystery man. *What now?*

While there might not be a single shred of evidence pointing to who's behind this theatrical show, I know in my gut who the mastermind is.

"Rionach! *Riona!*" my mother cries, but I'm not so mindless to believe she's screaming with worry for *my* safety. The use of my childhood nickname won't fool me.

No, even with a gun pointed at me and my life on the line, she's begging me to save *her*. If I didn't have said gun in my face, I may have lost it and laughed at this.

There's a crashing bang at the front door as more people enter the house. This time it isn't just masked goons. Standing in the forefront of the new group is a stunning woman in a well-tailored burgundy pantsuit. She's probably in her late thirties with shoulder-length dark hair. She might have a pretty face, but it doesn't conceal the "fuck around and find out" aura clinging to her.

I like it.

"What are you doing here?" my mother demands as she's hauled off the ground from under her arms. Her narrow wrists are now sporting a set of zip ties and the perfectly curled hairstyle she'd previously had is a wild disarray of red strands. I don't think in my twenty-four years of life I've ever seen her look so... unkempt. "Do you know whose fucking house this is?"

"Of course we do. We don't barge into just anyone's house like this, Mrs. Moran," the woman responds, face and tone conveying just how unimpressed she is. "Get her in the car. We're on a schedule."

The man holding my mom follows these instructions without hesitation. He produces a black cloth bag from his vest and yanks it down over her head before leading her out the door.

I watch, not making any move to help or stop them from separating us. When my mom is out the front door and out of sight, I look to the woman who's clearly in charge of this shit show.

"Where are you taking us?"

"To church," is all the information she offers. "Now, will you walk out of this gaudy-as-hell house on your own two feet, or do we need to sedate you? The boss would prefer we didn't have to do that, but he said to get you there by any means necessary..."

She trails off, leaving how the rest of this interaction goes up to me.

"I can walk."

"Great." She offers me a smile that doesn't reach her eyes. "Now, let's get moving."

I don't know what the hell Emeric Banes is up to, but something in my gut tells me I'm not going to like what happens next.

ELEVEN
EMERIC

Patience isn't something I excel at. Impulsivity is usually the lane I find myself driving in, but for this to play out how I wanted it to, I needed to wait. Seven weeks have passed since New Year's, and it's finally time. Excitement buzzes beneath my skin at the anticipation for what's to come.

The old church doors swing open, the wood banging into the wall behind them at the force. Nova and his team carrying in the precious cargo has a gleeful smile pulling at my lips. They're hooded, their hands zip-tied, but still they're fighting tooth and nail to free themselves. Let's see how much fight they have in them when I clip their wings.

Giuliana sticks her head out of the building's back office and nods her head at me. "We're just finishing up the final touches."

She's a cut-throat attorney and businesswoman. I brought her in twelve years ago when she was working for a rival corporation. She tried her hardest to fuck me over and got so goddamn close to doing just that, that I decided I needed someone like her on *my* team. Giuliana and Nova are the only two people I can trust to properly handle delicate and important matters such as this.

Giuliana disappears again while Nova forces our guests to take their seats in the front two pews. After all, they're the best seats in the house for tonight's festivities, and I don't want either of them to miss a single minute.

A small gesture of my hand has Nova ripping the black fabric from both of their heads and cutting their restraints. Matching sets of brown eyes widen at me when they find me standing behind the wooden pulpit.

With a shit-eating grin, I fling my arms out wide at my sides in an overexaggerated motion. "Welcome to church, boys!" I greet in my best southern minister accent "Who's ready to confess to their sins?"

"What the hell is the meaning of this, Banes?" Niall spits, his usual ruddy face growing monumentally more red. He's a stout man who's eaten one too many servings of pot roast and mashed potatoes. Rionach got her looks solely from her mother, while Tiernan is an unfortunate replica of his father with his dark blond hair and stocky frame.

"Hey now. Watch your mouth," I mockingly chastise, hands dropping back to my sides. "We're in a church. Have some fucking respect."

Tiernan Moran glowers at me as he snarls venomously, "I'm surprised you didn't burst into flames the second you stepped foot in here."

"You know what?" My fingers tap a couple beats into the worn wood in front of me. "I, too, was pleasantly surprised when this didn't abruptly turn into a Sunday barbeque. It appears even your god is smart enough to not fuck with me, but we can't say the same about you two now, can we?"

Tiernan's response is immediate and defensive. "I don't know what you're talking about."

His father at least has the decency to stay quiet and look worried. Niall knows where this is going because while he's struggled monumentally with his family's empire, his IQ is *just* high enough to know how to read a fucking room. His son, on the other hand? An imbecile. The overly cocky ones usually are. They think they can hide their lack of common sense and brain cells with an arrogant attitude.

Stepping to the side of the podium, I lean against it, my legs crossing casually at my ankles. "Here's the deal. I'm going to give you one more chance to confess to your wrongdoings. If you want to make this difficult, I'm more than happy to oblige. Actually, I'd prefer it if you did. I have about two months' worth of pent-up energy in me, and, boy oh boy, do I need an outlet."

"Tiernan..." Niall tries to pull his son's attention to him, but the cocky fucker seems to only have eyes for me. *I'm so flattered.*

"Fuck you." He spits at me, and it lands two feet from my leather shoes.

Classy.

Nova has been with me long enough now to anticipate my next moves. Like a well-rehearsed dance, we move in tandem. As I grab the item I stashed in the pulpit, Nova takes hold of Tiernan while his team members move in on Niall.

The Morans fight and yell, but I don't give a shit what they're saying. The storm around me now matches the ever-present one thundering in my bones. It's moments like these, when things are most hectic, that I feel most at peace. Calm. Steady.

The only other time I felt that way was when I was with Rionach in the cage. It was an unexpected and not unwelcome discovery. I was prepared to find only more chaos when I was inside of her, but instead I found myself feeling centered.

My second-in-command positions the kid's arm exactly as I need it. Never fazed by my actions, Nova doesn't flinch when the military-grade tactical tomahawk comes down, or when the resulting drops of blood splatter on our faces and clothes.

Trauma and shock do funny things to people. It's like their bodies and minds are momentarily disconnected, and their neurons need a minute to catch up to fully understand what's just occurred. When Tiernan looks down at his right hand, it takes him a solid five seconds to comprehend that it's no longer connected to his body.

The scream of horror that comes from him rivals the one that comes from Niall's windpipes. I'm sure there's been talented choirs in this building before, but in my humble opinion, their cries are the sweetest symphony to ever grace this church. A harmonic melody I plan to commit to memory. To repeat when I'm bored.

The color drains from Tiernan's face and his brown eyes are dazed as he holds his shaking arm in front of him. Blood pours freely from it, spilling all over his legs and the floor below him. Niall is still screaming, surely cursing my mother for daring to give birth to me, and no doubt promising pain to my own future children. This is just a calculated guess as I'm not really paying the Irish mobster any attention.

Kneeling in front of his thieving son, I rest my chin on the very ax I used to maim him.

"I warned you to not make this difficult, didn't I?"

His head bobs as he starts to lose consciousness from the shock and blood loss.

"Did no one ever teach you to not take someone else's toys?" I ask, knowing I won't get an answer. Not that I need one. Niall and Imogen did their son a disservice by making him believe he was above everyone else and untouchable. *God's gift to fucking earth, blah blah blah.*

Fueled by rage and desperation, Niall musters up enough strength to break free of the hands holding him at bay. He charges at me like a bull having a red flag waved in his pudgy round face. Standing just in time to face him head-on, I slam my fist into his sternum, a blow that instantly has him doubling over in pain.

Nodding at Nova, who no longer needs to keep the kid in place, I order, "Put Mr. Moran against the cross." My hand covered with the blood residue gestures to where the six-foot tall wooden religious symbol leans against the wall directly behind the pulpit. "I need him front and center, Nova."

Tears run down the father's face as he's manhandled away from his bleeding son. He's forced up onto the raised dais and pressed to the cross that sits against the wall painted with an absolutely hideous mural of the Garden of Eden.

"I'm going to fucking kill you, Banes. I'm going to skin you alive and—"

"And what? Feed me to your leprechauns?" I finish for him, completely unimpressed and unmoved by his threat. "Your son broke into *my* warehouse in New Jersey and helped himself to *my* shipment of weapons. The dumbass brought this on himself, and I'm only settling the score."

"He's just a boy, he doesn't know any better."

This has me throwing back my head and laughing hysterically. "Okay, sure. He's just a boy. In that case, he was in desperate need of learning a harsh lesson *his father* should have taught him decades ago. What I'm doing now is picking up *your* slack, Moran."

Niall thrashes against Nova's hold, but my right hand is built like a brick shithouse. A hurricane couldn't move him.

"But that only answers for your son's stupidity and actions. What about yours, Niall?" I press, my hands tucked casually in my jacket pockets. "Your son *told* you about his plans to steal

95

almost half a million dollars' worth of merchandise. You rushed to New Jersey that morning like a hellhound was on your ass but when you got there, what did you do? Did you stop him? No, you sat in your cushy hotel suite and waited for him. Your son proudly brought you his haul like a house cat bringing its owner a dead mouse, and you promptly found buyers for the entire shipment."

"He didn't tell me it was your warehouse. I had no way of knowing they were your guns."

My brows quirk and my head tilts. "Is that your final answer?"

Sweat pours down his sweaty face in fat drops and his whole body shakes as he nods. "Y-yes. Yes. I didn't know."

I ponder this answer for all of three seconds before shrugging my shoulders. "I don't believe you."

Nova's tattooed hand wraps around Niall's. He uses his brute strength to yank Niall's arm away from his thick body and pin it to the cross. The Irishman's head turns to the right to look at his hand. From the dread in his eyes, I know he thinks I'm going to cut it off and make him match his son, but I have other plans for Mr. Moran. Those plans require that he stay conscious. There's an important role he's yet to play for me tonight.

Pulling one of the five-inch long and quarter-inch thick nails out of my jacket pocket, I position myself in front of the hand that is palm up. He shrieks when I place the sharp point of the nail against his skin, and he all but screams when I pull the hammer from the back of my waistband.

"Please, no. God no. Don't do this, Emeric." His voice is hoarse from all his pleas and his body is trembling with fear. A delightful and expected response.

Holding the nail in place and the hammer over the top of it,

I ask one more time, "Tell me the truth. Did you know you were stealing from me when you accepted those guns?"

The internal fight he's having with himself is clearly written across his face. I know he's come to an answer when he nervously licks his dry lips. "Yes. I knew they were yours. I saw an opportunity and I took it."

No fucking shit.

"Thank you for your candor."

One harsh slam against the nail head, and it drives completely through the bones and tendons in his hand, and deep into the old wood of the cross. Niall hollers in pain, his eyes glued to the blood dripping down his palm.

Wanting his attention on me, I grip his chin and force him to look at my face. "That's right, scream. Make sure your wife can hear you from where she's bound and gagged. Let her know how your mistakes are costing you blood and body parts."

Switching to the other side, I repeat the process on his left hand. His cries are quieter this time, the shock and adrenaline coursing through his system shielding him from feeling the full effect of the pain.

Nova lets him go and steps back, leaving me alone to inspect my masterpiece.

"You Irish are really into the whole Jesus thing, aren't you? It must just tickle you pink that you get to emulate your god." Blood drips down the mural and into twin puddles on the dirty hardwood floor. It's a view I'd like to frame and mount on my fucking wall. "Go get the wife," I order.

This stops the pathetic whimpering coming from Niall. "Please, don't hurt her. She doesn't have anything to do with this."

"But she will," I correct, patting him on the chest like an ol' pal would. "The Moran women aren't sitting on the sidelines tonight."

The sound of high heels clanking unrhythmically against the floor has my head turning. A blindfolded and bound Imogen struggles to keep up with Nova's long legs as he drags her into the room. Stopping in front of her barely conscious son, Nova removes the bag from over her head.

The scream that comes from the sight of her precious boy is so loud and long, I'm utterly shocked that it didn't shatter the panes of stained glass in the windows. Any passerby would think that *she* was the one being maimed. Imogen drops to her knees in the pool of Tiernan's blood and presses her bound hands to the open wound in an attempt to stop the bleeding.

"While I'm sure this is all very shocking and tragic for you," I start, not an iota of sympathy or care in my tone, "I do want to move this along, as I have plans for the rest of my evening."

Blue eyes snap in my direction and if looks could actually kill, I'd be the one bleeding out instead of her boy. "What the fuck is wrong with you? You're a... *monster*."

"While flattery will get you everywhere, Imogen, we need to talk about how you want this to play out." Bloody hands tucked behind my back, I walk slowly toward the now sobbing woman. "Your husband and your son stole from me. Cost me a great deal of money, and I want to know how you intend to pay me for their crimes."

Her tear-soaked face twists in confusion. "Pay—pay you?"

"I'll give you the money," Niall hoarsely says from his place on the wall. "I'll need a few days to move the money into your accounts, but I can give you back every dime we made from the guns."

"You returning my money goes without saying, Niall." My eyes roll. Fool. "I'm asking your wife now what she is willing to pay to ensure that you and your son walk out of here alive and *mostly* in one piece."

"You've already taken your pound of flesh and now you're

asking me for more?" The high-pitched octave the distraught woman's voice jumps to is unpleasant, and, frankly, dramatic in my opinion. Her emotions are clear, there's no need to add theatrics to it.

"This..." I gesture between the two bloody men. "Wasn't my payment. This was my punishment. There's a fine line, but a crucial difference between the two."

"What else do I have that you could possibly want?" Imogen chokes out. Tiernan stirs and looks down at his mom from his slumped position on the pew. His mouth opens like he's going to say something but his eyes close again before he can. "For God's sake, you've already abducted me, tortured my husband, and disfigured my son..."

"I've also fucked your daughter." That malicious grin returns to my face at the sight of the matching expression of horror on her parents' faces. "Just thought I'd put that out there since you've yet to mention her name once or show any semblance of concern for her. She's safe, by the way, in case you were curious."

Imogen's head shakes in disbelief. "I don't believe you. When... when would you have been around my daughter?"

"Well, I'm not going to give you all the dirty details. I would hate to come across as crass or ill-mannered. I do have a reputation to uphold, after all, but I will tell you this. While your son was stealing from me, I was taking your daughter." Sending her away that night tested my restraint to an extreme I've never experienced before. For the first time in my adult life, I was depriving myself of something I wanted, and there was no doubt in my mind that I wanted more of Rionach Moran. To ensure that today went to plan, I needed to keep my distance. In the end, I know my reward will be worth the ache I've had in my cock for the past seven days. "Have you figured out what I want yet?"

"*Rionach?*" both Niall and Imogen mutter.

"Ding, ding, ding! We have a winner." Stalking closer to where Imogen and Tiernan sit, I yank his injured arm away from her caring grasp.

"Stop it!" she pleads. "He's going to bleed out."

Wagging his arm around like a puppeteer, I nod in agreement as blood drips onto my shoes and her clothes. "Yes, I'm very much aware. That's why you should answer this question quickly. I either take my payment by watching him bleeding out right here in this fucking church, or by taking your daughter as my wife."

"You want to marry her? *Why?*" Niall asks. I can't decide if the confusion in his voice is because he can't understand why I'd want to marry someone, or because he can't understand why I'd choose the daughter they have wrongly deemed inconsequential.

"That is for me to know. Now, ticktock, this offer has a time limit." Reaching for Tiernan's uninjured arm, I look down at the tacky gold watch on his wrist. "You have fifteen seconds to decide."

"You can't have her," Niall grunts. "She's already spoken for. A deal for her hand in marriage has been signed for weeks." *Yes, I'm aware, and I also know what filth you tried to pawn your daughter off to, you cocksucker.* "Even if I wanted to, I can't get out of—"

Imogen cuts him off, not caring what else her husband has to say because for her, this isn't a subject up for debate. "You can have her." Her expectant gaze turns to her husband, who, to my shock, is still hesitating to answer. "*Niall.* Tell him he can take her. He's already further *soiled* her. What is she worth to them now?"

Maybe I shouldn't let them all leave here alive.

With two seconds to spare, Niall nods his head. "Fine."

Unceremoniously, I drop the boy's arms and spin away from the pair. "I can't even pretend to act surprised by your answer." Nodding my head at the men waiting at the back of the church for my signal, they come forward to collect Tiernan and Imogen. "It's time for you two to leave. These men, believe it or not, are former combat medics. I've found it's good to have them on staff because this, as you know, is a very dangerous world to live in. They'll make sure your delinquent son is just fine and dandy." My cheerful tone has murderous rage flaring in the mother's eyes.

Picking up Tiernan by under his arms, they carry his limp body toward the back door.

Imogen turns to follow them but freezes at the sight of her son's dismembered hand. It sits discarded on the dirty and dusty concrete floor in a pool of blood. I almost laugh aloud when she begins to squat down, as if she plans on taking it with her.

"*Leave it,*" I snap, enjoying the way she jumps at the sound of my booming voice. "That belongs to me now."

For a moment, the strong Irishwoman's composure starts to break and her bottom lip wobbles. "But a surgeon might be able—"

"Do you *really* think I would go through all the trouble of hacking off his hand—ruining a perfectly good pair of slacks in the process, by the way—if I planned on letting you *reattach* the fucking thing? *No,* because that would have been a waste of my time, which you're also doing now by loitering."

I'll return the hand to them eventually, but it won't be in the way Imogen is hoping.

Back stiff and chin lifted in false bravado, she spits, "I hope you rot in hell, Emeric Banes."

"I'm sure you do." Waving my hand in a dismissal, I add, "I'll be sure to send you a Christmas card anyway."

"What about my husband? Get him off that fucking cross."

I look between the married couple with raised brows. "He's more than welcome to come down anytime he pleases once he's played the rest of his part. I'm not keeping him there."

Her mouth gapes in horror. "You... you expect him to pull himself free?"

"Correct, but only after he officiates the wedding. It's a good thing he was ordained for his niece's wedding last summer, or this plan really would have gone to shit. And besides, what little girl doesn't want her daddy there on her big day?" Lifting my chin at Nova, he understands my silent order and prowls over. "Time for you to go, Mrs. Moran. I'm afraid this is an invite-only event."

She periodically looks over her shoulder at her husband as Nova removes her from the building, but she doesn't fight him once.

"You're marrying her now?" Niall breathlessly asks. His chest is heaving like he's just tried to beat his best time for running a mile.

"Sure am. Is it too soon to start calling you Dad?"

I'd saw out my own tongue with a rusty grapefruit spoon before I called another person *Dad*. The taunt was just too perfect to not say to my future father-in-law. It helped make clear to him just how fucking serious I am about this whole thing.

Turning back to Niall once mother and son are gone, I cheekily say, "I'd ask you for marriage advice, but seeing how your wife just left you nailed to the wall like a chubby Irish Jesus without any argument, I'm thinking things aren't super cozy between the two of you."

His chin hangs to his chest in a pathetic fashion instead of offering me any kind of answer. That's fine by me seeing as I've always failed at small talk.

Minutes pass by in silence before Giuliana walks out the office door. My heart thuds against my ribs in anticipation for what's to happen next. This is the moment I've been waiting for since I saw her smiling up at the dark sky. I knew then she'd be mine and that she'd be my wife.

"We're ready," she informs me.

On cue, the wooden front doors covered in cracked white paint swing open, and I set my sights on my bride for the first time. Dressed in a long-sleeved black lace dress, Rionach stands between two guards with a look of pure fury on her face. The mask that is constructed of lies she forces herself to wear is nowhere to be found.

Rage and venom come from her like strikes of lightning, but she's never looked more beautiful, and I've never been so happy to call something I've stolen *mine*.

With a smirk pulling at my lips, and the storm inside me rattling my bones, I breathe a single word.

"*Finally.*"

TWELVE
RIONACH

THE ONLY PERSON who made a peep on the drive was my mother.

She begged and bargained for our captors to let her go. Even cried to really lay it on thick. I would have taken a picture if my hands weren't bound. Or if I still had my cell phone... that had been promptly confiscated before we were put in the back of the SUV. When tears didn't work in her favor, she reverted back to threatening them. Had we been in Ireland, and she was threatening them with the wrath of her father, her intimidations may have held more weight. The name Niall Moran doesn't carry the kind of fear required to make our kidnappers shake. I'm assuming they're all probably desensitized to shit because of who their psycho-as-hell boss is. All of Mom's attempts fell on truly unimpressed ears.

"Get out," the masked man who'd been driving us commands as he opens the door for my mother. When she refuses to move an inch, he sighs. Turns out the half an hour of her nonstop yapping has worn on his patience. "Lady, you either climb out on your own or I drag you out. From there, I will drag you through the fucking mud until we get to the building. Now, I know a pretentious woman like you would hate to get your clothes dirty like that. *Decide.*"

The man shoots me a look when Mom turns in her seat and tries her best to gracefully exit the car. My eye roll could be seen from space. *Of course, the threat to her designer clothes is what got her moving.* The look on the man's face tells me he's thinking the same thing. The second her heels hit the unpaved and uneven ground, he grabs her by her upper arm and yanks her toward the building.

Turns out the lady from the house wasn't kidding about us going to church. We are in fact parked in front of a really old, abandoned church with a steeple. From the looks of it, the only thing that accompanies the dated structure out here is the graveyard to the left. I have no idea how far away we are from the nearest town, but knowing Mr. Banes, he chose this location for that very reason. Debauchery is best done in private.

My attention is pulled away from the scenery when my door opens.

"Your turn." The woman looks as composed as she was back at the house. Like what is happening here is just another Tuesday for her. "We need to make you presentable."

My gaze flicks to the white oversized sweater and dark jeans I'd put on this morning when I thought my biggest problem for the day was going to be my family's luncheon. "What? Am I not dressed appropriately for church?" I point at the building covered in white chipped paint. "Doesn't exactly look like this place has a dress code."

"But you're not appropriately dressed for a wedding." She steps back, motioning for me to get out and follow her.

"*A wedding?*" I repeat, doing a superb impression of a dumb parrot. "Who the hell is getting married?"

"I AM *NOT* GETTING MARRIED," I growl at the team of people around me for the seventieth time since I was brought into this tiny office. Once upon a time I'm sure it belonged to a preacher, but right now it's been made into a makeshift dressing room. "And I'm sure as hell not marrying *him*."

I don't understand.

Any of it.

Emeric wanting to marry me doesn't make any sense. Him wanting to marry anyone doesn't make sense. He doesn't exactly seem like a man who wants to be locked down and wifed up. He has a wild and untamable soul, one that calls to mine, but is that reason enough for him to want to marry me? What could he possibly get out of that? Out of me being his wife? He's not doing this without some sort of angle, but I'm at a loss for what that could possibly be. From my experience, men like Emeric Banes want young naïve virgins. Seeing as he locked me in a cage and fucked me so hard I'm still sporting bruises a week later, he's well aware I'm not a virgin.

He doesn't need to marry for power or for alliances. A bride sporting the last name Moran won't strengthen his social standing.

"We're just doing our job, miss," says the middle-aged woman who stands behind me, lacing up the corset-style closure of the black lace dress I was all but forced into the second I stepped foot in here. "Now, please hold still so Monica can finish up with your makeup."

Monica offers me a small smile when I cut my glare to her.

"I'm almost finished," she whispers, but still, she avoids my stare. Good, at least someone in this room realizes how wrong this all is. "Just need to touch up your eyeliner. It got a little smudged when you..."

When I freaked the ever-loving fuck out and tried to escape. I was promptly halted by the men standing guard before I reached the door. I'd attempt it again if I thought there was any way I'd be successful at it. My best bet is to wait until I'm out of this shoebox of a room and try then.

And then what, Rio? Where are you going to go? Who's going to help you?

Mom and I were separated when we entered the back entrance to the building. I only bothered asking once where she was, but the woman in charge—whose name I now know is Giuliana—simply said, "She's fine," before going back to typing away on her phone. Business as usual.

"I. Am. Not. Marrying. Emeric. Fucking. Banes," I all but yell at the group surrounding me, and I might even stomp my foot, but you'll never hear me admit to it.

Giuliana sighs, finally looking away from the emails or whatever the fuck is so important on her phone. "You say that like you have a choice in the matter."

"I should!"

"Have you *ever* been offered a choice about who you were going to marry, Miss Moran?" Her words aren't malicious or meant to hurt, but still they cut deep. Painfully so because what she says is the truth.

Whatever I'm about to say is cut off when the sound of screaming cuts through the thick wooden door of the office. I whip away from Monica and her pestering eyeshadow brushes and turn toward the exit. The men standing guard don't seem fazed by the sudden commotion. All they offer are bored looks over their shoulders at the closed door.

"Who was that? What is going on out there?"

"Everything will be explained to you in due time, Rionach. Now, please, stand still so these ladies can finish their work. The faster that happens, the sooner you will get your answers."

I basically growl like an animal at the woman sitting so nonchalantly in her chair but end up doing as she says. What else am I supposed to do? There are five people in this room with me, I can't exactly fight them all.

The entire time they put their finishing touches on my makeup, hair, and outfit, I fidget. Occasionally, more shouting comes from outside the door and at one point, I swear I hear my mother's bloodcurdling scream. This only makes me shift anxiously back and forth in the expensive heels they've instructed me to wear.

While I'd never admit it to them, I can't deny that they've made me look... *beautiful*. The dress alone is a piece of art. The sleeves and bodice are made of intricately woven lace and the tulle A-line skirt flows weightlessly down my legs. It's several feet longer in the back, creating a train. My dark red hair has been curled and it falls down to the curve of my back in perfect waves. My makeup... part of me wants to ask Monica what she used on my eyes because my irises have never looked brighter. The rich green color is all but glowing now because of the smokey shadow and liner. Deep red, almost the same color as my hair, has been painted onto my lips, making them appear fuller than they are.

I look amazing and it only pisses me off more. I don't want to look amazing when I'm being forced to walk down the aisle to *him*. A burlap sack and Crocs seem much more appropriate for this sham of a wedding.

Wedding... *my wedding*.

Oh, God. I'm going to throw up.

"This cannot be happening," I whisper to myself while staring at my reflection in the antique mirror hanging on the wood paneled wall.

Giuliana, who had stepped out of the room a moment ago, returns and nods her head at the two guards. "It's time."

In perfect cadence, they turn to me and each take hold of one of my arms. The second we're out of the office and stepping through the back doors of the church, I thrash against their hold, fighting with everything I have to get away. *Maybe I can make it to the main road and flag someone down to help me*, I think, knowing already that doing so would just be putting an innocent life in danger. *Nope, that's a bad plan.*

"Miss Moran, please stop," one of the guards pleads, as they lead me around the building. It's the first time this one's said a word all day. Glad to know he's finally found his voice. "We've been ordered to deliver you unharmed. Fighting us will only result in bruises to your arms. Our boss wouldn't be thrilled with us if that were to happen."

Oh, so Emeric is the only one allowed to leave bruises on my body now. Got it.

I scoff at this and glare at the guard. "I'm so terribly sorry I'm making your job and *your* day difficult. For shits and giggles, should we review how difficult *my* day has been?"

"We're just doing our job," the other guard pipes up.

"If one more person tells me *they're just doing their job*," I repeat the sentiment mockingly, not bothering to hide the bite in my tone, "I'm going to run them over with a car, and then I'm going to reverse."

I don't miss the way the two men glance at each other.

"I get it now," the previously quiet one mumbles just as we reach the paint-chipped double doors at the front of the church.

"You get *what*?" I seethe, but I never get my answer because like a grand prize being revealed to the lucky winner, they're pushing the two doors open in front of me with a flourish.

Still simmering with anger, I lift my head defiantly and scowl at what waits for me inside. My rage quickly turns into

110

shock when I look at the raised dais at the end of the aisle. Nothing could have prepared me for what lies before me. Someone could have told me exactly what I'd find in here, and I probably would have thought they were lying.

In a choked gasp, I manage to get out, "What the fuck?"

THIRTEEN
RIONACH

HE *NAILED* my father to a cross.

This time when I shrug out of my guards' hold, they let me.

My walk down the aisle isn't a slow, elegant stroll with soft music playing, it's a wrath-filled and red-hazed march. There are no wedding guests smiling encouragingly at me as I walk to meet my groom. The only other people here other than Emeric and Dad are my guards and Emeric's tattooed hulk of a man, and the only person smiling at me is *him*. My fingers aren't wrapped around a bouquet of flowers, they're balled so tightly at my sides that my nails are dangerously close to cutting into my palms. My father doesn't walk arm in arm with me down the aisle, I walk alone with two armed men close behind.

Emeric is my target as I charge forward. I haven't quite figured out what my plan is for when I finally reach him, but my fist connecting with his smug grin sounds like a good idea to me.

That plan goes out the window when I reach the first row of pews and see all the blood splattered and pooled there.

And the *hand*.

There's a fucking hand just lying there.

Something bad happened here while I was locked in that tiny room being turned into mob princess Barbie.

"What the hell is going on? Whose hand is that?" I ask, my focus still locked on the appendage. Both of Dad's hands are currently nailed to the cross, so I know it doesn't belong to him, and it's too large to belong to my mom... "Is that *Tiernan's?*"

The gold pinkie ring with our family's crest on it is still wrapped around the smallest digit on the hand. I've always hated that ring—I mean, come on. A pinkie ring? Those don't look good on anyone—but Tiernan wore it with pride. Refused to ever take it off. Looks like he's holding true to that promise even now.

Footsteps moving on the raised dais have my eyes pulling away from the carnage and up to him. His hands, stained with blood, are clasped in front of him. It's a posture so nonchalant, it doesn't fit the current atmosphere of the room.

"I already told you, Rionach." His perfect sultry voice washes over me, and try as I might, I can't stop the chill from running down my spine. He shouldn't still have that kind of effect on me, not now. Not after today's charade. "I told you what happens to people who steal from me."

I don't allow people who steal from me to keep their hands.

"You said you'd take their hands..."

"Good girl." Emeric nods, a pleased look on his face. "That's correct. The only reason I didn't take both is because he's your brother. Which was a mercy on my part."

"A mercy?" My dad's strangled cry echoes through the hollow space in the rafters above. He pulls on the thick nails in his palms, making more blood pour from the wounds. "You mutilated my boy!"

My brain is trying to make sense of what I'm seeing and hearing. Usually, adrenaline rushes like today's make me feel awake—clear—but the constant state of anger I've been in since I found out what Emeric's plans are for me has my brain feeling cloudy.

"Tiernan stole from you..." I trail off as the frazzled and bloodied pieces begin to fall into place. "Last week, when you left to meet him in New Jersey..."

My father's eyes flare at this, his mouth parting just a tad before snapping shut when he realizes I'm addressing him.

"Surprise isn't a good look on you, Irishman," Emeric taunts, swagging closer to where Dad hangs crucified. "Is it really that big of a shock to you that your daughter pays attention? That she might know more than she lets on?"

How can he know something like that about me after spending barely one night together while my own parents continue to be oblivious?

"Underestimating people gets you killed," Emeric tells him before turning his attention back to where I stand. "Your brother stole half a million dollars' worth of merchandise from my New Jersey warehouse and then dear old Daddy here sold it off to my competitors."

I've spent the better part of the past decade building and strengthening the grip I have on my composure to ensure I never slip up in front of my family and allow them to see past my mask. Right now, all that self-imposed conditioning has gone out the window.

Have my family lost their ever-loving fucking minds?

"You stole from him. *From. Him?*" I'm taken aback by the low, dark register of my voice. My docile disguise is crumpling by the second.

My father stares at me like he doesn't recognize me and Emeric looks at me like I'm a prize. *His prize.*

"It... it was just business. This is how things are done in our world—" Dad's face, which has at least had the decency to show a morsel of shame since I walked down the aisle, shifts into that holier-than-thou expression I despise. It's the same one Tiernan inherited from him. "No. Enough. I don't have to explain myself to you—"

Dad falls into a fit of wheezing coughs as Emeric's fist collides with his ribs, effectively halting whatever other bullshit he was about to spew at me.

"Seeing as Rionach will be paying the price for your quote, unquote, "business dealings," I think it's more than appropriate she asks a few questions." Emeric bends down so he's right in my dad's face, forcing the panting man to look him in the eye when he asks, "Don't you agree?"

Dad tries his best to not shy away from him, but like a low-ranking wolf in a pack, my father submits and turns his head away. Emeric looks more than satisfied with this gesture when he turns back to me.

"Your father owes me a debt for stealing from me and I've decided what I'd like as compensation for my troubles." He prowls closer to me, that assertive swagger I appreciated in the past now grating on my nerves. "I'm sure you've already put together what that might be, haven't you, princess?"

"Me," I manage to grit out between clenched teeth. "You think I'm going to marry you to pay off their debt?" The scoffing sound that escapes my lips has Emeric's eyes darkening. Not in anger, but in hunger. It's the same look he got when I challenged him in that cage.

"I don't think anything." He continues with his slow, methodical prowl toward me. It's as if he doesn't have a single care in the world and what's happening here is just another day in the office for him. I suppose for Emeric it is. "I *know* you're going to be my wife, because I know what will happen to you if you don't march your pretty ass up here and let me watch those lips of yours wrap around the words *'I do'*. Do you know what happens if you leave here without my last name, Rionach?"

At my stubborn silence, he inclines his head at the tattooed beast of a man standing silently at the side of the platform. He's the same man who saved Emeric's life on New Year's. He looks like a Viking with his head shaved on the sides and his shorter but full beard. He also looks like he could crush someone's skull with just his fist if he wanted to. In other words, I wouldn't want to piss him off and end up on his bad side.

"Thank you, Nova," Emeric tells him, taking the file that is offered to him.

He rifles through the papers inside and as he does, that casual and laid-back attitude of his melts away. Something dark washes over the sharp edges of his features and the ever-present storm in his eyes turns glacial. That change in his features, it makes me wonder if Emeric Banes also wears a mask.

"Are you familiar with the name Koslov? Specifically, Igor and Bogdan Koslov?"

This has my spine stiffening. Both of my interactions with people sporting the last name Koslov were less than ideal. My dance with Bogdan gave me chills in the same way a hundred spiders crawling on you would, and Polina Koslov... something about that woman was just off.

"Why?"

"I was just curious if you were familiar with the man your father has sold you off to."

Sold me?

My confusion must be showing on my face because Emeric pulls one of the photographs out of the file and offers it to me. Stiffly, I accept it and find myself staring at the scarred-up face of Bogdan Koslov.

"That's a face only a mother can love, isn't it?" he

comments dryly. "Didn't your parents tell you about their deal with the Russians?"

"My parents don't tell me anything, but I think you know that."

I've already been forcibly brought to a church and stuffed into this dress. My brother's missing a hand and my dad's impersonating Jesus. At this point, why should I bother keeping up with the pretense that I own a filter?

"It was none of your concern—"

"It *was* her concern. It became her concern when Igor told you the price for an alliance with the Russians and you willingly paid it, knowing what kind of man you'd be marrying your daughter off to." The dangerous dark power that took over Emeric a moment ago blackens further. It's like standing outside during a lightning storm and tornado sirens are going off in the distance. Sane people would be rushing to find shelter, meanwhile I'm hating myself because even now, I'm drawn to the madness.

The sneer that crosses Dad's face is one for the books. "The hypocrisy of you—the notoriously deranged Emeric Banes—judging the character of another man is laughable."

"When have I ever claimed to be a good man? I'm as morally bankrupt as they come and getting my hands bloody is one of my favorite pastimes, but I have never cut a woman up for sport." Emeric holds the rest of the file out to me, silently ordering for me to examine its contents. "But can we say the same for Bogdan Koslov?"

Like the dutiful obedient girl I pretend to be, I take the offered folder.

"What are you showing her?" my dad demands, pulling on his nails again in his fit. The wounds tear and more blood pours from the wounds. He tries his best to sound outraged, but the unmistakable hint of panic is what has me anxiously opening the file. "What lies are you telling my daughter?"

"Stop. Fucking. Talking. Your voice is becoming grating, Niall. If you keep irritating me, I'm going to put nails in your feet too. That way we can complete the lord and savior look you've got going on."

I'm not sure if my father responds because my ears momentarily stop working and all I can hear is a constant droning noise. It reminds me of the sound of crashing waves on the shore. One after the other with no break, it blocks out the rest of the chaos surrounding me as I look at what's in my hand.

Despite my parents' best efforts, I don't consider myself to be a sheltered person. Growing up in the mob exposes you to a lot of stuff at a young age. I've been kept away from the true bloodshed, but I heard the men and boys talking about their escapades during gatherings. They boasted about their kills with pride. None of those stories could have prepared me for these photographs.

The women pictured are so butchered and bloodied, they're borderline unrecognizable as human beings. The only reason I know they were women is because of the few scraps of long hair still attached to their mutilated and disfigured scalps. The skin has been methodically removed from the heads of half the victims, while the others appear to have had their skulls bashed in until there was nothing but gore left of their once pretty faces. Their poor naked bodies don't appear to be in any better shape. I pray for their parents and loved ones that they never saw what became of them because no one should be remembered this way.

I can't tell how many different women are photographed. All the blood makes it hard to tell them apart. There are at least four. Four women who were mutilated and murdered for the fucking fun of it by a sadistic man. The same man my father planned to marry me off too...

"Did you know?" I don't recognize my own voice. The venomous edge is one I didn't really know I was capable of. "Did you know what Bogdan does to women when you decided to form the alliance with his family?"

My father lifts his head defiantly, looking down his nose at me. Even now, nailed to a wall and with no certainty he's going to walk out of this church alive, I'm beneath him. I'm not worth the truth. I'm not worth anything to him. It's something I've always known deep down, but having it confirmed hurts more than I'll ever admit.

"Answer me, dammit! Did you know who you were selling me to? Did you know what Bogdan does?"

His brown eyes flare. There's not an ounce of shame reflected in them when he admits, "I'd heard the rumors, but never thought it necessary to go through the trouble of confirming them. True or not, I believed it would be worth the risk if it meant we got to ally with the Russians. They could help us restore our family name. Regain the power we lost." Dad thrusts his chin to Emeric. "Together, we could be strong enough to take him on. Please, Rionach. That's why you can't marry him. You'll be ruining our chances of—"

"Shut up!" my cry revibrates through the room like a shrill scream.

My fingers release the photographs when I take my first step toward him. My designer heels clank against the worn floors. I'm a walking ball of fiery rage, I wouldn't be surprised if I looked behind me and found my footsteps scorched into the cracked concrete. I stop directly in front of him. So close the hem of my lace dress sweeps through the small pools of his blood gathering.

"How *dare* you?" I can't bring myself to feel ashamed of the way my voice cracks. "How dare you ask *anything* of me. You sold me to a legitimate monster without a single care for my safety. What he did to those women... if I married him, I could end up just like them and you. Don't. *Care*."

Dad's nostrils flare at my outburst. I've never felt more out of control than I do now. My perfectly crafted mask has turned into a pile of ash at my feet, and I can't bring myself to care. There's no coming back from this.

"You call Bogdan a monster, but you'll marry *him*? He might not do *that* to women, but that doesn't make him a fucking saint. He's the worst out of all of us. He takes pleasure in the destruction he's made of our family and families like ours."

I see his point. Emeric isn't a saint, but he isn't a fucking serial killer. We're walking a very fine line here. One I know he teeters on daily. Emeric has done terrible—horrific—things and he's more than likely capable of doing much worse, but peeling the faces off women to get his rocks off? Would he go that far? Something in my gut tells me no.

"You're right, I do," Emeric admits with a nonchalant shrug. "You're also correct about the whole saint thing." He sarcastically draws a halo around his head with an eye roll. "I'm certainly not one of those. What I am is a man who's owed a debt, and while I've loved watching that fire of yours peek through, princess, we need to get this show on the road. I've shown what would inevitably become of you if you left here and went with your father's choice in groom."

Bogdan now has a claim to me and if he gets his hands on me, I'll become one of the women in the pictures.

"You say the word 'choice' like I have one, Banes," I bite out, turning my glower to him.

This has his lips pulling up in a smirk. "You're right, that was misleading of me. You don't have a choice in groom. You

121

will pay the debt owed to me by leaving this church with my last name. The choice I am willing to give you is this: will you stand here on your own and recite your vows, or do I need to have my men hold you in place?"

"Fuck you."

Like a hunter with a kill in its sight, Emeric prowls to stand before me.

"I already did that, or have you already forgotten what it feels like to have my cock buried so deep in you, you can't breathe?" His fingers trail down my temple to my cheekbone. I despise the fact that I enjoy the trail of heat that follows his touch. Emeric's cocky grin only grows when I bat his hand away. "While the idea of other men touching you makes my trigger finger twitchy, I will have them hold you still until you say, 'I do'. It's your choice. Decide, princess."

FOURTEEN
EMERIC

"Emeric Alastair Banes, do you take Rionach Kara Moran to be your wedded wife, to live together in marriage? Do you promise to love her, comfort her, honor and keep her for better or worse, for richer or poorer, in sickness and health, and forsaking all others, be faithful only to her, for as long as you both shall live?"

I never planned on getting married. Tying myself legally to another human never quite appealed to me. If I'm being honest, dipping my dick in honey and fucking a red ant hill sounded more fun to me than marriage. Then she came along and now I'm uttering two of the easiest words I've ever said.

"I do."

All the church air I've been inhaling must be getting to me, because that furious fire in those green orbs of hers... I want to baptize myself in their flames.

Rionach is all but vibrating as the unadulterated anger rushes through her veins. Much to my delight, she made the choice to stand up here on her own even if she looks like she wants to scratch out my eyes while she does.

Come on, baby, show me those claws.

We stand before each other with Niall hanging between us. In my humble opinion, we look like a piece of fucking art standing up here. The setting sun's rays cut through the church's stained glass windows. The way the colorful light is shining on Rionach's pretty face reminds me of the night the fireworks exploded around her.

My soldier, Mathis, who's been acting as her guard all day, has taken up a position beside her weakening father. The adrenaline that had been keeping him alert and fighting against the nails embedded in his palms is crashing. The gun Mathis has pressed to Niall's temple keeps him focused on the very important task at hand.

Ordaining his daughter's wedding ceremony.

On top of his ever-declining attention span, he's still fighting against this union. Niall thinks by dragging his feet through the whole thing that I'll miraculously change my mind about wanting his daughter as my wife. I've waited since New Year's for this. I'm done waiting. My patience has run thin. Nothing is going to stop me from making Rionach mine.

When he doesn't prompt us to the next part of the ceremony, his eyes drifting lazily to the bloodstains in front of the pews, Mathis presses the pistol harder into his head.

Niall shifts his gaze to his daughter, his brown eyes a mixture of exhaustion and wrath.

"Your turn, Rionach." Despite the current predicament he's found himself in, he still doesn't have the decency to sound defeated. Gotta hand it to the Irish, they're tenacious fuckers. "Rionach Kara Moran, do you take Emeric Alastair Banes to be your wedded husband, to live together in marriage? Do you promise to love him, comfort him, honor and keep him for better or worse, for richer or poorer, in sickness and health, and forsaking all others, be faithful only to him, for as long as you both shall live?"

That same tenacity sits on Rionach's face like an unyielding shield. Her chin rises and those fiery eyes narrow, but still no vows come from her soft lips.

I lean in close and whisper darkly in her ear, "That's it, princess. Keep giving me reasons to punish you." Her breath catches in her throat when I trail my nose down the side of her face. I don't have to turn my head to know Niall's hatred is radiating from him in thick waves as he watches on. "Now, give me what I want. Let me hear those two little words."

My lips pull when she rises on her tiptoes and turns her head toward mine so she can mimic my stance. "I'm going to make you regret this, Emeric Banes," she promises in my ear.

"How could I ever regret making you mine?"

She pulls away and looks at me with her stunning wrath. "I do."

All mine. All mine. All mine.

Niall curses when Mathis shoves the muzzle of the gun against his temple again. "With the power vested in me by the state of New York, I now pronounce you husband and wife," he snarls between clenched teeth. He all but growls like a caged and cornered pound puppy when he's prompted *again* with the gun to say the next part. *The best part.* "Emeric, you may now kiss your bride."

Rionach's head snaps up at the same time her foot lifts off the ground to take a step back. While I enjoy a good chase and fully intend on making her run from me at a later date, I have no interest in prolonging this any further. I want my fucking prize.

"Till death do us part, princess."

Fingers threading through her dark red strands, I capture her before she can get too far and seal my mouth over hers. Her small hands push at my chest for a heartbeat, but the second my tongue traces the seam of her lips, she melts into me. Tasting her after this past week of no contact awakens something inside of me, and that something is hungry. The thought of possibly taking her right here in this church on one of the pews crosses my mind. Further sullying this holy ground with my corruption makes the demon in me grin, so does the idea of further rubbing this union in Niall's face. But I have plans for how I'm going to first take my wife, and those plans don't include this church or an audience. No, we need to be alone so I can savor my stolen bride. So I can make her scream and beg for me.

The soft groan that comes from Rionach has my cock straining harder against the front of my black slacks. Her fingers twisting the fabric of my bloodstained shirt as she holds me closer isn't helping with the depleting grip I have on my control. I'm contemplating whether a quick taste in the back of my SUV will truly force me to deviate too far from my plans when her perfectly straight white teeth sink into my bottom lip.

Hard.

Blood fills my mouth as I rear back from her. The smug smile on her face almost has me falling to my knees and lifting her leg over my shoulder so I can eat her alive right here and now. I don't even give a fuck it'd be in front of her father. She thinks she's done something by biting me, but she hasn't quite learned what a deviant I really am.

Sweetly, she wipes the smear of blood from her own swollen lips as she takes a cocky step back from me. That biddable and quaint girl who everyone's come to know is nowhere to be seen and I fucking love it.

"You should know something," I all but purr as I regain the space she'd just put between us. "Pain. Blood. *The fight*. It only makes me harder and right now, my cock is hard as fuck for you. Your little love bite only made me want you more." My hand snaps out and closes tightly around her jaw. The way her perfect lips part in a gasp gives me the perfect access. Bringing my bloodied mouth back down toward hers, I grin as her green eyes widen and then flare when I spit the mixture of my blood and saliva into her mouth. "Now you taste like me, *wife*."

Besides the way her chest heaves and her tongue swipes over her bottom lip, Rionach doesn't have time to react to what I've just done. The needle sinking into the pale skin of her slender neck steals the opportunity from her.

"What the fuck did you just do?" she cries, trying her best to shove out of my hold. Once all the contents in the syringe are injected, I throw it to the ground and wrap my arm around her waist. The sedative only needs seconds to take effect. "Why did you do this? I'm sorry I bit you. I did what you wanted. I married you..." Even as she berates me, I can see the haziness settling in her eyes.

I take more of her weight as her knees begin to give out. Swiping a long, curled strand of hair out of her face, I ask, "Are you scared?"

Her brows knit in confusion, but she still gives me a sluggish nod.

The kind of terror Bogdan Koslov could offer isn't the kind she craves. I can give her that. I can supply the fear her soul craves.

"Then you have your answer." I press my lips to Rionach's forehead at the same time her entire body goes limp. Swinging her up into my arms in a fashion very appropriate for today's festivities, I carry her bridal style off the dais and away from her quiet father. She makes one last weak-sounding protest before her head settles on my shoulder and consciousness is stolen from her.

"Niall," I call over my shoulder. "I don't know why we

waited so long to do business together because this was fun. We should do it again sometime. Don't stay up there too long. Temps are supposed to drop to below freezing tonight and I'd bet my left nut this hallowed shithole doesn't have insulation in its walls. From what I hear, death by hyperthermia doesn't suck, though, so maybe it won't be so bad if you pussy out and can't bring yourself to pull yourself free."

"Get me off this goddamn thing!" he roars, the fight reentering his body. Good, he's going to need every ounce of adrenaline if he's going to yank free of those nails. "I played your fucking game. I gave you what you wanted. I gave you my daughter!"

I can't stop myself from glancing at the sleeping woman in my arms. *All. Fucking. Mine.* "Yes, you did." There's no point in arguing. "If you make it out of here, I will be in touch within forty-eight hours about the money you owe me. If you fully commit to the Jesus thing and die on that cross, I'll be forced to go to your son and wife regarding my reimbursement."

Since his son and wife seem to be the only things he gives a shit about, maybe my silent threat to them will motivate him to get his ass moving.

I don't bother looking back to make sure Nova and his men are taking care of everything else and cleaning up the mess we've made here. He'll get everything squared away while I'm otherwise preoccupied for the rest of the night.

My wedding night.

FIFTEEN

RIONACH

My head is pounding, and my limbs feel like they're made of stone. It's a battle to fight the thick fog lurking around in my brain. It's an even bigger battle to get my eyelids to cooperate. Panic sets in when I finally manage to crack them open and I'm met with nothing but darkness. While the rational part of me knows I haven't gone blind, I still anxiously try to reach for my face to make sure. My leaden arms only manage to move an inch or so before the restraints wrapped around my wrists halt any further movement.

Okay... now I'm freaking out.

As the reality of my situation sinks in, the adrenaline coursing through my veins like fire burns away the drug-induced haze I've been left in. The memory of Emeric's stupidly handsome face—the blood on his lip only made him sexier, by the way—looking down at me as the needle sunk into my neck flashes in my mind. He drugged me, and now I'm restrained and blindfolded.

The recovered awareness I now have over my body tells me I'm spread out in the shape of an X on a bed covered in silk sheets. Thick cuffs are not only locked around my wrists but also my ankles, keeping me in this vulnerable—exposed—position. The cool breeze against my skin also alerts me to the fact that I'm very much naked.

So, to recap how my day's gone, I've been kidnapped, married off, drugged, and now I'm restrained while rocking my birthday suit.

That's it, it's decided. I'm going to kill my husband.

Husband.

Emeric Banes is my husband. What the actual hell? Today has been a fever dream and I—

"There you are," his voice comes from the dark void engulfing me. With my sense of sight stripped away, my hearing is amplified, and his rasp feels like a sensual caress against my skin. "I've been waiting for you to wake up so we can play."

"Play?" I growl, thrashing my body against the restraints. The material locked around my extremities isn't made of metal, but it still bites into my skin as I fight against them. "Sure, let me go and we can *play*. I can show you just how fucking fun I am."

My air gets trapped in my throat when his fingertips touch the center of my chest and begin to slowly trace down. Between the valley of my breasts and then around my navel. Goosebumps erupt in the wake of that light touch.

"Oh, my sweet Rionach. I already know how much fun you can be. That's never been a mystery to me." Emeric's fingers tread farther south. His touch is still featherlight as he traces a line back and forth between each of my hip bones. He doesn't delve any lower to where my pussy is exposed to him, even though I know he could. In this position, I am well and truly at his mercy. "What I do want to know is how far I can push you before you start begging. For me to give you more. For me to stop. I want to hear you *beg* for both."

Despite the anger simmering in my belly at him and the stunt he pulled today, my body still grows warm and my core clenches with a rapidly growing need at his words. I'm quickly becoming that problematic mixture of terrified and aroused that turns me into a puddle of goo at his feet.

"I already told you I don't beg," I grind out, my hips shifting in a futile attempt to evade his touch. I need my body and mind to get back on the same page about what we think about him, and the feel of his fingers against my warming skin isn't helping matters. "And I don't want this. I don't want *you*."

The bed dips to my left as his body comes to kneel beside me. I'm forced to choke down my gasp of surprise when his lips skim the shell of my ear. "*Liar*," he hums wickedly. "But that's okay. I know the truth. I know how your body comes alive at my touch."

"It does not." Do I sound like an indignant child? Maybe.

I all but come out of my skin when the fingers that had been constantly tracing that line across my pelvis trail lower and dip into that aching place between my thighs. A low groan rattles Emeric's chest at the same time I lose my battle and let out a desperate moan. Two thick fingers deliciously stretch me but it's still not enough. It does little to alleviate the ache that has been building since I first heard his voice.

"You can lie and tell me how much you don't want me, but this sweet pussy of yours will *always* betray you." The mouth on this man makes me feel like I'm going to spontaneously combust. It's not fair. He's not fighting fair. "Look how wet you already are for me, Rionach, and I've barely touched you."

He pulls his digits from my pussy. Any protest from me immediately dies when his fingertips, covered in my arousal, trace over my bottom lip, coating it. It happens without conscious thought when my tongue darts out and licks up the wetness there.

"Do you like the taste of yourself?" His question is followed by the unmistakable sound of him sucking his fingers clean. "It's been a week since I've last tasted you and every single day since then, I've thought about burying my tongue in your cunt. I'm like a heroin addict constantly thinking about my next fix." His palm comes down on my core in a punishing slap, making my back bow and all the air rush out of my lungs. "My drug of choice just happens to be this sweet pussy."

My only response is a low groan. It's the only noise I can manage to make as my brain short-circuits. I'll be the first one to admit that my sexual experience is basically nonexistent, but I've spent a fair amount of time fantasizing about what it *could* be like. Not once during any of those illicit daydreams did being slapped on my pussy cross my mind. The very thought of it sounds painful and borderline degrading. And yet, here I am *panting* over it.

His fingers return to where I need them most. This time he makes slow, methodical circles around my clit. It's not enough to tumble me over the edge. It's just enough contact to make me feel desperate.

The voice in my head keeps trying to remind me of the fact that I'm furious at this man and don't want him to be touching me like this, but with each torturous skilled touch, that voice grows quieter and quieter. Until it's silent.

Much to my displeasure, the mattress shifts again as he moves away from me, and a second later I hear him move to stand at the end of the bed. While I can't physically see him, the hairs rising all over my flesh tell me he's standing there staring at my bound and exposed body. My legs are pulled far enough apart that he has the perfect view of my most intimate places. At this vulnerable thought, my knees try to pull together again, but it's no use.

"Being shy around me is a waste of our time. You're now my wife. Each and every beautiful inch of your body now belongs to me, and I plan on meticulously spending my time making sure you and everyone else knows that." His hands skim up my calves, making me jump and shiver at the same time. "All of this is mine. It's all for me."

"I'm not yours." I manage to put a semblance of strength into my voice even though I'm quaking with need for this psychotic man. "You may have stolen me, but that doesn't make me yours, Banes. Now get your fucking hands off me."

I can't be sure if I sound believable. All I do know is that I don't believe myself.

The way he chuckles has my heart beating faster, pumping a new dose of delicious adrenaline into my system. That wasn't an amused noise. No, it was a laugh that promises something *wicked*.

"Okay, I'll take my hands off you." His easy agreement tells me I just fucked up and the sudden buzzing noise coming from where he stands at my feet confirms it.

He climbs back onto the bed and positions himself between my spread legs. I can barely hear the buzzing now over the blood rushing in my ears as anticipation courses through me. At the first touch of the vibrator against my aching clit, I yank so hard on all four restraints I know I'm going to walk away from this with bruises. The bite of them on my skin becomes a vague sensation as waves of pleasure creep through every nerve ending in my body.

"Oh fuck!" I cry out before sinking my teeth into my bottom lip. I don't want to give him the satisfaction of hearing the pleasure he instills. It's my weak and very desperate attempt to not give fully in to him.

Emeric presses the vibrating device against me and holds it there until stars start to form behind my eyelids. My entire body is shaking, building toward a violent release, but before I can crest the euphoric peak, he removes it from my pussy.

The distressed whimper that comes from me is a noise I barely recognize.

"What a pretty sound," Emeric praises. "Let's see if I can make you do it again."

"No," I breathlessly say, head shaking. "I won't."

"You will."

He doesn't press the vibrator back to my clit like before. The toy must be shaped in a U because Emeric slides one end of the silicone device into me and the other end rests against that bundle of nerves he left throbbing. It's a kind of pleasure I've never experienced before, but one I know is going to drive me fucking crazy. With my hands bound and my legs locked in place, I'm forced to endure every agonizingly delectable vibration until he decides I've had enough.

What a terrifying and exhilarating thing to be completely and thoroughly at Emeric Banes's mercy.

SIXTEEN
EMERIC

"While I know you have a knack for biting lips, I'd hate for you to make yourself bleed."

Rionach doesn't fight me when I pull her bottom lip free from her teeth. She's trying so hard to not make a noise as the vibrator I've placed inside her weeping cunt drives her wild. I know what angle she's playing here. She thinks if she doesn't show how much she's enjoying every second of this she'll remain on her moral high ground. That she isn't giving and accepting this situation as her reality.

I'm not so far gone I can't understand her reasoning for being angry at me. The problem is, I just can't bring myself to care. Not when I got precisely what I wanted: her, with my last name, writhing and shaking in my bed on the brink of an orgasm. Rionach doesn't see it now, the red haze of fury is obstructing it, but one day she'll understand.

I haven't just stolen her and made her mine. I've freed her.

The restraints her family have placed on her are gone. Now we need to work on removing the ones she's locked around herself in a desperate act of self-preservation. There's no need for her to pretend to be something she isn't. Not anymore. Not with me.

It will take time for her to see that. In the meantime, I'm going to have fun teaching her what freedom tastes like.

"Oh, God…" she cries, thrashing back and forth on the black silk pillow beneath her head.

Seeing her like this, restrained to the four posts of my king-sized bed with her red locks splayed out around her in a fiery halo, makes my cock hard to the point of pain.

With the toy in place, I crawl up the length of her body, leaving a trail of open-mouthed kisses as I go.

"Still don't have my hands on you," I tell her before biting down on her nipple. The gasp that comes from her parted lips goes straight to my dick. "Can't say I'm not a man of my word, princess."

Her chest heaves as she takes in shorter and more rapid breaths. I have no doubt the vibrator has her dangling on the edge of combustion, and I for one can't wait to watch her fall apart under me.

Rionach's squirming freezes when I come to a stop and straddle her chest. Not wanting to crush her much smaller body with my weight, I stay on my knees. The angle and position have my cock parallel with her chin, which is perfect for what I have planned.

Wanting to see those pretty eyes of hers look up at me while she sucks me off, I pull the black blindfold from her face. The mixture of heated arousal and ire in those green orbs instantly has a smile growing on my lips.

"Hello, my wife," I greet. "Don't you just look beautiful beneath me like this."

The makeup that had been perfectly applied to her face for our ceremony has turned to black smudges around and below her eyes. The red lipstick was first smudged during our first kiss as husband and wife earlier, and I only made a bigger mess of the pigment when I smeared her arousal over her lips.

She's a mess, but what a striking sight she is.

Her attention darts between my face and the head of my cock that sits directly in front of her face. "What do you plan to do with that?" Even on the cusp of orgasm, Rionach's insolence is strong as ever.

"First, I plan on fucking your mouth while you ride out a couple orgasms with that toy buried in your cunt, and then I'm going to fuck my bride." She bares her teeth at me when I drag the crown of dick across her bottom lip. "It's our wedding night, Rionach. Consummating the marriage is part of the tradition, isn't it?"

She tries to seem put off by my plans, but the dilation of her pupils gives her away. My dirty girl is more than enthralled by the idea of sucking my cock.

"What's stopping me from biting your dick right off if you try to stick that in my mouth?"

"You know what happens to people who displease me. *That's* what's going to stop you from biting me." Hands gripping the top of the headboard, I lower my head so I'm hovering over her. "You either open your mouth and swallow me down like a good girl, or I will force your lips apart, and I will fuck your throat like you're a whore for me to use and not my wife. I'm okay with either. The choice is yours."

"Fuck you," she snarls at the same time her hips roll and her fingers ball into small little fists. My wife is fighting for her life against an impending orgasm beneath me and I fucking love the view.

"Yes, my love," I coo. "I'll fuck you soon. All in due time."

This time when the head of my dick glides across her bottom lip, her tongue darts out, licking up the droplet of precum that had formed. I'm not even sure she realizes she'd done it. The sharp hiss of breath that slips from my clenched teeth has her eyes darkening and her jaw loosening.

For the rest of my life, I'm not sure if I'll ever find anything more beautiful than the sight of my wife's lips wrapping around my cock. We groan at the same time as I feed her inch after inch of me. She gags and her eyes widen with fear when I nudge the back of her throat. She tries to pull away, but with her restraints, she has nowhere to go.

She coughs and pants for breath as I pull out of her hot-as-sin mouth.

"You're doing so good." I wipe away the tears falling from her big eyes. "Have you done this before?"

That stubborn look crosses her face again. I knew Rionach's experience wasn't vast. The way she was raised didn't allow for much opportunity to explore her sexuality.

"I don't care if you don't know how to do this," I find myself reassuring her, "I like the idea of being the first and only man to fuck your mouth. Make sure you breathe through your nose. You have to relax your jaw and try your best to open your throat."

When I offer her my dick again, she doesn't hesitate to take me into her mouth. Her hot tongue licks and swirls as she explores and learns. For a few minutes, I keep my thrusts shallow, allowing her time to adjust to the intrusion.

Behind me, her hips rock and sway, and below me her chest heaves. She's so close.

"That's it, come for me," my fingers curl harder into the wood headboard. "Come while I'm fucking your hot little mouth."

In a display of pure beauty, Rionach succumbs to the roaring bliss. Her back bows and she throws her head back into the silk pillow. Her long, drawn-out moan wraps and vibrates around my leaking cock. As she shakes and writhes below me, she keeps me in her mouth the entire time. Even as she comes down from her high, she sucks on the tip like it's a fucking pacifier comforting her. This move almost has my eyes rolling back in my head and my cum shooting down her throat.

It's by sheer will alone I'm able to keep my own orgasm at bay.

Sensitive from her intense release, she lets my cock drop from her swollen lips as a distraught cry comes from her. Trying to evade the onslaught of vibrations between her thighs, her hips and restrained legs shift and kick violently.

"It's too much," Rionach whimpers. "I need... I need a break."

"No, you're going take it. I want to watch you come again." I reach behind me and press the toy harder against her overly sensitive clit. "Give me what I want. Give in to it, princess."

Tears run down her flushed face, further smearing her dark makeup. Trails of black run down her cheeks. *Stunning.*

She shakes her head violently left to right, and sobs escape her lipstick-smeared mouth. "I can't," she pleads, agony all over her face. "No more. Please, no more."

"Shh, yes, you can. You look so pretty when you beg, wife." I let go of the toy and guide my cock back between her lips to quiet her. "Suck my cock and come for me. I want to feel you moan around me again."

I take her mouth harder this time, my thrusts going deeper. Her throat tightens around me as she swallows me down. Her eyes flare when I keep myself buried, depriving her of air. She fights against the restraints at her wrists as panic sets in.

"Your throat. Your cunt. Your oxygen," I pant. "All of it belongs to me now."

Her eyes roll back as her second orgasm hits her like a freight train. I pull from the warm depth of her throat and watch her convulse beneath me. She sucks in greedy breath after greedy breath and rides out the waves of ecstasy.

Body spent and slightly dazed, she lazily gazes up at me when she's reentered her body. The growl that splits my chest when her tongue flicks the slit in my cock's head borders on primal. In jerky, unsophisticated movements, I move back down her body. The noise that comes out of her when I rip the toy from her soaked pussy is a mouthwatering mixture of a gasp and cry.

I've lost the desire to go slow. To draw our fuck out so we can savor each torturous movement. No, I need to be inside her the same way I need my next breath. This will be the first of many times, but I need to pound into her cunt like it's the last time I'll bury myself in her and I'm trying to brand her from the inside out. So she'll never fucking forget who owns her.

With a stifled groan, I slice into Rionach in one brutal thrust. Our muscles lock as we both tense and our breaths stall in our lungs. My teeth are gritted together so hard I wouldn't be surprised if I cracked a molar. The walls of her tight pussy clench around me, welcoming me home. The act has my body spasming as pleasure washes over me.

"Emeric..." My name is a broken sound that escapes her when she exhales.

"Are you still telling yourself you don't want this?" My hips draw back and then slam forward. Rionach's body tries to surge upright from the harsh intrusion, but the cuffs keep her firmly in place. "That you don't want me pounding into this pussy?"

That obstinate fury pinches her features as she glares at me.

"You want to know what I think?" I take her breast into my palm and squeeze it to the point it's painful. Her back bows, and she lets loose a wounded mewl. "I think even if you weren't tied to my bed, you'd be exactly where you are right now.

Trapped under me. Your greedy wet pussy wrapped around my cock, your muscles milking every ounce of pleasure out of me."

"Untie me. Let's test your theory."

"No." I nip her jaw. "I think I'll keep you at my mercy for a little while longer. I enjoy you like this. Forced to comply to my every want and need."

Whatever impudent retort she's no doubt about to fire back is silenced when I shove two fingers between her lips. Her breathing turns into ragged pants as I press my fingers down against her tongue. She gags once, then twice, and that's why my control truly snaps.

I pound into her. Each thrust is punishing and deeper than the last. My eyes remain locked on where my cock sinks in and out of her drenched pussy, enjoying the visual of being coated with her slick arousal. She's *dripping* for me.

Her cries and writhing become frantic beneath me. "I can't..." she tries to choke out around my fingers. "Not again."

I remove my hand from her mouth so I can collar her throat. Her walls are already starting to flutter and tighten around me. It's too late for her. She's coming whether she wants to or not.

"Yes, you fucking can."

My own release is barreling toward me. I've never come inside a woman. Before the night with Rionach at Tartarus, I've never not used a condom. It was a nonnegotiable for me. My brother, Astor, was trapped into marriage by a woman because he was foolish enough to bareback the bitch. Since I was a teenager, I've swore I wouldn't fall victim to the same fate.

But this is different. Rionach is already my wife and coming while buried in her cunt doesn't feel like a choice anymore. It's a necessity.

This fuck suddenly isn't simply about getting off, it's about *claiming* her. Marking her as *mine*. My growl is followed by a violet curse as my mind is taken over by thoughts and urges I've never once experienced before. It's a consuming and primal feeling, bordering on downright animalistic.

What better way to mark my territory than to fill her with my cum? To plant my seed deep inside her where it could take root and grow.

This very visual has me rearing back and a snarl ripping from my throat. Completely taken over by this primal need, I pound brutally into my wife. My hands, both now wrapped around her hips, grip her in a punishing hold as I force her to take every ruthless thrust. Over the thundering pounding in my ears, I think I can hear her strangled cries, but I can't be sure. I'm too far gone at this point.

White-hot, blinding ecstasy crashes into me like a tidal wave, it's a fight to keep myself from drowning in the exhilarating rush. My rhythm falters and becomes erratic. Her pussy clamps down on my length like a vise. Balls pulling up tight against my body, Rionach's muscles milk every ounce of cum from me. She lets out a hoarse moan when she feels me emptying inside her.

I never let up or stop fucking my wife through my climax, greedy for every bit of ecstasy I can get from her. Even completely spent and dick now at half-mast, I thrust shallowly. Each small touch forces a breathy gasp from her. She rears her head back into the pillow, her flushed and sweaty face frozen in a silent scream when I glide my finger through the mess between her thighs. The combination of our joined cum makes her center slippery as I circle her clit and force one last final orgasm out of her.

She explodes, calling my name as she does. It's a magnificent sound that has newfound blood rushing to my cock. If I wanted to, I could take her again, but my bride has had enough.

She has nothing left to give tonight. Even now, while fighting to regain her breath, her eyes are drooping, exhaustion settling in her bones.

I pull myself free from her beckoning core and kneel between her parted legs. The view of my seed leaking from her pink and swollen cunt has me biting back a groan. Rionach jerks, her flesh overly sensitive from the ceaseless attention it's been receiving as I gather the semen that has trickled out of her and push it back in. I have to ensure none of it goes to waste.

Satisfied she's been fully and thoroughly claimed by me, I climb from the bed and make quick work of releasing her limbs from their restraints.

Rionach doesn't stir once. Even when I pull the black sheet over her naked body, she remains deep in her blissful post-fuck slumber. The only noise she makes happens when I climb into bed beside her. I won't sleep, I rarely do, but that contented sigh of hers makes me want to stay and watch her for a while longer.

SEVENTEEN
RIONACH

I woke up alone in a bedroom that belongs in luxury interior design magazines. Between the blindfold and the sex-induced haze I was in last night, I hadn't looked around the room I'd been brought to after he *drugged* me. After our *wedding*.

Turns out the devil of New York doesn't live in an underground lair, he lives in a penthouse that is so many stories up in the sky, I can see the entirety of Central Park. All four corners of the tree-filled space that takes up fifty-one solid blocks are visible from his bedroom windows. And *windows* don't seem like an appropriate word to describe the walls of glass taking up two whole sides of his room. If we weren't so far up, I'd worry about people being able to see in.

Emeric's an incredibly elusive man. I know he wouldn't dwell somewhere his privacy would be threatened.

My screaming bladder is what finally pulls me from my post-fuck comatose state and out of the massive king-sized four-poster bed. *At least I now know what I was tied to last night.*

Every muscle in my body aches. I thought I had been sore after my last bout with Emeric, but it turns out that was just a precursor for the true havoc he could wreak on my pussy. Between the tenderness and stickiness left behind between my thighs, I'm in desperate need of a shower. My first look in the mirror hanging over the black marble and chrome sink vanity further confirms my rough state.

I look like I was fucked to *death*. Or at the least, I'm doing my best impression of a roadkill raccoon. The dark eye makeup Monica had painstakingly applied has migrated all over my face, and my lipstick? Yeah, there's no denying my mouth got thoroughly fucked. My hair is more tangled than the thoughts and emotions going through my brain, and my naked body is sporting a couple new bruises. As I'd guessed last night, my wrists and ankles are marked from how hard I'd pulled against the restraints, and my hip bones and thighs are dotted from where his hands gripped me. I hate that I *like* them, and I hate even more that I like that *he's* the one who left them there.

With one last disapproving look at myself in the mirror, I turn to the walk-in shower that's bigger than most New Yorker's bedrooms and turn the water on to "burn your skin and sins away" hot.

After standing under the spray of water and attempting to collect myself for a long moment, I reach for the alcove in the tiled wall where bottles sit. I freeze at the familiar-looking bodywash and haircare products. They're my brands. My *exact* brands. How the hell does he know what kind of shampoo I use?

Next to the bottles sits a razor with a lavender handle.

"That's mine," I whisper to myself after taking a closer look at it. Doing the same with the hair and body products, I find that some of them are half empty. Just like the ones I left in my own shower back at my parents' estate. "What the..."

Rushing through the rest of my shower, I climb out and

wrap myself in a giant fluffy black towel. *Black to match his soul... cute.*

One entire side of the bathroom is made of a long marble counter with two sinks. Between the sinks is a built-in vanity with a modern-looking stool in front of it. Opening the drawer in front of the leather seat, I discover that all my skincare and makeup have also been brought here and carefully organized.

And my electric toothbrush sits next to one of the sinks, like it's always been kept there.

Still dripping wet, I charge out of the bathroom and into the adjoining massive closet. Sure as shit, every single garment of clothing I own is hanging or is folded neatly in the drawers in the marble-topped island in the middle of the room. Even my panties are folded and tucked neatly away. Not only are my own clothes here, but it also looks like a personal shopper had a field day with Emeric's no-limit black card. *Dozens* of brand-new designer women's pieces have been added to my wardrobe. Their tags are still dangling off them and I just know if I looked at the price of them, I'd want to throw up.

The man has been *inside* of me—I mean, fuck, he came in me last night—and yet, seeing my clothes and his perfectly intermingled together seems too intimate. It's a jarring sight because until this very moment, I don't think the gravity of yesterday's events had really sunk in.

I'm married to Emeric Banes and now I'm living with him. This is now my *home.*

This is *really* happening.

"How is this going to work?" I ask myself like a lunatic because apparently on top of everything, I also talk to myself now. *Neat.*

That very question circles around in my head the entire time I dry my hair and apply my makeup. I still haven't come up with an answer to my question by the time I've pulled on my favorite pair of leather leggings and a ridiculously oversized black sweater that comes down to my fingertips. The only hint of skin that is showing is a bit of my shoulder where my top hangs loosely. *Good.* I need to talk to my newly acquired *groom*, and I don't need to give him any ideas while I do it. We both need to focus so I can get my answers.

Since my favorite pair of knee-high black boots are nowhere to be seen—another casualty to yesterday's festivities —I settle on a pair of chunky ankle booties. My mother despised them, which only made me love them more, but it also meant I rarely got to wear them. *She's not here. She can't tell you what to wear,* a little voice in my head excitedly reminds me. Imogen Moran would keel over if she saw me wearing this. It's too frumpy and casual for her elite tastes.

With no plan or idea for where Emeric even is, I decide my best bet is to just start wandering around the penthouse. Surely, I'll come across him at some point, and if that doesn't work, maybe I'll just start a small fire. That should have him running to me in no time. Burning one—or ten—of his bespoke suits is well deserved after the show he put on yesterday.

Devious smirk on my face, I leave the safety of his bedroom and brave the rest of his luxurious space. The first thing I discover is that this well and truly is a penthouse. I was kind of just making an educated guess before since I couldn't see Banes living in a two-bedroom apartment with a galley kitchen.

But nope, I was right. It's an enormous fucking penthouse.

This place is obscene. What a single man is doing with this much space is beyond me. I have to remind myself that we're not dealing with just any ordinary thirty-something-year-old male.

By every sense of the word, my parents are wealthy, but this home is calling them poor in about six different languages.

I'm not an architect—never cared much about interior design either—and even I know this place is a work of art.

Three stories are connected by a wide spiral staircase that is made entirely of shiny metal and glass. *Glass.* It's *everywhere*, between the abundant floor-to-ceiling windows and glass railings lining the various walkways on each story... one well-aimed rock could have this whole place shattering. The weirdest but prettiest chandelier I've ever seen hangs down the middle of the spiral staircase. I almost miss a step on my descent because I'm enthralled by the twisted metal and crystal monstrosity.

I make it down to the main level and am greeted by a very sleek and modern black and stainless-steel kitchen. It has the same vibe as his bathroom, and I can't say it doesn't match the property's owner perfectly. Dark and moody with a hint of opulence.

Beyond the kitchen is a sunken-in living room with the biggest white sectional sofa I've ever seen. *Does he have enough friends to justify this amount of seating? Doubt it.* It sits in front of a black stone fireplace that reaches the second level of the penthouse.

I'm about to venture down the hallway leading past the living area, when a low growl has me turning into a piece of stone where I stand. Too afraid to breathe, I turn as slowly and calmly as I can toward the source of the noise. Emeric is psychotic enough, for all I know he could own a fucking lion. If I turn around to find Simba snarling at me, I wouldn't be surprised in the least.

To my relief, it's not a giant cat, but it is a dog. A very large and very upset-looking Doberman Pinscher. I'm five-foot-four without any shoes on, and even in my thick-soled boots, the animal's pointed ears reach my rib cage. It's made of pure muscle—has to be at least one hundred pounds—and its teeth...

well, I can basically count every single one with the way its lips are pulled back in a vicious snarl.

I'm trying to remember what I'm supposed to do if I'm ever faced with a dangerous animal—do I make myself big and retain eye contact or do I run screaming?—when a sharp whistle slices through the tension.

The dog's menacing growling instantly ceases and its large head whips in the direction of the sound. I follow the animal's gaze and find the man I've been searching for leaning casually against the white-painted wall.

"Cerberus, *nein.*" His low, raspy voice wraps around me, making shivers run down my spine. "*Lass es. Freund.*"

Is that *German?*

Emeric stands in the hallway I'd been planning to search next, his arms crossed over his chest. The black button-down—an article of clothing that is a staple for him based on how many I saw hanging in the closet—is tight around his well-formed biceps and chest. Flashbacks of how his defined muscles had tightened and flexed under his golden skin as he pounded into me flood my mind. If it wasn't for the scary man-eating dog stalking closer to me, I may have succumbed to those illicit thoughts a moment longer.

"Oh... umm," I sputter when it pushes its cold wet snout into my fingers.

Emeric doesn't seem the least bit concerned. "Don't take the display of teeth personally, he's trained to corner and neutralize intruders." *Oh lovely*, he has an attack dog. "You should feel flattered that he hesitated like he did. Usually, he takes a chunk out of anyone he deems a threat without question. Just ask Nova. He's been on the receiving end of a love bite once or twice."

"Who the hell would be stupid enough to break in here?" Cerberus licks my fingers, making me jump back a step. Niall and Imogen have a strict no-animal policy. My experience with dogs is limited to the ones I've stopped to pet here and there on the street or subway. Most often than not, they were the size of stuffed animals and not the size of a small pony like this one is.

"The level of human stupidity never ceases to amaze me. Just take your father and brother, for instance." Emeric chuckles.

"Do you think what happened yesterday was funny?"

"Immensely." He doesn't hesitate a second with that response. "You don't have to worry about Cerberus. He knows you're a friend now."

The look on my face tells him I think he's full of shit. "You just told me he's bitten Nova. Isn't that Viking your lieutenant or something? That means he's here all the time. Meanwhile, I'm nothing but fresh meat."

"Fresh meat?" he repeats, a wicked grin pulling at his lips. "I've never told him Nova is a friend."

Cerberus walks around me in a slow circle, sniffing as he goes before returning to stand before me. This time he gives my hand a demanding nudge. Cautiously, I pet his head. The scary guard dog persona is completely gone when he plops down on his butt and happily accepts my attention.

"Why would you do that?"

"Nova isn't scared of much. Seeing him get nervous around my dog is amusing to me."

"Jesus, you're..." I trail off, not knowing how to finish that sentence. The options are endless. "Why do you give him commands in German?"

Emeric stalks lazily closer to me. His expensive leather shoes clicking against the light stained hardwood floors. "I don't want anyone else to try and tell something that belongs to me what to do. Orders should only be obeyed if they're coming directly from me."

It feels like there's a deeper meaning to his words and I'm going to dissect the possibilities at a later date, but not now. Not when I'm still looking for answers.

"I was looking for you."

This perks him right up, the wicked gleam in his eyes shifting to an arrogant one. "Oh? And what were your plans for when you found me?"

He's hoping I'll say something along the lines of, *Jump your bones and ride you until I'm weak in the knees*, so I tell him the opposite. "Stab your eyes out with a letter opener and then find your most expensive bottle of whiskey so I can propose a toast to this sham of a marriage."

I knew it when I said it that my taunt would have the opposite desired effect on him.

Emeric's stormy eyes all but twinkle as he traces his hand down the side of my face. "Vicious little thing, aren't you, Rionach?" His voice drops an octave, sounding dark and delicious. *Not fair.* Fingers threading into the strands of loose hair around my ear, he holds me firmly in place and leans his tall body down so we're eye level. "Nothing about our marriage is a sham. In fact, the official marriage license was signed and filed with the state this morning. My people told me your new social security card, driver's license, and passport should be delivered within the week."

"What? I didn't sign anything." Even as I say it, I know I'm being silly. A man like Emeric Banes doesn't need to go through normal—or legal—channels to get what he wants. "And why do I need new identification?"

His lips curl as his thumb swipes over my cheekbone in slow, methodical grazes. "Because you're no longer a Moran. You're my wife and your name is now Rionach Kara Banes." That sinister gleam returns to his eyes. "I like the way that sounds... it just rolls off the tongue, don't you think?"

Cocky fucker.

I gape at him. "What if I didn't want to change my name?"

"My bride can't have the same last name as my competitors —even if they are agonizingly pathetic," he explains. "Competitors doesn't feel like a fair word for your family, though. Then again, it's not Niall's fault. He's been fighting a losing battle for over a decade. Never really stood a chance."

He's right. My dad was never going to be strong enough to take Emeric on. I think his grand plan was to raise Tiernan to be strong enough to do it. With a single swing of an ax, Emeric proved how misguided that thinking was.

"You can change my last name, but you can't change my blood. Doesn't matter if my name is Moran or if it's Banes, I will always carry their DNA."

A look I can't decipher flashes across his striking features, but when I blink, and it's gone.

"You've never been one of them." He grips my face tighter. "The second they decided to sell you to the Koslovs, they forfeited any claim they had on you."

The anger I'd felt toward him yesterday while standing in the deteriorating church rears its ugly head. I shove his hand away and step back from him *and* his dog.

Or at least, I try to. Cerberus moves with me and lies his big body down basically on my feet.

"And what do you think that makes you? My savior?" I scoff at this. "That's a joke and you know it. You don't save people and even if you did, it wouldn't be out of the goodness of your black heart." At the root of my hair, my fingers tug at the strands as I shake my head at him. "I don't understand you. You could have married *anyone* at *any* time. You're powerful, richer than most small countries, and you're hot." Why beat around the bush? It's not as if he doesn't already know this. "You could have had your pick of the litter. So, I want to know.

153

Why now? And why *me*? It can't be because we fucked that *one* time at Tartarus. You're not a monk. Trust me, I'm fully aware that I'm another one of the many notches on our bedpost."

"But you are the only one to sleep in my bed." He shares this tidbit of information so casually, meanwhile I can feel my eyebrows hit my hairline. "You're also the first and only woman who isn't an employee to step foot in my home."

That can't possibly be true and if by some insane chance it is, then it's only going to make me more confused about why he chose *me*. What does he see in me that made him decide I was worthy of marrying him and sleeping in his bed?

Not willing to allow this information to completely derail me from my objective, I refortify myself against him. "Why did you force me to marry you, Emeric?"

Shoving his hands into the pockets of his black dress pants, he releases a long sigh. As he does, gray-colored eyes scan me head to toe. Just like that night in the hotel, I'm fully dressed and yet I feel exposed. That storm-cloud-filled gaze has a way of making you feel like it sees deeper than what's visible on the surface. They see past the walls and facades you build around yourself.

"Your father and brother stole half a million dollars in weapons from me," he starts, voice now hard and unemotional. "I was owed compensation for their thievery."

The way he says these words makes the whole thing sound so... cold and transactional. I guess that is the correct and *safe* way to look at the new status of our relationship. If we can even call it that yet. We're married, but are we in a relationship?

It's hard to reconcile that this was nothing more than another business deal when last night, when I was tied to his bed, it felt anything but. It was intense and passionate. The complete opposite of what business should be.

My arms cross tightly against my chest. "And finding another clever way to tell my father 'fuck you' was just the cherry on top, right?"

"What can I say? I never turn down a good time."

I stare at the mysterious man in front of me. Emeric's still a puzzle to me and I'm trying to put him together while missing the crucial corner pieces. All the information I have on him is from the rumors I've gathered over the years and from the short moments we've spent together. And during those very heated moments, we weren't exactly doing much talking.

The person I've married is a stranger to me, and what an alarming thought that is.

"So... half a million, huh?" I ask, shifting on my feet. The movement makes the Doberman's big head perk up. His brown eyes flick to me once before he returns to his relaxed state. "That's all I'm worth?"

And just like that, the impassiveness lifts from Emeric's face. "Niall thought you were worth that much." When he pauses, I'm ashamed of how my heart sinks. The pain of my parents' indifference is a wound I don't think will ever fully heal, no matter how hard I try to not let it affect me. "But me? I would have paid more."

I'm not sure if he's more surprised by my laugh that escapes or if I am.

He raises a dark brow. "Do you think I'm lying?"

"I don't know," I admit. "I don't know *you*. Shit, I don't know what we're doing. My entire life feels like a giant question mark right now. That's why I was coming to find you, so we could talk."

"What do you want to talk about?"

Oh, what a loaded fucking question. "Mainly, I just want to know how the hell this is going to work."

EIGHTEEN
EMERIC

Similar to how I felt last night watching her sleep in my bed, I get the oddest sense of rightness when Rionach makes herself comfortable on my couch. The sensation sits in my chest, right under my sternum. It's so prominent, I find myself rubbing at the spot. Once. Twice. Three times. I have to force my hand back to my side so I don't draw her attention to something I don't understand myself.

Aside from Nova and Cerberus, I don't enjoy having people in my space, and even then, Nova knows when he's worn out his welcome. My home is my haven away from the battlefield that is my world and all the bullshit that comes from it. Allowing another person—specifically a woman—to sully that was something I was never willing to do. Arranging meetings at the sex club below Tartarus kept that line in the sand between casual and commitment well defined. Commitment is something I was never able to offer, or something I wanted in life.

Until her.

My obsession for Rionach is something I'm not sure I'll

ever be able to fully comprehend, but I don't need to. Her parents barely put up a fight for their daughter, meanwhile I'd paint my city red with blood if someone tries to take her from me. My wife will need to be pulled from my cold dead hands for me to willingly give her up.

And from the looks of it, my dog—who's been trained to rip out throats and has more kills under his belt than some of my soldiers—is also completely enthralled with the pretty girl. Knowing he's not allowed on the furniture, he sits as close to her as he can get while resting his big head in her lap.

Without trying, Rionach already has Cerberus wrapped around her finger.

"So..." she prompts. "How do you see this working?"

I rest my arms on the back of the sectional and cross my leg over my knee. "What specifically are you asking? We're married. We'll live here together as husband and wife."

"We're going to, what? *Play house?* For how long?"

This has my eyes narrowing. "What do you mean 'for how long'?"

Either unfazed or unaware of my shift in tone, Rionach just lifts her narrow shoulders. "I just want to know how long you plan to keep this up—what your end goal is here. Will you decide you've had enough when the amusement of my father and brother being pissed at you wears off, or maybe you'll grow bored of me and that's when you'll realize you've made a mistake?"

She thinks I've made a mistake by marrying her?

While some would think that what she's saying makes her sound like a needy or insecure girlfriend looking for reassurance, I know that's not Rionach. It's not her character. If anything, I think she's asking these questions so she can plan and try to stay two steps ahead of the ending she clearly thinks is already barreling toward her.

"Did you not hear what I said yesterday?" My head cocks to the side as I greedily take her in. From what I've learned and observed during these past few weeks, her minimal makeup and casual outfit would never fly with her parents' standards. *"Till death do us part.* I would strongly recommend you stop anticipating our demise because one of our hearts will have to be still in our chests for this marriage to end. It's best you just accept it now."

She fidgets in her seat for a second, attention shifting to the dog staring adoringly up at her. *What a fucking sap.* "What? Don't tell me you don't believe in divorce," she says, still not looking at me.

"Quite the opposite. I'm a very strong advocate of divorce," I correct. The best thing my brother did was divorce the hag who trapped him into marriage, and to this day, I wish our mother had been strong enough to do the same and leave our father. She might still be alive if she had. "I just don't believe in ours. Not sure if you've noticed, but I'm a very possessive man, Rionach. I don't let go of things once they are mine. Not without a bloody fight, that is, and we both know I *always* win."

"Okay, so we're stuck married to each other—"

"Stuck?" I repeat, shifting my body so I'm leaning my elbows on my knees. "If that's how you see marriage, would you rather be *stuck* with me or with Bogdan? Either way, you were always going to end up married. At least as my wife, you'll get to live."

The second she pushed out a Koslov baby, her life expectancy would have dropped dramatically. If she lived to see the age of twenty-six, she would have been lucky.

"Do I?" she starts, green eyes sparking. "Get to live, I mean. What are you expecting from your wife, Emeric, because I'll tell you right now, being arm candy at fancy social events and being a subservient housewife isn't my idea of living. What am

159

I supposed to do? Wait around—alone—here in your penthouse all day, and have a scotch poured and waiting for you when you finally wander home? And then what? Once you're done eating the hot meal I no doubt prepared, I'm supposed to just spread my legs for you. Then we just repeat it over and over again until one of us dies? That's not living, that's *hell*."

"Do I look or act like the kind of man who would want that?" She really hasn't been paying attention if that's the case. "I'm not sure what I've done that's given you the impression that my dick gets hard for the pearl-wearing Betty-fucking-Crocker types, but that isn't correct. If I wanted one of them, I could have been married ten times over by now with all those aristocratic daddies acting like their daughters' pimp." The mothers are even worse.

The look on her face tells me she doesn't quite believe what I'm telling her. "It's been my experience that the innocent girls wearing a string of pearls are exactly the kind of wife men like you are looking for."

I know the second the expression on my face turns lethal because she sits up straighter on her couch cushion.

"This *one* time, I'm going to let you have a pass for grouping me in with the cocksuckers you were raised around." Those pseudo-alpha types who demand virgins and submissive wives are the very men who start crying the second I walk into my concrete room with a pair of pliers. No, I'm nothing like them. "As for what your daily schedule will look like as my wife, we'll need to figure that out. Contrary to what you're currently assuming, the only cage I want to keep you in resides under Tartarus. I don't want to keep you locked up at home because, you're right, that's no way to live."

The relief she feels hearing this washes across her face immediately. "So, if I wanted, I could leave whenever and do whatever I want?"

I find myself curious about what she wants to do with her freedom. She doesn't seem like the kind of girl who will spend her entire day in high-end boutiques shopping her little heart away. Perhaps I can find her a *safe* position somewhere working with me. That would solve two of our problems: her boredom and my very obsessive desire to keep her close to me at all times.

"Not by yourself," I correct, instantly stealing her relief. "The last name Banes offers you a level of protection you've never had before, but it also paints a target on your back. It's no secret I've amassed quite the list of enemies over the years. To get to me, they'll now try to use you." My obsession. My weakness. *My wife.* I knew when I gave her my last name that they'd try to use her against me and when they do, they'll quickly—and brutally—learn what a vast mistake that is. I thought I was creative before with my torture, but if someone comes for my wife, there's no saying what I'll do. "I'm working on finding the right guards to assign to your detail. It should only take a few more days. Nova is narrowing down the candidates as we speak." It would seem I'm having difficulty selecting a man I can trust to keep his hands and eyes off my girl. "Until that happens, you will have to stay in the penthouse unless Nova or I are available to escort you."

"Escort me? And ugh, *bodyguards*. The only one I ever liked was Brayden, but the rest were either mean as hell or pervy. Or *both*," Rionach groans, slumping farther into the couch. Sighing, she rests her head on the back of the cushion. After a second of contemplation, she says, "Promise it will only be a couple of days. I'm serious about this. While it's a very pretty cage, it's still a cage if you keep me locked up in here."

I nod. "I'll speak to Nova about it when I meet him in a bit."

She pats the top of my lovestruck dog's head. "Fine. I'll stay cooped up in your gargantuan penthouse with your dog." She gives me a pointed look. "For two days. *Only*. If you try to keep me in here longer than that, I'm warning you now, I won't be so compliant with your plan."

"Oh? Is that right? Do you worst, Rionach. I would love to see what you have up your sleeve." She's going to find out soon that the only way to access the elevator is with a key card. If she wants to leave this place, she'll need one of them, and since there's only five of them in existence, her chances of escape aren't looking too good.

"Don't say I didn't warn you." The not-so-innocent look that dances across her face almost has been picking her up and bringing her back to my bedroom.

"I heard you loud and clear," I counter, completely unconcerned with her threat. "Cerberus is better trained and more lethal than most of my soldiers. He'll keep you safe while I'm away at work."

"Then you should just hire him to guard me. He's cute and he can't talk. Sounds like a win-win situation to me," she offers with a small but *real* smile. It's the first one that's graced her lips since we were married. "Also, Cerberus and Tartarus... do you have a thing for Greek mythology?"

"I'm impressed you put that together." I incline my head at her.

She smiles again with a casual lift of her shoulders. "What can I say? I majored in hospitality and minored in myth studies at NYU. The Greek stories were my favorite."

This has my own lips twitching. This is just another odd but perfect way that Rionach's pieces fit with mine. "My mother was half Greek and spent most of her childhood in Greece. Instead of reading traditional bedtime stories, she told my brothers and I the myths she grew up hearing. They must have stuck because I named my guard dog after Hades's beast, and my brother Astor has a golden eagle named Periphas after a legend about Zeus."

Rionach's mouth gapes a little. "Your brother has an *eagle*? What kind of pet is that?"

I bark out a laugh. "Not a good one. Between the bird and his newly acquired wife's thoroughbred horse, he basically has a fucking petting zoo."

"Your brother recently got married too?"

"Yes, a few months back. Her name is Indie. Remind me to tell you about how he met his bride sometime. It's quite the story." Astor tries to pretend he's removed himself from the depravity we were raised in by becoming a prestigious member of academia in Seattle, but he's a Banes through and through. Stealing his own son's girlfriend is evidence of that. The fact that he also tossed his wife's stepfather out the side of a helicopter is further proof he's not as straitlaced as he tries to be. Flying out there to assist him with that endeavor was a bucket of fun... a true brotherly bonding moment for us, if I do say so myself.

She leans forward and considers me with a look I can't quite decipher.

"What?"

"This is just the first bit of information I've learned about you that isn't about your diabolical warfare or the havoc you wreak on the city. *Or* about what your tastes are like in bed," she explains, her eyes flashing at the mention of our more intimate time spent together. "This was just about you. Your family. It was real."

Talking about my family or personal details about myself always felt like a surefire way to give my enemies ammunition to use against me or my growing empire. It always seemed smarter to never allow someone to delve that deep. It helps that I scare most people shitless and they wouldn't dare try to pry for personal information about me. There was a time both Astor and I worried about my nephew, Callan. Just as I will do with my own children when the time comes, we kept Callan shielded and protected from the ugliness of this world for as long as we could. That came to an end last summer when he visited and informed me he was ready to be involved in the family business. At almost twenty-four years old, who was I to tell the young man no? By the time I was his age, I'd been running the Banes empire for nearly three years.

"You should do that more often moving forward. If we're really married, I'd prefer if I didn't feel like I was cohabitating with a complete stranger who occasionally fucks me." Her eyes flick over me from head to toe. "That's another thing I wanted to talk to you about."

"You want to talk about me fucking you?" I muse with a smirk. "I'm liking this change in subject already. Where should we start?"

This time she doesn't smile. "We can start with you telling me whether or not you're going to fuck other women while you're married to me. From what I've seen, faithfulness isn't something taken very seriously in our world. I might not have much to my name or to offer, but I have my pride and I'm not going to let you take that from me. I've seen the wives dangling off their husbands' arms thinking they're a prized possession while everyone else in the room knows he spends his weekends with his mistress. It's sad and embarrassing, and I swore I'd never end up as one of those women if I could help it." That stubborn look of hers settles across her face. "So far, you've demanded everything from me, and I haven't gotten a say in any of it, but I am going to demand this. Treat me with the respect I deserve and keep your dick out of other people."

"Keep my dick out of other people?" I repeat, rising from my place on the opposite side of the sofa. I close the distance between us and prowl to her. My dog ducks out of the room before I come to a stop directly in front of her legs. Her eyes flare when I lean over her sitting frame and take hold of the back of the cushion behind her, effectively caging her in. This isn't her first—or last—time being trapped by me and just like before, there isn't a glimmer of fear on her face as she tilts her chin up to look at me. "You think I want to fuck other people?"

I'm fixated by the way her tongue sneaks out and swipes across her bottom lip—a lip I very much want to bite. My own lip is still tender today from where her teeth sank into it yesterday at the church, I'm so very tempted to even the score now.

"How am I supposed to know what you want?" she asks, breath hitching in her throat when the tip of my nose trails from her temple down to her defined jawline.

"You *ask*," I whisper. "And I'll tell you *exactly* what I want."

I press my lips to where her pulse is thundering in her throat. Gasping at the contact, her hands, which had been sitting in her lap, snap out and fist my shirt at my sides.

"What do you want, Emeric?" With barely any contact, I've made her voice go from strong—demanding—to breathless. *So. Fucking. Responsive.*

I nip at the creamy flesh of her neck. "Princess, do you honestly think I would go through all the fucking trouble of making you my wife if I wanted to, as you so eloquently put it, *stick my dick* in anyone else? I'm a very busy man with a lot of options at my fingertips. Options I don't have to bloody or tire myself to obtain. I don't have to *work* to get what I want, but for you, I did. What does that tell you?"

"That you want me."

"Yes," I hiss, skimming my lips against hers.

She still doesn't know the entirety of my reasoning for

taking her as my wife. When she asked, I momentarily considered telling her about seeing her on the roof—about what I saw in her up there. That piece of her she keeps so well hidden calls to me like I am a moth to a flame, but I know she isn't ready to learn the whole truth. For now, her believing I wanted her because of what her family did is good enough. In time, when she finally comes into her own and spreads her wings, I'll tell her the truth.

Rionach pushes herself higher to try and deepen the barely-there kiss. I pull away before she can succeed at doing so. The frustrated look reflected back at me almost makes me grin.

"I'm not going to fuck anyone else." It seems trivial to vow such a thing when I haven't so much as thought about other women in nearly two months. "But, my dear wife, you must know by now that I'm not a man who shares well. I already showed you what happens to people who steal from me, and you..." I caress the side of her face adoringly before seizing it in a tight, unyielding hold, "Are my most priceless possession. If another man touches you, not only will he lose his hands *and* his cock, but he will also lose his life. And I will take them in that very order. Then I will bring them home to you gift wrapped like it's fucking Christmas. We haven't even begun to talk about what your punishment will be if you let another man's hands anywhere near you, Rionach."

She doesn't cower, doesn't even flinch at my threat. Instead, she stares up at me like she's considering allowing another man near her just so she can learn what her punishment could be. The possibility of pain and reprimand by my hands excites my wife.

"Glad we made that clear," she exhales, and the breath of air dances across my lips and chin. "And it's Rio. My friends call me Rio."

Unable to stop myself, I graze her bottom lip with my blunt teeth. "I'm not your friend." With one last slow, gluttonous perusal of her pretty features, I retreat and stand to my full height. "I'm your lawfully wedded husband."

"So you keep reminding me," Rionach quips sarcastically. She shifts to the edge of her seat when she notices me backing out of the room. "Where are you going?"

I check the Rolex on my wrist. Yep, I'm going to be late but getting to talk to Rionach is worth ruffling Nova's Boy Scout feathers. That man hasn't been late a day in his life. What a goddamn show-off. I already know I'm going to be walking into a room with an irritated and huffy tattooed not-so-Jolly Green Giant.

"Nova is waiting for me at the office. We have to go over a shipment we're expecting from our Turkish contacts. With your brother helping himself to my inventory, I'm trying to bring in new merchandise. Buyers were already lined up and waiting for those weapons to be delivered to them. While they'll be patient with my tardiness, it would be bad business to keep them waiting much longer."

Rionach's brows shoot up and she gapes at me a moment before clearing her throat and composing herself. "I can't believe you just told me that."

"Why not? You asked. I answered."

"I'm not used to getting a real answer when I ask questions like that one. Usually, I get some vague response... that's if I get a response at all." She stands from the couch and moves her waist-length hair over one shoulder. "I'm more accustomed to being kept in the dark about these kinds of things. A woman's place is in the kitchen and all that other bullshit, I guess."

Her family's antiquated belief system is going to be the thing that destroys them. It hinders their growth and keeps them in the dark ages. Some of the best business-minded people I've ever come across are women—just look at Giuliana. She can make grown men cry in courtrooms and she smiles while she does it. She's a cold-blooded shark who not only helps keep me out of federal prison but also helps me make hundreds of millions a year.

I want to allow Rionach to become something more than what she's been offered her whole life, but I also need to ensure her safety. If she gets in too deep with the murkier sides of my business, it will implicate her in the criminal activity, and orange is simply not her color.

"I'm never going to be able to tell you everything. It would be unwise and unsafe to do so," I explain. "But I will try to always tell you what I can."

Her head nods once. "Thank you." I find it interesting how providing her with that little bit of reassurance seems to put her at ease. "Okay. Well, I'll snoop around here for a while and find something to entertain myself with. Will you be home late?"

While it might not look like it, I feel every nerve in my body stumble at this question. When was the last time someone was *waiting* for *me* at home? It must have been when I was eleven and my mother was alive. When my father was unfortunately still breathing air and I was sharing a roof with my brothers, it was *never* this way.

I manage to shake off the unwanted memories that flood my head. That's twice today that I've thought about Mom, and I'm not sure if I like it. Sometimes our mind does us a favor by burying memories. It's a way of self-preservation.

"Most likely. Don't plan on me being home for dinner. My housekeeper and chef comes three days a week, and loads the fridge with meals. Help yourself to anything you want, and if you need anything, there's a new cell phone waiting for you on the kitchen counter. My number as well as Nova's is programmed into it."

"What happened to my cell phone?"

"Fuck if I know." I shrug. Truly, I don't have the slightest clue where it ended up after Mathias collected it from her. "It doesn't matter. I don't want anyone with the last name *Moran* to have a way of accessing you. A new phone number will help rectify that."

The new phone's location is also shared with mine, so I will be able to monitor her movements once she's allowed out of the safety of my home and able to wander as she pleases. *Wander within reason,* the possessive and newly protective demon inside me whispers.

I move back to her and press a kiss to her head. The scent of her shampoo floods my nose and I breathe it in deeply. I'm not ashamed to admit I smelled the citrus-scented shampoo this morning when I found it in my shower. While Giuliana and the guards brought Rionach to the church, a handful of men stayed behind and packed up every single item that belonged to Rionach. They were just finishing moving her belongings into my room when I arrived home with my unconscious bride. I wanted her to have her own things here to help make the transition easier, but here was no way in hell I was going to allow her to go back to her parents' estate to collect them herself.

"Have fun snooping."

"I'm going to start with your underwear drawer."

I bark out a laugh. "Good luck finding that. I don't wear underwear."

On that cheerful note, I leave my brand-new wife alone to explore her new home. During the entire one hundred and twenty-nine floor elevator ride down to the parking garage, I have to stop myself from going back up and bringing her to work with me.

Rionach Kara Banes has made me into a stage five clinger, and I can't say I'm mad about it.

NINETEEN
RIONACH

I SPENT my entire first day as a married woman exploring my new husband's home and as it turns out, the man wasn't joking. He doesn't own a single pair of underwear, but he owns everything else. I will *actively* have to try to be bored while I'm playing Rapunzel and I'm locked up in this penthouse for a couple days. I lost count of how many bathrooms are in this three-story monstrosity of a home. There's six bedrooms, though, not including the primary suit located on the third floor. I know that number because I counted each flawlessly designed room. *Twice.* There are two additional sitting areas aside from the living room I sat and talked with Emeric in, *and* there's an entire screening room complete with two rows of reclining leather chairs. Past the mini movie theater is a home gym that is fully stocked with every piece of equipment you can think of. The only room I didn't stick my nose in during my exploration was Emeric's office. While it was tempting as hell, something told me that snooping through there would be asking for trouble.

Every corner of the penthouse I wandered to, Cerberus

stayed right on my heels. At first his unwavering attention was intimidating, and I tried my best to not make any fast or sudden moves around the animal, but after two hours of this, I stopped thinking I was going to be puppy chow and relaxed. I found I really enjoy his company and the way he presses his big body into mine. It's comforting in a way.

I wonder what Emeric will think when I tell him his big scary attack dog is quickly becoming my emotional support animal. Might have to get him a vest and everything so I can take him places with me. I'm sure a highly trained protection dog will fit right in at Starbucks.

After exploring the interior of the house, I moved outside to the terrace that's off the kitchen and living room. No one in New York—especially residents who live this high up—have that kind of outdoor space, but Emeric does. *Of course, he does.* The L-shaped area has an outdoor dining table and a seating area that's situated around a glass firepit. There's even a built-in hot tub. Just like the inside, the railings that surround the terrace are made of glass so they don't obstruct any of the views.

Standing at what must be at least one hundred stories in the air with only glass surrounding me made me feel like I was in the clouds.

A man whose club is named after the underworld shouldn't live in a place that feels like heaven.

That doesn't mean that Emeric's dark aesthetic isn't all over the house. There isn't a single hint of color in the entire place and trust me, I searched. Even made a game out of it. Everything is neutral, black being the primary color. That amount of black should make the place feel dark and cavernous, but I never once felt that way while walking around. The numerous windows allow a ton of light to stream through and brighten up the place.

After finishing my exploration, I wandered back to the movie room. I selected a leather recliner in the middle of the room and found a soft gray faux fur blanket to sit under, and that's where I stayed for eight solid hours. I sat there and watched movie after movie, only getting up to go to the bathroom and to get more snacks.

And it was *glorious*.

I haven't been able to be that unproductive since college. My mother would never allow me to be so lazy. It could have been the most inconsequential or trivial task, but she would have found something else for me to do other than quote, unquote, "sit on my ass and rot." Today, there wasn't a disapproving look in sight, and I got to rot in peace.

After having a dinner that consisted of a bag of microwave popcorn and half a banana, I found my way back up two flights of stairs and into the suite that smells of Emeric Banes. Face washed and teeth brushed, I fell into the black silk sheets wearing my favorite cream-colored nightie feeling lighter than I probably should. *He forced you into marrying him. This isn't a real relationship,* the little voice of reason whispered to me as I shamelessly pulled Emeric's pillow to my chest and spooned it.

I fell asleep like that, snuggled up in his king-sized bed and engrossed in his scent.

That was hours ago, or at least I think it was. For all I know, I could have only been asleep for forty minutes. The midnight black skyline I find outside the window when I crack my eyes open does little to help with that mystery. Either way, I know I haven't slept near enough and something—or *someone*—has woken me up.

More specifically, a hot tongue running up the seam of my pussy has coaxed me awake.

I'm not sure when I released his pillow and moved onto my back, but it doesn't matter because Emeric is now lying on his stomach with his head buried between my thighs. I'm not sure how long he's been at this, but I'm going to guess it's been a minute because I'm already alive and buzzing with a desperate need.

"Oh my God," I choke out into the pitch-black room, fingers diving into the surprisingly soft strands of his equally dark hair.

The very idea that I was unconscious—and very much vulnerable—when he started this should anger me. Some, if not *most*, people would see this as a violation of some kind, but my body doesn't agree with that sentiment. Actually, if I'm being completely honest, this might be my new favorite way to wake up. Every other alarm clock pales in comparison to the great Emeric Banes's eating your pussy like it's the first meal he's had in days.

"Didn't mean to wake you, princess," he says, pressing an open-mouthed kiss at the crease of my thigh before he nips at the skin there. His tongue smooths away the slight sting of pain before he returns to where I need him most. "When I got home and found you asleep in my bed, I couldn't resist. I needed to taste my wife's cunt."

If he keeps this up, his words are going to turn not only my panties but me into a pile of ash.

With me fully awake and alert, he wraps his arms around my thighs and places them over his bare shoulders. This new angle instantly turns my core molten. Back arching and fingers clawing at the sheets, I unashamedly grind myself against his mouth.

"That's it," Emeric encourages. "Ride my face."

He licks and bites, his tongue alternating between fucking me and circling my clit. Within minutes he's got my inner muscles fluttering as I quickly climb toward an orgasm. The idyllic release is just within grasp when he suddenly pulls away and leaves me in that horrible needy place of limbo.

"No, please," I whine. If I wasn't so far gone, I might be embarrassed by how desperate I sound.

"Shh," he soothes, climbing up the bed to lie on his side next to me. "I've got you, baby. I'll take care of you."

His arms slip under me and gather me up so I'm situated on my side with my back in front of his much larger body. I'm not sure how many people in this city can say they feel secure in Emeric's embrace, but I have a sneaking suspicion I might be alone in that. Hands that are covered in more blood than I can possibly know roam over my body, pushing up the cream fabric of my nightdress to expose more of my skin. He runs one over the globe of my ass, pausing for a moment to squeeze the flesh there before he brings his palm down in a quick but punishing slap.

Where a shriek or gasp would be appropriate sounds to make after something like that, a throaty moan rattles in my chest instead. Which only encourages him to do it again. Harder.

"You had everyone fooled that you were an innocent mob princess, didn't you? Played the role like an award-winning actress," he murmurs darkly in my ear. "But you didn't fool me. I saw you."

Exposed. That's how hearing this makes me feel. Like I've been cut up and bared open for his viewing pleasure. When I fidget and shift anxiously, movements made beyond my control, he pulls my back tighter to his chest and his mouth skims across my cheekbone. With those simple little touches, my wariness melts away.

With one arm under my head and the other hooked under my knee, lifting my leg, Emeric positions the thick head of his dick at my painfully empty-feeling center. The previous times we've slept together, he's sliced into me with one unforgiving movement. This time he pushes inside in an agonizingly slow thrust, stretching my already sore muscles and stealing my ability to breathe and think in the process. Both are delicious and have me turning into a puddle of ecstasy, but something about the way he enters me now has every nerve in my body igniting.

He feeds me the last inch of his dick and thrusts deep, making me hiss out a breath of pain as my tender muscles yelp in protest. Emeric did a number on my body last night when I was tied to this bed. Instinctually, my hand flies down to where we're connected. To do what? I'm not sure. It's not as if I have any plans of pushing him away.

When my fingertips brush through my slickness and then the base of his shaft, he growls in my ear. "Keep your hand there," he orders, pulling out of me just as languidly as he entered until only the tip of his cock remains inside. "Play with your pussy and feel me as I fuck you back to sleep."

And then, like a flip being switched, the unhurried pace turns into the frenzy I know and love. And *crave*. It's terrifying how much my body needs him.

I don't know what he's doing to me, but just as surely as I know I like it, I also know this can't end well. He says this marriage is forever, which means this can only end one of two ways. He inevitably grows bored of me, and I'm stuck living the sad lonely housewife lifestyle I dread, or I fall in love with him. And I don't know which of those possibilities is more concerning. Is Emeric Banes the type of man you can love?

He pounds into me, the position we're in allowing me to feel every inch of him, and with every thrust, he hits that delicious place inside of me that I used to think was a myth. Whenever I tried to make myself come during those quiet and lonely nights, I could never achieve the right angles with my fingers to find it. Emeric doesn't have that problem. With each punishing movement, he brushes against it and forces a breathy gasp out of my lungs.

I follow his orders. While he fucks me, my fingers alternate between circling my swollen clit and stroking his dick. The orgasm that he'd let slip away when he stole his delectable mouth away begins to regrow as the pleasure swells. And swells

And then shatters.

I explode around him, throwing my head back into the crook of Emeric's shoulder as I do.

Forcing my face toward his, his warm mouth covers mine, swallowing my cry. Unlike our wedding, I don't try to bite him. Instead, I sink into the feel of his lips and the demanding caress of his tongue against mine.

When he follows me over the edge, his cock jerking and his hot cum spilling into my still spasming pussy, he keeps his mouth firmly on mine. His groan tastes delicious against my lips and I greedily eat it up.

Emeric continues to make shallow thrusts as we ride out the last lingering waves of our orgasms. Forehead now pressed to mine, he keeps up the slight rocking motion until our labored breathing has turned into soft panting against each other's lips. In the dark, I can't see his stormy gray gaze, but I don't have to, to know that he's looking just as intently at me as I am him.

With a pleased sigh, he presses one last kiss to my sweaty temple before he settles his head on the pillow beside mine. He wraps the arm that had been holding my leg hostage around my abdomen and holds me tight, but makes no move to pull his still half-hard cock from me.

"Go back to sleep, sweet wife," he commands in my ear.

Brow furrowing in confusion, I wiggle my hips to silently encourage him to vacate the premises. "Are you forgetting something?"

"No."

"Emeric." I shift again, this time harder. This has his hand clamping down on my hip bone, halting all further movement. "What are you—"

"I'm trying to sleep. I recommend you do the same," he says, like that answers the question of why he's still *inside* of me. His hold turns almost painful when I try again to shake him off. "*Enough.* Stop squirming."

"I'm not sleeping with your dick still in me."

"Yes, you fucking are." His teeth scrape against my earlobe. "I already told you. I own this pussy now. Just as you are, it's now my property and I will use it as I see fit. If I want it to warm my cock while I sleep, then that's what I'll do. Now, close those pretty green eyes and go to sleep, Rionach."

My lips part, a rebuttal primed and ready on the tip of my tongue, but he cuts me off before I can utter a single syllable.

"Fight me on this," he growls. "I fucking dare you."

After the events of yesterday and my sleep tonight being interrupted, I'm exhausted. And while I won't admit this to him, there's something oddly soothing about having him buried in me, even if it's not being used to currently fuck my brains out. One by one, I force my muscles to relax, and I sink into him and the mattress.

"Good girl."

TWENTY
RIONACH

I'm knee-deep in my fourth movie of the day and almost completely through a bag of potato chips, when the dog who's been resting at the base of my recliner rears up into a sitting position. Cerberus's attention is now laser-focused on the doorway of the movie room. Following his intent gaze, I find a blonde woman standing there.

If I had to guess, I'd say she's about ten to fifteen years older than me, and she's pretty and tall—*model* pretty and tall. Her all-cream outfit reminds me of something my mother would wear. All clean lines and sophisticated. I'm almost positive Mom owns the same leather slip-on loafers the mystery woman is wearing.

"My name is Anneli," she says, not making any move to step farther into the room. Her dark eyes keep flicking to where Cerberus sits. Wonder if she's just not a fan of dogs or if she too has been a victim to a couple of those "love bites" Emeric talked about yesterday?

Shifting to the edge of the leather chair, I give her a brief wave. "I'm Rionach."

"I know who you are." Her voice, which has a slight accent to it that I can't place, matches the same look written over her pretty face. Complete neutrality. She's neither impressed nor aggravated by my presence here. "I'd wager most of the city knows who you are, and if they didn't before, they do now. When the CEO of Banes Corporation announces he's taken a wife, people are going to stop and take note."

He *announced* our marriage? Jesus Christ, did he send it in his weekly newsletter or something? I can only imagine what was actually included in the announcement, but I'd bet my life it wasn't exactly *factual*. There's no way in hell Emeric can publicize the truth. Could you imagine what that statement would read like? *"The notorious Emeric Banes fucked an Irish girl once in a giant birdcage. She must have left one hell of an impression because a week later, he's stuffing her into a pretty dress and making her say "I do". Oh, and let's not forget about the small little detail of him chopping body parts off her brother and going biblical on her father's ass. May they live happily ever after and all that jazz."* Yeah, *no*. That, while an immensely more entertaining story, simply wouldn't work. It's best the public and whoever else might be reading his statement believe whatever fabricated tale he spun about our nuptials.

But what about the Koslovs? Isn't Emeric just rubbing it in their faces that he stole me from them and ruined the deal they had with my family? I might not be fully versed in the intricate dealings of this world but doing that doesn't seem like the brightest of ideas. Then again, when you're as powerful and psychotic as Emeric, you don't have to worry about retribution.

Though, I'm not sure if that level of self-assurance is a positive or a negative in this case. People at the top tend to stop expecting attacks or uprisings from their underlings. I hope for Emeric's sake that he's retained some sense of humility through his rise to power.

"Oookay..." I drawl, reaching out to stroke the top of Cerberus's head. "Well, you have me at a disadvantage then because I'm afraid I don't know who you are."

She clasps her well-manicured hands in front of herself. "Personally, I like to think of myself as Mr. Banes's house manager. His assistant of sorts, if you will." The unmistakable flicker in her brown eyes doesn't go unmissed when she says his name.

The way she chose to phrase that has my eyebrows rising. "And what title does Emeric use for you?" Anneli's neutral look falters at the same time I plant one of my well-trained smiles on my face. "I'm sorry. This is all new and my entire life has been turned on its axis. I'm trying to relearn what's up and what's down. I need to get my bearings and learn who's who. You understand, right?"

"Of course." She inclines her head, but her accented voice is now unmistakably tight. "Officially, my title is housekeeper and chef, but I do much more than cook and clean. I keep the house stocked with everything Mr. Banes requires and run errands when needed. I also keep track of his event and appearance schedule."

I feel my eyes widen. "You're in charge of cleaning this *entire* place? This penthouse must be over ten thousand square feet—"

"Seventeen thousand five hundred and forty-five square feet. To be *exact*," Anneli corrects. "And no. I don't clean the entire home. There are two other housekeepers who assist me. I'm only in charge of the kitchen and the primary suite. Mr. Banes doesn't allow anyone else into his personal bedroom. As you can imagine, a man of his caliber must take his privacy very seriously."

Ah. So, when he mentioned the only women to step foot in

his home were employed by him, he was talking about this Victoria's Secret model and her team. *Got it.*

There's no denying the very obvious fact that Anneli is a beautiful human and coupled with the fact that she's intimately familiar with Emeric's space—a space I still very much feel like an intruder in—I'm ashamed to admit there's a twinge of jealousy currently bubbling in my gut. Emeric and Anneli are both *stupid* hot. It wouldn't be an illogical to assume they've slept together, and I can't exactly fault Emeric for having a life before he decided I was to be his wife. That would be *insane* of me... right?

Getting jealous over a man who kidnapped you and then coerced you into marriage might be a new low for you, Rio, that dumb little voice living in the back of my head pipes in.

But it doesn't really matter how we got here, does it? We're already here. The papers are signed, I'm sleeping in his bed and my clothes are hanging next to his in the closet. At the end of the day, I'm married to Emeric. He's my husband and he promised me he'll remain faithful. Until he gives me a reason to believe he's not keeping up his end of the bargain and Anneli treats me with respect, everything will be fine.

I've been married to the fool for a little more than forty-eight hours, I can't go peeing circles around the man. A man who I'm not even sure I *like* yet. As a person that is. There's no doubt in my mind I *thoroughly* enjoy how he makes my body feel. I'm not sure how I feel about him in my head yet. Part of me believes if I truly allow myself to like him as a person, it'll put me on the fast track to developing real feelings for his crazy ass. And as it is, if he keeps me locked up in this place like he has, it's going to become a *Beauty and the Beast* situation and make me develop Stockholm syndrome, but at the end of this story, I don't foresee the sexy growly beast turning into a pampered-looking prince.

"I guess you were right," I say, returning my full attention to Anneli. "You really are like the house manager."

The blonde's pale pink lips flick up for only a mere second, but I don't miss it or the way she seems to relax. "That's why I came to find you. Mr. Banes called me. You are to attend a dinner meeting with him tonight."

"I *am*?"

"Yes. You are." It doesn't sound like there's much room for debate on this one. "He mentioned that he'd tried contacting you himself, but you didn't answer the call. He asked me to ensure the new cell phone is working properly." A perfectly waxed brow arches at me in silent question.

"Oh!" I search the blanket and leather chairs on either side of me. "It works fine, I think I must have left it in his bedroom this morning."

Without my full contact list and access to my social media accounts, I haven't seen much use for the device. I'm aware that I could sign into my accounts at any time, but it's been sort of nice detoxing from the internet for the last two days. I also have my parents' phone numbers memorized; if I wanted to, I could call them but they're the last people I want to talk to right now. I find I don't even want to know if Dad managed to pull himself free of those nails. After learning they were so willing to put my life in the hands of a man like Bogdan... I'm not sure if that's something I will ever be able to forgive. The whole thing really put in perspective how little they valued me as their daughter. As a *person*.

The only person I want to talk to is Ophelia, but I don't even know what I'd tell her. The situation I've found myself in is so insane it borders on unbelievable. I need more time to process it before I bring my best friend into the loop.

My head needs to be on straighter to fully explain the shit show that was my wedding.

"Hmm..." Anneli doesn't appear impressed by this. "I would recommend keeping it close by in the future. Just to ensure your husband can reach you."

"Will do," I vow with an awkward salute.

"Mr. Banes said he will be home at eight tonight. He requested that you be ready to leave then so you both will be on time for his meeting."

"I don't understand why I need to attend a meeting with him," I tell her. "Do you know what it's about?"

Anneli's head tilts ever so slightly. "Mrs. Banes, that information is above my pay grade. I'm simply just relaying the instructions that were given to me."

Mrs. Banes. This is the first time someone other than Emeric has called me that name and there's no way of knowing if the shiver zipping down my spine is caused by my lingering unease over the whole situation or from some kind of toxic thrill brought on by knowing I'm *his.*

"Okay... what time is it now?"

She glances at the gold watch around her wrist. "A little after six."

I had to take a shower this morning when I woke up because just like yesterday, Emeric's cum had left a mess between my thighs, but I didn't wash my hair. After a day of lounging and being a complete bum, I don't have to look in a mirror to know that I need to wash it to make it look presentable. It's well past dry shampoo and a curling iron.

I woke up alone in his bed again this morning. His side of the bed was stone cold and the sheets were barely wrinkled from where I'd assumed he'd fallen asleep next to me. I don't know what time he wakes up every day, but it has to be obscenely early because I'd rolled over just as the sun was peeking over the horizon and he wasn't there. It was so early I'd guessed he may have just been using the bathroom before coming back to bed. Hours later when my eyes had cracked up at a much more acceptable hour, he was still nowhere to be seen. That kind of sleep schedule can't be sustainable, not when most of his more *illicit* affairs take place after the sun goes down.

"All right," I pat the big dog's head once more before standing. "I guess I'll go get ready."

————

IT'S TAKING me longer to pick an outfit than it did for me to do my makeup and hair. I have no information about what kind of dinner this is. I don't want to wear the simple black dress I have pulled out if we're going to a fancier restaurant, and I don't want to wear heels if he's taking me to a dive bar. *Not* that I think the great Mr. Banes seems like a frequent flyer at dive bars, but then again, what the hell do I know? The man is a walking—albeit very sexy—question mark to me.

Anneli said this was going to be a business dinner too. Does that mean we're meeting clients or business partners? If that's the case, I want to make a good impression on them. The irony that I suddenly give a shit about the way I look or am concerned about which outfit will be most impressive to his people isn't lost on me. Imogen has been trying to instill this belief system in me for years, but I always silently fought against it.

I've just pulled a pair of black wide-legged and high-waisted trousers down from a hanger when every hair on my body stands on end.

I know what—or *who*—I'm going to find before I turn around.

Dressed in another black suit, but with a charcoal gray button-down today, Emeric leans against the impressive walk-

185

in closet's doorway. "I hope for the sake of every man we encounter tonight you're not planning on wearing *that* to this meeting."

I flick my eyes down to the only garments of clothing I've managed to put on. A basically see-through dark green lace bra and a matching thong. "Oh yeah? And why is that?"

"I don't get squeamish about much but eyeballs..." he trails off, taking two steps into the room. "I've never enjoyed dealing with eyes. The texture is rather off-putting, but if you insist on wearing that as an outfit, I'll have no qualms about plucking the eyeballs out of the heads of every man who sees you."

The delightful image he paints flashes in my head and has my face wrinkling. "Gross. Please don't." After a moment I manage to shake the overwhelming visual of a bunch of peeled grapes from my brain. "I'm obviously not going to just wear this. The information that Anneli passed along from you was vague. 'Dinner meeting'. I have no idea what kind of dress code that entails and it's not exactly like I've been invited to one of these in the past that I can use as reference." When he doesn't instantly give me any kind of guidance, I wave my hands in the direction of all the clothes hanging and folded neatly around me. "Don't just stand there and stare at me, tell me what to wear."

Stormy gray eyes lazily scan me, taking in every inch of exposed skin before he moves to stand before me. "But I enjoy staring. My wife makes for such a pretty view, after all." He uses his index finger to lift my chin up toward his face. My breath gets trapped in my chest when his lips skim over mine in a barely-there touch. Such a simple contact has my entire body coming alive for him. He keeps his mouth close to mine as he says, "I don't give a fuck what you wear, Rionach. It can be as revealing as your current outfit, or it can be a goddamn ski suit, for all I care. Wear whatever makes you feel beautiful."

No one has ever insisted I wear what makes *me* feel beautiful. Aside from those few stolen nights away with Lia, my wardrobe has been closely controlled by my mom since I left college. Selecting an outfit without being ridiculed is now a foreign concept to me.

"Okay," I manage to whisper back in a surprisingly steady voice despite the lightning storm he's ignited in my body. "I should only be a few more minutes, sorry if I'm making you late."

"I don't give a fuck if we're late," he assures me, pressing a brief kiss to my temple before stepping back. He does this as if it's the most natural thing in the world, like he's been showing me affection for a lifetime and not just a few days. "Our dinner companions will wait as long as I force them to. They're not going anywhere."

Of course. Why would I think otherwise?

Despite his reassurance, I quickly dress in a pair of black sheer tights and a formfitting thigh-length skirt. Over the silk tank top that I tucked into the waistband of the skirt, I put on an oversized blazer since it's still chilly out. The all-black outfit is fairly simple but the red-bottom stiletto ankle boots on my feet help make it appear more sophisticated. The only jewelry I wear are the various studs and loops already decorating up and down my ears.

Running my fingers through my freshly curled hair one last time, I turn away from the full-length mirror hanging on the wall and face Emeric.

I'm not expecting to find him standing shirtless on the opposite side of the closet with his back to me. I'm also not expecting to find the dark tattoo covering both of his defined shoulder blades. How could I have missed *this*? Thinking back to all the times he's been shirtless around me, I realize that either my back has been turned to him or his back was turned away from me. *Or* I'd been blindfolded. The dark—*black*—wings decorating his golden skin are beautiful. Emeric isn't the kind of man you'd think you could describe as beautiful and yet I find myself thinking it often. Beautiful body, face, eyes... and now with these wings on his back. I can't help but think of him as a fallen dark angel.

His muscles flex under his tattoo as he pulls on a fresh black button-down. I watch him with a sense of greed the entire time and only do I look away when he's pulled on a mid-length black wool coat. I couldn't tell you why, but for some reason I didn't want Emeric to catch me staring at him. Perhaps it's because we're only two days in and I'm struggling with trying to remember I'm supposed to be mad at him. He forced my hand at marrying him, but the alternative was far less appealing. Emeric is known as a vicious man—a monster—and yet, I haven't seen an ounce of that infamous wrath pointed in my direction. What has been directed at me is a delicious form of dominance and I can't get enough of that. I like the way he takes control and despite the pit of shame in my stomach when I think about it, I like it even more when he takes my choice away. The rush—the *fear*—that comes from it is my new favorite kind of high.

I even find it difficult to fault Emeric for what he did to my brother and father. Stealing from a man like Emeric Banes will go down in history as one of the dumbest choices one could make. My family paid the price for their stupidity.

"Okay, I'm ready," I say once he's fully dressed and facing in my direction again.

He gives me an approving nod and holds out his hand for me.

"Come."

TWENTY-ONE
EMERIC

I COULD SEE it on her face the second she put it together that this isn't going to be just any ordinary dinner meeting.

Rionach's first clue was the number of guards that are accompanying us on this endeavor. Perceptive green eyes noted the four-car caravan when we exited the building and despite the question written across her pretty face, she didn't dare ask it aloud. Her second clue was when we left Manhattan and entered a neighborhood with a heavy population of Irish in the Bronx. It's a neighborhood I knew she would be familiar with. And even then, as she shifted anxiously in the leather seat next to mine, she didn't utter a single word.

Ever the picture-perfect depiction of the poised and obedient mob princess.

The long-engrained mentality of being seen and not heard is going to take time to break. She'll learn soon enough all she has to do is open her mouth if she has a question. As I told her before, if it's within my capability to provide her answers, I'll be more than happy to oblige her curiosities.

The smirk that grows on my face is one of pride when I

hold my hand out to help her exit the bulletproof Escalade and she finally asks, "What the hell are you planning?"

"Good girl," I praise her, pressing my lips to the back of her cold but steady hand.

It's clear she doesn't understand what she's done to earn my approval based on the look she gives me in response.

"And why would that be?"

"By nature, you're a very observant person and I can tell you keep hundreds of questions locked up in your head because you've never been granted an opportunity to freely ask them," I explain. "I want you to be curious and I want you to ask questions. You're so much more than a pretty face, my wife. It's due time that not only does everyone else discover this but you also learn to accept it about yourself." I release her hand so I can tilt her chin up. "And since I'm almost positive no one has ever told you, and I'm pleased as hell to be the first, you're allowed to take an active role in your life, Rionach."

"That's rich coming from the man who forcibly saddled me with his last name."

Her jaw stubbornly sets but I know it's for show. There isn't a hint of such emotion in those jade eyes of hers. If anything, it's the opposite. Rionach doesn't yet believe what I'm saying, but she will. I'll make sure of it.

I hold her face in place when she tries to look away. "Despite what you're currently thinking, this marriage isn't another form of imprisonment, princess. I already told you I don't want to keep you in a cage. You'll learn soon enough that it's your freedom." Before she can hit me with another hostile retort, I reclaim her hand and lead her into the building we've been standing in front of.

Nova and Mathis walk in front and six other armed men trail behind us. If I hadn't decided I wanted Rionach to join me for this particular meeting, I wouldn't have brought as many guards with me, but I'm not about to knowingly put her in possible danger without taking all the necessary precautions. With the *delightful* way things were left between our two parties, I have no way of knowing the full extent of the hostile-filled environment we're walking into. While I very much enjoy the way a good ol' shoot-out or a knife fight gets my blood pumping, not having every possible protection for Rionach in place is nonnegotiable for me.

My team has already been told what will happen to them if a single hair is harmed on her head and to say I painted a very graphic picture for them is putting it mildly. My youngest guard, Camden, looked a little green around the gills by the time I was done. If my men weren't scared of me before, they sure as shit are now, but that's for the better. It's best they be well informed of the consequences if they fail to protect what is mine.

"My God, Moran, this place is a fucking shithole," I call in way of greeting once we enter the dimly lit dining area. "If all your businesses look as sad as this one, it's no wonder you need to pilfer from my warehouses to make any damn money."

The Irish Wife Pub was closed early tonight so we could have this meeting. Aside from the gaggle of men Niall brought with him and my crew, the establishment is dark and quiet. Depending on how this all goes down, that will work in our favor. We don't want any civilian witnesses or accidental casualties. Getting rid of bodies is *such* a hassle.

My grip on Rionach's hand tightens when her heels dig into the well-worn—and disgusting—carpet. I have to discreetly tug her forward to keep pace with me. The look I cut her is fleeting but my message is clear: *don't you fucking dare shy away from him or this.*

I return my full attention to the pudgy man looking notably worse for wear sitting alone at a round wooden table. A near empty tumbler of light brown alcohol sits between his two heavily bandaged hands with a pathetic-looking red bendable straw in it.

Poor guy can't pick up his own glass. What an absolute bummer for him.

Behind Niall, leaning against the wall covered in various framed photographs and flanked by four other Irish guards, is a tense-looking Brayden. His intense green gaze is zeroed in on the woman standing at my side. The way he examines every visible inch of her doesn't go missed. I cock my head at him in silent question when he shifts his focus to me. He expression turns into an impassive sheet of ice before his chin dips in a barely registerable nod.

"Jesus Christ, Niall—oh shit, that was a poor choice of words, wasn't it? My *sincerest* apologies." I give the defeated man my best playacting sympathetic smile before dropping the act with a casual shrug of my shoulders. "You're looking a little rough around the edges tonight, aren't you, old sport? I am, however, pleased as punch to see you managed to get free of those pesky nails. *Although...*" I wag a scolding finger at him. "I do believe the deal was you were to pull *yourself* free. You're lucky your devoted wife was kind enough to send you assistance because after you hung there like a pussy for six hours, I was really thinking you were going to turn into a Jesuscicle."

His round face turns a deeper shade of red.

"What?" I ask. "Of course, I know you didn't get free of the cross all on your lonesome. Did you really think we'd just leave you there unsupervised after we left? We had eyes on you the entire time, Niall. Had to have a team on hand in case your poor little corned beef and potato heart gave out. We couldn't just leave you there, you know? I'd hate to traumatize someone like that if they found your dead body."

"My daughter was right," a deep and thick Irish accented voice comes from the dark archway that leads to the other dining room on the opposite side of the pub. The looming figure takes a few easy steps forward until the scarcely available light illuminates his features. Tadhg Kelly might be well into his golden years, but he still stands strong as ever. "You do enjoy the sound of your own voice."

Beside me, Rionach stiffens and her hand flexes in mine at the same time her air catches in her throat.

I suspected her grandfather might be joining us for this meeting after I got word his private jet landed in an upstate airfield last night. Tadhg's attempt at being stealthy was admirable, but ultimately laughable. If he wanted to avoid my watchful eyes, he should have landed in Canada and crossed into the country that way. At the end of the day, despite that diversion, I still probably would have known of his arrival regardless.

His daughter, no doubt, called him with her sob story after she and Tiernan were dropped off at the hospital by my team of medics. I can't help but feel a sense of compassion for Tadhg. I heard the pipes that woman has on her in person and they were borderline deafening, I can't begin to imagine how shrill she sounded over the phone. That man's poor eardrums.

"Well, isn't this a charming impromptu family reunion?" I cheerfully note, looking at the two men related to the woman who now shares my bed. "Felt like you had to bring in the big guns for our little meeting, huh, Niall?" I ask, also sparing the seething man a quick glance.

Niall opens his thin-lipped mouth to finally speak, but his father-in-law beats him to the punch.

"He would usually bring his son to something like this, but seeing as my grandson is currently indisposed and recovering in a hospital bed from surgery, I thought it best I come in his stead," Tadhg explains, sounding neither angry nor irritated. He's calm, seemingly in complete control of his emotions, and that is why he's always held my respect. Or whatever the closest attribute to respect is that I can manage to feel. "Given the current turbulent history between our two families and the fact you're now married to my granddaughter, I felt it best we speak in person."

For the first time, Tadhg grants his grandchild his full attention. Just like Brayden, he thoroughly examines her. No doubt looking for any signs of damage. Which is laughable given who her family had originally planned on handing her off to. I'm no angel but I don't harm what is mine. At least, not in ways she won't find enjoyable.

"Pop," Rionach greets, finally finding her voice.

Given the situation, I wouldn't have faulted her if her voice wavered even the slightest, but my wife is strong, and her even voice reflects that.

"Lass," he responds. "You appear to be in one piece."

Can't say the same about your other grandchild, now can we?

Keeping her head high, she gives him a single nod. "I am."

I release an exasperated sigh. "*Fucking hell*, people. Did you think I was going to eat her alive or something?" A devious smirk settles on my face. "Don't get me wrong, I *did* eat her alive, but from the way she cried and begged for more, I think it's safe to say she thoroughly enjoyed being devoured."

A small hand reaching out and smacking the center of my chest has everyone in the room sucking in a collective breath and turning into stone statues. I know what they're expecting. They're all waiting for the legendary wrathful beast to rear its vicious head and punish Rionach for raising a hand to me. They'll be waiting a long time for that.

I catch her by her slender fingers before she can completely pull away. Her eyes widen and she fights me for a second before giving in to me as I bring her hand up to my mouth. If the room was silent before, it turns deafening when I press my lips to the thundering pulse point in her wrist.

Just like that, Rionach is the only relaxed person in the room.

"My apologies, my wife," I tell her with a subtle wink. "Talking about our extracurricular activities in front of your father figure and grandfather was crass of me."

She simply rolls her eyes. Another move that before she entered my life, only Nova could get away with, and even then, he had to catch me in a good mood. There's no need for Rionach to go through such measures to ensure she isn't on the receiving end of a bad reaction from me.

I love this side of her because it's *authentic*.

The obnoxious clearing of Niall's throat has my trigger finger twitching. "Can we move on from this circus and get to the real reason we're all here?"

"Ah, yes. Let's." I lead Rionach closer to the table and take a seat in the single chair situated across from Niall. She attempts to back away from me, but I'm not having it. Snaking my arm around her narrow waist, I forcibly bring her down on my lap. Rionach shifts anxiously and once again tries to leave the protection of my body. Like a vise, I lock my arm around her middle and force her to remain still. She does what I silently demand of her, albeit rigidly. "You owe me half a million dollars, Niall."

Tadhg slides into the chair next to him.

My new father-in-law—if we can *really* call him that—sniffs and glares at me. "It's here. I've brought you what is owed."

I rap the knuckles of my free hand against the slightly sticky lacquered surface of the table for a few beats before gesturing at Tadhg. "I'm assuming you're the reason behind this quick turnaround?"

My sources told me that while Niall had only recently sold the weapons off to my competitors, the money from those sales has already dwindled from his accounts. My assumption is the Moran family owed debts to people other than me.

Tadhg doesn't bother denying it, and with a sure nod, he says, "I was told that your messengers told my son-in-law you expected to be reimbursed within the week."

"A week was more than a fair amount of time," I explain.

Niall's entire body lurches forward so fast, my hold on my wife tightens. "*Fair?* You think you've been fucking *fair?*"

"I've been nothing but fair," I tell him, the dark edge I've managed to keep at bay thus far emerging. "By not putting nails through your eye sockets, I was being fair. When I only took one of your thieving son's hands, I was being fair. When I allowed you, the idiot who instilled the holier-than-thou and entitled mindset into your half-witted son, to leave that church alive, I. Was. Being. Fair." I swear, this clown keeps forgetting he's the reason he's in this situation to begin with. "Believe it or not, Niall, this is what my leniency looks like, but if you continue to push me, I will have no problem showing just how unfair I can fucking be."

Rionach shifts in my lap, her hand coming to rest atop my forearm. I can't be sure she's aware of making such a move and while the comforting gesture isn't needed, I find it endearing.

Tadhg raises a hand and cuts Niall a sharp look. "That's *enough!*" The pure authority in his voice is impressive. "You've already done enough damage. Keep your trap shut and stop digging yourself deeper into the shite you've found yourself buried in. Maybe then you can leave with whatever sliver of dignity you have fucking left." Yep. It's official, I like the grandpa. "Niall is incapable of supplying the amount of money that you're owed." If it were possible for words to physically bitch-slap a person, Tadhg just delivered one hell of a blow. "I will be footing the bill for his *mistake*."

My eyes narrow at this. "Why would you do that? And spare me the 'he's family' bullshit. It doesn't take a psychology degree to know you'd trade his flat-pasty ass for a sloppy blow job tomorrow if given half the chance."

Niall has the audacity to look revolted by this. "You don't know what the hell you're talking about. We are family. We—"

He's cut off by his father-in-law. Irritation and rage eat away at his expression.

"While it exasperates and confuses me greatly, Niall's demise would break my daughter. *She* is my family. No father wants to see his daughter heartbroken," Tadhg says matter-of-factly, not an ounce of emotion tangible. "I'm also smart enough to know I don't want you as my enemy, Banes. I respected your father." I take it back. I don't like the grandpa. "And I find I can't help but respect you in kind. The empire you've built, while impressive, is more powerful than anyone could have seen coming. You don't make an enemy out of someone you know you can't beat. You make them an ally."

"Smart man," I offer, still not sure what his endgame is.

Ignoring a fuming Niall at his side, he inclines his head at me. "For this very reason, I have brought you the money to cover my son-in-law's debt. Half a million dollars in untraceable gold bricks are in the back of our vehicle. Say the word, I will have my men transfer them into your custody." He leans forward in his chair, resting his arms on the tabletop. "I'm also prepared to include an extra hundred thousand as a sign of good faith if you're willing to accept this offer. I can understand your wish to force Niall to pay for his own debt whether it be in money or blood, but as I told you, I'm trying to protect my child's heart."

I look between the two men. "It's refreshing to know that *someone* in this godforsaken family gives a damn about their daughter's well-being."

Tadhg clears his throat and looks at his granddaughter sitting in my lap. "Your grandmother and I weren't aware of your engagement to the Koslov boy. If we had been, we would have—"

"You would have *what*?" Rionach interrupts, body going stiff against mine. "Put a stop to it? For some reason, I find that very hard to believe. If the Koslovs were *truly* the highest bidders, that's who you would have picked for me because *that's* how it's done. *Always* has been. Sons learn the business and daughters are sold off to whoever will make the strongest ally. Doesn't matter if he's a sadistic serial killer or a rapist, as long as he benefits the family, who cares, right?"

Both Niall and her grandfather stare at my wife like they don't recognize her, and I find my chest puffing with pride.

That's my girl. Show them your fangs.

"You're right," her grandfather concedes without a fight, meanwhile Niall looks like he wants to reach across the table and strangle Rionach. *Try it, buddy, see what happens.* "But that doesn't matter now, does it? You've secured a strong union to a much more powerful family than the Russians."

It's my turn to interject. "My marriage to Rionach will *never* be used as an advantage to the Moran clan. I am not an ally. Just as I've always been, I am the thorn in your side slowly dismantling your empire."

"What have we ever done to you?" Niall spits.

I shrug. "Until recently, nothing notable. You were simply just in my way."

You can't amass the kind of empire that I have without cutting out your competition along the way. Rarely is it a personal vendetta. It's the ugly side of an even uglier business.

Niall used to understand that when he still had his balls intact. Now I think they're kept in his shrill wife's designer handbag.

"I'm growing tired of this conversation and I'm growing remarkably more tired of looking at your pork roast of a face, Niall," I tell them while looking at the Rolex on my wrist. "Because of this, I will accept your offer of six hundred thousand in gold, Tadhg. Please have your men move it into my SUV immediately." With a nod of my head, Camden and Mathis move in tandem to oversee this exchange. They'll make sure there aren't any kinds of explosives or tracking devices within the package before putting it in the car. You only make that kind of mistake once. "Before we end this meeting, I want to make it abundantly clear that this is where my benevolence comes to an end. If your family moves against mine again, not only will I kill you, but I will also take you apart in such a way that not even your precious god would recognize you when you try to enter his pearly gates."

The easygoing facade is gone. The full extent of my wrath and promised pain is laced in every syllable I utter. Everyone in the room has grown deathly still except my bride in my lap. No, Rionach isn't afraid of me or my threats in the same way everyone else present is. The way her hips rock ever so slightly and her perfect round ass grinds into my suddenly stiffening cock is proof of how she truly feels about my change in demeanor. Her chest rises and falls in a more rapid succession and the hand that's been resting on my forearm tightens its grasp.

My free hand coming down on her hip and abruptly squeezing the flesh there has her jumping in her seat. Her head turns just enough that I get a peek at her widening eyes. The embarrassment reflected in those green orbs tells me she wasn't fully aware of the reaction happening in her body until I broke the spell with my rough grip.

I don't appreciate the sheepish look cutting across her now flushed features when she ducks her face away from mine.

It's now a task to return to the conversation at hand. "I will also remind you, Rionach is now my family. *Mine*, not yours." I let the silent threat linger between us for a long moment. She's my family and if all goes to plan, she will also be the woman who brings the next generation of our family into this world.

"I understand," Tadhg nods. "For what it's worth, I'm pleasantly surprised by how protective of her you are."

"It's worth nothing," I tell him without a second thought while patting Rionach on the hip, silently signaling for her to stand up. On steady legs, she gracefully removes herself from my lap and stands. I follow suit and loom behind her with an arm still protectively wrapped around her middle. "Niall here has firsthand experience with what I'm willing to do to protect what is mine, and that was just a drop in the very bloody bucket of what I'm capable of."

Her grandfather considers me with a look, head cocking ever so slightly to the side. "Your father would be proud of you."

This has me barking out a dark wicked laugh. "No, he wouldn't."

Niall apparently doesn't know when he's been well and truly beat, or maybe somehow in the last couple minutes, he's rediscovered his balls because he has the nerve to open his mouth again.

"The fact you're standing before me threatening me and my family with the full extent of your ire over an impure and broken-in whore is beneath you, Banes." If I thought the room had fallen silent before, I was wrong. A heavy—painful—quiet and stillness settles over the room like a suffocating fog. It chokes everyone present. Both Tadhg and Brayden have the sense to look very nervous as the dumbass before me keeps talking. "Do you know why I sold her to the Koslovs? They're the only ones who were willing to pay good money for a bitch they knew wouldn't bleed. Bogdan apparently has a thing for redheads and was willing to look past the fact that she'd already spread her legs for another man."

The sound of Rionach's pained gasp does something to my chest. Inside the cavity I'd long thought empty, something painfully squeezes. The only other time I'd experienced the sensation was the night I thought I was going to watch her leap from the rooftop.

What has she done to deserve the treatment she gets from her family?

"Keep talking, Niall. I dare you. You're so close to signing your death warrant and I've been itching to make you bleed since I walked into this shithole." My voice comes out deathly calm despite the violent storm building in my veins.

Of course, he doesn't listen.

"I know about the time you spent with Igor when you were a child. He told me all about it over a bottle of vodka."

Tadhg releases an exasperated sigh before he flies up from his seat and forcibly yanks his son-in-law up from his. The way Niall sways on his feet makes me wonder how many of those drinks he'd had before we got here.

"For fuck's sake, listen to the man, Niall."

He doesn't.

"Do you still have the scar on your back?" Rionach's father taunts. "That's right. I know about that too."

At the mention of the scar, the skin on my left shoulder blade burns. The same way the iron had when I was fourteen.

Like an animal with its kill in its sights, all of my attention is locked on Niall as I lift my hand and signal. The Irish guards behind the two men in front of me all jump to alertness. Brayden's reaction is much slower, but he still draws his gun. My men in the room with us don't flinch. The signal wasn't for them.

"You keep talking about the color red. Virginal blood. Redheads..." I pause, head cocking. "But I've got a say, I think it might be your color, Niall."

The red dot in the middle of his forehead has Tadhg releasing a violent curse and Rionach sucking in a shallow breath.

"What the hell are you talking about, Banes?" Niall asks at the same time the second sniper fixes their target on the middle of his chest. The realization of his impending peril has the blood rushing from his face as he staggers back a step.

"Say it again," I taunt. "Call my wife a whore one more time."

"*Emeric...*" Rionach's whispered warning is barely audible over the pounding in my ears. The *only* reason I'm not straddling his body while my fists connect again and again with his face is because she's here.

Niall's chin sets. "She's a—"

I hold two fingers up on my left hand and not even half a second later, window glass explodes and Niall screams.

As I said, with Rionach here, I am going to provide every possible level of protection for her, and that includes snipers.

Just like when the gun went off on New Year's, Rionach doesn't duck or run for cover. She merely flinches once from the sudden noise but otherwise stands still in my grasp.

Tadhg, however, ducks behind the table we'd vacated while Niall screams and the white of the bandage on his right hand is eaten away by a bright crimson. Blood pours from the new wound. He got off easy before with the wounds the nails caused. With time, I'm sure he would have regained almost full use of his hands. Not anymore. His right hand is a mangled mess from where the bullet sliced through it. A few of his fingers appear to be hanging on by sheer will alone.

"I warned you," I tell him, raising my voice over his own screaming to ensure he's heard me. "But you didn't listen. You better pray you can jack off with your left hand, because from the looks of it, your right hand's days of making you come are over."

Like bloodhounds locked on a scent, the Irish guards—Brayden excluded—surge in our direction. They don't get within five feet of where I stand with Rionach before my own men are meeting them head-on.

"*Enough!*" Tadhg's orders fall on deaf ears. "Stand down!"

To my left, in quick succession, Nova snatches a pistol away from one of the other guards and backhands the man across the face with it. The sickening sound of facial bones crunching and teeth hitting the ground accompany the chorus of grunts and yells now echoing through the empty pub.

Within seconds my men have each of the Irishmen incapacitated and on the ground.

To his credit, Brayden keeps his own weapon aimed in my direction as he takes a defensive stance behind a wailing Niall.

Repositioning my hold on Rionach so my body is now angled in front of her smaller one, I stare both Niall and her grandfather down.

"The *only* reason—a reason you should be *immensely* grateful for—I'm going to allow you to walk out of this building with your blood still pumping through your veins is because *she's* here." I shoot a dark look at Tadhg as I repeat the words he's spoken earlier. "I'm trying to protect my wife's heart. A daughter shouldn't be forced to watch the man who raised her be eviscerated." After the way she's been treated by her father, Rionach shouldn't shed a single tear for him, but at the end of the day, logic and emotion don't always see eye to eye. "Watching my father choke on his own blood and finally die will go down as one of the best moments of my life, but I don't think my wife would share that sentiment if I replicated what I did to him to *you*, Niall."

There's been rumors for decades Ambrose Banes was killed by his own children so they could usurp his crown and take over his kingdom, but never have they been confirmed. Until now.

Fuck it.

Rionach's fingers grip the wool fabric of my jacket. I allow myself one brief glance at her to ensure she's okay before returning to stare at the threat in front of me.

"We understand," Tadhg says.

"Do you?" I demand, voice raised. "I'm not sure your boy does because if he truly grasped the way his life is currently hanging in the balance, he would be on his fucking knees thanking Rionach for being the sole reason he's being spared tonight."

The grandfather nods his head stiffly. "You're right, he should be."

Still weeping and howling over his blown-apart hand, Niall mutters incomprehensible words, but he is silenced when his wife's father yanks him by the collar of his navy-blue sports coat and shoves him at Brayden. "Put him in the fucking car. *Now!*"

Brayden cuts me one last fleeting look before taking his boss by the arm and forcibly leading him out of the establishment via the back alleyway exit. With a discreet wave of my hand, my guards release the Irishmen they're still holding at gunpoint and return to their positions behind me.

All but two of the Irish guards remain and flank the legendary arms dealer in front of me.

Hands on his hips, Tadhg looks at the water-damaged

ceiling and releases a long, exhausted sigh before looking at his granddaughter. "I will tell your grandmother I saw you with my own two eyes and that you appear to be well."

Rionach is forced to look around my frame to see her grandfather when she says, "You don't have to do that."

"She asked I report back to her about the status of your well-being."

I swear, these people really thought I was going to maul her to death within the first forty-eight hours of marriage or something, and their artificial concern for her safety is starting to grate on my already shredded nerves.

When she tries to move out from behind me, I hold my arm out in front of her, blocking any further movement, and step partially in front of her once again. After that latest erratic display from Niall, I don't want her any closer to a family member than she currently is.

"Has Mom asked about me?"

I bite my tongue to stop myself from scolding her for asking a question I know is only going to wound her.

Forcing myself to remain where I stand so I don't give in to the desire to close the space between us and wipe the condescending look of pity off Tadhg's face, I reach behind me and lace my fingers through my bride's.

Her hand is limp in mine as her grandfather simply shakes his head and says, "No, lass."

"Okay," Rionach responds. Her ability to make herself sound unfazed by his answer is a skill I have no doubt she's been honing for years. "Tell Nan I said hello and that I'm not in any danger with Emeric."

We both know that's a lie, just as we know she craves danger.

"I will," he promises with a dip of his chin. "Give your

parents time, they'll see eventually that this union is a good thing for everyone."

I turn in time to watch her head tilt and an intensity settle in her jade eyes.

"Pop, I don't think you've been listening," she tells him, a cool and collected confidence reflected in her words. "Emeric already told you he will not allow our marriage to become something that my father or anyone else can benefit from, and *I* won't allow it either because I'm *done*. My final act of service for the Moran family was marrying Emeric—something that only happened because of my father and brother's desperate stupidity and blatant greed." There's going to come a time when she learns this isn't the full truth, but now is not that time. Especially not now as she's finding her voice and standing up for herself in front of her grandfather. "I've been told my entire life my only value is in what kind of marriage I can procure, but that's over. You and the rest of them are done trying to find ways to bleed my worth dry."

My wife has no idea how unbelievably intoxicating she looks right now as she slowly steps into her newfound power. I'm half tempted to bend her over and fuck her right here on the wooden table, whispering words of praise in her ear as I do. The way blood is currently rushing to my cock, I think it's safe to say that it's also on board with that plan.

Rionach doesn't falter or shy away as her grandfather observes her with a familiar intense perception. Seems he must be the one she inherited that trait from.

After a pregnant pause, he simply says, "You're right. You're no longer a Moran, Rionach Banes. Just as you no longer belong to us, neither does your loyalty." He turns his intense focus to me. "I just hope you're worthy of it."

Through narrowed eyes, I stare back at him but don't bother to dignify his retort with one of my own.

Hand tightening around hers, I begin to back us toward the front exit of the pub. "Come on, princess. We're done here, it's time for us to go home."

Home. I thought it would take longer to adjust to the idea of sharing my home—my sanctuary—with another person, but the idea that my penthouse is now *our* home settles something wild inside my soul.

Hands tucked into the pockets of his slacks, her grandfather dips his head in farewell. "Rionach."

My wife does the same, offering a quiet, "Pop," before turning around and allowing me to lead her away from him and her past.

TWENTY-TWO
RIONACH

When my paternal grandfather was still alive, the whole family—all my aunts, uncles, and cousins included—would go to The Irish Wife Pub on Sundays after church. This was during a different era of the Moran family when things weren't as cold as they are now. The dynamics and relationships changed when my grandfather passed away and Dad took over as head of the family. My memories of this now deteriorating bar were relatively fond ones, but after the events of tonight, those childhood recollections are now overshadowed.

There's a lot to unpack about what happened here tonight between my father's bitter ill will toward me now being fully in the open and my grandfather's surprising attendance. Not to mention the little glimpses of Emeric's less-than-pretty past. I have questions I want to ask about his father as well as his time with the Koslovs. One thing I know for certain is, whatever scar Igor left on Emeric's back must be covered by the black wings I saw earlier tonight.

The late winter air wraps around us in a bitter wind as we push through the creaking wooden doors. Despite the adrenaline still soaring through me from the chaos that was that so-called "meeting", I move toward the large black SUV in an almost floaty sense of autopilot. Emeric's hand, which has been holding mine captive since we left Pop inside, pulls me to a stop before I can reach the back passenger door.

Over my shoulder, I regard him with a questioning look.

"We're not taking a car home," Emeric explains.

I'm even more at a loss now. "You don't seem like the cab or subway type."

I have no idea what the full extent of Emeric's net worth is. Between the vast generational wealth he was born into and the way both his legal and illegal businesses have grown over the past decade and a half, I know his pockets are *deep*. It goes without saying I'm a fan of the subway myself but riding the subway with a hundred other civilians seems like something he might view as beneath him.

"I'm not," he says, confirming my slightly snobbish assumptions. But then again, do we really think it's wise to trap a poor cabby or a crowd of unsuspecting people in a tight space with Emeric? In hindsight, his fancy—private—car service is probably for the best. He leads me past the line of three matching SUVs and stops when we reach a sleek-looking black motorcycle with *Ducati* written across the side in bright white lettering. "I am, however, the fast car and faster bike type."

Staring at the high-powered machine in front of me, I discover it fits his personality to a T with its dark and powerful design. Where it came from or who brought it here for Emeric is a mystery, but asking these kinds of questions when it comes to my new husband seems like a waste of time and energy. At any given time, I know this man is pulling more strings than most people know exist. He's the puppeteer and we're just along for the ride.

"Why does that not surprise me?"

"Have you ever been on a motorcycle before?"

"No," I answer, head shaking. "I've always wanted to, though. It seems dangerous but exhilarating."

"Your favorite combination," he muses, tipping my chin up. The amber light from streetlamps casts shadows across his face, making the angles of his bone structure appear sharper and his gray eyes darker than they truly are. The way his turbulent gaze is examining me now makes it seem as though he's trying to deconstruct and see past the mask I'd felt slip firmly into place the second I saw my father sitting at that table. I must be doing a bang-up job keeping my external emotions in check because he asks, "Tell me what you're feeling right now, princess."

"Everything," I tell him honestly. "And nothing."

It's such a weird place to be in mentally. I'm numb but there's also a kaleidoscope of emotions wreaking havoc inside of me. It's like feeling hot and cold at the same time. Hot because watching Emeric exude that kind of power is alluring in a way it shouldn't be and cold because I'm mourning a family who didn't value or cherish my existence.

I'm angry and I'm heartbroken because of it.

My head and my heart are in very different places at the moment.

It's one thing to assume what your father—the man who is supposed to love and protect you—truly thinks about you; it's another thing entirely to actually hear him say it out loud with unbridled disgust and *hatred*.

Do you know why I sold her to the Koslovs? They're the only ones who were willing to pay good money for a bitch they knew wouldn't bleed.

When that bullet had pierced through Dad's hand, tearing it apart in the process, something I've never felt before blazed through me. It was dark—inky black—and unholy. It had a malicious grin threatening to spread across my lips and a matching laugh bubbling in my chest. I would have called the gunshot divine retribution if I hadn't been standing in the king of the underworld's embrace. There is nothing *divine* about him or his actions.

The cynical side of me whispers Emeric orchestrated it because having his new bride be called a whore reflects negatively on him. The other side—the side I really want to believe —insists he ordered that shot on my behalf because he wanted to *defend* me.

"Do you want to feel more or feel less?" Emeric asks, his unwavering attention locked on me and any miniscule emotions he can see reflected back at him. I'm quickly learning that this position, my face held captive in his hands and our focus solely on each other, is one of his favorites. "Or do you want to feel something else entirely?"

My response is immediate.

"Something else."

"Glad to hear you say that because if I keep feeling what I'm feeling, I'm going to hunt down Niall and force him to eat those gold bars your grandfather just kindly gifted me." Releasing me, he reaches for the leather jacket laid over the seat of the expensive-looking motorcycle and hands it to me. "Put this on."

No sooner have I complied with his order and pulled on the oversized jacket that smells like him does he hold a full-face helmet out. Knowing I have no interest in painting the pavement with my brain matter, I allow him to help me pull it over my head. He does the same with a matching one but keeps the reflective visor up so I can still see his eyes. Gracefully, he swings a long powerful leg over the machine before holding a hand out for me.

"Come here, wife." I don't have to see his mouth to know

he's smirking. I can hear it. "I want to feel that body of yours pressed against mine while I show you just how fast this thing can go."

Between my shorter legs and the tight skirt restricting my flexibility, my movements aren't as smooth as his were when I climb on behind him. His hands remain on the sides of either of my thighs until he knows I'm settled and balanced. Emeric hasn't yet started the engine, and I'm already humming with a newfound and different kind of adrenaline rush than the one I had inside the pub.

He only lets go of my legs so he can capture my wrists and circle my arms around his solid middle. The heat that radiates from his body is delightful and a stark contrast to the cool winter air still nipping at my skin. Had I known we'd be going on this joyride, I would have worn pants.

"Are you okay?" he asks, looking at me over his shoulder while giving my wrists a quick squeeze.

"I think so."

"Good," he says with a nod. "Don't let go of me. If you want me to stop or slow down, just tap my chest."

This has me smiling. I won't want either of those things. "And if I want you to go faster?"

Emeric's eyes glow with a mischievousness I know means trouble is coming. "That's my girl."

His girl. His *wife*. It still doesn't feel real.

Squeezing my wrists one last time, he lays my palms flat to his chest and turns on the bike. The loud and rumbling sound of the engine matches the chaotic rush starting to build in my veins.

"Ready?" he hollers over the purring roar.

I open my mouth to tell him yes, but instead what comes out is, "Why did you bring me here tonight, Emeric?"

He stares at me intently for a moment. "They don't deserve you. I needed you to see that."

I think the little girl who was constantly cast aside and overlooked held on to a sliver of hope that one day they'd open their eyes and realize I'm worthy of their devotion too. Tonight, hearing the pure vitriol in my father's words and seeing the repulsed look in his eyes burned away the remaining fragment. My grandfather told me tonight I'm no longer a Moran, but after what my dad said about me, I wonder if I ever truly was.

"And what about you, Emeric Banes? Do you deserve me?"

He doesn't take a second to ponder his response. It's immediate and there's a rawness to it that tells me he's speaking nothing but the truth. "No, I don't, but I made you mine anyway." Not waiting for a reply from me, he slides his visor down and orders one last time, "Hold on tight, princess."

With that, like a bullet exiting the chamber, Emeric revs the engine and we take off down the dark street.

———

HE TOOK the long way back to the skyscraper I now call home. Through busy and empty streets alike, Emeric sped through the city, and I clung to him—feeling alive and blissfully out of control—as the buildings we passed turned into fleeting blurs. Car horns blared at us and pedestrians yelled their displeasure, but he didn't stop and he didn't dare slow down. I've lived here my entire life and never has the bustling city ever felt more electric than it did while speeding through it.

At one point as we soared between two lines of traffic, the euphoric paradise I'd plummeted into was interrupted when red and blue lights erupted behind us. My heart plummeted into my stomach and the man I was wrapped around like a backpack didn't so much as flinch. For ten blocks, the police car wailed and raced after us, and still Emeric's speed never faltered. Just as another cop car had joined the chase, the sirens went silent, and the flashing lights ceased. The two blue-and-white cars simply turned down another street. My confusion only lasted another block before the realization hit me. Emeric has every powerful government office in this city in his pocket. Those cops would have made a grave mistake had they succeeded in pulling him over.

Emeric rumbled with his own chuckle when I couldn't help but release an exhilarated laugh of my own. For only a second, he'd released one of the handlebars to gather my hand in his and give it a quick squeeze as well. Something about that simple move had butterflies swirling in my chest cavity. From the outside looking in, one could assume that his world looked similar to the one I grew up in, but Emeric Banes is in a playing field of his own. He's managed to make himself untouchable. Godlike, even.

Now, rounding the street that will lead us to the underground parking garage, Emeric slows his pace just enough that I can let go of his torso and spread my arms out wide at my sides. It's the same thing I do when I stand on the ledges of high places and want to feel the wind whip around me. It's like free falling without the crash.

Unable and unwilling to stop myself, I tilt my head back as far as the helmet will allow and let a delighted cheer out. It's mostly lost between the reverberation of the engine and the commotion that always accompanies these streets, but Emeric can hear it. He glances at me over his shoulder, making me wish we didn't have visors so I could see his face.

The guard sitting in the little office next to the security gate recognizes Emeric immediately and presses the button that allows us to drive through. At a much safer speed, we drive through the main level of the garage before entering a private area that is a level lower that I learned is reserved solely for Emeric and his many vehicles. One of his men, I think I heard someone call him Camden earlier, is already standing there with the secondary gate open for us. The younger man nods his head in greeting at us as we pass.

Two other men, looking like soldiers with their hands clasped behind their stick-straight backs and black tactical pants, are standing at the glossy silver elevator doors. They give the same nod as Camden. From what I've seen—and granted, it hasn't been much—Emeric's men respect him. The way they move and operate as a well-oiled and deadly machine is exactly what I would expect of men on Emeric's payroll. Organized, efficient, and lethal.

Just like him.

Emeric pulls into a spot next to an expensive-looking matte black sports car. I'm sure the price of that thing would make most of the world sick to their stomachs and it's not even close to the only one he owns. I did a quick count when we were leaving the building earlier and between the caravan of black Escalades, there's five other cars varying in size and shades of black and gray. Their sizes range from a small two-door Audi R8 to a large Mercedes-Benz G-Class.

Cutting the engine, he holds his hand out to assist in my less-than-elegant dismount. Between the adrenaline rush and never having been on a bike before, my legs are slightly shaky once both my feet are on the ground. Emeric follows me off and removes his helmet. His dark hair is more mused than I've ever seen it and the sight of it has a smile tilting my lips upward.

He removes mine and places both helmets on the top of the black coupe behind him. I try to bite my lip to hide my grin, but I know I'm failing miserably when his stormy eyes lock on my mouth.

"What's this for?" he questions, tapping under my chin once.

"Your hair."

This has his brows pulling together. "What about it?"

I surprise him *and* myself when I reach up and brush my fingers through the slightly wavy and awry strands. I'm pretty sure this is the first time I've initiated physical contact. In the past it's always been him, and I've been okay with that thus far. Until now, regardless of the fact that I'm now married to him, it's felt wrong to touch him first. Just like it's not a wise idea to go around petting random dogs, you don't just go around touching men like Emeric. That seems like a surefire way to get bit.

"It's messy," I explain, taking my sweet time fixing his hair. I'm not so worried about getting bit now, and besides, I'm quickly learning I quite enjoy his mouth on me. "It makes you look younger—boyish—and maybe just a tad bit less scary."

"You think I'm scary?" The subtle change in his voice has my body reacting immediately. Legs already trembling, I have to lock my knees so I don't flat-out stumble into him.

"Terrifying."

He captures my hand and brings it down to his mouth where he then presses a kiss to the center of my palm. "It's a good thing you get off on fear then."

I don't know when I'll get used to him talking about my darkest secret so freely and without judgment. It's such a stark contrast to the internal struggle I've had around it for so many years. With him, it's no longer about achieving a simple rush during those stolen moments when I sought out fear. Emeric's elevated it into something darker and sexual. And I can't get enough.

He drops my hand and prowls closer to me until my butt hits the back of the Ducati. In a smooth but predatory move-

217

ment, he rests his hands on the motorcycle's seat on either side of me. Caging me in. I lift my chin and stare into his face that is only mere inches from mine now.

It would be so easy to just lift on my toes and kiss him, but I stop myself.

"You shot my dad tonight," I tell him.

As expected, there isn't a single flicker of remorse in those turbulent eyes of his. "Yes, I did," Emeric confirms just as his lips skim across my cheekbone and then my jaw. Heat and desire begin to swirl in my lower stomach. "He disrespected my wife. No man, not even the clown who raised you, is permitted to do that. Not unless they want to end up hanging from my ceiling while I get creative with my knife."

Without my permission, my head tilts to the side as his barely-there kisses evolve into more passionate ones as he begins to move to my neck. Eyes fluttering shut, I relish in the feeling of his lips against my now thundering pulse point.

"You're a confusing man," I tell him on a long exhale.

"I'm not," he insists against the skin of my throat. "Everything boils down to me protecting what is mine or what *will* be mine. My methods may seem a bit more... *innovative* than what most have deemed socially acceptable, but I don't care how much blood paints my hands." His teeth nip my earlobe and pulls on the small silver loop there before whispering darkly, "I will *always* win, and I *always* get my way."

"It didn't seem like you got your way tonight when you let my dad live," I counter, my fingers trailing up the buttons of his shirt. The itch to grab the fabric and tear it open so I can feel his bare chest is palpable.

"My business with your father is far from over. There's still plenty of time for me to get my way."

He takes hold of the leather jacket that's three sizes too big for me and pulls it from my frame. Without care, he tosses it off to the side in the parking garage. He lifts his chin at the guards who I'd completely forgotten about that are still standing by the elevator. His mouth has a way of making my mind go blissfully empty. My blazer and tank top go next, joining the jacket on the pavement.

In nothing but a see-through lace bra, short skirt, and sheer tights, I should be freezing but instead I'm on fire. For him. Watching him unleash his viciousness back at the pub had ignited something inside of me and he knew it. How could he not know the effect he was having on me when I'd been unconsciously grinding against his lap? There's a time and place to get turned on and watching your new husband threaten the patriarchs of your family is *not* an appropriate time. In my mind I knew this, but my body wasn't listening. It was basically humming with greedy need as Emeric went from cool and collected to dark and commanding. It's as if a switch had been flipped in him when he'd completely dropped the facade.

That coupled with the uninhibited and fast-paced motorcycle ride home, it feels like he's pumped me full of lightning. My bloodstream is electric. The open-mouthed hot kisses to my face and neck have only made me feel more charged. If he doesn't put his hands on me soon, I swear I'm going to burn up.

I don't believe in God, but I find myself sending up a thankful prayer when Emeric's hands land on my hips and my world spins. In the span of a single breath, I'm leaning over the seat of the expensive motorcycle and Emeric is on his knees behind me.

"I want you to keep your hands right where they are, princess. Don't move," he orders just as my skirt is shoved up my hips. His instruction doesn't sound difficult to follow until the unmistakable sound of a switchblade flicking open echoes through the concrete space. Instinctually, I begin to turn around, but his palm coming down in a punishing slap on my left ass cheek has me yelping in surprise and halting. "What did I just say?"

"Don't move."

"Correct." For a moment his hand slides over the spot he'd just slapped and soothes away the sting. The sensation of his warm palm is replaced by a blade running ever so lightly down the vertebra of my exposed spine. "We don't want to make you bleed, now do we?"

My brain screams no, my now throbbing pussy begs for it, and my lips? My lips say, "Why not? What's a little blood?"

If it weren't for the delicious-sounding moan that emits from him and makes my skin tingle, I may have momentarily regretted those unfiltered but amazingly honest words.

"You're perfect for me, Rionach Banes, and you don't even know it yet," he groans, his mouth pressing briefly to the curve of my ass. I've just relaxed into that light touch when the blade catches the fabric of my tights. The sound of them ripping coupled with the sudden cool air on my sensitive hot flesh has me gasping. Methodically, he cuts the sheer material until the only thing covering my ass is my dark green barely-there thong.

"Hey!" I scold when the lace is also sliced from my body. "This was a matching set."

"They were in my way," Emeric says as way of explanation. "I'll buy you a goddamn lingerie store if it means I can cut as many pairs of lacy thongs from your body as I please."

"I'm going to hold you to—" My snarky reply is violently cut off when there's an unexpected and distinctive sensation of cool metal sliding through my pussy lips. I'm torn between pulling away or leaning into the dangerous position he's just now put me in. One wrong move and that sharp blade could nick something important. Instead of doing either of those things, I turn into a piece of stone and freeze. I don't even dare breathe.

His movements are slow and so very careful. I remind myself that Emeric plays with knives often. He's skilled and precise when he's dismembering someone, and in an incredibly odd sort of way, that knowledge allows me to relax enough to exhale. The blade moves backward, grazing between my butt cheeks until he reaches my tailbone and pulls away. Gliding it a few inches to the right, he trails it over my cheek and when he reaches the roundest point of my ass, that's when the sharp tip of the knife slices through my skin. It's a quick and sharp kind of pain that has me sucking in a breath. It burns more than anything, but his tongue swiping over the small wound sooths it away until I feel nothing but warm.

The fact that at any given moment he could hurt me if he wanted to has my knees trembling, my heart racing, and my pussy dripping. I'm so far past feeling any shame for my body's reaction. When you're playing chicken with a train, your life is in your own hands, but right now, I've handed it all over to Emeric, and *that* is a different kind of fear entirely.

"And Niall said you wouldn't bleed," Emeric remarks sinisterly. "Your bright red blood against your pale skin is beautiful, princess."

"Oh God..." I can't stop the moan that escapes my throat as I drop my head to hang between my shoulders, but when his lips once again touch the place he cut at the same time I feel something foreign at my entrance, my neck snaps straight back up. "What—"

"Shh... you're being such a good girl," he soothes, his free hand trailing from my hip to my thigh. I'm back to not breathing when he pushes the cool metal inside just an inch before retracting. He does this a couple times. It's not till the fifth time do I figure out he's not teasing me with the blade, but with the handle. The second I relax, he pushes it deeper until I gasp. "You look so beautiful dripping all over my knife."

221

He fucks me with the knife handle in slow and measured thrusts, and I about come out of my skin when his other hand wraps around my body and finds my clit. The combination of both has me nearing that idyllic pinnacle within minutes. Fully aware there's still a sharp as hell and exposed blade between my thighs, my muscles begin to lock in preparation of my impending climax. I don't want to thrash about or move too much and end up causing the blade to unintentionally slice me.

While I'm making plans for staying as still as possible as I fall over the edge, Emeric has his own. I'm mere seconds away from toppling over when the handle is pulled out and he's now standing behind me. There's the telltale sound of his zipper lowering and the shuffling of fabric before the thick head of his cock is at my entrance.

The hand with the blade comes to rest against my sternum, the point of the knife now just inches below my chin at the same time he slices into me in one fluid but volatile thrust.

With a knife at my throat and Emeric buried inside me so deep I know I'll be feeling him for days to come, I ignite.

TWENTY-THREE
RIONACH

He's a big fat, no-good, dirty liar.

Okay I'm over exaggerating the "big fat" part. The only thing that's fat on Emeric Banes's body is his dick and I am not ashamed to admit I'm quite a fan of that. But the rest of it, I wholeheartedly stand by.

Emeric told me it would only take a couple days to secure me a bodyguard and after that, I would be free to live my life outside of this gilded cage, but here we are, a week and a half later, and I'm still doing my Rapunzel impression.

After the two agreed upon days came and went, I said fuck it and tried to leave on my own. In hindsight, it was foolish of me to think a man like Emeric wouldn't have a state-of-the-art security system attached to his hundred-million-dollar fortress looming in the clouds. I made it as far as the elevator doors when my grand escape was halted. A key card scanner on the wall next to the up and down arrow buttons mocked me and since that day, my irritation and anger has slowly but surely been growing. And after tonight, when I'd waited for him downstairs to come home until nearly two in the morning so I could demand he hold true to his promise, I think I've finally reached my boiling point.

After the turbulent night at The Irish Wife, Emeric's seemed on edge. The few times he's taken me out to dinner or to the café down the street for a latte, he's been tense, but I still found myself enjoying his company. Sitting across from him while having a meal or our morning coffee feels... easy.

The same large number of guards that accompanied us to the meeting with Dad travel with us too. Have you ever ordered an iced vanilla latte with almond milk and a sprinkle of cinnamon while eight armed men are watching you and all the possible exits? I can tell you right now, it's not an enjoyable or relaxing experience. I was raised with guards, but there were never this many on rotation at once, and I at least knew them to some degree. Emeric's men are still strangers to me, and it only makes me miss Brayden more.

The irony that the only person from home I seem to miss is my dad's head of security isn't lost on me. I actually think it really puts into perspective just how broken my relationship with my family members truly was. I haven't found myself longing for the comfort of my bedroom or the familiar faces of my family once.

On top of Emeric being on guard and tense when we leave the penthouse, he's seemed off the last couple days. His mood seems to shift on a dime and there's something about the storm brewing in his eyes that makes me believe there should be tornado sirens blaring. On multiple occasions behind the closed door of his office I heard him yell at people over the phone and yesterday morning, he got angry at the brunette named Liv who works with Anneli because she walked into his office without knocking.

Even with this change of behavior and him lashing out at

other people, he hasn't raised his voice once to me. The only change—if we can really call it that, seeing as he's always had a certain *vigor*—is that the ruthlessness in which he's fucked me the past couple nights. It's hard, fast, and oh-so very deep. Last night when he'd finally decided to join me in bed, Emeric slipped between my thighs with a desperate kind of hunger and he pounded into me until I orgasmed so hard, I think I almost blacked out. When he'd followed suit close behind, coming inside me with a mouthwatering growl, he didn't pull out. Just like that night after we'd first gotten married, he'd pulled me into his chest and within minutes, his ragged breathing had evened out.

For the second time since I became his wife, I fell asleep with his cock snug inside of me and once again, I was shocked by how comforting being filled by Emeric was.

When I woke up this morning—sore as hell and looking like he'd painted me with bruises—and all alone, my anger had reignited. I spent the day waiting for him to show and while I did, I got to know Anneli a little better. Turns out the accent I couldn't place was Scandinavian and she's worked for Emeric for nearly eight years. I *also* learned with that long tenure comes access to a key card. That was a nugget of information I tucked away while she told me about her childhood in Scandinavia.

My respect for the woman grew when I learned what she'd been through. She was brought to the States by a man promising her a job in modeling—see? I was right about the modeling thing. Turns out he, too, was a liar and for nearly a decade, she was forced into sex work. That changed when one of her repeat customers brought her to Emeric's club and got a little too drunk and way too aggressive with her. Emeric's men intervened, and she was brought before the big boss. Emeric offered her a job in the basement of Tartarus or to come work for him personally at his home. She wisely chose the latter and as they say, the rest is history.

I don't know if we'll ever be the best of friends, but I do think it will be nice having another person to talk to when Emeric is gone. And he's gone *a lot*.

After Anneli and her two other girls, Liv and Maja, had left for the day, I'd taken up position on the giant sectional so I could know the second Emeric got home. Cerberus stayed at my side, curled up at my feet until midnight rolled around and he went and put himself to bed in the dog bed that's in the upstairs sitting room. Exhausted myself, I forced myself to stay awake for another two hours before I gave up and got ready for bed.

I had been peacefully asleep until the bed shifted behind me a second ago. Eyes barely cracked open I find that the sky has just started to wake up and light pink and orange decorate the clouds we reside in. His hand settles on my hip at the same time his lips brush across my shoulder blade.

Emeric's fingers gather the silken fabric of my nightie and he pulls it up until he has unrestricted access to my ass.

I mumble a sleepy sound of displeasure over the fact he's woken me up. Blindly, I reach for his hand resting on my hip and capture it in mine.

"Shh..." he soothes in my ear, his naked chest pressing against my back. "It's just me."

"Who the hell else would it be?" I croak, forcing my eyes to remain shut. It's too goddamn early. "Now, shoo and let me sleep."

He chuckles as he brings our now gathered hands to my pussy. I'm mad at him—I remember that clearly—but the second he brushes his fingertips through me and begins to methodically and torturously circle my clit, my fight abandons me. Like a *traitor*.

Within a minute, he's got me rocking my hips in rhythm with his movements. A gentle but still enjoyable orgasm washes through me. Yep, doesn't matter how mad at this man I am, this will continue to be my favorite kind of way to wake up. *The bastard.*

When the head of his aforementioned fat-as-hell cock nudges my entrance, I'm instantly yanked out of my post-orgasm haze.

"No," I tell him, still sounding drowsy. "No fucking. Not tonight—this morning—or *whatever* the fucking time is right now. You wrecked my poor pussy last night when you came at me like an *animal*. I'm still sore."

"Oh, how you flatter me," he hums in my ear as he increases the pressure at my opening. "It's a good thing I don't plan on fucking you."

"It sure *feels* like that's your plan, Banes."

He kisses along my shoulder blade again and then to my cheekbone. "I just want to sleep," he explains slowly, starting to push inside. My breath catches in a gasp as my sore muscles involuntarily clench around the thick invasion. It's tender, but not bad enough that I want to shove him away. "I'm exhausted, Rionach, and it turns out I sleep best while I'm inside of you."

His words instantly get added to the very niche list of things that shouldn't be flattering or hot, but for some bizarre fucking reason they are.

I tighten around him again, forcing a sharp inhale of air from him.

"Behave," he scolds. "Go back to sleep, love."

Love.

It's so very hard to remember I'm pissed at him when he says things like that while he's *inside* of me.

Relaxing myself against him, I tell him on a long exhale, "Good night, Emeric."

TWENTY-FOUR

EMERIC

"She's pissed at me," I tell Nova as I duck to avoid one of his meaty tattooed fists.

Sparring with Nova has been a long-held tradition between the two of us. In the past we had more free time to train than we do now, but we try to squeeze in a session—whether it's a quick round in the ring or a trip to the shooting range—once a week. We're not about to allow our honed and well-earned skills to grow rusty by becoming lazy or too complacent in our current ranking. People and organizations are constantly circling looking for a way to deliver a debilitating blow. Weakness of any kind isn't allowed if you want to stay at the top, and I fucking do. I earned my throne.

Nova uses a wrapped hand to push some of the brown hair that has fallen from the stupid fucking man bun he put the longer strands of hair in to keep out of his face. The sides and back of his head are shaved, allowing for his tattoos to expand and be visible on parts of his scalp. Most people find the hulking man intimating, but I find that difficult to do when he looks like a Yorkshire terrier with his little topknot.

"Of course she is," my second hand scoffs while blocking a jab and then cross from me. "You told Rionach almost two weeks ago that you'd find a man to put on her security detail so she can leave this place, and you haven't. I'd be pissed at you too. She's a human, not a pet, E."

"I *know* that," I snap.

Full of a wild kind of pent-up energy and emotions I'm currently too far removed from myself to fully recognize, I let it all fuel me as I lunge at Nova. I don't hold back and he doesn't balk or falter. He meets me with his own vigor and we trade blows back and forth.

I'm having one of my "bad days". Personally, I've never referred to them as that, but that's what Nova has called these *episodes* for over a decade. He knew the second I called him this morning at four-thirty a.m. what he'd find when he walked through the doors of my penthouse elevator. And if my ungodly early phone call didn't alert him, the wired state he found me in clued him in immediately.

He showed up with two black coffees and his gym bag an hour later.

We talked in my office for over an hour going over upcoming shipments as well as the meetings we'll need to attend in the coming month for our more legitimate businesses. Banes Corporation has its hands in many pies to ensure that our power and reach are well spread out. From hotels and clubs to technology development and politics, the Banes family's income comes from many sources. I've expanded our brand into places my father could only dream of and because of it, I've made billions. I hope that knowledge makes him roll in his grave.

Once that was taken care of, we both changed into workout clothes and headed to the home gym. The makeshift boxing ring is nothing more than a large black floor mat, but it suffices our needs just fine.

We spar and battle it out until we're both sweating and panting like dogs. We both succeeded at landing blows to each other, and I already know my ribs are going to be sore from Nova's knee making contact, but I relish the muscle strain and the fatigue.

That is the end goal here, after all.

"How are you feeling? Have you had enough yet?" Nova asks before taking a long drink of his water when we finally take a break from trying to beat the shit out of each other.

"No, not yet," I exhale, wiping sweat from my brow with the hem of my black T-shirt.

"Okay," he says with an understanding nod as he begins to recheck the wraps around his knuckles so he'll be ready for round two once we've both caught our breaths. "Are you going to tell me why you haven't put a team on your wife yet and why you still have her locked up in this joint?"

"I haven't found anyone I deem trustworthy enough to guard her," I tell him simply despite there being anything *simple* about it.

He throws me a bottle of water, an incredulous look on his stern face. "That's not the full reason and you know it."

Of course I fucking know it.

I drink half the bottle in one go. "It's not safe for her."

He stares at me for a long moment. "It's never safe in our world, Emeric. You know this."

"My contact at the hospital told me both Niall and Tiernan have been discharged. It's only a matter of time before they're done nursing their boo-boos and come up with a plan to retaliate. You saw how Niall acted at the pub, he's going to be out for blood and for that to happen, he's going to need support."

Nova positions himself back at the center of the mat and

motions for me to do the same. "Are you thinking Tadhg will step in and help in his vendetta against you?"

"I don't think her grandfather has any interest in going to war with me. The full weight of his power is in the UK. Bringing his men here will only weaken his stance back at home. He doesn't seem like the kind of guy who would be willing to jeopardize that, and he's already admitted to my face he couldn't win against me." He at least has the sense to know when he's been beat. His son-in-law, on the other hand... "Niall's going to go to the Russians and reinstate the original deal they had but to make that happen, he'll need to take Rionach from me to give to Bogdan."

Nothing makes a man like Bogdan want something more than when he's told he can't have it or when it's taken away from him. At that point it becomes a matter of damaged ego and by me stealing his future bride out from under his nose, the younger Koslov's ego must be hurting something fierce.

I move to stand before Nova and tap my wrapped knuckles with his before we start circling each other.

His strong brow quirks and a skeptical look flashes across his pale eyes. "And you know that will be his plan, how? Do you have men watching both families?"

"I have men watching everyone," I say as way of explanation before I dodge his tattooed fist and throw a jab of my own at his ribs.

Nova grunts at the contact but his raised hands don't drop an inch. He's ready for whatever else I'm going to throw at him.

"Between Niall and his son, they have two good hands and nowhere near enough money to fund a war against you. The Koslovs will see this too, and I can't imagine them still wanting to keep up their end of the bargain even if they were able to get their hands on Rionach."

On a normal day, my temper is always on a short leash, but

on days like this when I'm actively feeling everything all at once, my hold on it is near nonexistent. My vision turns red at Nova's choice of words, and I unleash myself on him.

"No one is putting their fucking hands on *my wife!*" I may have roared this, or I could have snarled it, I can't be sure which. The only thing I can hear is the blood rushing in my ears like an angry current. "She's *mine* and *I'm* going to keep her safe."

Nova lets go of his control too and we attack each other. This time, it's not a friendly spar, it's a full-out bloodbath. By the time I get him on his back on the mat and the heel of my shoe is in his jugular, we're both sporting matching split lips and bruises. I spit a mouthful of blood on the mat and glare down at my friend.

"All right, that's enough for today, brother," Nova says calmly, signaling for me to remove my foot by patting my shin twice. When he calls me brother, I'm reminded of the fact I have two brothers by blood and yet I'm closer with Nova than I am with Astor, or with Ledger when he was still around. This tattooed beast of a man had played a big part in my life for a long time.

Grunting, I pull my foot from his neck and offer him my hand to help him up off the ground. Nova slaps me on the shoulder once he's on his feet and offers me an easy smile. We never get angry when we put each other on our asses. He knew when he found me in this state he was more than likely going to end up in this position.

"How many days has it been?" he asks, regarding me with an inquisitive stare.

I grab both of our waters and unscrew the cap off mine. "Days since when?"

He rolls his eyes because he knows I know what he's asking me. "How many days has it been since you slept, and I'm not talking about just an hour-long nap here and there. I mean *sleep*."

I once told Rionach I always win in a fight, but in a way that was a lie. I've been losing my battle against sleep since I was fifteen. Back then, the memories and thoughts I tried my hardest to avoid when I was conscious snuck into my unconscious mind and infiltrated my dreams. My plan then was to just avoid sleep altogether for as long as possible. I'd go days before I'd finally crash. That plan evolved and became a severe case of insomnia midway through my twenties.

Some of my most erratic and renowned acts happened because I was severely sleep-deprived. I've found lack of sleep may affect my decision-making skills and aggravate my already unpredictable disposition, but it also brings out a certain flair when I have a knife in hand and an enemy in my sights.

"I think I slept for almost four hours on Tuesday night, and I got an hour in on Wednesday on the couch at the office between meetings."

"*You think?* Jesus, Emeric. It's Friday," his tattooed fingers pinch the bridge of his nose. "You can't do this anymore—not with *her* living here with you now. You know how you can get when you don't sleep." Erratic—more than I already am, which is saying something—irritable, paranoid, and if I go too long, hallucinations join the party. It's a swell time for everyone. "I've said it before, but you need to address this. Find some kind of solution that allows you to fucking rest so you don't lose whatever's left of your goddamn mind. It's different now because you're not just putting yourself in danger."

I don't dare tell him that I've already found something that lulls me to sleep better than any drug we've tried. The best sleep I'd gotten in years was the first time I fell asleep with my cock still in my wife. I had still woken up early the next morning, but five hours of uninterrupted sleep was unprecedented for me. My original objective by staying buried in her was to keep any of my cum from escaping her womb, the sedative-like effect it ended up having was a welcome surprise. Tuesday night when I climbed into bed beside Rionach and slipped inside her warm welcoming pussy, I discovered it wasn't a one-off thing. No, having her wrapped around me and in my arms put me right to sleep.

By the time I finished dealing with the shipment of weapons from my contacts in Turkey on Wednesday, it was already morning, and she was awake when I got home. I got caught up again last night at Tartarus, and didn't make it home until after four a.m. this morning. I was too wound up to go to her and that's when I called Nova in. In the past, sparing a couple of rounds exhausted me enough to knock me out, or at the very least take the edge off.

And if that doesn't work...

"I brought a sedative," Nova says like he's read my mind. "I wasn't sure what we were dealing with and figured it couldn't hurt to have the option."

I give him a look that has him holding his hands up in front of him.

"Look, man, it's not a strong dose. It will knock you out for a couple of hours and allow your body and mind to rest and reset. You know you're running on fumes and close to going over the edge. What do you say we just avoid that dog and pony show?"

I contemplate what he's saying and know he's right.

The volatile and wired energy coursing through me makes me feel dangerous in an out-of-control kind of way. People like to tell stories about how uncontrollable I am because it's easier for them to believe I do the things I do because I can't help myself. I can't honestly say that hasn't happened in the past, but in most cases, I'm in *complete* control of my actions, and if you ask me, this makes me ten times more dangerous. It means I'm fully aware of how depraved my deeds can be and actively seek opportunities to do more.

I know what kind of man I am, but the sleep-deprived side of me is one I'm not sure I want my wife seeing. I promised I would protect her, and I'm now starting to understand that also means even from myself. And if I'm being honest, getting to the point of exhaustion where I hallucinate is something I'd like to avoid. In the past when it's happened, I have found myself thrust back into the memories I'd much rather forget.

"I don't want Rionach knowing."

The image of her walking in and finding I've had to be medically sedated crosses my mind, and I find I don't like it.

Nova nods in understanding. "We can go to the office or the hotel." He's talking about the hotel we own on the other side of Central Park called The Daria. After my father died, we changed the family-owned hotel to my mother's name. She always loved the tearoom there, and we were searching for new ways to honor the great woman and mother who had been taken from this world. It doesn't feel like enough, though. "Hell, we can go to my place, and you can crash in my spare bedroom."

"Your place," I choose, knowing it'll be the most private of the three options.

Nova wastes no time scooping his gym bag off the floor as he heads toward the double glass doors leading out of the gym. "Okay, let's go. The sooner that brain of yours can shut down, the better it'll be for everyone, but especially you."

Scrubbing my hand over my sweaty face, I push my hair back from my forehead with an exhausted sigh. "Yeah, all right." I begrudgingly follow.

We've barely made it down the hallway when a panicked-looking Anneli rushes toward us. In all the years she's worked for me, I've never seen the willowy woman look as distressed as she is now, and I rescued her from her abusive john. *Something is wrong.* Every fiber of my being is instantly on edge and painfully alert. My eyes scan the vast living room area, surrounding it for signs of danger, but the only person present is my housekeeper.

"What is it?" Even if I tried, I couldn't keep the aggression from my tone. Not now.

She nervously shakes her head back and forth, pale blonde strands of hair flying about. "I don't know how she got to it. I *always* keep it in my back pocket."

"What the hell are you talking about?"

"Got to what?"

Nova and I speak at the same time.

Anneli looks between us, eyes wide. "Mrs. Banes."

My heart instantly turns to stone in my chest, and this time I can't stop myself from reaching up and touching that tight spot on my sternum. "What about her?" I grit out between clenched teeth.

"She somehow managed to steal my key card," the Scandinavian woman before me touches the empty back pocket of her beige trousers. "She left. She's not here, Mr. Banes."

For the second time in an hour, my vision goes red, but this time, my world tilts along with it. "What the fuck do you mean *she's not here?*" my raised voice bounces off all the glass in the room, reverberating around us. "Where is my fucking wife?" My question comes out as a violent roar, making Anneli flinch.

"I don't have the slightest clue where she's gone, sir," she whispers. "I'm so sorry... it was in my pocket. I would have *felt* if she'd taken my key card from me, right? I don't see how it'd be possible to not—"

"Stop talking," I order as I push past her and head for my office. Other than the bedrooms and bathrooms, there are

237

cameras around the penthouse. I also have access to the ones outside the building and up and down the street. It won't take me long to find her... that's if I find her before someone else does. *Fuck!* "Nova, call your men. Put them on standby. We'll need them here shortly."

"On it." Nova already has his cell phone to his ear.

Feeling a mixture of blinding anger and nauseating dread, I surge through my office doors.

You're going to regret this, princess.

TWENTY-FIVE
RIONACH

"Okay, let me get this straight. You just *left*?" Ophelia asks from the other side of the park bench for the third time since we sat down. "Alone?"

I wave the black leather leash in my left hand at her and gesture at the on-alert dog sitting in front of my legs. "Clearly I'm not alone."

Lia gapes at me. "The dog does *not* count, Rio, and you know it."

"Why not?" I ask, taking a sip of the coffee we'd grabbed before making our way to this park. "Emeric himself said Cerberus is highly trained."

"Rio!" my friend scolds, an aghast look on her pretty face. "I really don't think you're grasping the full magnitude of the man you're now married to. A dog, even if he's as trained as you say, does *not* offer you the kind of protection you now require as his wife." Lia's head shakes in disbelief. "God, you're in so much deep shit. Not only did you go against *Emeric Banes's* orders and leave, but you also kidnapped his dog."

"I didn't kidnap Cerberus, I simply borrowed him," I argue, patting the Doberman's big head.

What I'm doing is foolish, I can admit that, but I'm not a *complete* idiot. I brought the dog as a safeguard, just in case Emeric's seemingly paranoid rationale proves correct. It's not like I plan on gallivanting around the city all day. I just wanted to see my friend and have a moment outside of the Emeric bubble.

Not to mention I warned him two weeks ago what would happen if he tried to keep me locked up. If anything, my escape is *his* fault. He wrongly underestimated me when he thought I couldn't figure a way out of his cage.

"Do you worst, Rionach. I would love to see what you have up your sleeve." This is what he told me with that goddamn arrogant smirk on his face. Well, buddy, I did my worst and now I'm free.

I'm aware I'm going to be walking into a shitstorm when I go back, but I felt like I was going crazy locked up in there.

When I woke up alone, *again*, and later heard Emeric locked away in his home gym with Nova, I said "fuck it" and decided to go through with the half-baked—and anger-fueled— plan I'd come up with yesterday when I was waiting for him to come. The perfect rectangle shape in the back pocket of Anneli's light brown and tight pants told me exactly where she kept her key card this morning. A simple maneuver in the kitchen that involved accidentally spilling a cup of orange juice gave me the opportunity to put my self-taught pickpocketing skills to use and swipe the card from her. With it safely hidden in my bra, I went upstairs to grab my long camel-colored coat and the dog leash I'd saw hanging in the laundry room above Cerberus's food bowls.

After that, it was just a matter of waiting for Anneli to move to another part of the house so I could walk past the kitchen and into the elevator. With my head down and Cerberus at my side, I breezed through the immaculate and fancy-as-hell lobby of the skyscraper.

A thrill settled in my tummy when I breathed in the crisp morning air and headed in the direction of the pole dancing studio Ophelia teaches at a couple of times a week. I know she teaches early morning classes on Fridays, and I sent up a little prayer to whoever might be listening that she'd still be there by the time I walked my butt ten blocks.

I all but did a happy dance when I got to Twirl & Tease Dance Studio and saw her demonstrating a complicated move to her small class.

Lia's poor jaw nearly hit the polished wood floor of the studio when I walked in.

"You *married* him?" she'd screeched at me the second her last student left. "You're Emeric Bane's *wife*? What the hell happened, Rio?"

I was confused about how she had already known about the teeny-tiny changes in my life, when I'd remembered the announcement Emeric had put out. Anybody who is anybody knows about the change of my last name.

After helping her lock up the studio, we'd walked to our favorite coffee shop down the road before we made it to this park bench.

Lia sighs while running a hand through her dark hair before pushing it over her shoulder. "I just think you're playing with fire by making Emeric mad." An incredulous look settles on her face. "We've all heard the story about how he is, and after what you told me happened at your wedding... I just don't want you to get hurt, Rio."

As if it's second nature, I instantly and without so much as a single thought, tell her, "Emeric isn't going to hurt me." *At least not in a way I don't find enjoyable.*

Something settles in my soul when I realize I truly believe what I've just said. Even if he's going to be big mad when I get home, I know in my core I'm safe with Emeric. How many people can say that?

"I still don't know..." She shakes her head. "You know the guy who shot him on New Year's?"

It doesn't surprise me that Ophelia knows about that. I'm sure everyone that witnessed it ran off and told their friends. Gossip spreads faster than wildfire in our communities.

"Of course I do. I was standing right there when the gun went off."

Lia's nose wrinkles. "Apparently Emeric sent a fruit bouquet stuffed full of the gunman's fingers back home to his boss and family."

I don't know what the appropriate reaction should be to hearing something like this, but I'm going to assume by the horrified expression on Ophelia's face that busting out laughing isn't it.

"Rio!"

"What?" I ask, choking back another fit of laughter. "All these dumb fucking men keep going after Emeric, thinking they will somehow get the better of him, and then everyone is surprised when he chops off their body parts." *Looking at you, Dad and Tiernan.* "What did they expect? They fucked around and they found out the hard way. Emeric has been on top for over a *decade* for a reason. I just don't understand why people are still desperate enough to try."

Lia's dark brown eyes widen as she stares at me like she doesn't know me.

I don't like that look. It's the same look my dad and grandfather gave me the other day at the pub. My first instinct is to shove my painstakingly crafted mask on, but I don't want to do that anymore because I don't have to. Being married to Emeric means I don't have to hide who I am. Not anymore.

"*What?* Why are you looking at me like that?"

Her narrow but strong shoulders rise. "I'm just shocked to hear you defending him like that after he's—"

"All he's done is protect the empire he's fought hard to build. People are fully aware of the kind of man they're going up against and they continue to challenge him. It's not Emeric's fault people never seem to learn."

My dad's antics that night at the pub is proof of it.

"I was going to say after he's forced you to marry him."

Despite my anger at him for dragging his feet on getting me a bodyguard so I can freely come and go as I please, my time so far as Emeric's wife hasn't been awful. From the outside looking in, that might make me sound like I'm cuckoo bananas crazy, but for me the past two weeks have given me the gift of just... *being.* I get to exist. I don't have to pretend to be someone I'm not, and I don't have to walk around his home on eggshells like I did at my childhood home.

I was to be seen and never heard. Until *him.*

My soul is now free.

Lifting my chin, I tell my closest friend the God's honest truth. "I don't hate him, Lia. Emeric is violent and erratic, but he doesn't scare me. Not like he scares everyone else. What does scare me is the fact that if I let myself, I think I could one day love him." And then where do I go from there?

Ophelia wraps her slightly callused fingers around my wrist since my iced coffee is still in my hand. "Trust me when I tell you I understand—maybe better than anyone—what you're feeling right now. Banes men have a way of crawling under your skin and then into your heart, and no matter how hard you try to move on, they're just *stuck* in there."

It's my turn to stare at her like I don't know her.

"You have a past with a Banes?" I feel my stomach flip violently when I remember the way she knew her way around Tartarus so well. "You and Emeric..."

Her face falls and her hand grips me tighter. "Oh, God no! No, not him." She looks away and releases another long sigh. "I never told you because it was never relevant and it was *so* far in my past, but I have a little bit of history with the Banes family. When we lived in Seattle, I was neighbors with Astor Banes and his son Callan. You remember Bash, my older brother? He was best friends with Callan in middle and part of high school, so I spent my fair share of time around him."

I gape at my friend. "This definitely feels like something that should have come up before *now*."

She lifts a shoulder. "Like I said, it was ancient history and when we moved here, we lost all contact." Lia gives me a small smile. "Come on, don't fault me too hard for this. It's not like you've told me about *every* friend you had in your awkward teen years."

I give my stunningly beautiful friend a dubious look.

"Don't lie to me. You never had an awkward phase in your life." Ophelia is the perfect combination of her French-born father and her Filipino mother. I've met her mom, Salome, a couple of times and not only is she an amazing nonprofit director, but she's also gorgeous. Her brother, Bash, was also blessed with good looks. When I met him, he was wearing his Marine Corps uniform and as they say, there's just *something* about a man in a uniform.

"I had braces in middle school."

"Shut up. We all had braces in middle school." I wave her off just as a thought occurs to me. "But, *hey*! Wait a minute! I know for a *fact* Callan is here in New York now."

Last week, Emeric mentioned his nephew does accounting

for the family business now when he got home late from a meeting he had with him. "Have you seen him yet?"

The tips of Lia's high cheekbones turn bright red.

"Aha! It would appear it is not as far in the past as you say it is. Now spill."

I know Emeric's going to be mad, but it'll be worth it. I needed this time away, and more than anything, I needed to talk to someone outside of his household. I needed my friend.

———

IT WASN'T long after we'd finished our coffees that Ophelia had to leave to meet a friend of hers who attends Julliard. Apparently, the poor girl's father has been ill for a while and it's looking like she's going to have to return home so she can be closer to him.

With the treatment I've received from my own father, I can't imagine packing everything up and moving across the country so I could be with him. After the way he talked about me and called me a "broken-in whore", I don't think I'd care how sick he was, I wouldn't be lifting so much as a finger. I don't want to help him and having him play an active role in my life is now out of the question, but Emeric was right when he said I wasn't ready to watch my father die. In my heart, I know that if he keeps pushing Emeric, that's how he's going to end up. I also know there is nothing I can do to stop him from going further down the path he's created. Dad's digging his own grave and he's too stubborn to see that the dirt is already up to his neck.

Cerberus's attention locks on a fluffy white dog that's yipping at him from across the quiet street. The leather leash goes taut in my hands when the black dog connected to it lunges.

"*Nein!*" I don't know how to say *leave it* in German, but simply telling him no seems to have done the trick since he's now back to walking calmly. "Good dog."'

When I left the park Ophelia and I had been sitting in, I chose to take the longer route home. The weather has finally decided to act like it's spring and not winter, and I'm enjoying the blue sky peeking through the clouds and the absence of the bitter chill in the fresh air. Well, as fresh as city air can get. This way will only add about fifteen minutes to my walk, so it's not as if I'm deviating too far from my original plan of heading straight home after visiting with Lia. The sidewalks aren't as busy with morning commuters heading to work or classes. It's quieter. It gives me some time to come up with what I'm going to tell Emeric when I see him.

If reason and rationality don't work in my favor, I can always pull out the big guns. Distract him with sex. *"I was a very bad girl. Please don't punish me too hard."* With a couple bats of my eyelashes and a little pout on my lip, I'm sure I can have him forgiving me in no time. And depending on what my punishment could be, I might find I thoroughly enjoy it. If that's the case, then it's a win-win for both of us.

Completely lost in thought over the possible punishments lying ahead me, I don't hear the dark van skidding around the street corner until it comes to a violent and crashing stop at the curb next to me. The windows are so deeply tinted I can't see who's inside or how many there are. Cerberus's hackles rise and a deep growl I've never heard from him rips through his throat as the van's back door rapidly slides open. Three men wearing balaclavas surge from the vehicle and barrel toward me. They're dressed in head-to-toe black with no distinguishing markers that can tell me who they work for, but there are two very strong possibilities for who could have sent them. Or *one* if

246

Dad's men and Igor's crew are continuing with their alliance and working together.

Cerberus lunges at the same time I drop his leash. I don't see which of the men he grabbed but I do hear the scream of pain when I turn. The only thing I can think as I try to sprint away from the masked men is that Emeric was right about it not being safe. I was arrogant. And I was dumb to believe leaving without him was a good idea. No, let me reword that. I always knew that it was stupid to leave protection, but I simply wanted to do it anyway.

Your recklessness really did it this time, Rio.

I silently thank my past self for choosing to wear my white leather tennis shoes over the pair of heeled boots I'd originally pulled out. The soles of my shoes pound into the pavement as the sound of two additional—much heavier and faster—pairs of footsteps gain on me.

My mouth opens with the intention of screaming for help. At the same time, a strong arm grabs me and encircles my waist. My body is lifted from the ground as a leather-gloved hand slams down on my face and muffles the shrill scream currently trying to slice through my throat.

Oh God, Oh God, Oh God.

I kick, thrash, and fight the man with all my strength but when his teammate appears at his side and they hold me between them in vise-like grips, there's nothing I can do. The three hands on my body keep me still and the hand over my mouth keeps me silent.

Fear like I've never experienced cascades through my bloodstream like a noxious cloud and when it ceases my lungs, it chokes me. In the face of genuine fear, I'm not humming with the addictive adrenaline I've come to love and crave, instead I feel like I'm suffocating.

I know what's happened has occurred in the span of thirty

seconds, but it already feels like it's been minutes. My bleary eyes search my surroundings, hoping that someone will walk by and see what's happening here. The only other figure I can find is the man standing by the open van door with a blooded hand cradled to his chest. It's Cerberus's handwork, but my beloved dog is nowhere to be seen.

This has a newfound wave of strength pulsing through me. As hard as I can, I sink my blunt teeth into the meaty part of the hand covering my mouth. My attacker hollers and drops me, which causes his companion to fumble and lose his grip on me. I stumble to my feet and waste no time bringing my knee into the closest one's junk. It just so happens to be the one I didn't already bite, so now I've got both of them whimpering in pain. Good.

I've turned only a quarter of the way to face the one who isn't currently nursing his ball sack with, when the telltale sound of a gun cocking echoes in my eardrums. The cold, hard metal of the barrel pushes into the base of my skull. This time, I freeze and don't fight.

"We were warned you might be a feisty one." The man with the gun chuckles darkly behind me.

I swallow hard and set my jaw as I force my mask of indifference to fall into place. Allowing these men to see that I'm scared isn't an option. I would rather lick a subway bench seat than give them that satisfaction. There's a very strong likelihood they're employed by the psychopath Bogdan Koslov and if they're anything like the Russian, they'll probably get off on my tears and screams.

No, I have to keep it together for as long as it will take Emeric to find me because I know in my gut he *will* come for me. He's said on numerous occasions he protects what is his—and *I am* Emeric's.

A hand grabs my shoulder and forces me to spin around to face the open door of the black van. My heart soars when I spot Cerberus already sitting in the back in a wire crate with a muzzle strapped to his face. He's pissed and growling, but he isn't hurt, which is all I care about. I wouldn't be able to live with myself if I got him hurt by bringing him along on my little adventure this morning.

So fucking stupid, Rio. You're. So. Fucking. Stupid.

The men behind me take advantage of me having my back to them and they yank my arms backward. Cold metal hand-cuffs encircle my wrists. The clicking sound of them locking has me fighting a flinch.

"You can either climb in yourself, or I will have my men throw you in," the one with the gun tells me. The free hand hanging at his side drips blood onto the sidewalk every few seconds. My dog got him good.

Not bothering or willing to dignify him with an answer, I glare at him and step into the large vehicle. I've no sooner taken a seat next to the large cage when someone forces a black bag over my head. On our wedding night, Emeric bound my hands and blindfolded me too, but right now, the vulnerability I experienced that night pales in comparison to this.

"Sit tight," someone says, sounding irksomely pleased with himself. "It'll take us a little more than an hour to reach our destination."

An hour? My parents' estate is nearly an hour away from the city. Is that where they're taking me? It would be really unwise to take me there because that is one of the first places Emeric is going to look, but then again, we're talking about my brother and father. Their planning skills as of late have been less than stellar.

I could have just stayed in bed this morning and slept in, or

I could have snuggled up under a blanket and watched a movie. Instead, I just had to prove Emeric wrong and defy him.

What was I thinking?

TWENTY-SIX
RIONACH

THEY PLAYED rock music at such a deafening volume the entire drive that I could hardly hear my own heartbeat let alone my thoughts. I did my best to work through the possible scenarios I could find myself in once the van stops. It all comes down to who will be standing on the other side of the door when it opens.

If it's my dad or brother, as depressing as it sounds, trying to appeal to the fact I'm still their blood will more than likely be my only option. That, and getting on my knees and begging for their forgiveness even though I haven't done *anything* wrong. If it's Bogdan and Igor, I really don't know what my play will be. Just like I did with the men who grabbed me, not allowing myself to show them any kind of fear is vital. If it's all four of them... I'll need to come up with a plan C on the spot.

Either way, I will just have to hang on long enough for Emeric to show up. I can do that.

I can be strong until then.

The van bounces and sways as we drive over uneven terrain. The sound of rocks and dirt crunching beneath the tires tells me we're no longer on a paved road and we're not in the city. A window in the front slides down when we come to a stop. The scent of fresh earthy air tickles my nose.

Cerberus, I don't think we're in the overpopulated and smog-filled city anymore.

My parents' estate sits on a good-sized lot with many trees for privacy. While I have no way of knowing if that's where they've brought me, something in my gut tells me it's not. The drive was too long, and we didn't hit much traffic on the way here. Unless they took the scenic route?

Finally, the music is turned off just as someone outside the van asks, "How'd it go?"

I listen closely for any hints of Russian or Irish accents. The only person so far who has the slightest hint of an accent is this newcomer, and I can't place his. Maybe Spanish or Portuguese? Meaning he's definitely not an employee of my father's then.

The driver laughs. "The bitch sunk her teeth into Yates and made him scream like a pussy, and the dog took a chunk out of Westin."

Someone in the van coughs and awkwardly clears his throat. "I wouldn't call her that if I were you, man."

"She *bit* you," the driver argues.

"I'm just saying, I don't think it's wise," the mystery man, who I'm now assuming is called Yates, explains.

An awkward silence falls over the inside of the vehicle for a drawn-out moment before the man with the accent grumbles, "Get moving. He's waiting for you down at the tree line."

He. That doesn't exactly help me narrow down my choices for who's behind this mess.

The sound of metal screeching and grinding fills the air. It's not until it ceases does the van start moving forward once more. A gate. We're driving through a gate. Now I know we're not at my parents' place. The gate in front of their home doesn't make much of any noise when it opens. If it did, I wouldn't have been as successful at sneaking out as I was on those rare occasions.

The dirt road turns into gravel once we're past the gate, and the only sound inside the van at this point is the sound of it beneath the tires. Now that I can hear my erratic heartbeat, I find myself wishing they'd turn the god-awful music back on. The frenzied pounding in my chest and ears is only making my anxiety climb. I tug on the metal wrapped around my wrists knowing full well it's not going to budge. The fifty other times I tried on the drive here already proved that. At this point, I'm just hurting myself. The way the metal bites into my skin makes me appreciate the leather ones Emeric used on our wedding night more.

The car comes to a stop again, but this time on uneven ground that makes me feel unbalanced in my seat, and the parking brake grinds into place. The engine turning off completely has the hair rising on the back of my neck as I brace myself to face whatever—and whoever—is waiting for me outside.

Cerberus moves restlessly in the wire cage next to me and emits a low growl when the men sitting in the back of the van with me move closer. Gloved hands grip my upper arms and pull me up into an awkward standing position just as the door slides open.

This time there's no threats about getting out of the car of my own volition or being forced from it. Everyone is deathly silent. I'm doing my best to do the same by clenching my teeth together and slowly forcing oxygen out of my lungs in slow measured breaths. If I let myself, my breathing would be nothing but ragged panting sounds as dread claws at my throat. The worst-case scenario here is that I'm about to come face to face with my—unbeknownst to me—previously arranged fiancé. The pictures Emeric provided at the church of the atrocities Bogdan instilled on women flash in my head like a horror-filled slideshow.

I will not become one of them.

I will not become one of them.

I will not become one of them.

My silent mantra is repeated over and over as I'm escorted out of the back of the car. I promised myself I wouldn't show the Koslovs any fear and I will do everything in my power to remain true to that, but I will also fight like hell if it comes to it. I refuse to make it easy for Bogdan. Or his father. The odds will be against me, but I won't let them win so easily.

With my new resolve strengthening me, I keep my shoulders back and my head held high despite the black fabric still concealing me.

But that all goes to shit when the handcuffs are removed from my wrists and the bag is lifted from my head.

I have no idea where I am, and I don't bother looking around for clues because my focus is locked on the man standing in front of me with a furious lightning storm flashing in his eyes.

In a single heartbeat, my terror and dread morph into white-hot rage.

"You *motherfucker!*" I shout, completely forgoing my detached mask and not caring that his men are witnessing my meltdown.

"Hello, princess."

Fueled by anger and the fear-induced adrenaline still pumping in my veins, I do something that would result in an immediate death sentence for anyone else.

I lunge at my husband and slap him across the face. The men—*Emeric's* men—standing around us all suck in a collective breath and then hold it as they wait to see how he will react, but I don't allow him time to do so. With my palm still stringing, I slam my hands into his hard chest and push him with every ounce of my strength.

"What the *hell* is wrong with you?" I seethe, shoving him again because to my annoyance, he barely moved an inch the first time. "Do you have any idea how fucking scared I was, you deranged psychopath?"

Just for good measure, I slap my palms against his black Henley-covered chest and push again. This time, though, he doesn't let me pull them away. In the blink of an eye, Emeric has my wrists captured in his hands and we're stumbling backward at a pace my shorter legs can't keep up with.

My spine slams into the paneling of the van with such force, the air is knocked out of my lungs. I've just barely managed to suck in a rush of oxygen when his hand slips around my throat in a domineering hold. He's done this before, but in the past, it's been in a sensual way. A way that made my toes curl and a thrill flash through me.

This time, he's not teasing or taunting me with the promise of pleasure, he wants to punish me.

"I know *exactly* how scared you were, Rionach." his words come out as a raspy growl that rattles his chest. He's pissed, I knew he would be, but there's something else—some other emotion mingled with his ire I've never heard come from him. "Because if you were *half* as scared as I was when I learned what you had done, then I know you felt like your heart was going to beat out of your goddamn chest as terror ripped you to fucking shreds."

Fear.

That's the other emotion in Emeric's dark, sinister voice.

Oh, God. What have I done?

TWENTY-SEVEN
EMERIC

THE FEEBLE HOLD I've had on my deteriorating control for the past few hours has finally snapped. I'm riding shotgun in my own body and mind. This is exactly what I feared would happen when I called Nova this morning. Rionach leaving the safety of our home thrust me violently over the edge I had been trying desperately to avoid.

Green eyes resembling precious gemstones widen and stare pleadingly up at me as my hand tightens around her throat. The relief of seeing her alive and unharmed with my own two eyes was fleeting. The toxic combination of fury and terror are now governing my actions and I am completely at their mercy as they burn through me.

Desperate for air, her free hand claws at my wrist, trying to break the unyielding hold I have on her airway. I don't flinch or so much as acknowledge the red scratches now decorating my skin. The pain doesn't register in my turbulent and frenzied nervous system either. I'm past the point of feeling physical pain.

My fingers dig into the soft skin of her neck, the arteries on either side pounding beneath my fingertips.

"That's it, my boy," a familiar, heavily accented voice praises from over my shoulder where I know cold, dark eyes are observing my every move. "Just as I taught you. Keep applying pressure just like that on the carotids and the bitch will be out like a light in no time."

My stomach rolls when his rancid breath, caused by the combination of his hand-rolled cigarettes and a steady diet of pickled foods, hits my nose. The scent plummets me further into the memories already crawling out from the depths of my mind.

He's not really here. Wake up, Emeric. Wake up!

I shake my head, trying in vain to regain a semblance of clarity, but it's no use. With each passing second, I'm pulled deeper and deeper into that dark place.

My wife's face grows redder, and her plump lips are parted but make no noise. So beautiful and to think I could have lost her because of her blatant stupidity. I thought she was smarter than her family. Her actions today have me thinking otherwise.

"I told you it wasn't safe," I snarl, bringing our faces together so we're at eye level. "And then you knowingly put yourself in danger by defying my clear instructions. Anyone could have taken you from me today. It was so fucking easy to have my men scoop you off the street. Like a darling lamb to slaughter."

My terrified wife tries to speak to me but can only manage to emit a strained gurgling sound as my hand continues to deprive her of oxygen. Already her eyes are starting to lose their focus.

"End her," he whispers, hot breath washing over my ear. "Finish this and you will be rewarded."

Rewarded. He means fed real food and not just the protein

bars he chucks into my room—cell—twice a day, a bath, and clean clothes. Basic necessities are now my rewards.

No! They *were* my rewards. I'm not there anymore and. He's. Not. Here.

His chuckle, a vile, humorless sound that has always made the hair on my body stand on end, washes over me. "Don't lie to yourself, baby Banes. I'm always here because I'm ingrained in you." A dry, callused hand gripping the back of my neck makes my anger rise further. I hated his hands on me. "She has to pay for what she did. Keep going."

"I don't understand how you can be so fucking reckless when you know what is out there waiting for you." While I'm struggling to decipher what is reality and what are memories conjured by my sleep-deprived brain, I know for a fact the fear that's been churning around in my gut like a snake since Anneli told me what happened is seeping into my tone. For all I know, it could be written across my face too. I usually have a better handle on keeping my emotions at bay, but that skill fails me when I'm in this state. "My goal was only to keep you safe, and you refused to listen. Does your life mean so little to you, Rionach?" I ask, knowing full well that she can't answer me in her current state. "Your life means too much to me for you to behave this way. You are too valuable to me for you to be so careless."

I warned her that she now has a target painted on her back. Making her my wife when I was fully aware she could be used as a token against me makes me a selfish bastard, but can't she see she now means everything to me? Rionach is the most valuable thing I've ever had the privilege of calling mine and she put that at risk today.

Everything around us moves like we're underwater. Movements are slow and floaty, and there's a halo-like light around the dark red strands flowing from her head. The drumming sound in my ears has reached a fever pitch as the life shining in her big jade eyes begins to dim.

"That's it," he encourages in my ear again. "Just a little bit more."

The hand that has been incessantly clawing at my wrist and forearm falls away and lands limply at her side, and her knees start to buckle under her weight. Her lips sluggishly mouth a singular word. I can't be sure, but I think it's my name.

"Look at her try to beg," Igor mocks with a dark chuckle. "Pathetic. Just like the others, and you thought she was strong."

She is strong, a voice in my disconnected and foggy brain argues. *She's brave and she's special. What are you doing to her, Emeric?*

The fight leaves Rionach and her limp body crashes into mine. I wrap my arms around her smaller frame, catching her before she can land in a heap on the ground. Her dead weight against my chest makes my heart seize—a sensation only she can make happen. Keeping her upright with one arm, I brush her messy hair from her forehead so I can look at her pale face. She's alive, but she's unconscious.

"The dumb whore deserved that for disrespecting your authority like she did," Igor clucks, the telltale sound of his lighter clicking open quickly following. The distinctive scent of burning tobacco and cloves fills my nostrils.

This wasn't supposed to be about my authority over her. It was about showing her how unsafe our world is, that going off on her own like she did put her in the direct path of our enemies.

"I didn't want to hurt her, I only wanted to teach her a lesson," I tell him while keeping my attention on her. Bruises will start to form around her throat soon. This isn't the first time I've left marks on her skin from my rough handling, but the previous ones were results of our intense fucking. Those were different and they weren't given with the intention of purposely hurting her. I can't say the same about the ones that will blossom on her neck soon.

"Lessons are best learned when pain is involved. I taught you that," the Russian man's voice floats through the air along with the smoke of his cigarette.

The type of pain Rionach enjoys is the same kind that I like. Pain mixed with pleasure. That had been my plan with bringing her out here, but I crossed a line. I allowed my anger and Igor's taunting to pull me into a place I didn't intend to go with her.

An emotion I can't recognize settles in my very soul like a boulder. and a bitter taste floods my mouth. Guilt. Is this guilt?

Too far. You went too far.

A hand slaps and shoves at my chest, and over the drumming in my ears, someone is calling to me. My arms try to curl tighter around Rionach's suddenly weightless form but when they do, I find that they're now holding nothing but air.

Where is she?

Startled, my eyes dance between my now empty arms and the space around me. The bright aura that had been around her head moments ago has grown and given everything a bright, disorienting glow. It takes me a minute to realize that the shining figure currently standing before me is my wife.

Slow blinking and deep, measured breaths have everything coming back into crystal-clear focus. As this happens, the clove-tinged smoke vanishes along with the looming presence that's been behind me, coaching me like he did when I was a teenager.

Rionach, pinned between my body and the van, is still a ball of ferocity and is wide awake.

"Emeric. That's enough, let me go."

I look between her angry face and her throat—a throat I'm

still indeed grasping, but my hold isn't meant to strangle, only to control. Her airway is unobstructed and the only reason her breathing is currently labored is from the array of emotions currently wreaking havoc on her.

Hallucinating. You hallucinated all of it.

Given the Russian guest that was along for the ride, it should be obvious that none of that actually happened, but when I get like this, it's difficult for my brain to untangle what is real and what's not. Just to be certain, I release my hold on her neck and search for evidence of strangulation. The perfect pale skin of her throat doesn't sport a single red mark.

Relief that I didn't nearly choke the life out of her crashes down on me at the same time I remember why we're at my property an hour outside the city to begin with. With my newfound—albeit shaky—clarity, I refocus my attention to the original plan I had in store for her.

"Emeric..." She searches my face with an inquisitive gaze. While I imagined my fingers compressing her arteries, what was I *actually* doing, and how long was I doing it? "What—"

"You put yourself in danger today," I say, cutting her question off.

That defiant aura of hers firmly settles around her. "You promised me it would only take two days to find me a bodyguard and from there I could come and go as I please. You didn't do that, and I do believe I warned you what would happen if you didn't uphold your end of the bargain, buddy."

She's right, she did. I was cocky and didn't believe she'd find a way around my security system. Color me surprised to learn my princess is quite the skilled pickpocket. I can't wait to ask her where she learned that skill and for what purpose. She doesn't exactly strike me as the type to walk around Grand Central Station stealing loose change and knockoff Rolexes from tourists.

"That was before our meeting with Niall," I snarl, dipping my head closer so she can see the full extent of my anger reflected in my eyes. "Niall, despite my warnings, has no intention of rolling over and showing me his submissive, fat belly. He's letting his emotions govern his actions, which means he's going to do something beyond idiotic in a misguided attempt to exact his revenge on me. I could have taken care of the problem right there in that shithole he calls a pub, but I didn't because the thought of you witnessing his organs splattering on the dirty carpet didn't sit well with me. I was protecting you then, just as I was when I kept you from leaving our home unattended, but you're too goddamn stubborn to see it."

Rionach crosses her arms in front of her chest. "So, your marvelous solution was to stage my kidnapping and make me think my father or, worse, the Koslovs came for me? This was you teaching me a lesson or something?"

She's trying to hide it, but I can see the lingering terror still residing in her body from being abducted. Even if she wasn't in any true danger with my men, up until the bag was lifted from her head, it was real to her. My wife gets off on fear, but this isn't the kind she finds enjoyable. For all she knew this was a genuine life-or-death situation. Which was the whole point of this charade.

I tap under her chin with two fingers. "That was precisely what that was. You needed to learn how fucking easy it would be for someone to take you from me." While this seems like a repetitive conversation for me due to my hallucination, I have a strong inclination it isn't for her. With the way none of my guards still loitering nearby are staring at me like I've grown a second head, I believe it's safe to assume I wasn't standing here having a conversation with myself while I imagined choking her. "Just like you're about to learn what happens to those who defy my orders."

Her perfectly shaped brows pull together. "What does that mean? You haven't already done enough?"

"Oh, sweet Rionach, we're just getting started." I take her arm in my hand and pull her with me into the thick trees that surround us. "You chose a very bad day to decide you want to be punished, my wife."

TWENTY-EIGHT
RIONACH

AFTER WALKING in tense silence through the woods for fifteen minutes, he takes my long wool coat from me and hangs it over a low-hanging tree branch nearby. The trees here are tall and the dense canopy above us blocks out much of the early afternoon sunlight. It was already struggling to break through the thick clouds in the sky to begin with, this combined with the foliage makes it seem darker and later in the day than it really is.

In my simple jeans and lightweight gray pullover, I give my husband a questioning look. "Okay, now what?"

As a precaution, I check the surroundings for anything that he might be planning to ambush me with. With Emeric, I think it's safe to always assume the unexpected from him. You never know what kind of crazy-ass shit he has up his sleeve. His behavior already seems off to me as it is. For a moment there while he held me against the door of the van, I swear he checked out for a minute. His gray eyes lost their focus, and they darted around like he was hearing something. This deviation in his demeanor didn't last a full minute before he snapped back into his ol' domineering self.

He comes to stand before me with a relaxed posture that is palpably artificial. The wild look in his gaze gives him away immediately.

Oh, so casually, he pushes up the sleeves of his waffle-knit Henley as his head cocks at me. "Now you run."

My eyebrows lift and my crossed arms drop listlessly to my sides. "Excuse me?"

That wicked smirk of his makes an appearance. "You're going to run and I'm going to chase you. If you find my cabin before I can get my hands on you, I will allow you to walk away without punishment. *But*, if I find you before you can reach your sanctuary, you will be completely at my mercy and you will accept everything I throw at you with a smile on your fucking face."

Instantly, a chill of awareness snakes down my spine.

My tongue swipes out to lick my suddenly dry bottom lip. "What exactly do you plan to do if you catch me?"

His eyes darken as his grin grows. "I plan on making you beg for mercy."

Haven't we already been over this?

"I won't beg."

Emeric chuckles. "You will when I use and stretch you, and then leave you feeling empty and needy for more." He takes a slow, easy step toward me. "I'm giving you a chance to evade your punishment if you can outrun me, but if you can't, I'm fucking you until you're so desperate to come, tears are running down your face, and your pussy is weeping for my cock."

Oh. Holy mother of God.

My knees feel weak already and he hasn't touched me yet.

"You're not fucking me. Not right now, not after you had

me abducted off the street and thrown into the back of a goddamn van with a bag over my head!"

"If you don't want to get fucked, you better run. Fast," he retorts sinisterly, completely unfazed by my refusal. "I own over one hundred and fifty acres of land, most of which is covered in trees just like this. It's going to take you a while to reach the cabin—if you can find it, that is—but I'm willing to give you a head start. What do you think, does a minute sound fair to you?"

"Emeric..." I say as he looks at the expensive silver watch around his wrist.

"If you don't want to end up on your hands and knees in the dirt with my cock buried so deep inside you that you can feel me in your chest, I recommend you start running, princess." Gray eyes flick to mine. "Your time starts now."

The adrenaline shooting through me is like a live wire. My skin hums and my heart thunders madly against my sternum.

"Emeric, you're not hearing me. You're not fuck—"

"You're wasting time," he tsks. "You have fifty seconds left."

"This is ridiculous," I continue to argue even though my feet are already moving me backward of their own accord and a thrill is shooting through me. "I told you no."

Yeah, but did you honestly mean it, Rio?

I've said it before, but Emeric taking control and with-holding my ability of choice from me does *something* to me. The very idea of him hunting me down and then taking what he wants from me has my body on the verge of convulsing and my insides turning into a puddle of horny goo. Not once in all my years of searching out things that scare me did a scenario like this ever cross my mind. Now, I know without a shadow of a doubt it's not only something I want but something I *need*.

I nearly trip over my feet at the sight of the menacing

expression darkening his face. For how many people was this the last face they saw before they died?

A shiver of fear joins the one of arousal already cascading down my body.

"And I told you that you weren't permitted to leave the house alone and you did it anyway. I suppose we're both ignoring each other's wishes today." His hand reaches into the back pocket of his dark jeans. The glint of metal catches in the minimal sunlight coming through the branches overhead. It's the same switchblade he used on me after our motorcycle ride. "I hope you're not attached to your clothes because when I find you—and I will *always* find you, Rionach—I'm cutting them off your body." The sound of the blade swishing open has me inadvertently flinching and backing up another foot. Knife twisting in his palm, he reclaims the space I'd just put between us by taking a foreboding step in my direction. "You have less than forty seconds now. I'd get moving if I were you."

The disconnect my brain has been having with my body finally catches up.

Twisting on the balls of my feet, I take off between the trees like a skittish deer. If I wasn't splitting my focus between searching for signs of the cabin and making sure my path is clear of any tripping hazards, I might find this animal analogy amusing. In our current predicament, it's more than fitting. Emeric is a predator, and I am his frightened prey.

I run as fast as my legs will take me. Even when I hear him start to charge through woods behind me, I don't stop, and I don't dare look behind me to see how close he is.

The entire time I dart between the good-sized tree trunks, I curse myself for not paying better attention to my surroundings when I first got here and when Emeric was leading me deeper and deeper into the woods.

On gut feeling alone, I keep heading straight on my chosen path, hoping and praying that I'll get lucky.

A twig snapping not too far behind me has my heart skipping a beat and my stomach clenching to the point of pain. Knowing I won't have a chance at evading him as long as I'm in his direct line of sight, I push my legs to go faster before ducking behind the thick trunk of a cottonwood tree.

Spine pressed to the rough bark, my chest heaves for my next breath. Not wanting to give away my position by letting him hear my unpleasant and slightly embarrassing wheezing, I force my chest to inhale and exhale painfully slow lungfuls of oxygen.

His steady footfalls crunching in the dirt slow down as he draws closer to the area I'm hiding in.

As gently as I can, I take measured steps to slowly ease to the other side of the tree so I can avoid detection if he stalks by. The quiet—but noticeable—snap of a small stick below my right sneaker has every nerve ending in my body lurching. I turn into a piece of stone as I wait to see if he heard it too.

My gaze anxiously darts between my left and right to make sure he's not creeping around to apprehend me.

I hold my breath and listen to my surroundings. Rustling movement a little ways away from the tree I'm using as cover tells me I have a couple seconds before he's close enough to successfully sneak up on me. This allows me to relax just enough that I'm once again able to form coherent thoughts and create a plan for my next course of action.

There's still no sign of this cabin. As far as I can see in any direction there are only trees and the occasional shrub. Emeric said he owns over a hundred acres of land. For all I know, he's dumped me in the farthest corner of the property from the cabin. He doesn't play games he can't win, and what better way to get what he wants than to set me up for failure?

You've been standing here for too long. Move!

On a steadying exhale, I dart out from behind the safety of the large tree and head in the direction that is more eastbound than my original trajectory. My plan is to run this way for a while and once I've put some space between us, I'll swing back and continue down the first path I was on. One of these directions has to be right—

He moves like a dark blur—a phantom—between the trees and by the time I realize he's found me, his strong arms are wrapping around my middle. His hold is steadfast and it almost hurts with the way he compresses my ribs. Half a second later, my world is spinning rabidly. We're going down. Emeric takes the brunt of the fall as we land on the dirt and leaf-covered forest floor.

Before my brain has a chance to catch up with the change in our position, Emeric is rolling us again. This time he ends up above me, straddling the backs of my thighs. Instinctually, I immediately try to get up but his hand shoving into the middle of my back locks my torso in place.

I thrash and kick my legs beneath him like I'm a bull and he's the idiot in the cowboy hat and matching chaps I want to buck the fuck off me.

"*Argh!*" I scream in frustration. "Get off of me!"

"No. I quite like the view from up here."

I twist and turn my body, trying my best to dislodge him.

The cold edge of a blade pressing into the vertebra of my exposed spine because of my askew pullover has the fight going silent inside me. One by one, he drags the sharp tip over each bone of my spine and as he does, he pushes my top farther up my back. He pauses when he reaches the band of my bra. It's a simple cream silk today, and just like the last time we played with a knife, he cuts the smooth fabric from my body without pause.

The switchblade slashes through the cotton of my gray pullover next. From the back of my neck to the hem of the shirt, he slices it all the way open. The cool early Spring air bites into my exposed and heated skin as he starts to press open-mouthed kisses down my back.

I'm angry he caught me so fast, but I'm more frustrated by how my body reacts to him—how easily it yields. He incites a desperate kind of need in me, even when I don't want him to. Logically, I know I should hate being stuck beneath him, but there's just something about him taking my choice away that has my blood running molten.

Refusing to give in to him or my unexplainable reaction to being captured, I fight against his hold with a newfound vigor when I hear the knife thudding to the ground next to us. It takes everything in me to do it, but I manage to roll over and topple him off my thighs. With an almost animalistic snarl, I slash my hand out at his face and feel an odd—but not entirely unwelcome—sense of triumph when my nails rake across his upper cheekbone. I don't wait around long enough to see how deep the wound is before I kick my legs and shove my body the rest of the way out from under his weight. I manage to pull myself upright and onto my knees, a shift in position that has the shreds of my bra and top falling completely off my shoulders.

I've just managed to get a foot underneath me to stand when his hand wraps around my ankle and yanks. I tumble forward and my chest and elbows hit the cold, hard earth with an *oof*.

"I love your fight, princess," he purrs as he knots his fingers through the loose strands at the back of my head. Pulling my hair tight, he presses the side of my face into the dirt and leaves beneath me as he straddles my hips. As he does this, he grinds his rock-hard arousal into the roundness of my ass. It's a move that has both of us choking on groans and my thighs pressing together like my life depends on it. "But I think I love it more when you submit to me."

His mouth closes over my shoulder in a hot kiss. I relax into the contact for all of two seconds before his teeth sink into the skin there. He doesn't bite me hard enough to actually break the skin, but it's enough that I know I'm going to have a mark there tomorrow. And maybe the next day, too.

The idea of wearing his claiming mark has me trying and failing to bite back a soft moan.

In quick succession, he removes his weight from my body and pulls me up onto my hands and knees. The rocks and debris in the damp dirt below me dig into my palms. The dull pain nearly vanishes completely when his fingers wrap around the waistband of my jeans and he wrenches them—along with my thong—down my ass and thighs. In this position, this is the farthest he can get them down my legs, but this doesn't seem to be a problem for him because the part of me he wants to play with is fully bared to him.

There's no teasing or slow buildup.

His thick, long fingers push inside of me, and he lets out a growl of approval when he discovers I'm already wet for him. Emeric should know by now it doesn't take much for him to turn me on. He's seemingly unlocked something inside of me and by doing so, he's set free that hidden piece I've kept tucked away from others. Not only has he found a way to access the secret side of my soul, but he also gets along with it oh-so very well. I can't help but aimlessly wonder if that piece of me was simply waiting to come out until I met Emeric. That it was made for him.

This fast and fleeting thought disappears just as quickly as it entered my head when his fingers, coated in my arousal, graze over my swollen clit.

I didn't fully realize how far gone I already was until the walls of my pussy begin to flutter and my inner muscles tighten as an impending orgasm threatens to erupt. He keeps working me, alternating between sliding his thick digits into me and then around my sensitive bundle of nerves until my very being is quivering.

"Oh, fuck!" I cry out, not bothering to try and stay quiet out here in the woods. "I'm so close... I'm going to come."

My breath quickens into uneven pants and my entire body tremors as it prepares to topple over that heavenly edge. It would seem Emeric has other plans because when I'm one mere caress away from exploding around his digits, he pulls them out of my greedy core and withholds his touch completely.

"Good girls are rewarded with orgasms," he explains, sounding way too pleased with himself for my liking. "Bad girls are deprived of what they need, and you, my dear wife, have been a *very* bad girl."

His palm comes down on my right ass cheek in a blow that has my back bowing and my breath catching in my throat. It hurts, and yet, a choked moan escapes me and the walls of my pussy clench.

"Maybe this will have you thinking twice about putting yourself in danger in the future." He spanks the left side of my ass with the same kind of ferocity as before. The strangled cry that claws out of my throat is interrupted with a mewling sound when his attention returns to my humming center. My face burns when I can hear just how wet I am for him as he slips his fingers back inside. "Your cunt is ravenous for my touch, isn't it, Rionach?"

"Y... yes," I sob. His thumb pressing down on my overly sensitive clit has what feels like electricity shooting through every nerve of my body. "*Please.*"

"Please, what?" he taunts, his skilled fingers not letting up.

"Please, let me come."

"Look at you, asking so nicely." His admiration is nothing but another taunt, but my body doesn't seem to care. It likes being praised by him. Emeric continues to tease me and as he does, that ball of tension returns in my lower stomach. It pulses and grows with every stroke of his fingers. I'm once again teetering on the cusp of ecstasy when his dark chuckle washes over me and joins the shivers already dancing across my skin. "But no, I don't think I will. Not until I can be sure you've learned your lesson."

He leisurely pumps two fingers into my soaked channel twice more before removing his hand again.

"*No!*" My hands claw frantically into the ground and tears of desperation leak from my tightly closed eyes. "Emeric, *please*. I've learned my lesson. I learned it when I thought I'd been fucking kidnapped."

The sound of his jean's zipper lowering tickles my eardrums.

"You haven't learned shit until I'm sure you've experienced the same level of desperation as I did when I didn't know where you were this morning."

Another pang of guilt that I'd forced those kinds of emotions onto him by leaving tugs at my chest.

"I wasn't running away from you this morning. I wasn't leaving you." I don't know why I have the sudden urge to make sure he knows this, but something in my chest tells me it's important he hears it. It's the stone-cold truth, after all. Since we've been married, not once has the thought of leaving him crossed my mind. It probably should have. For a normal person, I'm sure they would have been forming an escape plan since the moment they were forced into saying *"I do"*, but I haven't because I don't hate being Emeric Banes's wife.

My very soul shudders and shakes when the long, thick length of Emeric's cock slips through the wetness between my thighs. I'm incapable of making a single noise. My mouth just parts in a silent gasp, and I just about come out of my very skin when the head knocks against my aching clit. I know he knows what he's doing to me when he does it again. Twice.

"It doesn't matter if that had been your plan because I'm not fucking letting you go, Rionach. *Ever*. You can run and I will chase after you. You can try to escape to the ends of the earth, and I will follow you there. I will follow you anywhere. Do you know why?" He doesn't bother waiting to hear my answer. "Because. You. Are. *Mine*."

I've never been claimed by someone as much as I have been by Emeric, and I don't just mean in a sexual way. He tells me every chance he gets that I belong to him. It makes me feel wanted in a way I've never felt before. Since my birth, my parents had been searching for who they would pass me off to when the time came.

They never wanted *me*. They wanted what they could get *for* me. I wasn't a child nurtured with love. I wasn't cherished. I was simply a bargaining chip in a game I didn't want to play.

Emeric doesn't just desire me, he wants me. Just... *me*.

The fear in his voice and expression today solidified that for me, and something about this knowledge has my emotionally neglected inner child settling. The little girl who just wanted to be wanted is finding peace because of Emeric Banes.

"I know," I whisper breathlessly to him.

"Do you?" He punctuates his question with another slicing thrust through my pussy lips.

"Yes."

His hands take hold of my hips. "Say it. Tell me so I know you understand who you are."

I turn my head, making my long, debris-covered hair fall

over one bare shoulder. I need to look him in the eyes as I tell him, "I am yours."

Those storm-filled eyes of his have bolts of lightning flashing in them when he nods his head once in approval and growls, "Yes, *only* mine."

Without warning or preamble, he drives into me in one long, punishing thrust. He doesn't give me time to recover or to adjust to his intrusion either, he slices into me again and again with rapid, breath-stealing movements. All I can do is lock my muscles in place and dig my fingers into the damp dirt below me in a desperate attempt to hold on.

The orgasm that has been threatening to go off since he first touched me minutes ago awakens in the depths of my lower stomach. It builds and grows at a speed I can't keep up with. Waves of heat that originate from between my thighs race through my body like licks of flames. The inferno continues to expand and I'm nearing the point of no return when Emeric's hand slaps my already tender ass cheek again and he pulls out, leaving only the thick crown of his cock inside.

"No." His order comes out sounding more animalistic than human. "This isn't about you. I already told you bad girls don't get rewarded for their disobedience."

"I'm sorry." I don't bother hiding the despair in my tone. It's not a secret anyway. This is the third time he's brought me to the brink and then denied me. He's fully aware I'm hanging on by a fucking thread. "I was being careless when I left without you. It was dangerous. I know that now and I won't do it again."

He thrusts shallowly, taunting me with his gentle strokes. "I know you won't, because you're going to remember this punishment, and what it feels like to be left painfully wanting."

Emeric's hand wraps around my throat. He pulls me up until my bare back presses against the cotton shirt still covering his chest. This position has him sinking deeper into me and my head lolling back against his shoulder. His hips start to flex upward, creating slow but achingly deep thrusts.

The hold he has on my neck may remain loose, but there's still no doubt who's in control here. Where he could easily increase pressure and threaten my air supply like he's done in the past, he doesn't. The pad of his thumb swipes across my pulse point in a way I find endearing.

"Emeric," I whimper, the frantic tears from before reemerging and falling down my face in warm drops when I squeeze my eyes closed. "*Please.* I'm so close."

He ignores my plea and continues to pound into me. This new angle has the head of his cock scraping against the sensitive front wall of my pussy, which has stars starting to form in my vision.

"Refrain," he grumbles in my ear before his teeth close over the silver hoops decorating my earlobe. "If you allow yourself to come now, I'll be forced to do this over and punish you again. You don't want that, now do you?"

Oh, God no. I can't do this again.

My cry of anguish rings through the trees. To my own ears, it sounds like a pathetic wail. I told him I wouldn't beg, and I've been doing just that, but it didn't work. He's not interested in relenting this time. No, he wants me to suffer.

It takes every ounce of concentration and all the shaky willpower I have left to not cross that line. It would be so easy to allow myself to fall into the white-hot pleasure beckoning me, but I fight against its invitation because I don't think I would make it if he made us start this over. As it is, I'm already a painfully exposed nerve.

I'm full-on sobbing by the time Emeric's fluid thrusts become uneven and erratic. The hand resting on my hip digs into the flesh there and the hand at my throat shifts upward to grasp my jaw. He turns my head, and his mouth closes over mine in a messy and nearly violent kiss. I'm fairly certain the groan of pleasure that rumbles up from his chest could sustain me for life. Like a woman starved, I swallow the sound and match it with one of my own when his hot cum fills me.

Our ragged breathing is in sync as he presses his forehead to mine. My heated face is wet from tears, and I'm caked in dirt and mud, but the look of approval in those gray eyes makes me feel beautiful. More importantly, they make me feel wanted. And that's all I've ever needed.

.

When Emeric said he had a "cabin", what he really meant was he has a completely renovated and modernized A-frame house that, just like his home in the city, belongs on the cover of an interior design magazine. While I was expecting a log cabin decked out in flannel and a genuine wood-burning fireplace, what I found is an architectural designer's wet dream with its black siding and floor-to-ceiling windows. The interior is decorated similarly to his penthouse with its dark and moody color palette, but this "cabin" is cozier.

I could imagine coming up here in the winter and watching the snow blanket the plethora of surrounding trees while cuddling up on the couch. It'd be like a Hallmark movie scene, but without the slightly religious undertones and with a lot more kinky sex.

Already showered and dressed in clean clothes that consists of only a white button-down shirt I found in the primary bedroom's closet, I stand at the large window overlooking the forest I'd run through an hour ago. In case you were wondering, it turns out I hadn't been headed in remotely the right direction when I was searching for the cabin. Quite the opposite, actually. Emeric had smirked at me when I realized my mistake as he carried me here. The cocky fucker.

With the sun starting to drop below the tree line, I thank my lucky stars that Emeric hadn't forced me to run from him in the dark. Then I really would have been fucked.

I see him coming up behind me in the glass reflection before his large hand grasps my shoulder and turns me around.

His dark hair is mussed and still slightly damp from the shower we'd shared. I'd almost wept with joy when he'd dropped to his knees on the tile and buried his tongue in my pussy. The relief alone of finally being able to come nearly had me collapsing. If he hadn't kept a steadying arm around me, I'm positive I would have ended up on the shower floor next to him.

He's dressed in a black hoodie and joggers, both things I'd yet to see him wear before. Today was also the first time I saw him in jeans, which I also quite enjoyed. With his disheveled hair and casual outfit choice, he doesn't look like the kind of man who enjoys making his enemies beg for mercy before he forces them to choke on their own blood. I can't help but wonder how many people have been granted the opportunity to see this more relaxed side of him. I feel special and slightly territorial that I've been gifted access to this side of the illustrious man in front of me.

He passes me the cup of coffee he holds. "Almond milk with vanilla syrup and a dash of cinnamon."

Eyebrows raised, I accept the glass mug from him.

"What?" he asks, shoving his hands into the front pocket of his sweatshirt. "Didn't think I paid attention?"

"To the big things? Without a doubt, but to the small things like my coffee order? No, not really," I tell him honestly.

After taking a sip of the steamy-hot, sweet drink, I move to sit on the king-sized bed that's the focal point of the room.

Between the way it's positioned and the wall of windows, you'd feel like you're going to bed in the trees every night. I don't know what his plans are for the rest of our evening or if he needs to get back to the city for work, but I'm silently crossing my fingers that we'll be able to spend the night here. I want to wake up surrounded by the trees. It's also nice to be away from the bustle of the city for a minute. Don't get me wrong, I thrive in the chaos and noise, but there's something about stepping away that resets the soul.

Emeric nudges me forward so he can sit behind me with his back against the headboard. His arm snakes around my middle, holding me against him as his thumb instantly begins to caress back and forth across my ribs.

"You should know by now I know everything about you, Rionach Banes," he murmurs into my now clean hair before pressing his lips to the side of my head. The simple act of affection has my heart fluttering in my chest. He catches me off guard when his chest rumbles with a low chuckle. "Though, I will admit I didn't know you were quite the pickpocket. That was a surprise."

"Your secret is safe with me. I won't tell anyone I was able to surprise the all-powerful Mr. Banes." The grin I'm hiding with the brim of my cup falters when the guilt from earlier has my abdomen clenching. The fear that was tangled in his furious voice replays in my head. "I know I already said it, but I want you to know I truly am sorry for today."

Emeric stiffens around me. "It was beyond careless of you to leave. Putting yourself in danger like you did..." he trails off. "You're smarter than that, princess."

"You're right, I am," I agree easily. "But—and that's a big *but*—that doesn't change the fact that you cannot keep me locked up like you are. You promised me you wouldn't put me in a cage, and for the past almost two weeks that's exactly what you've done. I'm your wife now, not your prisoner, Emeric."

He tightens his hold around my middle. "Yes, you're my wife and that means your safety is now my responsibility. It's a responsibility I take very fucking seriously, too. I'm not willing to put your life in the hands of someone I can't fully trust to keep you safe. As it stands, the only person I trust with such an important task is myself." His free hand brushes the hair off my temple so he can tuck it behind my ear. Chills scatter across my shoulders and down my spine from the gentle touch. "You can be as pissed at me as you'd like, Rionach, but I won't apologize for putting your well-being before a promise I made."

Emotions swirl in my gut at hearing him say this. When have I *ever* been a priority in anyone's life? "My family wanted very little to do with me when I shared their last name, I just don't understand why you think they'd care about me now."

"That's simple," he says, fingers tracing over the side of my neck. "They care because they know I care about you. I could lie and say I usually have a better hold on my temper, but I showed my hand to Niall when I blew apart his hand for disrespecting you." He pauses for a beat. I can hear the smirk in his voice when he adds, "Seeing as I had him shot in the hand and not between his goddamn eyes, I suppose I was exhibiting some level of restraint that night."

I scoff and roll my eyes at this. "Would you like a gold star for not putting a bullet in my father's head?"

"I'm not very motivated by stickers, no matter what whimsical shape they might come in. I will, however, gladly take a blow job as my reward."

I nearly choke on a mouthful of coffee. Once I manage to swallow—pun not intended—I can't help but laugh at his absurdity. "If I blew you every time you refrained from putting a bullet in someone who simply annoyed you, I'd never get off my knees, Banes."

"As fun as that sounds, I'm afraid you might be underestimating how many people I shoot in a week, dear wife."

Other people might find this news a tad bit alarming, but all it does is make me laugh harder. Ophelia's horrified face when I'd laughed earlier crosses my mind. That's twice in one day I've laughed at something others would balk at, and I can't say I give a shit. It's nice to emote the feelings and thoughts I usually keep safely tucked away from others. Expressing myself without fear of judgment is freeing.

Emeric cups my cheek and turns my head so we can look into each other's eyes. The amusement flickering in his is nearly drowned out by the exhaustion staring back at me. I didn't notice it earlier, but the dark circles under his turbulent eyes are prominent. The last time he was in bed with me was... days ago.

"You really don't fear me, do you, princess?" There's a distinctive air of surprise in his tone as he asks this.

My head shakes once. "I don't fear you in the same way others do because I know you're not going to hurt me. When people see you, they think they're looking death in the eye. I look at you and know I'm staring at a wild and dangerous thing, but we both know I run toward those things, not away." I skim the pad of my thumb across his lower lip. "I think I'm addicted to the kind of fear you give me. You're my favorite adrenaline rush."

I've seen it on his face before but right now, it's more evident than ever. Emeric regards me like I'm the greatest prize —no, not prize, a *gift*—he's ever possessed. This simple expression on his face has my heart plummeting into a dangerous territory, a territory where it might end up getting shattered into pieces if this all goes south.

He doesn't say anything back, but he doesn't have to. I smile against his mouth when he presses his lips to mine in a fleeting but still toe-curling kiss.

I'm still grinning like an idiot when I pull back and look around the room again. It is pretty here, and the view out the window is serene. It's a bit stereotypical, but when you grow up in a concrete city, you tend to appreciate the simplicity of nature more.

"Why do you own this cabin and all this land?" I want it noted, I still don't think "cabin" is the appropriate term for this place.

He relaxes further into the pillows against the headboard with a content-sounding sigh. "Do you want the partial truth or the whole truth?"

That's stupid question. "If you're going to tell me that this is your secret love nest and you've fucked women on every surface in this joint, you can go ahead and keep that to your-fucking-self."

His genuine, unhindered chuckle has my lips twitching with my own smile. "No. Just like our home in the city, I've never brought a woman back here." *Our home.* That's not the first time he's referred to it as such, but it still has my heart panging. "I own a sex club. There was never a reason to bring them home."

And it better stay that way...

"Okay, so then what's the real reason you own this place?" Coffee now gone, I lean over and place the mug on the dark wood nightstand.

Emeric takes my free hands and entangles our fingers together in my lap. My attention is glued on the way he runs his fingers over my knuckles in gentle unhurried strokes. After the way he chased me and then pinned me in the woods earlier, you wouldn't expect such gentleness from the same man. I appreciate both sides of him equally, but I like it even more that the softer side is reserved exclusively for me.

"I bought it for two reasons, but both have to do with privacy. There's a concrete room in the basement of Tartarus I have people delivered to when they've wronged me or they have information I need. That's where the Italian who shot me on New Year's was brought. It's soundproofed and secure but occasionally I appreciate having the option to prolong my torment. Having space to get creative with my... punishments is something an isolated property like this allows for." I asked for the full truth and he's not holding back. He told me before he will always give me the truth if he can, and it seems he's holding true to this promise. I mentally tuck away the knowledge he has a torture room in the same basement he operates a sex club in. That just seems very on brand for him, and I can't say I'm totally shocked to hear it. "The second reason is, I wanted a place away from the city that was kept off the books. No one other than my most trusted men know of its existence. I like that for a couple reasons: it guarantees my privacy, but it also means if shit goes tits up and I need to get somewhere safe, I can come here."

"So, it's like your safe house?"

"*Our* safehouse," he corrects me immediately. "I'll give you directions on how to get here when we get home. Keep them somewhere safe and don't share them with anyone. If something happens and I can't get to you, this is where you'll come."

"Emeric..." I interject, not enjoying the sudden spike of anxiety coursing through my veins.

"I'm serious, Rionach." His sharp tone has me flinching. "We have to think like this. As long as I hold power, people will try to come for me and what's mine. Half-wit people just like

Niall. I already told you he isn't going to let this go—that was the risk of allowing him to live. If he hasn't already, it's only a matter of time before he crawls back to the Russians for help. Igor and Bogdan will agree to reenter the alliance because in their eyes, I've humiliated them by stealing you out from under them. I'm very familiar with how they operate and think, which is another reason why I haven't allowed you to leave the penthouse without me."

My father's cutting remark about Emeric's history with Igor crawls back to the forefront of my mind, along with the beautiful tattoo he has across his shoulder blades.

Squeezing his fingers tighter between mine, I nervously release a long steadying breath before asking, "Will you tell me about your history with Igor?" My body turns into a piece of stone as I wait for him to lash out at me for asking such a personal question. My brother and father didn't appreciate it when I asked them anything, so I'm mentally preparing myself for Emeric to react similarly. "I think I might understand better why you're so adamant about keeping me at home if I knew more about it."

With the small amount of information I already have, I know the father-son duo is deranged in ways Emeric isn't. Emeric isn't a moral man by any means, but he doesn't slaughter innocent women for sport.

Emeric's body mirrors mine by going painfully rigid.

"You don't have to tell me," I rush out before he can so much as inhale his next lungful of air. "I shouldn't have said anything, I don't have the right to pry about your secrets."

The minute that passes in tense silence is one of the longest of my entire life. My mind races with a million thoughts and my heart pounds wildly against my sternum. With each pump of blood, more and more regret and anxiety filter into my system. When he remains quiet, I wish I could rewind and stop myself from opening my big dumb mouth.

"You're my wife, Rionach. You and you alone have the right to ask me anything," he finally says. His words are quiet, but steady and they instantly put me at ease. "My father, Ambrose, wasn't a good man. I know that's rich coming from me, but it's the truth. He never should have had a child, let alone three of them, and he shouldn't have taken a wife, especially one as softhearted as my mother, Daria. I can't remember a time when he didn't lift a hand to us. One of my first memories is his fist cracking a rib when I accidently spilled my orange juice during a Sunday family brunch. Anything set him off and if we cried, our tears only made him hit us harder. When he wasn't slapping us around over small things like spilled juice, he was inflicting the unimaginable on my mom. For eleven years, I watched him leach the life out of her and rob her of her will to live. She was too gentle and kind for our world. They tried to tell us she threw herself down the stairs and broke her neck, but my brothers and I knew the truth. When Ambrose got drunk enough, he would all but admit to the role he played in her death. He'd sound proud of himself for finally freeing himself of his weak wife."

The coffee I'd just ingested curdles in my stomach and my throat tightens. A wave of nausea washes over me as the visual of Emeric as an innocent child being beaten by his own father forms in my mind. And his mother... she didn't deserve that fate. Emeric didn't deserve to lose his one loving parent in such a horrific way, and by his own father's hands, no less.

I don't know what to say, so I simply bring our joined hands up to my face and press a kiss to his knuckles.

"I stopped fearing him and his wrath after that. At the ripe age of eleven I was just... numb. I'd laugh when he hit me, which would thoroughly piss him off, and the angrier he got, the harder I laughed. My brothers Astor and Ledger begged me to stop goading him, but I didn't care. They hated seeing the bruises all over my body from his fists and whatever else he deemed suitable as a weapon. I. Just. Didn't. *Care*. For six months straight, I think I had matching black eyes. We were homeschooled by tutors during this time, so there weren't any adults who could raise concern on my behalf. Not that they could do anything. The Banes name wasn't as prominent then as it is now, but it still carried a lot of weight. People weren't going to go against Ambrose Banes. I was apathetic toward his abuse and everything else until the night of my initiation."

"Initiation?" I repeat, my voice barely a whisper.

"It's a tradition of sorts in our family that my great-great-grandfather started. When the Banes boys turn twelve, they're officially brought into the family business after they prove they are worthy of carrying the name. A random person is selected and we—the kids—are instructed to shoot them in the head. They could be a homeless person they found under a bridge somewhere or it could be a nurse walking home after a sixteen-hour shift at the hospital. It didn't matter to them. They weren't picky."

I can't hold back the gasp of horror that creeps out from between my lips.

His heart is beating so viciously inside his chest cavity, I can feel it through the two layers of clothes between us. I can't be sure at this moment if I do it for him or me, but I clumsily twist around in his lap. His muscles lock when my legs and arms wrap around him like a vise. For a moment, I think he's going to push me away, but to my delight, his arms encircle me in a fierce hold that rivals mine.

"I was yanked out of bed and dragged to the basement of my father's estate one night. I still remember the tops of my feet scraping against the concrete of the basement staircase as two men carried me down. They brought me to the back room we were never allowed to go into. My father was waiting there with a hooded figure curled up into a ball in the corner of the room. The gleeful smile across my father's face as he handed me the gun is something I'll never regret."

My own father has his faults, but Ambrose's treatment of his children and wife makes Niall look like a pretty good guy.

Then again, he did sell me to a serial killer, so perhaps they both just fucking suck?

"My brothers told me about their initiations. Their victims had gags in their mouths the entire time. They never got the chance to speak—to beg for their lives. My father removed the woman's gag after he took off her blindfold. I didn't understand why he'd do such a thing until she started begging." Emeric's entire body shudders against mine, and all I can do is hold him tighter. "She was a mother. She pleaded with me to let her go so she could return home to her young children. Ambrose didn't select a person at random. He selected a mother because he knew how it would affect me."

Emeric's words from The Irish Wife replay in my head. *Watching my father choke on his own blood and finally die will go down as one of the best moments of my life.* I find a small sliver of peace knowing that Emeric already eliminated his father, and I can only hope that Emeric did too when he plunged the knife in.

"My hand holding the gun shook violently as my father yelled at me to pull the trigger and the woman begged to go home to her babies. At one point, he got sick of watching me hesitate and backhanded me across the face. Once I managed to get back to my feet, I turned the gun on him. He laughed and laughed at this. He stopped when the bullet ripped through his shoulder, though. I took my worst beating that night and the mother still ended up with a bullet in her brain. To this day I don't know her name."

The tone of his voice has turned emotionless. Revisiting these memories is painful and disconnecting is how he's protecting himself.

"Bloodied and broken, he threw me in the trunk of his car and took me to his friend's house. He told me if anyone could teach me to behave correctly, it would be Igor. He said, 'Igor will show you the way'. I was kept in a crypt below Igor's family cemetery on his property in New Jersey. If I wanted to eat, I needed to earn it. If I wanted clean clothes, I needed to earn it. If I wanted to use a real toilet instead of the bucket in the corner of my stone cell, I needed to earn it. The only way I earned any of those things is by executing the teaching he beat into me. I rebelled and refused him, but that only lasted a week. A hot iron poker with his family's insignia pressed to my shoulder had me falling in line without any more fight. Igor taught me how best to inflict pain on a person with a blade. He showed me the fastest and the most efficient way to strangle a person." His voice catches in his throat when he says this. "I learned how much blood they could lose and how much of one's body could be dissected before they finally died. I discovered the most painful and effective ways to get information out of people. For three years, I was nothing but Igor's weapon. I cut and sliced where and when he told me to, and I never hesitated again after the weeping mother in the basement. Igor helped me become the killer I am today, but I took his teachings and evolved into something more."

If people knew this story, I know without a shadow of a doubt they would look at my husband differently. In a good or bad way, I'm not sure. On one hand, he was an innocent child forced to do horrific things. This could make them feel sympathy for the boy he once was like I do now. On the other hand, he was only a child when he first learned and began to excel at the carnage he's known for today. This could incite even more fear and further darken the lore that accompanies Emeric.

"I don't think Igor or Ambrose expected I'd put my new skills to use so soon after I finally returned home. The shock on my father's face as my blade sliced him open from his navel to his throat was proof of how much he underestimated me. I'd played the part of the dutiful soldier for three years perfectly, never once giving them a reason to doubt my loyalty. With my brothers' help and support, I showed my father what he'd actually created. In those final moments as he choked on his blood, I saw in his eyes that he knew what a grave mistake he'd made."

I pull back so I can see his face. In the span of him telling his story, the circles under his eyes have darkened and the color in his usually golden-tan face has turned ashen. The same unfocused, wild look that was in his eyes earlier today when he had me pinned against the van has also returned. Clasping his face between my palms, I gently stroke my thumbs back and forth under his fatigued eyes. In slow, rhythmic order, I press kisses to his forehead, nose, both cheekbones, and then finally his mouth as I do.

It takes a couple minutes of this for the haze to lift from his face and for him to return to the present with me. I wait until I know he's fully back before whispering, "I hope his death was slow and agonizing."

I want to know why he hasn't taken out Igor yet, but refrain.

He blinks, but the bleary look in his gaze remains. "It was."

"Good," I tell him, pressing my forehead to his briefly before pulling back so I can continue to examine his face. "Are you with me, Emeric?"

I'm expecting another one of his usual self-assured

responses, so when a choked-sounding, "No," comes from his lips, I nearly flinch.

"What's wrong?" feels like an extraordinarily stupid question to ask given the traumatic history he just divulged to me, but I don't know how else to find out what's going on in that head of his.

His wild eyes drift to stare over my shoulder. "Koslov is standing behind you right now and he's telling me to strangle you. Just like he did when you first got here."

I nearly topple off his lap and the bed because of the breakneck speed in which I turn around to search the room for signs of a sadistic Russian. To my relief, but also horror, the only people in the room are the two of us. "Emeric..."

"He's not actually here, I know this," he explains, his voice sounding distant. "But this is what happens when I haven't gotten enough sleep. My brain conjures him up to torment me more."

Eyes wide and pulse racing, I scan his face and once again linger on the agonizingly dark circles residing there. "When *was* the last time you slept?"

He pulls his focus away from the hallucination that is apparently occurring behind my back. "With you, the other night."

"Emeric! That was days ago." My brain races as I try to figure out what I can do to help him. He seemed okay until he deep dived into his past and between unearthing those bad memories and the lack of sleep, he's spiraling right before my eyes.

He nods once. "I struggle with sleep. Have since I was sent to Igor. It turned into severe insomnia about a decade ago. I can usually manage it, but I think dealing with Koslov again has aggravated it."

My heart is breaking for the boy who was sent to that

monster and it's breaking for the man who is still sporting the physical and mental scars over twenty years later.

"Okay. It's okay," I say more for myself than anything. "Emeric, you have to tell me what to do to help you. Do I need to call Nova?" I have no clue where my cell phone is, but I'm sure Emeric's is around here somewhere. "What will help you fall asleep? You fell asleep the other night, what helped you then?"

"You."

"Me?" I repeat like a confused and panicked parrot. "I don't understand." But I'm willing to help him in any way I can to make the apparition of his tormenter vanish.

"I don't either," he admits. "All I know is, when I'm inside you, not only do I fall asleep, which is a feat all on its own, but I *stay* asleep. The longest I've slept in years was our wedding night. That's when it first happened."

It takes me a moment to fully register what he's saying.

"Oh..." I murmur. Flashbacks of him coming to bed late the other night and getting me off before slipping inside me play in my head. I also remember how comforting it'd felt to have him so intimately close to me as we fell asleep.

"I know how it sounds—"

I cut him off with a quick wave of my hand. "It sounds like you've found a way to ward off the ghosts that haunt you, Emeric." Another woman might not understand him and think this is some perverted ploy, but I know it isn't anything like that. Emeric doesn't need ploys to get between my legs. I let him enter there freely and as often as he likes. Tricks aren't required. "You could have told me sooner."

He barks out an unamused chuckle. "Didn't exactly know how to tell my new wife that I get insomnia-induced hallucinations if I go too long between REM cycles, but I discovered falling asleep with my cock buried in her warm cunt seems to be my own personal sedative. I'm my very own mouthwatering brand of crazy, I'm well aware of this, but that makes me sound certifiable, princess."

"I've stolen hundreds of thousands of dollars' worth of jewelry from New York's high society because I like the rush of slipping diamonds and other precious gemstones off the bodies of the people who've always refused to acknowledge my existence. I don't even keep the money, I donate it," I explain in a rush. He's told me his secrets. I think it's fair that I divulge a few myself. "I once stood so close to the edge of a subway platform that a patrol cop tackled me to the ground because she thought I was trying to kill myself. I had to escape and run from her so my parents wouldn't be notified. That's when I found out running from the police is way more fun than it should be. You know and accept that I crave things that scare me, and that's why you tie me to beds and have me run from you. You give me that, so I can give you this. Isn't that what marriage is about?"

He stares at me for a long moment. "I had you run from me as punishment."

"No," I shake my head. "Withholding orgasms was my punishment. You knew I'd get off on being chased and pinned down." I untangle myself from him and stand from the bed. With steady fingers, I begin to unbutton the shirt I'd stolen from him. "And besides, it's not really a burden to sleep with your dick in me. It's comforting. Safe feeling." My attention turns downcast as I quietly admit, "I like being close to you."

His gaze heats when I stand before him naked and reach for the hem of his hoodie. He allows me to pull it over his head and throw it to the ground to join my discarded shirt. Emeric shifts down the bed until he's lying flat. Once he's gotten his joggers over his hips, I help pull them the rest of the way off.

Already, his cock is half hard and I haven't even touched him yet.

Bending over, I press a kiss to each of his hip bones before walking away and quickly turning off all the lights in the bedroom and connected en-suite bathroom. Double checking the bedroom door is shut and locked, I return to him.

The sun has a couple hours before it'll fully set, but still shadows surround us. As I crawl up Emeric's body, pausing to kiss either of his defined thighs as I do, I can feel his intense gaze watching my every movement. Straddling his hips, his hardening cock nudging my pussy, I bend down and press my lips to his thundering heart.

Rising up on my knees, I fist him in my hand until his hips are rocking and matching each languid stroke. I feel powerful—in control—as I lower myself onto him. I work him into me an inch at a time, until only the very tip is inside before sinking down and taking more of him in. I repeat this until I'm fully seated on his cock.

My muscles clench around him, begging for me to start riding him, but that isn't what this is about. This is about giving him the refuge he needs to fall asleep without his demons inter-fering. We have plenty of time to chase our orgasms later, but for now, he needs rest.

Lowering my body, I press my naked chest to his and wrap my arms around him the best I can. His heart pounds under my ear as his head dips and he presses a kiss to my hair.

"Go to sleep, love," I whisper, eyes closed. "I'm not going anywhere."

"I'd chase after you if you did."

"I know."

My eyes flutter closed when he drags the nearby soft blanket over our naked forms and his strong arms cocoon around me. Intimate. This is so incredibly intimate.

We lay like this in serene silence for so long, I think he's passed out already. It's the softly offered, "I like being close to you too, princess," that tells me he's still fighting off sleep.

I smile into the shadowing darkness and snuggle my face tighter against his sculpted chest. I think I'm still smiling when his breathing evens out and he succumbs to his exhaustion.

THIRTY
RIONACH

I'VE OFFICIALLY BEEN Mrs. Banes for a month now and we've fallen fairly easily into a routine after the day he brought me to the cabin. Emeric opening up about his childhood and the history he shares with the Koslov family helped me understand him on a level that's more... *human*. The lore of Emeric Banes is so vast and occasionally edges on otherworldly that it's sometimes easy to forget at the end of the day, he's still a just a person. He's a human who has scars and trauma like the rest of us.

Now that I'm privy to the ghosts still haunting him from his past, I can help him keep them at bay. He's still not a good sleeper by any means, but he's fallen asleep in the same bed as me more times in the past two weeks than he did when we first got married. We've had many nights where he comes home as the morning sun is starting to peek over the horizon. It's become second nature for me to crawl over to him and situate myself so I can easily slip him inside of me. It takes him only minutes to fall asleep, and he stays that way anywhere from three to six hours. According to what Emeric's told me, this is the most uninterrupted sleep he's had since he was a child. And the fact he's getting that kind of rest on nearly a daily basis is monumental for him.

We started cock warming—yes, I googled the correct term for it. I have a lot of free time on my hands—to help him sleep, but over the weeks, I've discovered I also sleep sounder when he's intwined with me. When I have no choice but to go to bed without him while he's still out working, I find myself feeling painfully empty. In such a short time frame, my life and my body's needs have become dependent on him. It's not completely one-sided either. Emeric depends on me now too, and I find that equal parts terrifying and calming.

Not only do I understand my husband more, but I also better understand his almost paranoid worry about what my family will do if they end up allying with the Russians again. Desperate people act recklessly, and Emeric has left my father in a *very* desperate state. Every day I struggle with the weight of knowing the extra trepidation Emeric is carrying around is because of me. If I gave the word, Emeric would eliminate my father, and subsequently my brother, without hesitation. I can't bring myself to call it. After everything, anyone with the last name Moran doesn't deserve my benevolence. There's a big difference between not wanting someone in your life anymore and wanting them dead. I don't know if I'll ever reach the point of wishing death upon the family who failed me so bad, but the ball is in their court. If they do something as stupid as Emeric is predicting they will, they'll be signing their own death sentences and there won't be anything I can do to help them.

The morning following our night in the cabin, I finally got the courage to ask Emeric why he hadn't ended Igor when he killed Ambrose. I can't help but believe it would have been therapeutic and healing for him to watch Igor bleed out just like he did with his father.

It turns out two decades ago the Bratva that Koslov is affiliated with to this day was a bigger force than the Banes were at that time. Emeric's eldest brother, Astor, who took the reins of the family's empire after Ambrose's death, struck up a deal with the Russian *Pakhan* to avoid creating more conflict between the two families. Astor was unexperienced at leading the family and knew a battle with the Russians wouldn't have ended well for them. As a sign of good faith, the Bratva gifted the Banes family a highly sought-out piece of real estate on the Upper East Side and Emeric vowed to leave Igor alone as long as the Russian did the same.

It was a shaky understanding, but it's seemed to have held for over twenty years. At least it had until Emeric stole me from Bogdan Koslov. The lines in the sand are now a little blurry.

It's because I now know the whole story that I'm not as irritated as I was before about not being allowed to come and go from the penthouse as I wish. Emeric still hasn't selected a team to be my official security, but he's made more of an effort over the last couple weeks to take time out of his schedule to accompany me on various errands and outings. As promised, on an impromptu shopping trip he replenished the supply of lingerie he's shredded off my body. On that same shopping trip, I dragged him into a pet store and picked Cerberus up a couple new toys. Emeric argued that the Doberman wasn't a house pet and my response to that was to throw in another squeaky toy.

He even took me to Ophelia's studio so I could take one of her beginners' classes. The entire time I tried my best to gracefully glide around the silver pole, I felt his gaze raking over me. The hour-long class led to a very hot and heavy moment in the studio's bathroom. Lia hadn't been the slightest bit amused when she caught us leaving with our hair still mussed and Emeric's shirt untucked. Laughing at her sour face, I kissed her on the cheek and promised her I'd see her soon before escaping through the front doors.

It's been good.

I've been happy.

Emeric makes me happy.

But I still spend a lot of hours of my day bored. There's only so many movies and TV series you can watch before your brain turns into Swiss cheese. I tried to switch it up by downloading a book on the iPad Emeric got me, but my attention span doesn't seem to be cooperating long enough for me to get through a chapter.

"Wow, this place looks a lot different in the light of day," I muse, spinning around the empty and eerily silent space. The lack of pounding music and gyrating bodies has my voice echoing through the high ceilings. "When you said you were taking me somewhere, I didn't think you meant here."

Tartarus at eleven in the morning on this random Tuesday looks a lot different than it did the night I was here last. The night I thought would be nothing more than a momentary escape from my dull reality but ended up being the start of something else entirely instead.

Emeric's expensive dress shoes click against the black-and-white marble floors beneath as he moves closer to me. "My only hope when I bought this building was that I'd own a club successful enough that I could run a portion of my operation's dirty money through it. Washing money is what I use all my legit businesses for." This isn't exactly a shocking revelation for me to hear. That's what most crime families do. They just work on much smaller scales than my husband. "This nightclub is one of the most popular hot spots on this side of town. The VIP rooms are sold out eight months in advance and we turn away hundreds of people every night at the door because we simply do not have the capacity to allow anyone else in. Between the popularity of the main club and the members-only sex club in the basement, it's safe to say Tartarus has grown into something I never expected or planned for."

I admire the original detailing etched into the marble columns before looking over my shoulder at him. "You need to be careful how you word things like that because someone might overhear you and accidentally mistake you as a humble man." My face morphs into an exaggerated look of horror and my words drip with sarcasm. "And we can't have that. Your scary reputation couldn't possibly survive it."

The way his eyes narrow in pretend aggravation has me laughing.

"I don't want you to worry one hair on your pretty little head, princess. While you may not find me scary, most would not agree with that sentiment. Not only have I secured my reputation, I've fucking earned it." Knowing the true story of how he ended up becoming the man he is today, I couldn't agree more with this. "But as I was saying, Tartarus has evolved over the years and there is still room for more potential growth. We have a running interest list of people and organizations wanting to rent the whole club out so they can host private parties here. The kind of money we could charge for something like that would allow us to run a great deal more of the dirty money through the books."

The sound of the heels of my over-the-knee black suede boots clacking fills the quiet void around us as I turn and close the space between us.

"It sounds like you've got it all worked out in your head, so why aren't you doing it?" I ask. I'm still not used to business plans like this being disclosed to me. He does it so casually, like we're having a conversation over a cup of coffee. It's the complete opposite of how Dad or Tiernan behaved.

"I didn't have anyone on my current staff that had the time or ability to coordinate events like that." Thunderous gray eyes scan my face. "But now I have a wife who majored in hospitality, and I thought it would be a perfect job for her."

I think my jaw just hit the fancy marble floor. "What?"

He taps my chin, silently urging me to close my mouth. "I told you weeks ago I had no interest in being married to a pearl-wearing housewife. You need a life outside of our home, Rionach, and as much as I love calling you my wife, you need a purpose in life outside of that title. It isn't feasible for me to allow you to go find some random job in the city, but I thought a job here at Tartarus working alongside me could be a good compromise."

"I'd be working alongside you, huh? So you wouldn't be my boss?" My teeth bite into my bottom lip as I fight a smile.

He reaches out for me, hands grasping my sides. "Don't you know I'm everyone's boss? Your office here will be directly next to mine, so I'll be able to step in and *boss* you around anytime I damn well please."

My own office? How long has he been planning this?

"As long as I can come to your office and cause trouble anytime I want, I don't see a problem with that."

"You can cause all the trouble you want, princess. In fact, I encourage it."

Laughing and unable to hold back my growing smile any longer, I stare up at the man who is known for taking what he wants, and yet through it all, he hasn't taken a single thing from me that I haven't been willing to give. In fact, Emeric has handed me everything I didn't know I wanted.

His reflexes are wicked fast when I launch myself at him with an excited squeal. His hands catch the backs of my thighs as my legs wrap around his middle. Eye level with him, I push strands of his dark hair back and ask, "Do you mean it? Do I really get to work here?"

"You've been a Banes for a month now, it's time you start working for the family business, don't you think?"

My head is still nodding when I kiss him.

THIRTY-ONE
EMERIC

"I'm still trying to understand why you thought it would be a wise decision to get married, Emeric," Astor repeats for the third time since I finally answered his phone call on the drive home.

Just like the rest of the people in our social circle, he saw the marriage announcement that went out over a month ago and I've been avoiding his calls like a bad case of herpes since. I might be the head of this family now, but Astor is still my big brother, and he thinks that title grants him the right to scold and lecture me.

After I plunged the knife into Ambrose's gut, Astor became my legal guardian until I turned eighteen. He was in the middle of leaving a terrible marriage and being the father of a little boy he wasn't ready to have. It wasn't easy on him, and I sure as fuck didn't help. I wasn't exactly a walk in the park after I returned home from Igor's, but he took me and my bullshit on along with everything else. At that time, he was running the business basically alone since Ledger had mostly checked out at this point. To this day, I don't know how Astor managed everything and I owe him a lot for keeping me out of the deep end.

That being said, I don't have any interest in listening to him question my decision to get married. Nothing he could say is going to make me change my mind about my bride or make me give her up. The only thing he'll succeed at doing is pissing me off, and I would prefer to skip that step.

"You married your son's ex-girlfriend," I retort as I step into the elevator of my building. The watch on my wrist tells me that I'm home twenty minutes later than I told her I would be. Hopefully, Rionach is almost finished getting ready so we can leave as soon as I change into my tux. "I don't know if you should be questioning me and my relationship choices when you don't exactly have the moral high ground on the topic."

A desk chair squeaks on his end of the line. I can picture him sitting at his desk in his home office that overlooks Lake Washington. That stern look, the one I'm fairly certain he was born wearing, firmly in place.

"That was different. I loved her."

Yup, I can hear the scowl in his tone.

"Exactly. You loved her and you wanted her, so you claimed her as your own. You weren't going to allow something as trivial as *morals* to get in the way of you obtaining what you need. I understand that now."

There's a long pause before he asks in a voice that is surprisingly gentle for Astor, "Is that why you did it? You need her?"

"Like oxygen," the wholly honest answer slips from my lips before my brain has a chance to catch up. "You can tell me it's a bad idea or believe it's a mistake—though, I'd strongly advice you against saying those things to my face—but nothing, and I mean *nothing,* is going to make me give her up. It's done. She's mine."

"Okay," Astor agrees without argument. "I hear you and I understand."

I know he does because my big brother is just as possessive as I am, and his very heart now beats for the woman he stole from his son.

The shiny elevator doors open, and I step into my silent and still home. My dog, who is usually quick to greet arrivals at the door is nowhere to be seen, an occurrence that has become more frequent as of late. Instead of guarding the property like he was trained to do, he's taken to guarding my wife. Where I find Rionach is where I'll also find Cerberus. I can't bring myself to be irritated at him for deviating from his intended job. Keeping Rionach safe is far more important to me these days.

"I figured you would," I tell my brother as I start walking up the winding staircase in search of my bride.

"Indie has never been to New York. I've been thinking about bringing her out there for a weekend trip when she has her next break from classes."

I bark out a laugh. "Oh, what a marvelous family reunion that will be. I'm sure your son would love to see you and his new stepmother."

"You're an ass," Astor grumbles.

"Stop flattering me, Astor. It's going to go straight to my head," I mockingly chastise. "I would hate for my ego to inflate. Can you imagine how utterly unbearable I'd be?"

The only light in our bedroom comes from behind the cracked en-suite door where the shower is still running. I guess she isn't, in fact, dressed and ready to leave. We're definitely going to be late to Senator Holloway's presidential campaign fundraiser.

Cerberus lies with his head on his front feet beside the doorway, vigilant eyes watching my every move as I walk toward him.

"Oh, because you're so tolerable *now*?" he scoffs, "Good-bye, Emeric."

The line goes dead.

I'm laughing at the fact my grumpy big brother didn't bother waiting for me to say my own farewell before he ended the call when I enter the steamy bathroom. Rionach, with her long hair piled on top of her head, is stepping out of the shower at the same time. She reaches for one of the over-sized black towels hanging on the towel rack, but I beat her to it. Towel in hand, I step behind her dripping wet, lithe body and wrap her in the soft fabric. Unable to stop myself, I press my lips to her shoulder speckled in water droplets before I do the same to her sensitive neck. She tremors as I take in a deep, greedy lungful of her citrus-smelling bodywash.

"Who were you talking to?" she asks.

"My brother," I answer against her throat.

"Astor, I'm assuming?" She leans her damp back into my chest. "I know you said you haven't heard from Ledger in a while..."

If *"in a while"* is synonymous with nearly twenty years, then *yes,* it's been a while. "The night before he left to join the Navy was the last time I spoke to Ledger in person. The last form of communication I had with my brother was when he sent a letter years later when he became a Navy Seal."

Ledger wanted nothing to do with the world we were brought up in or the empire we were destined to inherit. The second he saw a chance at a life away from the bullshit, he took it. It was less than six months after Ambrose died that he went to bootcamp and never came back.

Ledger was always the best of us. He smiled easier and he laughed louder. Something changed in him after his initiation. His smile faded and his laugh went silent. Both Astor and I tried to get him to tell us the specifics of what happened that night, but he was vague and never gave us a real answer.

When he got out and found freedom, I was happy for him. Some of us just aren't meant for this life, and it's better to learn that early on than to discover it later when you're in too deep.

"Have you tried to find him?" Rionach asks, twisting in my arms so she can rest her chin on my chest and wrap her arms around me. I plan on changing in a minute but even if I wasn't, I wouldn't mind the water from her damp body seeping into my clothes.

"I have on many occasions. With all my resources and connections, I still couldn't find him. So, what does that tell you?"

"He doesn't want to be found."

Or he's dead, I think but don't say aloud. Both Astor and I have thought the same thing over the years, but neither of us has dared speak it into existence. Ledger was smart, maybe the smartest one out of all of us, and he was observant. He could have used the skills he was taught in the first eighteen years of his life to disappear.

Just like Nova did after his stint in the military, Ledger could be hiding out in some off-the-grid cabin in Alaska, for all I know. What I do know is if Ledger wanted us to know where he is, he would make his location known. If he's alive, he's staying an untraceable ghost by choice.

"No, he doesn't." That doesn't mean I'm going to stop my yearly searches. I need to know one way or another if my brother is alive or not. I lean back so I can see the entirety of her bare face. She looks much younger without any makeup on but just as beautiful. "You were supposed to be dressed and ready to leave so we can go to the senator's event."

Her nose wrinkles as she pulls away from me and moves to stand in front of the vanity where all her products now sit. She leans her back against the marble counter and crosses her arms over her towel-covered chest. "Do I really have to go with you?"

"You're my wife. I told you that you'd have to attend some events with me," I say, positioning myself in front of her. "Why don't you want to go?"

"I don't really feel well," she explains with a forced nonchalant shrug.

"What's wrong? Do I need to call the doctor?" My hand instantly reaches out to touch her forehead, but she bats it away before I can see if she's running a fever.

She doesn't look pale or like she's on the verge of tossing up her cookies. I never saw myself as the compassionate type of person who would hold a woman's hair back while she was sick, but for Rionach, I know I'd happily do it.

Which is funny in an ironic kind of way because I once put a knife through a man's cheek when he barfed on my Italian leather shoes. In his defense, he was on hour sixteen of being tortured for information and was feeling a bit queasy. Long story short, he didn't live long after that. My shoes were burned along with his corpse.

"*What*? No, you don't have to call a doctor. While it's adorable to see you fussing like this, it's nothing that serious." She brushes away my hand again when I reach for her, which causes me to snarl at her and try again. "Will you stop? I'm fine. I started my period this morning and now I'm crampy and bloated. I feel like I look gross, and the idea of shoving myself into a long and tight formal gown sounds about as appealing as a Pap smear. Or eating gas station sushi."

My concern for her health seamlessly transitions into disappointment. It's been well over a month since we were first married—since the first night I filled her with my cum. I've lost track of how many times I've spilled my seed inside her. With our new sleeping arrangements, more times than not, my cock remains buried in her after I come. This ensures not a single drop escapes.

I knew this is what I wanted, but learning I've failed to put my baby in her hits me harder than I could have predicted.

Rionach's eyebrows scrunch when I pick her up and place her on the countertop in front of me. Her confusion only grows when I step between her spread knees and trail my hand up her soft and warn inner thigh.

"What are you—" Her question is cut off by a stunned gasp as two of my fingers dip inside her. She shoves at my hands, horror reflected in her eyes. "Stop. The blood..."

My eyes stare at the crimson-painted digits when I pull them from her heat.

"Emeric?" My name on her lips is a barely audible exhale of air.

It's only been a month. This can take time. You have to be patient.

"This could have been... I wanted this to be my baby." The disappointment in my tone is obvious to my own ears, and I have no doubt Rionach is also picking up on it. That primal urge that roared to life the first time I came inside of her is clawing at me as my head fills with visions of her stomach swelling with the life I will put in her. A life that is the perfect combination of both of us.

"Your baby," she repeats slowly, like she's struggling to wrap her mouth around the two words. For a moment, in complete stunned silence, Rionach joins me in staring at the streaks of blood on my fingers. The second she comes out of her disbelief-induced fog, her palms slap against my chest and she shoves me backward. "Emeric fucking Banes, are you trying to knock me up?"

"You're my wife. Would that be so wrong of me?" I retort after I reclaim the space she just tried to force between us.

The pink flush that has been sitting on her cheeks from her hot shower has deepened and her glaring eyes are glistening green flames.

"Yes!" she all but screeches. "We've been married for a little over a month. We can't have a baby *now*." A shadowy look falls over her face as she quickly adds, "Or maybe ever."

An emotion I can't place seizes my chest hearing her say this. Jaw muscle clenching, I place my hands on either side of her on the black stone countertops and cage her in.

"You don't want to have my babies, Rionach?" A fleeting look of sadness joins the shadowed expression marring her lovely features. It's gone in the span of one breath. "I want you to have my babies, I want to watch your stomach grow with our child. My dick is hard just thinking about how beautiful you'll be."

She rolls her eyes at this and shoves at my chest again. I don't budge an inch. "Your horny dick is *not* a good enough reason to have a fucking baby."

I dip my head and run my tongue along her bottom lip before whispering, "It's going to happen one day, princess. Sooner or later, my seed will take root in your womb, and you will bring our baby into this world."

"You really think so?" The overly confident and knowing look that flashes in her eyes has an alarm bell ringing in the back of my head. "I guess we'll have to wait and see about that."

Well before she came to my club and ended up in the cage with me, I had Nova gather all the information he could on her. From the name of her first-grade teacher to her most played song on her preferred streaming platform to the number of times she had strep throat as a child, I know everything about her.

You didn't know she was a skilled pickpocket, so maybe you don't know everything, the taunting voice in my head says.

"Are you keeping secrets from me, dear wife?" I ask, trailing my lips along her jaw and down to her throat.

"I wouldn't dream of it." Her fingers twist into the fabric of my shirt and tug me closer. "Do we still have to attend the fundraiser?"

"Unfortunately, but since we're already going to be more than fashionably late..." I tear away from her and grip her hips. She yelps when I yank her nearly to the edge of the counter. Her confusion morphs into unease when I drop to my knees between her spread thighs. "I read once that orgasms help with menstrual cramps. If I'm going to make you join me tonight, making you feel better is the least I can do."

I tear away the black towel so her perfect pussy is fully on display to me.

"You—" She jerks in place when I kiss the place where her thigh and hip meet. "You can't do this. Not right now. You'll get blood—"

I silence her with a quick nip of my teeth. "If you think I'm going to be bothered by a little blood, princess, you haven't been paying attention."

All reservation and fight leave her at the first swipe of my tongue through her sweet pussy.

THIRTY-TWO
RIONACH

"Stop," Emeric murmurs in my ear as his hand tightens around mine.

The Metropolitan Museum of Art's beautifully preserved architecture is plastered in tacky red, white, and blue decorations and various-sized banners that boast Senator Robert L. Holloway's smiling mug. I don't care how attractive a person might be, no one looks good when their face is blown up to the size of a Mini Cooper.

Patrons are dressed to the nines in their designer suits and dresses. Fake smiles and surface-level small talk fill the crowded room. It's like every other fundraiser and charity event I've been forced to attend over the years. Contrived and reeking of enlarged and unjustifiable egos.

I hate it, and the second I stepped through the glass doors on Emeric's arm, I felt my well-practiced blank mask slip effortlessly back into place. Seems a month away from this bullshit wasn't enough time for my skills to grow rusty.

"Stop what?" I whisper back.

We've only made it twenty feet into the building and

already I can feel their stares. The looks on the guests' faces as they stare at us—*me*—range from confused to appalled to angry. The latter sits predominantly on the faces of young women. It takes me a minute to figure out what their problem is, but when I do, I have to fight a smirk. They're jealous of me because I'm *his*. Without even trying, I landed the most elusive and eligible bachelor in the state. Emeric told me he's had fathers offering their daughters to him for years, but he's always turned them down. He rejected these women and then chose me, the girl who's always gone unseen.

Emeric pulls us to a stop, and he shifts so he's standing directly in front of me, his wide shoulders blocking out everything in the crowded room behind him. "Stop trying to make yourself small," his voice is quiet but still holds every ounce of his power. "Remember who you are. You're a Banes now. You're my wife, and that fucking means something, so act accordingly. We both know you're not the reserved girl you pretended to be for so many years. Drop the disguise and show them who you are."

Throat feeling oddly tight, I look directly into the storm flashing in his eyes. "How have you always been able to see the real me, but they never could?"

I don't have to elaborate on who I mean by "they". He knows.

He twists the lock of hair I left loose to frame my face around his finger. The rest of my hair is twisted into a messy but still elegant braid that hangs down my exposed spine. I had ended up choosing a simple midnight blue dress that has thin straps and is nearly backless. My lower stomach is still bloated, but luckily the fabric hangs tastefully from my shoulders and doesn't cling.

• "Because they didn't want to," he answers simply. "The real you—the version you tried so damn hard to hide—is *all* I want, princess. I told you this once already, but I'll say it again because it's as true now as it was then. Your family doesn't deserve you. Their blatant disregard is something they'll come to regret. I'll make sure of it."

It's ridiculous to think there was a time not that long ago I thought I could control my feelings for this man. We're so far past that now. The train has left the station and we're barreling toward something that scares me in the best way.

Peeking around his frame, I find inquisitive eyes locked on where we're having our private conversation. "People are staring."

"Let them." He returns to my side and wraps his arm around my waist. "Come on, I want to show off my wife."

For the next hour, I stand beside Emeric with my head held high and my shoulders back. I don't retreat into myself like I've been conditioned to do. A few times I caught people whispering and not so subtly gesturing in our direction. They were too busy gossiping at first to notice, but the color leeched from their embarrassed faces when they realized I'd caught them staring. Their worry multiplied when I had narrowed my eyes at them. Emeric is an intimidating entity, and by association, I guess I now am too. That's something I've never experienced before, and it gives me a sense of power that's always been foreign to me.

"Rionach," Emeric says, breaking me out of the thoughts I'd fallen into. His fingers thread through mine again. "This is my nephew Callan."

Oh. On top of obscene wealth and influence, the Banes men have been blessed with achingly good looks. If Emeric gets his way and manages to knock me up—something that hadn't appealed to me prior to him admitting his devious plan but is now consuming a large portion of my brain's bandwidth—our babies will be beautiful.

Callan Banes is around my age, maybe a year younger, and he's handsome as hell. Built similarly to Emeric with his tall frame and wide shoulders, he stands with a confidence that must be hereditary. The only pictures I've seen of Astor Banes have been on the internet, but the facial resemblance he has to his father is uncanny. His dark brown hair is tousled but doesn't appear unkempt, and there's a seriousness in his blue eyes. He's got that all-American hottie vibe but there's an obvious air of danger hovering around him too. Another trait I believe comes with his bloodline.

I can see why he once appealed to Ophelia, but I prefer the violence and wickedness that clings to my husband.

"Rionach," Callan repeats, an easy grin on his face. "It's good to finally put a face to the name." He bends and presses a friendly kiss to my cheek. "I was betting my uncle was going to scare you off before I could meet you in person and welcome you to the family."

"I don't scare easily," I tell him, returning his smile.

"That you don't," Emeric chimes in under his breath.

Ignoring his cheeky comment, I keep my focus on his nephew. "Emeric told me you moved here from Washington to do accounting work for the businesses."

Callan nods as he takes a drink of the scotch or whiskey in his glass. "I graduated early with a degree in forensic accounting. We thought we should put my education to use and help keep the books in order." In other words, Callan helps launder the dirty money through the legit companies the Banes family owns. I'm sure this is precisely what his professors thought he'd end up doing with his private school education when he sat in their classes. "I heard you're also joining the family business and you're going to be working at Tartarus."

Anticipation shoots through me as I squeeze Emeric's hand, silently thanking him again for the opportunity. Having been pulled into another conversation with an older gentleman, he can only squeeze my hand back in acknowledgement.

"I am! I guess I'll also be putting my expensive college degree to use. I'm actually really excited to get to work. Being a kept housewife is *so* boring."

"Has Emeric brought you to the club during operating hours yet? If he hasn't, make sure he does. You'd have fun."

I bite my lip to refrain from telling him that his uncle personally gave me a tour of the club and the secret one residing in the basement. Instead, I give him my best blasé look as I casually tell him, "I've been before. I attended the masquerade party held there before we got married. My friend, Ophelia, managed to snag a ticket and she brought me as her plus-one. Do you know her? Ophelia? I think she mentioned once that she knew you when you all were kids, but I might be remembering wrong," I play dumb to see what he'll say.

A symphony of emotions dance across Callan's face before he reins them all in and replaces them with a neutral expression. "That's correct, I did know her when we were younger. I was good friends with her brother, Bash." *Yeah, whatever you say, buddy, but that isn't all you two were, and we both know it.* There's more history between Callan and Ophelia than either of them is letting on, and one day soon, I'm going to get the full story out of someone. I make a mental note to ask Emeric about it once we're home. "She's actually here tonight. I saw her an hour ago or so."

"She is?" My head instantly starts pivoting on my shoulders as I search for my best friend.

"From the looks of it, she's on a date."

At the bitter and venomous change of his tone, my eyebrows skyrocket to my hairline. I force myself to school my features. I have no idea if I should be on Team Callan or not since I don't know their full history, but either way, I decide to stoke the flames of Callan's obvious jealousy.

"Really? Good for her."

"Yeah, sure. It's great." In one swallow, he drains the remaining contents of his glass before he shifts on his feet and looks around the room. "There's someone I need to catch up with, but it was wonderful meeting you, Rionach."

Oh, he's big mad. I need to find Ophelia so I can tell her.

"Rio," I correct before he can walk away. "You can call me Rio."

"Okay, Rio." He nods his head in farewell before slipping into the crowd.

I do another slow perusal of the giant room we're in, but I still don't see my friend. Sighing, I step closer to Emeric and give his companion an apologetic smile.

"Sorry to interrupt, but I'll be right back. I need to run to the restroom," I tell him quietly.

"Camden will escort you." Emeric turns and lifts his hand. The young soldier I didn't noticed lingering close by appears at our side a moment later.

I feel my face wrinkle as I ask, "Is that really necessary?"

The dark, unswayable expression on Emeric's face tells me this isn't up for debate.

Raising my hands in mock surrender, I start to back away from him. "Ugh. Fine, whatever, just stop looking at me like that." With a cheeky grin, I duck away before he can say something back.

———

BETWEEN THE WOMEN reapplying their lipstick and fighting with the zippers on their formal gowns, it takes me longer to get out of the bathroom than I anticipated. Also, nothing aggravates pee fright quite like knowing there's an armed guard standing in the hallway waiting for you to be done. The added pressure wasn't working in my favor there for a minute.

Stepping around a pair of women who seem to be close in age with me, I push open the heavy wooden door. Before I slip though, I pause and glance at them over my shoulder. "You know, you two would probably enjoy your evening more if you'd stop staring at me like I stole your favorite toy during playtime."

By the way their perfectly painted faces drop and then contort up into unjustified distaste, I know they weren't expecting me to say something.

The bottle-blonde wearing the blood-red dress speaks first. "My father has been trying to discuss a possible courtship between Emeric Banes and myself for over two years, but Banes turned my father down every single time. And Dad isn't just some random suit on Wall Street. People *know* who he is." The way her arms uncross and recross in rapid succession give her away. She's not as confident as she's pretending to be.

"The same thing happened with my family," the blonde's friend huffs. "And we own an airline, and I'm not talking about some small private one, I mean an entire commercial airline. Do you know how wealthy that makes us? It didn't matter because Banes still snubbed my father's messages."

Emeric wasn't kidding when he said he could have been married ten times over with all the suitors that were being shoved his way.

This is what happens to women's minds when they're told from girlhood their worth is dependent on who they marry and have children with. It corrupts their heads and blinds them to their true value. My heart bleeds with sympathy for them

321

because they never stood a chance but that doesn't mean I'm going to let them try to run all over me.

Equal parts annoyed and sad for the women standing here, I raise a brow and ask, "Is there a question in there somewhere?"

The blonde looks at me down her perfectly sculpted nose. "We know who your family is and that they stopped being relevant years ago. What we don't know is what makes you so special that he chose you. Why would he want to marry *you*?"

Okay, *ouch*. Fixing my sweetest, most condescending smile on my face, I say, "That seems like a question for Emeric. Why don't you go ask him? I dare you." Their indignant expressions don't change until I add, "Or, better yet, I can ask him for you. Don't worry, I'll be sure to make it crystal clear to him that it's you two questioning his decisions."

Like rehearsed choreography, the blood drains from their faces at the same time and matching gasps come from their plump red lips.

Head cocking, I examine their visible and tangible fear. "*This*. This is why neither of you could have married him. The fear dripping off you right now is proof you couldn't survive being his wife. You wouldn't last a night in bed with Emeric. He would eat you alive and smile while he did it." Luckily for me, I fucking love that smile. "We're currently standing in a building that is filled to the brim with wealthy and powerful men. Go find yourself one and stop fucking glaring at me for having something that was *never* going to be yours."

Not bothering to wait around to hear what they have to say, I turn back around and leave them to stew in their misplaced envy.

The bathrooms are located down a long hallway away from the main exhibit where the bustle of the function is taking place. A man's voice that I'm assuming belongs to the man of the hour and future presidential candidate echoes through the corridors. He's speaking into a microphone and by the time his words reach me, they're garbles. I don't have to be present to know what Senator Holloway is saying. He's making all kinds of outlandish promises about how he's going to save America when he becomes president, but for that to happen, he needs everyone here to write a very big check for his cause. *Yawn.*

With the attendees wanting to listen to the speech, the hallway that was populated with people when I first went to the bathroom is now empty. Completely empty. As in the guard who Emeric assigned to me is nowhere to be found.

I'm worrying about the young guard's overall health and safety for when Emeric learns Camden abandoned his post and *me* when footsteps sound behind me.

My head has just barely had the chance to turn in the direction of the noise when an arm wraps around me from behind and a hand clamps down on my mouth. Due to his aptitude for chasing and abducting me, for a single heartbeat, my body thinks it's Emeric's arms around me. But the body pressed against mine as it starts to drag me backward feels wrong. The warm, slightly clammy hand covering my mouth is wrong.

Adrenaline floods my veins and fight settles in my bones because this isn't my husband hauling me away. A knowing twinge in my gut tells me he's also not behind this. I haven't done anything that would warrant being taught another lesson like the one in the woods. I've been good.

My legs search for purpose, or any kind of traction, and my elbows thrust backward until they connect with a set of ribs.

His back slams into a nondescript white door that is meant for employees only and he rushes us inside the dimly lit space. With my struggling and hysterical thrashing, I vaguely take in the room I've been brought to. There are rows of metal shelving with carefully placed boxes and items organized on them. We're in one of the museum's archive rooms.

The man chuckles when I try in vain to grab one of the items placed on the shelves when he drags me past them. With the disarray happening in my head and the panic-induced haze overtaking my focus, I can't be sure what I was even reaching for. Anything can be made into a weapon if you hit someone hard enough with it, right?

The room is deeper than I initially thought, and he weaves us back farther between the shelves. It's not until we reach the last stack of items does his hold on me loosen. Regaining my balance, my now bare feet—apparently, I lost my stilettos at some point—stand on the cold tile floors at the same time the hand releases my face.

I've just managed to suck in a breath so I can demand to know what the hell this is about when another figure steps out from behind a shelf. My words turn into sawdust on my tongue and I nearly choke on them when the figure moves out from the shadows.

It's been over six months since our dance this fall and the damage to the left side of his face is just as horrifying as it was the first time I saw it. The skin that looks to have been shredded from his skull and down his neck before being sewed back on is made of ugly raised pink and silver lines. His eyelid, which also appears to have been reattached, doesn't move when he blinks. I still don't know if he can see anything with the partially hidden, milky eye that sits beneath it.

"We're sorry to take you away from the festivities." The smooth timbre of his voice could be considered pleasant if I didn't know it was a lie. Or a tool he uses to lure women to their horrific and bloody ends. "As you can imagine, it's been a difficult task to find time to speak to you alone. Banes hasn't made it easy on us by keeping you locked away in his stronghold in the sky."

Fear, and not the fun kind, wraps around my diaphragm and squeezes until it hurts. Images of butchered women swirl in my head, causing my stomach to roll. As if Bogdan Koslov can read my mind, an evil grin spreads across his fucked-up face.

It takes a moment for what he said to register in my brain. *We. Us.*

"What are—"

I've been so focused on the butcher standing before me that I momentarily forgot about the person who carried me in here until he speaks.

"Hello, little sister."

Chills erupt down my spine like a hundred spiders scurrying across my skin. I spin around at such a violet speed I nearly topple over.

"Tiernan," his name catches in my throat as I choke it out.

He's my brother, I know this, but raking my eyes over him now, I barely recognize him. Tiernan's always taken pride in his appearance. Was borderline fanatical about keeping his dark blond hair neatly trimmed and styled, and I've never seen him with more than a day's worth of facial hair. It looks to me like he hasn't cut or shaved either since the church. The taupe blazer he wears is wrinkled and a size too big because of the weight he's lost.

The deranged side of him that I always saw but everyone else ignored is on full display.

"What are you doing? Why are you..." Once again, my words are stolen from me. It shouldn't be a shock to see him without his right hand. I mean, for fuck's sake, I saw the carnage lying on the dusty floor of the church, but there's something jarring about seeing his jacket sleeve hang empty for the first time.

Tiernan follows my gaze, and a bitter grin lifts his lips. "Appreciating Banes's handiwork?" He shoves the sleeve of his blazer up his forearm and presents the wrapped stump to me. "He sent it back to us. My hand, I mean. Did you know that? It was left on our porch and Mom opened the box. She thought it was something she ordered online. It was a big box, after all. But no, it was just my hand with a 'get well soon' balloon tied around it. She just screamed and *screamed*, the damn balloon floating in her face. Dad had to have her sedated for days after that. She's still not back to herself."

The way he's staring at me... he's waiting for me to be outraged by Emeric's actions. He's going to be waiting a very long time for that kind of reaction from me. After the way my family behaved in the church, I think Emeric has every right to taunt them further by returning the severed hand. Doing so in such a colorful manner is completely on brand for the man I now share a life with.

"What the hell did you think was going to happen? Did you think you'd get away with it?" I grit out, hands balling into fists at my sides to conceal the way they shake. I'm not sure if it's from the fear or the rage now humming within me. "You. Stole. From. *Him*."

"And then he stole you from us!" Tiernan points between his chest and Bogdan's.

From us. Interesting.

The weird conversation we had the morning he came into my room back at our family estate reemerges in my head. *Marrying outside our heritage is what's weakened our bloodline.* He was visibly angry at the prospect of me being married off, and now he's teamed up with Bogdan, the man I was supposed to marry?

He's up to something and based on how well his last scheme went, I don't foresee whatever this is ending well for him.

Stupid, stupid man. Do you want to lose another body part? Perhaps your head this time?

"He stole you from us and ruined everything we had planned between our families." His face turns red as he takes a step closer to me.

I lift my foot to back up a step but stop when I remember that will only put me closer to Bogdan. Not liking the fact my back is already to the Russian, I shift away and position myself so they're both somewhat in front of me. I want to see both of them at all times until I figure out how to get the hell away from this.

I've been gone too long, it's only a matter of time before Emeric notices and he comes searching for me. I just have to make sure these two pricks don't try to take me to a secondary location. As long as I remain in the museum, it'll be fine. *I'll* be fine.

Emeric has men everywhere. Someone will find me.

"Where's the man who was guarding me?" I ask instead of acknowledging his retort. Arguing with him isn't going to get me anywhere. All it will do is further piss him off and I know what Tiernan can be like when he's angry.

"Why do you care?" Tiernan snaps. "He's just one of Banes's lackeys."

"I'd prefer to not have an innocent man's blood on my hands because you decided to throw a tantrum in the middle of a political fundraiser." *Oops*, there goes my plan of not pissing him off.

Bogdan chuckles. It's a dark, sinister kind of sound that has alarm bells sounding in my head like a category five tornado is imminent.

He stalks toward me. I try to stand my ground, but when he closes in on me, I end up with my back pressed against the shelving.

Idiot, I scold myself.

His hand reaches out, and his calloused fingers drag down the side of my face. Bile starts to rise in my throat. The blood that coats Bogdan's hands might not be visible now, but it still drips from them. Emeric's hands are also bloodstained. That's never been a secret to me, but I've never shuddered at the thought of his touch. I've never shied away because I know in my very soul I'm safe in his hands.

Rough fingertips trace across my jaw.

"Mmm, such soft skin," he mumbles mainly to himself, before pinning me with his gaze. "I appreciate your spirit, Rionach." His praise and touch have my entire body heaving in disgust. "I prefer my women to have a decent amount of fight in them. It keeps things exciting. *Lively*."

"I'm not your woman," I instantly snarl back, refusing to allow him to see the fear that is racking my insides.

His light blond brows pull together—or whatever remains of his left eyebrow tries to. "Because you're his?" The tsking sound he makes is mocking. "No. You were promised to me *first*. I chose you. You're not Banes's, you belong to me. I have a contract signed by your father saying just that."

Thick inky dread twists my insides, but still, I lift my chin to meet his eyes... eye? "I have a signed marriage license that says I'm his." A marriage license my signature was forged on, but whatever. Semantics and all that. That's information he doesn't need to know.

Tiernan scoffs loudly. "License or not. It's a sham of a marriage."

It may have started out that way, but it's not anymore. My

marriage to Emeric is more real than I ever thought it would be. It's evolved into something I didn't see coming... something I didn't know I needed.

"Emeric won't agree with that sentiment," I warn my brother over Bogdan's shoulder.

"We aren't concerned about Banes," Bogdan snaps. "His days on top are numbered. We're coming for him." He moves on from petting my faces to the long braid hanging down by back. He wraps the woven strands around his palm and tugs. My head is forcibly snapped back, and my throat is exposed to him. I fight against the submissive position he's forcing upon me, but all I succeed in doing is making him yank on my hair harder. The bones in my neck have reached their limit. My neck cannot physically go back any further, but still he pulls. "That's why we're here. Either way, you will be rightfully mine, but I'm giving you the option to make it easy on yourself. If you voluntarily leave here with us tonight, I won't punish you too severely for willingly spreading your legs for Banes all these weeks. But if you decide to stick around at his side like the obedient whore you are, I'll make sure you regret it after we annihilate him and you're left unprotected." The way he examines my exposed throat feels like he's imagining what it'd be like to slice a blade across it. "When you're nothing but sweet fruit ripe for the picking."

I think it's a reflex when my eyes dart to where my brother stands behind Bogdan. Of the two evils in the room with me, Tiernan is the safer option and I think that's why I look at him for help. It's pathetic and if I get out of here, I'll find time to feel shame over it.

"I'm not going anywhere with you," I grind out.

A smile that could be the cause of nightmares tugs at the corners of his mouth. "Like I said, I prefer women who have fight in them." He leans in close so he can whisper in my ear. "I think I just like beating it out of them. Nothing gets me harder than when they finally beg for their lives."

The terrifying smile vanishes and twists into liquid fury when he pulls back and I snarl, "Fuck you," before spitting in his face.

Hand like a vise wrapped in my hair, he pulls me by the braid and whirls me around. The unforgiving metal of the shelf crashes into my chest and thighs when I'm slammed against it. The bones in my sternum scream in pain and I just barely manage to swallow my cry.

The full length of the front of his body presses into my back as he forces me to discover what kind of affect I'm having on his body. My breathing stills in my chest and every muscle in my body goes agonizingly rigid.

Oh God... the fear I felt when Emeric staged my kidnapping pales in comparison to what is currently wrapping its clawed hand around my heart.

"Bogdan. This wasn't the..." My brother's warning comes just as an insanely loud and high-pitched ring cuts through the turbulent space. Lights on the ceiling and over the doors flash with each eardrum-rattling beep.

The fire alarm. Someone pulled the fire alarm.

Despite Bogdan's hands still being on me, I calm down and a weight lifts from my chest. And then I start to laugh. I laugh because I know who's behind this and I know what that means.

"You're fucked," I tell the pair of men standing at my back between giggles. The Russian's hold on my hair hinders me from turning my head. To make sure they're hearing me over their own concern and the deafening noise, I raise my voice and say it again, "You're so unbelievably fucked!"

"We need to move," Tiernan shouts at his new companion.

"Leave her here for now. We'll get her later. Just like we talked about—"

"Stop talking!" Bogdan's yells his demand over the alarm.

Emeric's coming for me.

"So, can I count on your support, Mr. Banes?" Robert Holloway's smile is so well rehearsed, it drips with sleazy insincerity.

It's no different than the other politicians I've had to deal with during my climb to the top. They sit on their high pedestals and paint themselves as morally superior humans who wouldn't dare get their hands dirty. In reality, they're just as corrupt as I am. For four generations, the Holloways have hidden their depravity behind their shiny veil of religion and simulated altruism. But I know the truth and I also know how they've managed to possess political power for so long.

His smile falters when I blandly glance at his offered hand.

He's trying his best to conceal it, but the trepidation he's experiencing in my presence is plain as day. The way he's blinking more than necessary and his throat bobs betrays him. Robert's been cultivating and growing his political career since he was chasing co-eds in college. You'd think after all this time he'd be more skilled at reining in his emotions. *Pathetic. And this guy wants to run the country?*

I was originally pleasantly surprised he was brave enough to approach me after Rionach had slipped away to use the restroom. My surprise has already turned to ash and now I'm just unamused. My wife should be returning shortly and once she does, we're blowing this political Popsicle stand.

I smirk at him when he awkwardly returns his arm to his side. "I wouldn't hold your breath, Robby," I tell him while casually stuffing my hands in my pant pockets. "I don't have any interest in putting the West Coast's Italian mafia in the oval office. You can see how that might negatively affect me and my personal interests, can't you?"

It's taken me nearly a decade to get my hooks into players in the United States government. Like everything else I do, it was a meticulous game of strategy and planning. I've carefully placed people in jobs of power that will serve me and my goals. If the walking, talking Ken doll standing in front of me ends up sitting pretty in Washington, D.C., he will royally fuck up what has taken me years to do. Especially if he has the Italians in his ear calling in the favors they've collected from the Holloways over the years.

Robert coughs and then forces a fake chuckle while his dark blue eyes dart around to make sure no one overheard what I said. "Mr. Banes... if you're insinuating I'm anything other than a devoted husband and father, and a humble servant of the United States of America, you are *sorely* mistaken." He steps closer as he quietly adds, "For God's sake, I am not a member of the mafia."

Already bored with this interaction, I sigh exasperatedly. "Using the company line on me of all people is not only a mistake, but it's also a colossal waste of both our times. You know what kind of man I am, and I know what kind of man you are. Let's just skip the monotonous part where we pretend we don't, shall we?" I've already seen what I came here to see tonight, and now I'm ready to take my wife home. The taste of her I had before we left wasn't enough to satiate me. It's never enough. I always end up wanting more of her. "The Holloways and the Valentino crime family have been sucking each other's cocks for nearly forty years. That's no secret."

Robert's face tightens and pinches around his eyes and mouth. His shiny forehead doesn't so much as flinch, but that's normal for him. Up this close, the tiny scars near his ears from where he got a face lift years ago are visible.

My hand gives him a condescending pat on the shoulder. "Careful. There're cameras everywhere tonight. We don't want tomorrow's headlines to read, *'Hopeful presidential candidate seen looking tense while deep in conversation with a man known for making his enemies wear their entrails like a stylish scarf'*, now do we?"

The color drains from his face but he forces another one of those fake million-dollar smiles back on his face. "Correct me if I'm wrong, but didn't one of your cousins marry into this so-called 'crime family'? I would think you'd be in support of whatever ongoing business relationship my family has with them seeing as you, too, have family involved."

"You've assumed incorrectly." A cousin I haven't spoken to in decades does not outweigh my business's need to keep its stronghold in the country's capital.

"If you're not here to support my cause, why are you here, Mr. Banes?"

My attention flicks around the room, landing on a few familiar faces.

"I wanted to see firsthand whose lives I'm going to need to fuck up to ensure they pull their support for your bothersome campaign," I tell him honestly. "You claim your loyalty is to your god and country. Mine lies with the needs of my empire." *And my wife.* "That's all I give a shit about, and I'm not about to let your slimy ass and ill-conceived policies endanger it in any way."

Indignation flares in his eyes. "You're a respectable businessman and your power is vast, Mr. Banes, but you're not strong enough to alter the outcome of a presidential election."

"You don't think so?" My head cocks to the side as I slowly examine him with calculating eyes. "Well, I suppose if I can't sway the votes, I can always just eliminate the problem altogether."

"Did you..." he sputters, ignoring the pair of young men signaling for him to join them near the stage. "Did you just threaten to have a United States senator *executed*?"

"Good luck with your speech, Senator."

I give him one last knowing smirk before I nod my head in farewell and turn away from the gaping man.

Satisfied that my task for the night has been completed, I search the room for signs of my wife. She should have been back by now, but Callan did say that Ophelia was here. Perhaps she's found her friend on the way back from the restroom? While this is a very strong possibility, my intuition tells me to keep looking. The crowded throng of attendees all push toward the stage as Holloway begins his speech. I don't pay attention to a word he's saying. My sole focus is on finding her distinctive red hair amongst the gathering people.

Tension snakes down my spine as a rock forms in my gut. Jaw set, I push my way through the chatting patrons and make my way across the room toward the bathrooms. She wouldn't have run off, certainly not after learning the truth about my history with the Koslovs. Rionach wouldn't risk her safety like that. Not again.

Camden is with her. I watched him escort her away. The guard is young, but he's good at his job. I wouldn't have assigned him this task if I didn't think he could fucking handle it. The kid also knows what the consequences would be if he lost my wife. He wouldn't risk my wrath.

When I stalk around a stone column just outside the exhibit where the party is happening, I find Mathis, concern written across his features like neon paint, rushing in my direction. The way he frantically speaks into his walkie-talkie confirms that someone is going to end up dying by my hands tonight.

"Start talking," I grind out before he has a chance to say anything. "Where is my wife?"

His head shakes. "I don't know."

I take hold of his jacket's lapels and viciously whirl him around until his spine collides with a nearby wall. Mathis doesn't fight me off. I lift him until he stands on his tiptoes, and still, he doesn't struggle against me. The hallway is empty because everyone is engrossed in the senator's speech. This is good because I don't need witnesses to the possible murder I'm about to commit.

"If you ever string those three words together in my presence, I will ensure they're the last words you ever speak," I snarl my threat out close to his now pale face. "So let me ask again, where is Rionach?"

His head fucking shakes *again*. "We found Camden in the emergency exit stairwell. It looks like someone got the jump on him. They broke his neck and dumped him there." Flames of rage ignite in my bloodstream, but I can't bring myself to mourn the young life that was taken. Not yet, not while Rionach is missing. "We searched the stairwell and the bathroom for Mrs. Banes, but she wasn't in either. We're trying to do a more extensive search while remaining discrete, but that's hard to do when there's so many people in the building."

Drawing attention to our more illicit dealings in such a public and crowded space would be foolish. People in my line of work thrive in the shadows. When there's too much light pointed in our direction, that's when shit tends to go south.

"Then clear the fucking building, Mathis."

"Sir?"

Without care, I drop the man trapped in my hold and march ten feet down the corridor to where the red fire alarm sits starkly on the white wall. The commotion taking place in the exhibit multiplies tenfold as the blaring alarm cuts through the senator's speech and the emergency lights start flashing.

I stalk back to where Mathis stands wide-eyed. "Find my fucking wife."

———

THE METAL DOOR of the archive room slams against the wall behind it. My hold on the gun I'd taken from Camden's dead body tightens when my attention locks on the discarded high heels on the floor.

Rionach is here. Or she was here.

The room is vast and maze-like because of the rows of shelves. I step inside, Mathis and Yates flanking me on either side. Two other teams of three are searching other parts of the museum. Behind me, I'm vaguely aware of Yates telling the other two teams searching different parts of the museum our location.

Nova and additional men are heading to us now for extra backup, but we're working on a time crunch. After retrieving Camden's weapon, I'd sent a message to the city's police commissioner and warned him to keep his people and the fire department away as long as possible. There's always some young cop who believes their shiny badge is synonymous with a superhero's cape and they ignore orders by charging into a scene. If that happens and they walk in on what's happening inside this building right now, they'll be effectively ending their career and possibly their life early.

Weapons raised, we ease into the room and search for any more signs of her. Since the second I saw Mathis's alarmed face, I've been silently reprimanding myself for insisting we attend this fucking thing tonight. Rionach doesn't feel well and still I made her come with me.

It's my fault she's in harm's way right now.

You also trusted someone else to guard her tonight.

All my fault.

I nearly lose my very grip on reality and every ounce of self-control I have when we clear the second row of shelves, and two familiar figures emerge from the darkness of the third one. Between their much bigger frames, stands a smaller one. The glint of the silver pistol held to her temple catches in the flashing light.

Bogdan Koslov is holding a gun to my wife's head and Tiernan Moran has his remaining hand wrapped tightly around her upper arm.

A murderous red haze falls over my vision as my world begins to tilt on its axis. In tandem, Mathis and Yates point their guns at the men's skulls.

Igor's son makes a disapproving *tsking* sound as he wags a mocking finger at us. "Be smart about this, Banes," he shouts. "I can put a bullet in her head a lot faster than your goons can shoot us."

I ignore his mocking warning and focus on my wife. The lighting is dark, and I can't make her out in great detail, but from what I can see from fifteen feet away, she doesn't look injured. The only sign of damage is the way her artfully crafted braid is now loose, and more pieces of hair are falling forward around her face. And she's barefoot. With a gun to her head and two men holding her captive, a panic-stricken appearance would be more than warranted, but she seems surprisingly composed. With her ability to tamp down and hide her emotions, for all I know she could be on the verge of hysteria. If that happens, every tear that escapes my wife's beautiful eyes will be another slice of my blade across her captors' skin.

"Talk to me, baby," I call to her as I lock my gaze on the man holding the gun. "Are you hurt?"

Ignoring her brother's warning growl to remain quiet, Rionach answers me. "I'm fine." There's an edge to her tone that I love. In the face of danger, she's holding on to that wild-fire burning inside her. "I want it noted for the record that this wasn't my fault this time. I didn't do anything wrong."

"I know you didn't, princess," I assure her. "Everything is going to be okay. This will be all over soon."

If Nova had accompanied us tonight, he would already have bullets between their eyes. His years of being a sniper for the army makes him deadly with a gun. Some of the shots I've seen him make should be considered impossible. Under normal circumstances, my aim is also impeccable, but with my wife standing in the crosshairs, I can't bring myself to pull the trigger.

Tiernan, who should know to keep his mouth shut around me, interjects. "You're right. This is going to be over soon because you're going to move out of the fucking way and let us pass. If you don't, we'll be forced to make Rionach pay the price for your stupidity."

"The only stupid people here are—" Rionach's words are silenced when Bogdan shoves the barrel harder against her temple.

I don't miss the way she winces. The beast living within me rattles the bars of his cage.

"If you return her to me with a single bruise, I will take a play out of your book and skin you alive, Koslov." I pin him with a glare. "Before you, I was your daddy's student, and just like you, he taught me where to cut to induce the most pain. I will gladly demonstrate my skills on you."

Igor's son chuckles humorlessly. "He may have taught you, but we both know I've practiced more. I've perfected my skill. Made it into fucking art and if you don't get the fuck out of our way, I will carve her face until we're matching."

For the first time since I arrived, Rionach shows her fear. It's quick, barely a flash across her face, but I saw it and it only makes my wrath grow.

"Okay, we'll let you leave. You can take her," I tell the pair, the words tasting like ash on my tongue.

The way Rionach's face falls breaks my heart.

It's okay, baby.

"Bullshit!" Tiernan spits. "I don't believe you."

"Your partner just threatened to carve up my wife's face," I remind him. "We'll let you pass. No catch." To show them that I'm serious, I drop my gun to my side. My trigger finger all but screams at me to use it, but I refrain.

Koslov's free hand takes hold of Rionach and he tugs her so she's placed directly in front of him like a human shield. Tiernan's eyes nearly bug out of his head at this and like a scared child ducking behind his mother's legs, he maneuvers himself to stand partially behind Bogdan.

Acting like she doesn't have a pistol pressed to her skull, my wife dramatically rolls her eyes when she watches her brother do this. I'm almost positive her lips also mouth the word *"pussy"*.

Oh, how this woman was made for me.

I don't think she realizes it yet, but Rionach owns my heart.

"He's lying, he's not going to let—"

"Stop fucking talking," Bogdan snaps at the nervous Irishman. "We need to get the fuck out of here and your yapping isn't helping."

"You should listen to him," Rionach mumbles under her breath with a disgruntled sigh.

Bogdan grips her harder and yanks her closer to his chest. "You too. Both of you need to keep your mouths shut."

For every step they take toward the door behind us, we mirror them and take a step back. Allowing this to play out is testing my patience in a way I've never experienced before. It's painful. All I want to do is charge forward and return her to the shelter of my arms. And once I know she's safe, I want to force bullets down Bogdan's and Tiernan's throats.

When the fear she's fighting to keep at bay rears to the surface, I softly shake my head at her. "It's okay, princess. Just keep those pretty eyes on me." She does as she's told. "We'll be going home soon."

"Don't lie to her!" Tiernan shouts, his face turning red in the flashing lights. "That isn't her home! It never was. Just like she was never yours!"

With my arms held causally behind my back, I take two steps forward and cock my head at them. "I didn't lie."

Because he never seems to learn, my wife's brother opens his mouth to spew more bullshit but he never gets the chance to speak them out loud.

While they were so focused on us standing in front of them, they kept their backs to their exit. Rionach was right. They are stupid. Trying to steal what is mine was their first mistake. Selecting a room with only one door was their second one and their downfall. While the bar is set about an inch off the ground, Koslov is the smarter of the two and their mistake dawns on him five seconds too late. He spins, taking Rionach with him at the same time Nova and his team cut them off at the door.

Tiernan is tackled to the ground while Bogdan struggles to keep my wife tucked against his body. He raises his gun to fire but at the same time, Nova launches himself at the entangled pair.

All three go crashing to the tiled floor and my world momentarily ends when the gun goes off.

I'm surrounded by chaos. The lights flash. The fire alarm blares. More of my armed men rush into the room. And yet, everything is deathly quiet and still inside of me. My eardrums can't register any noise and my eyes refuse to see anything but the place where she disappeared between two bodies. Nobody moves.

My knees suddenly weak, I stumble forward two steps. I think I say her name, but I can't be sure.

Please be okay.

I force myself to take more steps toward her, and this time when I open my mouth, I know I manage to really get her name out because my roar echoes through me as everything snaps back into focus. The world around me speeds up and returns to its normal pace.

"Rionach!"

I reach them just as Nova pulls himself up from where he was partially concealing my wife's body. Barely able to give my friend more than a passing glance until I know if Rionach is injured, I take her in my arms and lift her bridal style off the unconscious Russian's body.

For the first time since the gunshot went off, my heart beats in my chest as her shaky arms circle my neck and she pulls herself tight against me. The only sound she makes is her labored breathing.

"Talk to me, baby," I urge into her hair when I drop my head against hers and inhale her. "Are you okay? Does anything hurt?"

She shakes her head in answer.

I gently try to urge her to loosen her grip on my neck so I can see her face, but she refuses.

"Rionach," I murmur. "Let me look at you. I need to see that you're okay with my own eyes. *Please*."

The please must be what finally does it because her arms relax their hold on my neck just enough that I can finally see her face and chest. My heart goes back to malfunctioning when I find her pale skin streaked with crimson. Unceremoniously, I place her back on her unsteady feet in front of me so I can trail both of my hands over her body. I search for the source of the blood but can't find anything.

"It's not mine," she finally speaks. "I didn't get shot."

My eyes shoot to her slightly dazed ones. "Then who—"

"Don't worry, E, it was just a through and through," Nova announces behind me.

Turning, I find my second-in-command holding his right hand over a gunshot wound in his upper left shoulder. He's a little pale but doesn't look to be hovering anywhere near death's door. Thank fucking God.

"Nova, if you wanted matching gunshot scars, you could have just asked," I deadpan. With my arm securely around my wife, I move us closer to him. "You didn't have to go through the theatrics of letting a Russian shoot you."

He barks out a laugh and accepts my offered hand with his free one. He winces when I squeeze his hand in mine but returns the favor. I'll tell him soon how thankful I am to him for taking a bullet for my wife when I can find the right words. Until then, he knows what I'm trying to say now.

"He's out cold," Yates, who's squatted beside Koslov, tells us. "It looks like Nova's big-ass body colliding with his made the back of his head smack the ground. He's breathing, so I'm guessing he's just got a wicked concussion."

"I can confirm that Nova's body packs one hell of a punch," Rionach chimes in, her voice sounding clearer now that the adrenaline-induced fog is lifting. "I think I need a chiropractor to put my bones back where they belong."

Nova's face blanches further, but not from pain. "I'm so sorry, darlin'."

Darlin'? We'll be talking about that nickname later when he doesn't have a gunshot wound gushing blood. I grant him that time to recover, but once Doc puts stitches in there, we'll be having words.

My wife waves him off. "I'd rather have a sore spine than..." She points at where his dark gray T-Shirt is turning crimson. "*That*, and I'm pretty sure you just saved my life. So, please don't apologize, big guy."

Near the door, Mathis is helping the guard who tackled Rionach's brother restrain him. Due to the missing appendage on his right arm, handcuffs are out of the question. Another guard joins Yates at Koslov's side.

"We need to get moving," I tell everyone. "The authorities are going to show up here any minute. Yates and Mattis, take these cocksuckers to the cabin. I want them strung up and waiting for me in the basement."

"The van is parked in the alley." Nova digs in his pockets and tosses the keys to Yates. "I'll meet you there once I'm stitched up."

The men nod at both of us before carting the stars of this shitshow out the door.

"I need someone to get Camden." Nova's head whips in my direction when I say this. "We can't leave him here for the cops to find. Take him to Doc's office. We'll notify his family tomorrow."

Nova's face goes from murderous to sorrow and back to murderous in the span of a single heartbeat. My second-in-command is the one who picks who will join the team and then spends months training them. He knew Camden better than any of us. Stiffly, he nods his head in agreement before exiting the room.

Scooping Rionach in my arms, I follow him out. "Come on, princess. Let's get you home."

She drops her head on my shoulder with an exhausted sigh. "I told you I didn't want to come tonight."

My chest tightens at this, guilt clawing at my insides. "I know."

THIRTY-FOUR
EMERIC

"I'M SORRY ABOUT YOUR TATTOO." Rionach's voice comes from the doorway of the spare bedroom where Nova is currently being tended to by the doc. "You're going to have a scar through it now."

My friend doesn't so much as wince or flinch when the good doctor threads another stitch through his skin. As always, he elected to not receive any kind of anesthetic while his bullet wound is being repaired. If I didn't know better, I would say my friend likes pain, but since I do know better, I know for a fact he has an interesting relationship with pain. Hence the reason he's covered chin to toe with tattoos.

"It's all good," Nova assures her, lifting his attention away from his damn iPad for just a moment so he can offer her a quick smile. Only Nova would continue working while he's receiving medical attention. "It's not my first scar and it certainly won't be my last. Especially while I'm employed by this one right here." His chin tilts in my direction.

Only offering him a bland look, I push away from the wall

347

I've been leaning on while I observe the doc work and move to stand before my wife. "I thought I told you to go to bed."

Green eyes, that still reflect a sliver of the distress she endured earlier, roll at me. "And then I told myself I'm not a toddler and my husband doesn't get to dictate my bedtime. If *you're* tired, I will be more than happy to tuck you into bed, though."

She crosses her arms defiantly in front of her. When we got home, she changed into a tank top and a pair of cotton shorts. The bruises that have started to darken are fully on display to me. I fixate on them and as I do, the dark cloud of fury that had started to lift returns. It blankets over my shoulders like a heavy cloak.

She told me on the drive home what Koslov and Tiernan had planned for her. Learning they'd given her the option of leaving with them now or being punished if she waited until they came for her after they succeeded in eliminating me had me almost ordering the driver to follow the van with the twin idiots in it. I have a plan for what their next three days will look like, but I was more than willing to deviate from the schedule if it meant I could spill their blood right then and there. It was Rionach talking me down that had me returning home with her.

Noticing where my attention has drifted, Rionach's palms shift over the marks decorating both her upper arms. "I'm fine. They're just bruises. In a couple days, they'll fade. No biggie. *Nova* is the one who had a bullet go through his shoulder."

I capture her chin in my hand and bend so my forehead is nearly pressed against hers. "*No biggie?*" The two repeated words come out as a menacing grumble. Using my larger body to crowd her, I back Rionach up into the hallway until her back touches the white wall across from Nova's recovery room. "Fine. If you're going to elect to act so cavalier about your well-being, I'll just have to be concerned enough for the both of us. Tonight, two men had their hands all over you and one of them had a goddamn gun pressed to your skull as he tried to take you from me. In my book, I would consider that to be a *very* big deal. I don't take threats made against my realm lightly, but to have threats made against your life? *My wife's life?* I won't accept it." Like a living entity taking shape inside of me, the venomous combination of fear and anger gains control over me. "They've been calling me a monster for years. They have no fucking idea what kind of monster I can really be, but if your life is ever put in danger again like it was tonight, they will be forced to learn the deadliest lesson of their lives. I will show them what happens when my wife is hurt. I don't care if it's *just a bruise* or a paper cut, no one causes you harm and gets to live." My hand tightens its hold on her face to make sure she's truly paying attention to what I'm saying. "Do you understand me, Rionach? No one."

She doesn't balk or tremble at the venom lacing my words. Rionach simply removes my hand from her jaw and holds it between her two smaller ones. It's then I realize I'm the one trembling. My hand quivers in her firm, calming grasp. Eyes locked with mine, she brings our joined hands to her mouth where she then presses her lips to my knuckles.

"You're not a monster," my wife whispers. "Monsters don't care about the health and safety of others. There's a difference between being a monster and being willing to do monstrous things to defend the ones you care about. That makes you a protector, Emeric, and at your core, that is what you are. I can see that now. I know who you are."

I know what kind of man you will become, my son, and I know you and your brothers will make me proud. It's been decades since my mother's voice has played in my head. The chill running down my spine that accompanies it feels akin to being visited by a ghost.

"I'm not a good man," I tell my wife and the memory of my mother.

Rionach removes one of her hands from mine so she can place her palm over my erratically pounding heart. "But you're a good man to me and that's all that matters. Every jagged and bloodstained piece makes you who you are, and I wouldn't change a single thing because I've grown fond of those flawed pieces."

The magnitude of what's just happened isn't lost on me. The girl who's been waiting her entire life to be accepted by someone has switched our roles and is now standing before me declaring her acceptance of me and my flaws.

"You have?"

She nods. "Yeah. We... *fit* together like a really fucked-up puzzle, but I think you figured that out before I did."

If there was ever a better time to tell her about the night I found her on the roof, it would be now. She said we're a puzzle and telling her this bit of information will give her the corner piece she's been missing. Without it, she can't see the full picture that paints who we are together.

My name being called from the bedroom cuts off the words that were sitting heavy on my tongue.

"Hey, Banes," Nova's starts. "You're going to want to see this. They got the boys strung up in the basement."

Rionach's face pinches. "Is he talking about Bogdan and my brother?" Hand still captured in hers, she walks us back into the bedroom where the good doctor is just about finished with his handiwork and Nova's unaffected attention is still locked on the screen in his lap. "What do you mean strung up?"

Nova raises a brow at me in silent question. *Do you want her to see this?*

I incline my chin. Rionach's a permanent fixture in my life now and it's important she gets familiarized with what comes with that. A large portion of my schedule revolves around sitting through boring-as-hell board meetings for Banes Corporation and attending events like tonight's to ensure my interests are being protected. It's no secret the other half of my time is spent in the depths of depravity, and that's the half I much prefer.

Rionach doesn't make a sound of surprise or worry when Nova turns the screen. She stands there, silently accessing what's being done to her brother and the fiancé she didn't know she had. When she finally does speak, she only grumbles, "I could have gone my entire life without seeing my brother naked. Thanks so much for the warning."

Nova laughs so hard, he has the doc jumping in place. He mumbles a quick apology before fixing my wife with a perceptive stare. "That's all you have to say?"

Her shoulders casually rise and fall. "What would you like me to say? They're just naked and hanging from the ceiling by their wrists. Or *wrist* in Tiernan's case. They look like human piñatas." They're not suspended completely off the ground. Their bare toes are still able to touch the concrete floor. Rionach leans in closer to the screen before glancing at me. "Is this at the cabin? When you said basement, I thought you were talking about the club. Why didn't you take them there? It's a lot closer." It takes her a long moment of examining the serious expression on my face before it finally clicks for her. "Oh, right... The cabin is where you bring people when you want to stretch out their pain and punishment."

I don't miss the way Nova's arctic-hued gaze cuts to mine in astonishment. "You told her?"

Rionach answers for me.

"I'm his wife," is all she offers as explanation, but that's all she has to say for him to understand. She's my wife and I vowed I would answer every question of hers as long as the knowledge wouldn't jeopardize her. Making Rionach an accomplice in our illegal activity isn't on my to-do list. She may not be innocent at heart, but she will remain that way in the eyes of the law. "What's the plan? What are you going to do to them?"

"The cellar they're in is temperature-controlled. I used to store my imported wines and expensive bottles of alcohol in there before I decided the room would be better utilized if I stored cocksuckers like Bogdan and Tiernan in it. We've dropped the temp in the room to the lowest possible setting. They'll shiver and shake so violently they will think their exposed dicks are going to freeze off. It's *just* warm enough to prevent anyone from actually developing hypothermia." I tap the screen where a black box is mounted in the upper corner of the room. "There are speakers in every corner. All four are turned on to max volume and the most annoying songs you can think of are playing on repeat. This will prevent them from sleeping. For the next seventy-two hours, they are going to hang there without food, water, clothes, sleep, or heat. It will be—"

"Torture."

"Yes." *And they've only got themselves to blame.*

She looks away from the live footage streaming on Nova's iPad. "What happens after seventy-two hours?"

Rionach says I'm not a monster, but when the visual of my blade slicing across their skin—repeatedly—fills my mind, the bloodthirsty beast that resides in my soul purrs with anticipation. "That's when I'll go visit and teach them that lesson I was telling you about a moment ago," I tell her honestly. "I know Tiernan is your blood—"

She raises her hand and silently cuts me off.

"Our shared blood didn't matter to my family when they

352

willingly sold me off to Bogdan Koslov. Our shared blood didn't matter for all those years I silently begged them to look at me and see me as a person. As a member of their family. And our shared blood certainly didn't matter to Tiernan when he assisted in trying to kidnap me and allowed someone to hold a loaded gun to my temple." The sliver of fear that was lingering in her eyes has morphed into molten rage.

"You're right." Pride swells in my chest as I swipe my thumb across her cheekbone where her skin has turned flushed.

"I'm a Banes now. I don't owe him anything." She may say this quietly, but the intensity in which she declares this isn't lost on me. "And the world will be better without Bogdan Koslov roaming freely in it. I won't lose any sleep over his death."

"Amen," Nova murmurs under his breath.

She looks at Nova. "They're also the reason Camden is dead. He didn't deserve that."

Tomorrow I'm going to have to personally call his mother to inform her that her son died. Along with paying for his funeral, I'll also pay her three years of Camden's salary. Doing that won't bring back the life that she lost, but it's all I have to offer. Well, that and the promise that her son's killers will be brought to justice. That is if what I plan to do even counts as "justice".

With the front of his shoulder stitched up, Nova shifts on the bed so the doctor can begin working on the exit wound on his back. For the first time since he stepped in this room, I see him wince in pain. Thank fuck. I was starting to worry that the not-so-Jolly Green Giant was a robot.

"I still don't get it," he mumbles so lowly I think he's talking to himself until he turns his head to meet my eyes. "Camden was good. I trained him myself. The building was full of witnesses, and he knew what both of those fuckers looked like. He would have been on the lookout for them. How did Koslov and a one-handed Moran manage to get the jump on him and snap his neck?"

The same thought has already crossed my mind.

Both our heads snap in my wife's direction when she shifts on her feet and says, "I've been wondering this too."

"You have?" Nova's astonished look sets my teeth on edge.

The glare that settles on Rionach's face could turn someone into a pillar of salt and I love to see it. "I know women in our world are typically just nice lawn ornaments for men to look at, and they're kept around because they fall to their knees and suck cock like their lives are on the line." For the first time tonight, the good doctor's attention is pulled away from his task. Behind the small glasses that sit on the tip of his old, crooked nose, he gapes at my wife. "But I actually have a brain. A brain that I occasionally like to use. So, if you could wipe that look off your face, Viking, I'd appreciate it."

Nova's expression only turns more confused as he openly gapes at my bride.

"What now?" she snaps.

"How did you do it?" he asks.

"Do *what*?"

"Pretend to be someone you're not for so long? How did your family miss... *this*?"

They didn't miss it. They simply chose to ignore it, just like they did with everything else that has to do with her.

Rionach visibly relaxes next to me. "I'd stand on the edge of rooftops until I felt like me again and then I'd shove it all back down. Rinse and repeat as needed." Nova already knows about her proclivity for rooftops, but I don't think either of us were expecting her to admit it so openly to him. I'm proud of her for doing so. It means she's learning how to freely and unapologetically be herself. She's owning it. "But whatever, back to Camden. I think there's more to what happened to him. Maybe there was a third guy there tonight no one saw? Regardless, you should look into that."

I cock an eyebrow. "Did you just tell me what to do?"

"Sure as shit did." Her grin drips with fake sweetness. "Anyway, I'm going to go take a shower. I need to wash the smell of the Russian's cologne out of my hair."

I have to remind myself again that three days of systematic punishment before I slowly and artistically end his life is what Bogdan has earned because the knowledge that my wife currently smells of him has me chomping at the bit to get it over with now.

"I'll join you once the doc is done putting Humpty Dumpty back together again."

Before I release the hand that's been wrapped up in mine since we entered the spare bedroom, I tilt her chin up and press my lips to hers in a fleeting kiss. I do the same to her temple next and I have to fight back a growl when the faint scent of Koslov's cologne tickles my nostrils.

She nods, her bottom lip between her white teeth. "Okay, try not to stay up too late. You need to sleep."

If anyone else had said this to me, I would have taken it as condescending as hell and ripped their head off because of it. Instead, her concern has my black heart tightening in a way only she can cause.

"I won't be long."

"Good." She backs away toward the open door. "You know I struggle to fall asleep without you these days."

Being dependent on someone is something that would have scared the ever-loving shit out of me twenty years ago. The very idea of it would have made my skin crawl and my balls shrivel into raisins. It went against my very nature to need someone like that.

But with Rionach, I couldn't give a single fuck and I know

I'm no longer alone in this thinking because we need each other now.

"I know, princess."

She smiles at me and then waves at Nova. "Thank you for saving my life tonight, Viking."

"Anytime, darlin'," he calls after her.

I wait until her footsteps move down the hallway before my hand slaps against the back of Nova's shaved and tattooed head. "Call my wife darlin' one more time. I dare you."

He laughs so hard the white-haired curmudgeon of a doctor at his side grumbles in irritation.

"She cares about you," Nova observes, a soft grin lifting his lips.

I turn my head toward the door she'd just escaped through. "Yeah, I think she does." As I say this, echoes of the panic and fear when I couldn't find her earlier tonight slither through me.

When this business with her family and the Russians is finally put to bed, I will no longer be her only source of protection. I will have to finally build her a team that I can trust her with. Though, tonight's events don't make the thought of doing that an easy one to swallow. It's impractical and unfair to her to think I can always keep her in my sights. There will be times when she's away from me living the life I promised her I'd provide her. For my own sanity, I need to find a way to ensure I always know where she is. "Hey, Doc. When you're done with this, there's something I want to talk to you about."

The doctor glances at me over the wire frame of his glasses. "Okay."

I snap my fingers when Rionach's comment from earlier tonight comes back to me. With all the chaos that ensued tonight, I nearly forgot how our evening started. "Oh, there's something else I need you to do. I need you to look deeper into my wife's medical records."

He frowns at this. "I believe I had my people already deliver that information to Nova months ago."

"You did, but I don't think you found everything." I ignore the confused look on my second-in-command's face. "I'm pretty sure my sneaky bride is hiding something from me."

Something that will put a big kink in my plans if my suspicions are true.

THIRTY-FIVE
EMERIC

I TRIED to be home tonight before she fell asleep, but I couldn't get away from dealing with the mess at the Red Hook shipping port in Brooklyn. Some brave souls at the port authority decided it would be wise to investigate the containers I had delivered from Bolivia earlier this week. Needless to say, those brave souls lost their lives and have joined the other corpses floating along the bottom of the Hudson River.

I've been operating at the port for nearly a decade and haven't had an issue like this in years. My ongoing deal with the director of New York's port authority is supposed to ensure that I don't have to deal with bullshit like this. The director's face when he realized a handful of his men had stuck their noses where it doesn't belong would have been comical if I wasn't standing in front of one of my shipping containers with so many of the hidden bags of cocaine cut open it looked like it fucking snowed in there.

Nova and I were both at a loss for what their endgames were. It would have been really ill-advised since I have my own security planted in the container yard and cameras posted

359

nearly everywhere for them to try and steal from me. All four port employees had been searched when they were caught by my men and none of them had pilfered a single gram of the drugs. From the looks of it, all they'd succeeded in doing is destroying my property.

When pressed about what they were doing there, they stayed strong and didn't break. Their unwavering resolve was inspiring but bothersome. With more than a day and a half left before I can take out my ever-growing wrath on Tiernan and Bogdan, the vandalizers took the brunt of my pent-up energy.

When I'd left Nova and his guys with the mess to clean up, my right hand was just as stumped as I was about what we were dealing with.

Two things we could agree on was, this wasn't done at random or without reason. Someone is attempting to play a game with me, and I can't begin to accurately describe what an epic mistake this will end up being on their part. We also agreed we needed to double our surveillance on Koslov and Moran Senior. By now, they know I have their sons in my custody and if they're smart, they know I have no plans on returning them. *Yet.* Once I'm done breaking and bloodying my new toys, I will gladly deliver them back to their rightful homes. And once that happens, I'll transfer my attention to dealing with the pissed and grieving fathers.

I'll be able to breathe better once I know the threat against me, and subsequently Rionach, is eliminated. My reasons for not doing so are still valid to this day, but it would have been so much better for everyone had I put a bullet in their heads at the church. That way, Moran wouldn't have crawled to the Koslovs to help him exact his revenge. Niall is still so blinded by emotions that he's forgetting that this is all entirely Tiernan's and his fault. The victim mentality has grown incredibly old. I gave him a second chance that night at the pub to put an end to this, but he refused.

I arrived at the penthouse feeling wired and volatile, but when I entered our bedroom and found her wrapped around my pillow sound asleep, the turbulence humming beneath my skin quieted.

Her sleeping form calls to me to touch her, but all I allow myself is a brief kiss pressed to her soft lips. I can't put my hands on her yet. Not when they still have the dried blood of four dead men still caked on them. Yanking off my blood-stained clothes, I enter the bathroom and make quick work of washing the depravity from my body. I stay under the spray of the showerhead until the water swirling around the drain runs clear. The symbolism of my sins being washed away might hit me harder if I were truly done committing them for the night.

No, there's still something I need to take care of before the sun rises. Had I been home on time, it would already be taken care of by now.

With my towel wrapped around my waist and the item I'd asked Nova for in my hand, I return to my slumbering wife. Her pretty face scrunches in a way that is almost childlike when the weight of my body makes the mattress dip.

"Shh, baby," I sooth while carefully brushing a ribbon of hair off her closed eye. The way her nose twitches when the strands brush against her nostril has a small smile forming on my face. Just being around her—conscious or not—puts me at ease like nothing else ever has been able to. "I'm here."

Drawn to my voice even in her sleep, her body presses closer to mine. Pulling the towel from my body, I discard it on the floor, and I shift into bed behind her. Wrapping my body around her smaller one is like coming up for air after being trapped underwater. It revives and relaxes me at the same time.

Pressing my mouth to her shoulder and then to the side of

her face, she makes a contented sound in her sleep and shifts in my embrace.

"I've got you." The cap of the syringe I'd brought to bed with me silently falls to the silk sheets between us. I run the back of my hand gently over the roundness of her ass nestled against me and push up the lacy nightie she wears. At the same time I stick the needle into the muscle there, I whisper reassuringly in her ear, "Just sleep, princess."

She stirs again at the sharp bite of pain, but the sedative Nova usually has to use on me is fast acting. In less than a minute, Rionach is dead to the world, and she'll stay that way for a couple more hours.

That gives me plenty of time to execute my plan.

As if on cue, the good doctor knocks on my bedroom door. "Mr. Banes?"

THIRTY-SIX
RIONACH

"HEY!" I charge into the kitchen where Anneli and Mathis are talking by the massive marble island. In synchronized movements, both of their spines snap straight and their heads whip in my direction. They must have been in a really deep conversation because based on their matching wide-eyed stares, it appears I scared the crap out of both of them. "Why is that guy —Yates or whatever his name is—putting Cerberus in a travel crate?"

Anneli, looking as model-esque as ever in her dark blue outfit and gold jewelry, steps away from Emeric's man and goes back to whatever she's cooking on the stove.

Mathis rubs the back of his neck as he comes around the kitchen island. He's dressed in the black tactical cargo pants and formfitting pullover that all Emeric's security wear. The only time I've seen him out of this uniform was two nights ago at Holloway's event. Mathis is probably in his forties, and the way he holds himself and wears his dark hair screams *military*.

"There was an incident last night at one of the shipping ports we use. I suggested we bring the dog in to help our team there guard the shipments the boss keeps in the container yard."

"You suggested it?" I cross my arms and pin the man standing before me with a glare.

He at least has the decency to appear uneasy as he nods his head. "That's what we've always done before when we've run into issues like this."

"Did Emeric sign off on this?"

"Yes?" he answers. "This is what the dog is trained to do, after all."

"*No,*" I snap at him and once again catch him off guard. "He's not going. Get my dog out of that fucking cage."

His eyes nearly bug out of his skull. "The boss—"

Already spinning away on the balls of my slipper-covered feet, I cut him off, "I don't care what the boss said." I storm down the hallway in the direction of Emeric's office. He's been working in there most of the morning. "Cerberus is staying here."

Never could I imagine talking to one of Brayden's guys like this. It feels good. They would have gone running to him or Mom so fast if I'd quote, unquote, "disrespected" them like this. My relationship with Brayden was never like that. I never had to walk on eggshells around him. He was the one person on my father's staff I could actually talk to.

"*Ma'am...*"

"Don't call me ma'am! I'm, like, twenty years younger than you," I shout back over my shoulder.

I woke up this morning feeling like shit. The second and third days of my cycle always hit me the hardest, but the cramps I've had all morning have me wanting to crawl into the fetal position at the bottom of the shower. My head has also been pounding. The over-the-counter pain medication I took over two hours ago hasn't done jack shit in helping relieve either ailment.

It is not my morning. I don't feel well, I'm hormonal, and now they're trying to take my damn dog?

Hell no.

I don't bother knocking when I reach the closed office door. Pushing inside, I find Emeric standing before the floor-to-ceiling windows behind his massive dark wood desk. His phone is pressed to his ear, but before I have a chance to close the door, he ends the call with whoever he's talking to.

"Rionach just walked in," he tells them, attentive eyes raking over me from head to toe in slow passes as he does. "I have to go. Call Nova if you have any issues."

I step behind one of the modern chairs placed in front of the desk and place my hands on the leather back of it. "You didn't have to hang up. I could have waited."

"You're my wife. You don't wait. If you want my attention, it's all yours." How long have I waited for someone to tell me that? Warmth washes over my body and momentarily eases the dull cramping in my lower abdomen. Stormy eyes zero in on my face and a frown pulls on his mouth. "You aren't feeling well, are you, love?"

I ignore his question and focus my energy on the reason I came in here in the first place. "Yates put Cerberus in a crate and is planning on taking him to the docks or somewhere."

It's obvious he wasn't expecting my reasoning for coming in here to be this.

"I'm aware."

"Well, that's not happening," I huff. "He's staying here."

Emeric's eyebrows nearly crash into his hairline. "Is that so?"

"Yes. Now go tell your goons to let my dog out of that crate."

"*Your dog*?" This time a smile joins his quizzical expression.

"Stop responding to me with questions, Banes!" I growl.

He presses his palms into the shiny surface of his desk and leans his weight forward. "Cerberus was trained to do tasks like this. It's his job."

My chin lifts and my arms clamp around my middle when my uterus twinges again. *Goddammit.* "Well, I only want his job to be guarding us from now on. Here. At home. Go find another dog, because this one is staying here with me."

My husband chuckles at this. "It doesn't work that way. I can't just go find another dog and have him trained with a snap of my fingers."

"You have hundreds of millions of dollars. Go buy one. Hell, I'm pretty sure I can find the spare change needed to get you a brand-new fully trained scary guard dog in your fancy couch cushions alone." When he just stands there staring at me like I'm speaking another language, I sigh and admit, "Okay, so clearly, I've gotten a little attached and the idea of him being sent away is breaking my heart. What if he gets hurt? Please just let him stay here."

Emeric regards me for a long moment before his head tilts. "Okay, he can stay."

"He can?"

His grin reappears as he rounds the desk to stand at my back. His arms engulf my upper body, and he pulls me back against his warm, safe chest. "I don't think you realize how wrapped around your finger you have me, princess."

Biting my lip to keep my own smile at bay, I softly say, "Thank you."

I lose my battle when he presses his lips to the top of my head.

"If it's within my capabilities to do so, I will always give you what you want." Taking hold of the fabric of my oversized hoodie, he forces me to turn around so he can see my face. With how icky I feel, I didn't bother putting on real clothes today. Or makeup. Stretchy leggings and this hoodie were the best I was going to do. "You don't feel well." This time it's not a question. "How can I help?"

I sigh and shake off his concern. "It's fine. I'm just thriving in the joys of being born with a uterus."

Something flutters in my chest when he slides his palm over my abdomen and rests it over my lower stomach. The act isn't the slightest bit provocative, and yet, it's intimate in a way I haven't felt between us before. Our conversation from the other night where he admitted to wanting to put his baby in me hasn't been far from my mind since, but with his hand placed where it is, his words surge to the forefront of my thoughts. *It's going to happen one day, princess. Sooner or later, my seed will take root in your womb, and you will bring our baby into this world.*

Delicate shudders racking over the entirety of my body have him examining me closer. "Are you okay?" His free hand slides up my spine to collar the back of my neck. Another wave of goosebumps erupts across my skin.

"Yeah, I told you I'm fine," I assure him again, mouth feeling suddenly dry. "Just crampy but that's not anything new. I think I'm going to ask Anneli where a heating pad is and maybe go hang out in the theater room for a bit. I know you're working, so I should probably stop distract—Emeric!" My arms loop around his neck out of pure instinct when he suddenly scoops me off the ground and into his arms. "What are you doing?"

"We can do better than a heating pad."

———

I RELAX further into the scalding water of the bathtub and into his chest. When he brought me into our bathroom and started to fill the deep soaker tub up with water, I didn't think he'd be joining me in it. Not that I'm complaining. It wasn't until he slid his strong and very naked body in behind me that I began to consider myself a bathtub person. Until that moment, I had been strictly a shower person. Chilling in my own bathwater never appealed to me, but if Emeric plans on making this a regular thing, I think I can get on board with it.

He was also right about this being better than a heating pad. Sitting between his legs with my knees pulled up toward my chest, I'm starting to feel better already.

Collecting some of the bubbles that surround us with my hand, I say, "You didn't have to do this. I know you have work that needs to be done, and I'm sure your people are wondering where you've disappeared to." Men like Emeric Banes don't take time out of their schedules to take bubble baths, and yet, here we are.

He lazily drags a soapy washcloth from the nape of my exposed neck down to my light pink painted fingernails and then back up again. "There will always be work that needs my attention, just like there will always be people who need something from me." Dunking the cloth back into the hot water to warm it up, he repeats the process on my other arm. "But you and your needs will always come first. You don't feel well, and I want to help. That's what's important right now."

How can this be the same man who locked me in a cage, and chased me through the woods until he caught me and pinned my body to the ground?

People have no clue that this side of Emeric exists, and I want to fiercely protect it from their prying eyes and greedy hands. This version of him is for me and me alone.

"This is already helping," I tell him as I close my eyes and drop my head against his shoulder. "I'm starting to feel a little better."

"Only a little?" His breath tickles my earlobe and makes shivers dance down my spine. "I can make you feel a lot better." He idly drags the washcloth across my chest, grazing my nipples as he does. Tauntingly slow, his attention gradually drops lower beneath the line of bubbles and hot water. My abdomen muscles flutter when the soft fabric circles my navel before he once again goes lower. His free hand slides over the outside of my thigh until he reaches my bent knee. "Open for me, love," he instructs into my ear as his hand hooks around the back of my knee, and his gentle tugging encourages me to spread my thighs for him. "That's it. Just like that."

Between my legs, the washcloth drags over my bare pussy in barely-there grazes. Emeric repeats this act twice more. The third pass of the fabric is done with more purpose and with a firmer touch. Caught off guard by the sensation of the terry cloth dragging over my clit, I can't stop the sharp inhale of breath between my lips.

Something I learned the other night when Emeric sat me on the counter and put his mouth on me was that I'm a hell of a lot more sensitive when I'm on my period. My responsiveness had only spurred him on, and he devoured me until I was a weeping mess. The mortification I'd first felt when he dropped to his knees turned foggy as I succumbed to the gratification he forced out of me.

Emeric isn't remotely bothered by the fact that I'm bleeding, and I force myself to remember that when my shame creeps to the forefront of my brain. I feel better about it now since we're sitting in the bathtub than I do when we're outside of it. Something about knowing the water is washing away most of the crimson evidence puts my conflicted mind at ease.

When the washcloth is replaced by his palm and fingers, I choke on another moan.

"How's this?" His lips skim across the damp skin of my neck and shoulder. "Do you feel better with my fingers playing with your swollen clit?"

"Yes," I breathe.

"Good," he praises. "I hate seeing you in pain."

The water sloshes around us when my hips violently buck against his hand. Thick digits slide into my pussy and the heel of his palm applies pressure against my aching bundle of nerves. He works me at an unhurried pace, taking his time to caress the tips of his fingers against the hidden spot inside of me that makes my toes curl and my ability to think go by the wayside.

I grind in rhythm with his fingers as the ball of buzzing heat grows and expands in my core. He hums in approval when my arm lifts up and my fingers stroke the slightly longer hair that curls around the nape of his neck. I appreciate that he wears his hair long enough that I'm really able to sink my fingers into it, and I love when the black strands fall forward to frame his forehead and temples. The messy, boyish look when that happens humanizes him.

Head turned to him as far as the vertebrae in my neck will allow, I graze my lips along his stubbly jaw. "Kiss me." My request is nearly lost in the soft moan he solicits out from me. "Please."

Emeric doesn't have to be told twice. His mouth seals over mine and I nearly whimper with how good it feels. He's enacted all kinds of pleasure on me, but something about the simplicity of a kiss has my insides warming further. He licks along the seam of my lips, demanding entry, and I don't deprive him.

His tongue thrusts into my mouth in tandem with his

fingers in my pussy. Emeric doesn't let up once or doesn't allow me to pull away so I can catch my breath as it transitions into ragged pants against his mouth.

When the building ecstasy peaks and then implodes, the waves of pleasure rolling through me, he consumes the cry that spills from my throat.

My brain is still a malfunctioning, gooey mess when he tears his mouth away and pulls himself up from where he sits. He moves so quickly that the water sloshes over the sides of the tub. He doesn't seem concerned about the mess in the least as he lifts me up by under my arms with just as much vigor.

Not bothering to reach for a nearby towel, Emeric steps out of the tub and turns to grab me. With ease, he lifts me out and into his arms. With me wrapped around his naked torso like a damn koala, he carries our dripping wet bodies out of the bathroom and into the bedroom.

"Wait, what about the sheets—"

He places me on my back atop of the neatly made king-sized bed. "I don't give a fuck about the sheets," he all but growls as his hands wrap around my ankles and he yanks me until my ass it at the very edge of the mattress. Holding the place where the backs of my thighs meet my calves, he spreads me open for him by forcing my knees up toward my chest "All I care about is burying myself in you." Not seeming to want to waste any time, the thick crown of his dick prods at my entrance. "I want to watch your sweet-as-sin cunt swallow every inch of my fat cock."

One day, his words are going to make me contentiously combust into flames, and I already know I will relish in that fire.

Whatever retort is on my tongue is replaced by a heady moan when he pushes forward and stretches my muscles with the first addictive inch. Teasing me, he thrusts shallowly, but still refuses to feed me any more of his length. When I writhe and plead for more beneath him, he ignores me and placates me with gentle shushing sounds.

"Emeric..." I mewl, hands reaching for his sculpted and tanned chest. The only body hair he has is the neat strip from his navel down to the impressive part of him I'm currently desperate for. "Please—*ah!*"

In one fluid and strong movement, he pulls completely from my deprived pussy before he surges forward. The swift invasion has my back bowing and my muscles stretching to the point of delicious pain around him. He doesn't grant me time to adjust before he rears back again and drives forward with just as much force. With each deep punishing stroke, he picks up speed until he's pounding into me like a man starved.

I gladly and selfishly take everything Emeric gives me, and while he does, I unabashedly beg him for more. He complies, the pad of his finger pressing tight circles to my clit. I feel myself become more aroused—wetter—for him when he does.

Eyes alive with lightning collide with mine. "You take my cock so good, princess." I whimper in desperation when he steals his hand away from my clit, and his fingers drag downward to a place that's never been touched. I nearly fly off the bed when his thumb applies pressure against the tight ring of muscle there. "One day, I'm going to take your ass too and you're going to be such a good girl while I do. Just like your cunt and throat, I'm going to mark my claim here as well."

My favorite kind of fear floods my system with adrenaline at the thought of him fucking that forbidden place. Emeric was blessed in many ways, the size of his dick being one of them. There are days when he feels like too much for my pussy, I can't even begin to imagine the burning stretch of him entering my ass. The very thought terrifies me as much as it invigorates me.

The way his thumb is increasing pressure nearly has my eyes rolling back in my head. "I'm close," I pant my warning. "Oh fuck, I need to come."

The hand still holding my leg up presses the limb higher, which allows his thrusts to go deeper. Something I didn't know was possible. "Come on, love, let go. I want to feel you milk every drop from my cock."

Seconds later, I'm taken out by the violent force of my orgasm. My body shakes and quivers both under and around him. My muscles clamp down on his swelling length and hold tight until he follows my lead and delves over the edge of blissfulness.

My shouted name coming from his lips sends another wave of pleasure ricocheting through my nervous system. I don't think I've ever liked my name more than I do hearing it rip out of his throat.

He grips both of my hips, his fingers digging into the soft flesh there as he rides out the rest of his release. Emeric keeps going until he curses and the weight of his upper body collapses atop of me. Breathing heavily in my ear, he snakes his arms around me, and I do the same to him. We hold each other tight and get lost in our little cocoon. My fingers trail over where I know the dark wings are tattooed on his upper back.

His body turns into a piece of solid stone around mine when I graze the burn scar that the inked feathers conceal.

"Rionach..." My name is a low warning mumbled directly into my ear.

I turn my head so I can pepper the side of his face with soft, reassuring kisses. "It's okay." The pad of my finger traces the raised skin and the painful evidence of what happened to him as a child. "It's okay. He won't ever be able to hurt you again. Real or imagined, I'll make sure of it. I'll keep his ghost at bay."

His hold tightens around me, but he relaxes into my gentle

touch. I trace the lines of the Koslov family's crest and with each pass, I hope I'm healing some of the pain he's carried for over two decades. I'll never be able to erase the mark from his skin, but maybe I can help him heal from the memory this burn symbolizes.

We stay like this, entwined in each other, with Emeric's semi-hard dick still inside of me, until the water-soaked sheets below me turn cold and goosebumps start to erupt across my skin as I shiver from the change in temperature.

"Emeric," I whisper. "I'm cold. We need to get up so we can change the sheets. I don't know about you, but I don't want to sleep in damp sheets later tonight." And there's no way there isn't blood on them now too. Thank God they're black.

Trying to warm me, his big hands slide up and down my arms. "Do you feel better now?"

I take stock of my body. Just like the other night, a couple orgasms have seemed to have momentarily relieved the cramping in my lower stomach. "Yeah, I do."

Rising onto his forearms, he looks down at me and says, "Good," before pressing a chaste kiss to my lips. I gasp beneath my breath when he pulls himself free of my body and tendrils of pleasure trickle through me.

I'm about to follow suit and sit up, but his hand pressing to my lower stomach stops me. Confused by what he wants, I look down my body at Emeric and find his gaze fixated on my no doubt swollen pussy.

Self-consciously, I attempt to bring my knees together, but his other hand stops me.

"I'm sorry, we both have blood on us now." My cheeks turn hot when I say this. "We probably need to shower..." I trail off when his fingers swipe through my overly sensitive pussy lips. "What are—"

"Watching my cum drip out of you is like viewing an

exquisite piece of art, but I think I like the idea of it being stuffed inside of you more." Fingers coated in a mixture of our releases and blood slip into my slightly tender channel. He gathers more of his spilled cum and pushes it inside of me. "We can't let a single drop go to waste."

My body feels hot—too hot—when I realize what he's doing. With his hand gone from my stomach, I manage to pull myself up into a sitting position. "Are you still trying to get me pregnant?"

He doesn't answer me. Instead, his turbulent storm-like gaze locks with mine as he brings the two fingers he'd just had inside of me up to his mouth. Such conflicting emotions rage in my body when he wraps his lips around the digits. In my head, I'm horrified. Up until a second ago, my pussy was spent, but now it's waking back up and a dull throb drums between my thighs. The throbbing only intensifies when that smirk of his grows on his handsome-as-hell face.

My mouth gapes open at the same time Emeric captures my face between his two hands. I can't be sure if I'm frozen in place because I'm so utterly surprised by what he's just done, or if I'm too morbidly curious about what comes next to pull away from him when he tilts my head back and brings our faces close together.

All I can manage to do as he spits the combination of our cum and my blood between my lips is take a shallow breath. The sinister look of approval shining back at me when I swallow down what he's offered me nearly has me falling to my knees for him.

"We taste good together, princess," he murmurs before sealing his lips over mine. We lick and sip from each other's mouths until we're both breathless. With my face still held between his hands, he breaks away and presses his forehead to mine. "To answer your earlier question, yes, I am."

My foggy brain needs a minute to understand what he's saying. He's trying to get me pregnant. In the past, I viewed being knocked up as another way my future husband was going to use me for his gain. That thought always turned my stomach and broke my heart a little bit. It turned me off the very idea of having children because I knew with what my future looked like, I didn't wish to subject my babies to that. They didn't deserve that life, just like I didn't.

My feelings toward the whole situation have been shifting since Emeric brought it up two nights ago. It's been heavy on my mind, and it has awoken a need in me I'm finding hard to ignore. It's a need I never thought I was going to have, but I still don't know if I can knowingly bring a child into this world. Even if it's half of the man I've fallen hard for.

Swallowing down a steadying breath, I tell my husband, "You can keep trying, but you're going to have a very hard time achieving that goal."

Dark brows pull together. "And why's that?"

I struggle to meet his gaze. "I have an IUD…"

My spine stiffens and my muscles lock in place as I brace for his reaction. In my parents' eyes, I was put on this earth for one reason only. To get married and birth the next generation of our bloodline. If they knew I had elected to prevent my body from doing the one thing it was destined to do, I would be feeling my mother's palm against my cheek for the second time in my life.

Emeric has admitted he's actively been trying to put his baby in me and unbeknownst to him, I've been sabotaging those advances. For all I know, he's going to be just as upset as my parents would be.

"Do you?" His head tilts and I can't decipher the emotion that's settled in his gaze as he leisurely examines me. A long, drawn-out sigh escapes between his lips and he backs a step away.

I nod. "I do."

Without a word, he turns his back to me, and I feel my heart squeeze in my chest. *Oh, this is bad.* He doesn't say anything else as he opens the bedside drawer on his side of the bed. There's about a hundred possibilities for what he could be grabbing from inside there, and I would wager it's something to punish me with for inadvertently deceiving him. The chances of it being something like that are so high, it's basically guaranteed.

His fingers close around the object before I can get a good look at what it is. Returning to stand before me, he motions for me to give him my hand. Reluctantly and with shaky movements, I do as I'm told.

Emeric places a glass specimen jar with a blue lid in the middle of my offered palm. I'm beyond confused what he's showing me until I do a double take at the object inside the glass jar. The reality of what is happening slams into me like a hurricane and with it comes every emotion under the sun. They twist and turn, wreaking havoc on my insides while all I can do is stare at what he's handed me.

"You *had* an IUD," he explains to me with a casualness that makes my head spin. He sounds like he's telling someone what the weather forecast will be for the next forty-eight hours, and not *this*. "As of last night, you are no longer on any form of birth control."

The container starts to shake in my hand as a mixture of hurt and betrayal crawls up my throat like a venomous spider.

"Are you keeping secrets from me, dear wife?" That's what he said two nights ago. Is that when he figured it out?

"H... how?" I don't like how weak my voice sounds to my own ears. "What did you do?"

"You were smart going to the free clinic on the other side of town. It took us a minute to find the record of your doctor's appointment. Which, I suppose, is a good thing because I can't imagine your family would have been supportive had they found out."

The way he's being so cavalier about what he's done only makes my anger boil harder. "When did you... You took it out last night?" It makes sense now why I woke up feeling like I did. The cramping that happens after getting an IUD removed is similar to how you feel when it's first inserted. I just thought it was my cycle. And the headache that was pounding in my skull... "Did you drug me?"

He inclines his head. "I heard how it could be uncomfortable to have them placed and removed, and I didn't want you to feel any pain."

"Don't!" I fly off the bed and my free hand shoves at the center of his chest. He stumbles back half a step and that's how I know I surprised him. Good. "Don't you dare make it sound like you did me a *favor*. Can you even hear yourself right now? You made a decision about my body and then sedated me so you could do what you wanted. You basically drugged me and then operated on me! Do you know how incredibly violating that is?"

"The doctor didn't see anything; I wouldn't let him that close to you. He talked me through how to safely remove it."

This does make me feel marginally better, but just barely.

I glare at him and move back a couple feet so I can pace at the end of the bed. I'm struggling to reconcile all the things I'm feeling right now.

"Am I supposed to thank you for not allowing another man to see my cervix?" My fury begins to boil over and without thinking it through, I hurl the glass container at his head. He ducks at the very last minute and the jar ends up crashing into the wall many feet behind him. Glass explodes when it makes contact. Shards shower down on the hardwood floors. "How dare you," I choke out, my throat feeling tight.

Emeric returns to his full height and looks between me and the mess I just made. As if he's tired of my *theatrics*, he just sighs and takes a step toward me. I mirror him by taking a step back. Keeping distance between us right now is important to me. "I told you I wanted to have babies with you, and I warned you it was going to happen sooner or later. You having a secret IUD was preventing that from happening."

I throw my hands up in exasperation. "This isn't about me having babies with you, Emeric. This is about how you violated me and my body when you decided to remove my IUD without asking me first. I was already coming around to the idea of having your babies all on my own."

His gray eyes narrow and his jaw switches. "You were?"

It's my turn to sigh. Head tilted back and my arms crossed tightly in front of my still naked body, I take a moment to collect myself before I return my attention to my husband. "I need to take a shower." Between my thighs is sticky with blood and cum. When he makes a move toward the bathroom door, I throw my hand up. "*Alone*. I need to be alone."

"Why?"

This man can be so fucking frustrating.

"Because right now, I'm so pissed at you, I'm struggling to remember that I like you—that I *care* about you." The truth hurts him. I can see it in the way his eyes dim, and his arms fall to his sides. "I just need time to be alone so I can remember."

He doesn't stop me when I walk past him into the bathroom, and he doesn't follow.

———

EMERIC GIVES me twenty or so minutes alone before he pushes open the bathroom door. I think he was waiting for me to be done with my shower—a shower I spent a majority of the time just standing under the stream of water—before he came in. From the looks of it, he took a shower of his own in one of the other bathrooms and is now dressed in a pair of well-worn jeans that hang low on his hips. Wordlessly, he stands at the glass door of the massive walk-in shower with a fresh towel in his hand. Just as he'd done before, he wraps the warm, fluffy towel around my body the second I step foot outside.

Once the towel is secure around my chest, he grabs another one and carefully helps squeeze the water from my drenched waist-length strands.

My heart constricts at this gentle gesture because I know what he's doing. In his own way, he's trying to make amends for upsetting me.

Emeric Banes isn't the type of man who says things like *"I'm sorry"* or admits when he's wrong. It's not in his nature to do so. I told him last night I wouldn't ask him to change and that I've grown fond of all his jagged pieces, but that doesn't mean some pieces aren't easier to love than others.

I allow him to lead me to the vanity and I sit down on the stool in front of it when he silently instructs me to do so. Emeric pays attention to things I wouldn't think he'd notice, like my coffee order and my haircare routine. Without any assistance, he brushes out the knots in my hair from the shower before he applies each of the leave-in products I use before blow-drying. He shocks me further by gathering the strands and weaving them into a long braid down my back.

He breaks the silence first. "I'm not going to apologize."

"I know you're not."

In the mirror's reflection in front of us, I watch his head nod once.

Gnawing on my bottom lip, I watch him a moment longer before saying, "I got it when I turned eighteen."

"I know. I saw the date on the paperwork." He meets my gaze in the mirror. "What made you decide to get one in the first place? Mob princesses are usually kept on tight leashes and don't have a lot of opportunities to have sex."

The memories already starting to bubble up in the back of my mind make my stomach churn. "You're right, we don't. It was preached to me from an age that was far too young to be talking about things like sex and future marriages that I needed to remain pure for my husband. The older I got, the more resentful I became about the whole thing. I resented what my life was going to look like, and I hated that my virginity was just another thing used to determine my value. *My worth* as a human and a future bride to some random man."

Talking about this brings me back to being that angry teenager who felt trapped in a life she didn't want. I was still resonating with that girl up until recently. Now, I wish I could go back and tell her that we'd find our freedom in the least likely of places and she just needed to be patient.

"I knew I wasn't going to be able to choose who I got married to, but I thought I should be able to pick who I allowed inside my body. When I got to attend NYU, I decided to use that sliver of freedom to my advantage. I knew it was reckless and that one day, it would bite me in the ass, but I didn't care. I just wanted to live a little before I was sold off to whatever man my parents would pick for me. I had four years of freedom before me and a campus full of strangers at my disposal. I went to the clinic and got an IUD the week before school started because what I was planning on doing was already dangerous, I didn't need to add the risk of an accidental pregnancy."

Admitting to my husband that I originally got an IUD because I wanted to sleep around during college is not something I saw coming, but I guess I should have. Nothing stays hidden from Emeric for long.

"I met a boy on the first day of orientation. He was nice. A little dorky with a crooked smile. We went to a dorm party, and I ended up letting him finger me in some random closet. He was clumsy and didn't know what he was doing. I left him in that closet not long after. Two days later, I met Isaac during our shared first period math class. He was charming. Confident. He wanted to be a district attorney, which I found funny since he would be fighting on the opposite side of the law as my family. We talked on and off for a week before we decided to get a hotel room. We both had roommates and as stuck-up as it sounds, I didn't want to lose my virginity on a crappy twin-sized mattress. The whole thing was awkward and comically fast, but I was happy. I was happy because I chose Isaac. It was my decision to sleep with him. He had just gotten up to throw the condom away when the door flew open, and my dad and brother showed up. Turns out my dad had been paying my roommate to spy on me and she told them where I was and what I was doing. Isaac never stood a chance. Tiernan had him in his grasp before Isaac knew what was happening. My father yanked me completely naked out of bed and made me watch as Tiernan slammed Isaac's head into the bathroom mirror until the glass shattered. Isaac was out cold after three blows and on his stomach on the bathroom floor, but Tiernan kept going and my dad didn't stop him. My brother slammed Isaac's face into the tile until he was unrecognizable and dead."

I tried to scream, but my father had clamped his hand over my mouth to keep me quiet. Watching Isaac die was my punishment and the guilt of putting that innocent boy in harm's way for purely selfish reasons is something that will never fade. I will carry that weight until the day I die.

Emeric's eyes flash and I don't have to ask to know he's

imagining doing the same thing to Tiernan tomorrow night when his three days of torture are up.

"Word spread that I'd whored myself out, and my prospective husband pool dried up into a puddle. That's why at twenty-four, I wasn't married yet." That's what my mother was the most upset about. The loss of increasing her social status by having her daughter be married to a high-society gentleman. She had been sobbing for the perspective life she lost when her palm struck my left cheek. "But apparently Bogdan Koslov wasn't turned off by my lack of virtue and, well, you know the rest."

"Yeah, I do," he grinds out as he nudges me with his hand. "Come one, let's get you dressed."

He waits for me in our bedroom while I dress into my second pair of sweats today. While I was in the shower, he had changed the sheets on the massive four-poster bed. The black silk has been replaced with a dark red that makes me think of the bed inside of the cage below Tartarus. He sits on the edge of the mattress with his elbows resting on his knees.

"You didn't fuck anyone else for six years until you met me?" he asks when I climb to sit on my side of the bed. This forces him to shift on the bed so his back isn't to me.

"Can you blame me?" I counter. "The one and only man whose dick went anywhere near me ended up with his brains splattered on the bathroom floor of a three-star hotel."

A flash of anger crosses his face as he settles against the headboard. "If you weren't sleeping with anyone else for all those years, and you knew the next man who was going to fuck you would be whatever husband you ended up with, why did you keep the IUD?"

"Because I decided I was no longer willing to bring a life into this corrupt-as-hell world just because it was expected of me when I became someone's wife."

Emeric pins me with a stare that makes my knees shake and has me second-guessing why I'm not letting him impregnate me right here and now. "You're not *someone's* wife. You're mine and I want to put my baby in you. You said you were coming around to the idea."

My suddenly very empty uterus twinges at the blunt honesty of his words.

Down, girl, remember we're mad at him.

"I don't want my babies to be raised like we were. I want them to be loved and protected. *Cherished.* And most importantly, I want them to enter this world knowing they were created because they were *wanted,* and not because the next generation of Banes needed to be born or because you decided you needed an heir." Of its own accord, my hand moves to lie over my lower stomach. Emeric's eyes lock on this like a predator, and my breath catches in my throat when his much larger, tanned hand rests over my pale one.

My chest constricts to the point of pain.

"I'm already prepared to burn down this entire fucking city for you if I have to. You don't think I'd protect our children just as fiercely? You don't think I'd cherish them as much as I cherish you? If that's the case, I have failed at showing you how important you are to me." His fingers entwine with mine and hold tight. "And I don't want children with you because I need an heir."

"You don't?"

"Before he retired and left to do whatever the fuck he's doing these days in the world of academia, Astor was the rightful next head of this family. Just because he abdicated the throne so he can play with textbooks and co-eds doesn't mean Callan loses his birthright."

I've never heard of a family's hierarchy working this way. Leadership is always passed down to the oldest son of the current head of the family. "If Callan is your heir, what role will you be expecting your child to play in this empire you've built for your family?"

"Whatever role they want." His tone is surprisingly gentle. With his free hand, he brushes a couple strands of loose hair behind my ear. "I won't force my child to become like me. As you already said, I don't want them to be raised like we were. They deserve better than the hands we were dealt, and I know we can give them that."

Unable to stand it any longer, I roll over onto my side and bring myself closer to his bare chest. My lips are a hairsbreadth away from his as I whisper, "I'm still really fucking pissed at you, and I will be finding a creative way to make you pay because what you did is *not* okay."

"It's okay, princess, I can take it."

And then he kisses me.

THIRTY-SEVEN

EMERIC

I FIND her on the terrace, lying in one of the lounge chairs under the late morning sun. She's still dressed in the same pair of black sweatpants and cropped long-sleeved top she changed into yesterday after her shower. The one she took alone after our... *disagreement* over her use of birth control. Knowing her reasoning for getting it in the first place and then keeping it for all these years didn't make me second-guess my decision to remove it from her body. Her concerns about bringing a baby into this world were once all valid, but they're not anymore. Not when she's married to me, and I'll be the one fathering her children. I'll be able to meet every one of her requirements for having a baby and then some.

I'll prove to her that our children will be loved and safe in our home and that they'll be shielded from the bloodshed in our world for as long as possible. My childhood made me into the ruthless man I am today, but I would never wish for my child to be taught those same lessons. I want to do better by them than my father did for us.

Due to the ongoing problem at the Brooklyn shipping port,

I had no choice but to return to work soon after our conversation ended. Rionach had let me kiss her again before I left, but she was still distant.

When I returned home around one in the morning, she wasn't in our bed. The same panic that had rocketed through me when I couldn't find her at the fundraiser reverberated through me until I finally located her in the screening room. She was curled into a ball in one of the leather recliners while the credits to whatever movie she was watching played on the projector screen.

Two things stopped me from picking her up and taking her to our room.

The first was the fact she'd brought her pillow and the blanket she prefers from our bed with her. She didn't simply fall asleep while watching a movie. She fully intended to sleep in the recliner and not with me. Seeing as we're both now fairly codependent on each other for restful sleep, her refusal to share a bed with me spoke volumes. She hasn't yet fully forgiven me for what I did.

The second reason I didn't take her to bed is because of the menace that was once my goddamn dog. I raised Cerberus since he was a puppy, and I put hundreds of hours into training him. His loyalty has always been to me and me alone. Until now. The bastard had the fucking nerve to bare his sharp canines at me when he deemed I had gotten too close to my sleeping wife. I would have reprimanded him for his behavior if I hadn't been comforted by the knowledge he will keep Rionach safe if something were to happen while I'm away from her. She made the right call when she demanded that he stay home with her.

Needless to say, I didn't go to our bedroom last night either since I knew sleep wouldn't come without her body there to pacify me. Instead, I elected to spend the night taking shots of espresso like I was a spring breaker taking shots of cheap tequila while I sat at my desk and worked.

I did that for hours until Nova called to inform me about the three dead men strung up outside of my warehouse in Queens, and each corpse had *B*'s carved into their foreheads.

With what's happened at the port with my containers full of destroyed merchandise and now the bodies, both Nova and I concluded that someone is trying to play a game with me.

And it's not exactly a big mystery to us who the illustrious masterminds are.

A preschooler could connect these giant, glowing dots.

What I don't understand is how Tweedledum and Tweedledee are operating in my blind spots. I've gone years without having incidents at either of these locations, but in less than forty-eight hours, both have been hit. This has both Nova and I revisiting how Camden died at the fundraiser and how it shouldn't have been that easy for them to eliminate him. Doc had inspected his body and found no defensive marks on Camden. This leaves us with two possibilities. Either the person who ended his life was just that good, or Camden knew his attacker and he was caught off guard because of it.

My gut tells me it's the latter, which opens up a whole other bucket of fun for me to deal with. Traitors caught within my organization are made into violent lessons that teach my other soldiers what will happen to them if they betray me. My methods are meticulous and sadistic enough that most wouldn't dare toe that line, but if my hunch is right, my teachings didn't stick for someone and they're not just toeing the line, they're tap-dancing over it.

After we spent hours dealing with the mess left on my warehouse's doorstep, I returned home with Nova, Yates, and Mathis in tow. We need to go over my employees and narrow down who might be the mole, and we also need to come up with a plan to increase the amount of security posted at my properties as a precaution.

Most importantly, I wanted to check in on Rionach and see that she's still okay with my own eyes. Igor and Niall, spurred on by the fact their sons are currently in my custody, are about to do something drastic and I don't know what it is yet. Their attacks so far have been so small and seemingly random that it's clear there's a bigger play at hand. According to my wife, Bogdan had been very confident in his plan for how he'd claim her as his once they succeeded in eliminating me.

Waiting until after I'm finished with their sons is no longer an option. I'll have to take care of them all at the same time, and that's why I have instructed the surveillance teams assigned to both to bring them in. They'll be taken to the cabin where their sons are waiting. Because I'm a big supporter of charity, I'll even allow the four of them to share a few last moments of oh-so sweet father and son bonding time before I carve them up into pretty little pieces.

Rionach lifts her head from the paperback in her hand when she hears me approaching. She wears a pair of dark round sunglasses but with the sun nearly at its highest point, they're not enough and she has to use her free hand to shield her eyes further.

"You're back."

"I am." I kiss the top of her head before gathering her ankles in my hand and lifting her legs up so I can sit. With her legs situated across my lap, I ask her, "Did you sleep well?"

She frowns at me and dips her chin to her chest. "No. Did you?" Her light pink painted nail picks at something on the cover of her book.

"I knew I wouldn't be able to sleep without you, so I didn't bother trying. I ended up getting called back into work early this morning, anyway."

Head snapping back up, her brow furrows as she stares at me from behind her sunglasses. Wordlessly, she drops the book in her lap and extends her arm. The back of her left hand tenderly trails down the side of my face.

I capture it in mine and bring it to lips before she can pull away.

"Do you remember?" I ask after pressing my mouth to her knuckles. The empty ring finger, something I've never paid much attention to before, catches my eye. Once I've dealt with her family and the Russians, I'll make a point to remedy this problem.

"Remember what?"

"Have you remembered that you like me yet?" *That you care about me.* Hearing her say that yesterday caused me pain in a way I've never felt before. It wasn't an ache that you could ice or use heat to alleviate. It hurt in a place that isn't tangible.

She regards me again for another drawn-out and tense moment before she sighs. "I'm pretty sure for the rest of our lives, I will like you beyond all reason or common sense, Emeric Banes."

I hadn't realized that the ache from yesterday was still lingering within until now because, like a knife being yanked out of my sternum, the pain fades. Pulling, I slide her closer to me so I can drop my forehead against hers. "I don't think that's true at all."

Rionach tries to yank back, but I don't allow it.

"What? Why do you think that?"

"You're not always going to like me, because one day I'm going to make you love me." I tuck the loose strands of hair blowing around us behind her ears and then hold her face between my hands. "It's going to be soon too."

The first smile I've seen grace her face since yesterday pulls at her mouth. "Soon? You think so?"

"Yeah, I really do." I can't stop myself from touching my lips to that stunning smile of hers. "No more going to bed without me, princess. You can scream at me all you want, and you can break things, but when it's all said and done, we don't go to bed apart. Understood?"

Her nose slides against mine as she hums, "I understand." She tilts her head just far enough that I can see the entirety of her striking face. "You know, one day I'm going to make you love me, too."

In the past—meaning before her—I fought tooth and nail to avoid situations and conversation like this one with *anyone*, but especially women. Commitment wasn't something I was capable of or willing to give, and the gooey-warm sentiment that is *"love"* felt like a trivial thing that was manufactured more times than not. It was something I never wanted because it seemed like a colossal waste of my time, and I didn't believe in the authenticity of it.

But just like in so many other ways, my wife has forced me to have a change of heart. My views have shifted, and I now know without any doubt that when you fall in love with some-one, it's an all-consuming kind of experience and when it happens, it's completely out of your control. You're at the mercy of your emotions, and I think that's what scares people the most. I know it scares the ever-loving shit out of me. Needing someone so you can breathe, or sleep, is daunting, but needing someone so you can simply just function is slice-you-to-the-bone terrifying.

It makes you vulnerable, and that's something I was never allowed to be.

But for her, I'm willing to learn.

"Of course you will," I tell her. "You won't have to try very hard, either."

"I won't?"

My thumbs swipe across the soft edges of her cheekbones. "No, you won't. I know no one has ever done anything to make you believe this about yourself, but falling in love with you is as easy as breathing, Rionach."

Behind the dark lenses of her glasses, her eyes grow wide and her pink mouth parts as she exhales a shuddering lungful of oxygen.

"Boss."

Our tender moment is blown to bits by Nova and Yates charging out onto the terrace. By the looks on their faces, I'm not going to fucking like what they're about to say.

I pull back a bit from Rionach, but don't remove her from my lap yet. If my mood is about to be shot to hell, then I want to savor her proximity for as long as possible before I'm forced to leave her again to deal with whatever bullshit is happening.

"You're about to ruin my day, aren't you?" I groan, hand scrubbing over my face. The nearly three days of facial hair growth scratches across my palms.

Nova passes me his handy-dandy iPad. "Moran and Koslov slipped the surveillance detail you've had on them before our boys could pick them. We've had teams checking the feeds of all the nearby CCTV we have access to for signs of them. To at least figure out what direction they headed in." His tattooed finger points at the screen in my hand. "Five minutes ago, they caught them on the city's traffic cameras."

Grainy, black-and-white screen grabs of two different video feeds are displayed on the screen. One is of Igor walking across a street with a hood pulled over his thinning blond hair and the other is of Niall stepping through a very familiar set of antique revolving doors.

My head snaps up to look at my second-in-command. "Moran is at The Daria Hotel?"

Rionach leans over to look at the picture of Niall. "Of all

the hotels in the city, why would he be staying at the one you own…" Her words trail off as realization dawns on her. "Oh. He's not spending the night there, is he?"

"No." My answer is forced out between my clenched teeth.

"The problem you've been having at the port, he's behind that, right?" Her face pales at my stiff nod. "What's he going to do to your mother's hotel?" The night I told her about how my mom died, I also told her about how we'd changed the name of our family-owned hotel to honor her. I didn't think when I was telling her about my mother's love for the tearoom there, that in a few weeks' time Niall would be headed there to possibly desecrate the place that holds so many memories of her. "And I thought my dad and Igor were working together on all of this."

"They are."

She points at the candid shot of Igor. "Then why is he about two blocks away from Tartarus?"

When I glance at Nova for confirmation, he nods once. "That's what we were coming out here to tell you. We can't tell what their plans are, but it's something. I think the cargo containers and the warehouse were both just meant to be distractions while they organized whatever it is they're planning to do to the hotel and club. They're much bigger and more lucrative businesses. Hitting them will affect you and your bottom line harder than the port or the building in Queens."

Yates stands like a soldier with his arms held behind his back and his stance wide. "They're also splitting our resources by choosing two locations—locations they know are important to you. They know you'll send people to both establishments."

This plan is too well thought-out to be a Niall Original. This has Igor written all over it. Perhaps if Niall had made the Russian an ally ten years ago, his family's legacy and empire wouldn't metaphorically look the same as a depressing child's birthday party no one showed up for, where the cake is stale and the singular, sad balloon is half deflated. Absolutely pitiful.

"Divided or not, we have three times the man and fire power as they do. They knew this and that's why they had to try to weaken us by going to both locations." Reluctantly, I remove Rionach's legs from my lap and pull myself off the lounge. "Make the calls, Nova, and get our men divided equally between the two places. I'll going to The Daria, you and your boys take Tartarus. Everyone needs to keep their radios on. I want there to be constant communication between our teams. If there are any updates on your end, big or small, I want to know about them immediately. Got it?" I look between Nova and Yates.

"Yes," they answer in unison. Plan decided, they head inside to start getting things in order.

With them gone, I'm able to return my sole focus to Rionach. "I'm going to have Mathis stay here with you while I'm gone. He and Cerberus will keep you safe."

The unmistakable air of worry pouring off her pulls at the place inside of my chest. "Don't you need Mathis? He's one of your best guys."

"He is. I'll focus better on the task at hand out there as long as I know you're here safe. Far away from this bullshit. In my eyes, no one will ever be good enough to guard you, but my back's up against a wall and I don't have a choice. I have to take care of this. I've had too many opportunities to end this in the past and I was more lenient than I should have been. That needs to stop."

She stands from the lounge chair and pushes her sunglasses atop her head. Coming to stand before me, she softly agrees, "I know it does." Rionach loops her arms around my neck, and she holds me close. "Just like Tiernan, my dad brought this on himself. He has no one to blame but his own idiocy, and Igor's been living on borrowed time since the moment he put his hands on you when you were a child." The ruthlessness in her tone makes me proud of her and the way she's slowly coming into her own. "We won't be able to move on with our lives until they're gone, and whatever future family we may have one day won't be safe if any of them are walking this earth. They'll always be a threat to us. Do what needs to be done, Emeric. My conscience is clear."

I hold her so tight to my body, I wouldn't be surprised if it edged on painful for her, but she doesn't complain. "You remember what the plan is if shit hits the fan, right?"

"Go to the cabin."

"Good girl." I touch my lips to her temple. "If it comes to that, I'll meet you there as soon as I can. This goes without saying, but if you do end up at the cabin, stay out of the basement. I'll deal with the guests down there when I'm done with the fathers."

"Everything is going to be fine." I don't know if she's reassuring herself or me. "Now, go teach those bastards what happens when they fuck with the Banes family."

THIRTY-EIGHT
RIONACH

As it turns out, waiting for your husband to kill your father and then come home to you isn't as fun as it sounds. *I know,* who could have seen that coming? It was a disappointing discovery for me as well because I really thought this was going to be my version of Disneyland. *Insert warning for sarcasm here.*

It's the opposite of fun. It's torture because while I'm stuck up here doing another rendition of my princess locked in the tower act, he's out there doing God knows what. He's been gone for over an hour, and there's still no update. From anyone. The exasperated look on Mathis's face when I asked again if he'd heard from Nova or Emeric was proof of how incessant I'm being.

But I don't care. I don't think I'm going to be able to breathe normally again until my husband is standing directly in front of me.

For the first half hour he was gone, I tried to make good use of my time. I showered and changed out of the clothes I'd been wearing for nearly twenty-four hours.

My brain is a hornet's nest of different thoughts and emotions.

It's because one of those thoughts said something about looking nice for Emeric when he gets home that I changed into a dark floral-print dress and my favorite black jacket. Is this really a situation in which you need to look your best in? Nope. Did I spend an extra five minutes on my makeup than usual just to get the winged eyeliner perfect anyway? Yes.

Dressing up didn't make any sense, but all I know is it was a lot better when I was actively doing something than now when all I'm doing is pacing in front of our bedroom windows. The very thought of having to participate in surface-level small talk if I go hang out in the kitchen with Anneli and Mathis keeps me upstairs. I can't go talk about how the weather is changing from winter to spring, when what I really want to talk about is how they think Emeric will choose to kill my father. And that, my friends, is what we call an inside thought. You have to be very selective about who you share those with because people can be judgmental little shits.

So, instead, I pace, and while I do, Cerberus watches diligently from his place by the bedroom door. I think he knows something is going on because he seems to be on higher alert than usual. When I had briefly gone downstairs to ask for an update, his pointed ears flattened closer to his head and his lip curled up to show off his sharp white teeth when he'd looked at Mathis and Anneli. The pair had balked back a step as they shared an uneasy look between them. It didn't seem to put them at ease when I told them the dog is probably just reacting to the energy I'm giving off.

With the entire width of Central Park visible from these windows, I've been periodically looking toward the east side where I know The Daria is only a few blocks from. I can't see the actual building from here, but that hasn't stopped me from looking in its general direction as if I'm miraculously going to get a clue about what is happening there.

I've lost count of how many laps I've made of this side of the room, but I've got to be closing in on two hundred when I look up from the wood floors and out the window again.

My boot-covered feet turn into lead blocks, and I almost fall on my face as I stumble through my next step. Barely recovered and still unstable on my legs, I surge toward the window until my hands and forehead are pressed against the cool glass.

That spot I've been staring longingly at in the distance now has black clouds of smoke rising above it. My optimistic side tries to tell me anything could be burning and it's not The Daria with Emeric trapped inside of it, but the logical and slightly cynical half knows the chances of that smoke belonging to anything else are slim to none. The timing would be too weird for a building nearby to randomly catch fire when my father was seen sniffing around the hotel.

Heart a cold lump of stone in my stomach and my throat suddenly tight, I force myself to turn away from the window. I need to go to Mathis. He'll know what's going on.

I make it to the second floor of the penthouse just as the soldier comes sprinting up the stairs from the main floor.

"Is it the hotel?" I ask breathlessly before he has a chance to open his mouth. "Is The Daria burning?"

His nod is robotic. "There was an explosion in the basement of the building. The chatter on the police scanners is that almost the whole building came down."

I can't mourn for the now scorched memories Emeric shared with his mother at that hotel. Not yet. Not until I know whether or not my husband was in that building when it came down. "Have you heard from anyone? Is anyone hurt?" *Are they all dead?* "Was Emeric—was my husband—in the building when it exploded."

The way the stoic soldier's face pales makes my insides twist painfully. "I haven't heard anything, but we need to go. *Now*." He shifts down a stair step and motions for me to follow him.

"Go where?"

"Just like he told you; you're to go to the cabin outside the city. That was Emeric's order to me if anything like this happened. It's my job to get you there safely. If he's okay, your husband will meet us there as soon as he can."

If he's okay… I forcibly swallow the bile rising.

He's telling me the exact same information that Emeric told me before he left but still, my gut tells me we should wait here. At least for a little while longer, just until we hear something. *Anything*. If Emeric is injured, I don't want to be over an hour away from whatever hospital he'll end up at. What if I can't get back to him in time?

My head starts shaking as all these thoughts twist and turn through my dread-soaked brain. "No, not yet. We need to wait until someone calls us."

I swear he looks mad at me for refusing. "Mrs. Banes. That is not what the boss wanted you to do, and you know it. Now please, we have to go. Anneli is waiting downstairs already."

"Anneli is going too?" I mumble mainly to myself. This is a new kind of fear. This isn't an 'I'm worried for my own health and safety' fear. This is a deliberating, soul-soaking type of fear that has me feeling frozen in place.

He isn't hurt. He can't be. He'll be home soon and then we can live out the rest of our messy lives together.

"Of course she is." Mathis's eyes turn scrutinizing. "Mrs. Banes, please don't make me carry you out of this building. I don't want to do it, but I will if you force my hand. I don't have time for this—*we* don't have time for this. We have no idea what is happening over there, and we can't stay here much longer. We need to move."

It goes against everything my soul is screaming at me, but reluctantly I nod. "Okay." Forcing my feet to move, I turn away from the staircase and move down the hallway toward the laundry room.

"Ma'am, where are you going?"

I snag the leather leash off the hook just inside the doorway before releasing a short but sharp whistle. "Cerberus, *hier!*" *Here*. The large dog bounds down the hallway and sits patiently at my feet while I connect the clip to his collar. Since the day I took him on my little field trip to see Ophelia, I've been secretly learning German commands. I figured it may come in handy one day and I also found myself wanting to impress Emeric. Which I suppose is a little silly considering what we've been dealing with all these weeks.

The same uneasy look that was on Mathis's face earlier when the Doberman bared his teeth at him is back, and this time it's more severe. He coughs nervously. "I don't know if bringing the dog is a good idea. Emeric didn't say anything about him accompanying us."

"Cerberus goes where I go. If you want me to voluntarily leave this building, the dog is coming. If not, I'm more than happy to stay here while you take off to the cabin by yourself, but I'll warn you, if my husband does show up and he finds that I'm not there with you..." I raise a challenging brow and wait for him to draw his own conclusion about how that will go over for him.

"Fine," he grits out. "Let's go. I'm already late."

I start to follow him down the stairs. "Late? I didn't realize that this was going to be a timed event."

He doesn't answer me.

INTUITION IS A FUNNY THING.

These days, I think a lot of people mistake it for simple anxiety and disregard it, but in reality, it's an innate skill that's helped keep humanity alive for thousands of years. It signals to your body that something is wrong before your brain has a chance to catch up.

I can't tell you specifically what's making me feel this way, but I know in my very bones that something isn't right. Well, duh, something isn't right. There's a chance that Emeric is trapped under the rubble of a collapsed building, and my father and his crazy Russian sidekick could be coming for me so I can tie our families together through a less-than-holy union with Bogdan.

It's wild to think that for so many years all I longed for was to be wanted by my family. By someone. And now I have four men fighting to retain me from the man who stole me away. No, not stole. *Saved.* Emeric saved me.

The hour-long drive out of the city is an agonizingly slow and silent one. In the front seats, Mathis and Anneli shared a couple looks I couldn't fully decipher. The one thing I managed to confirm is that there is definitely something more to Mathis and Anneli's relationship than just coworkers. Those two know each other on an intimate level. You can't have full conversations consisting of only shared looks without knowing each other deeply.

We turn down a familiar dirt road lined with tall, sun-obstructing trees. The last time I arrived on this property I was handcuffed and blindfolded, but when I left the following day with Emeric, I took in all the details that I'd been forced to miss. Given the reasoning behind my arrival now, I'm struggling to find the same serene beauty in the land as I did before. It's dark and ominous without Emeric here.

When we reach the impressive metal gate, Mathis rolls to a stop and leans out the window to enter a code.

It's not until we've driven through, the metal clanging shut behind us, do I notice what's so clearly missing. "Why isn't there a guard posted at the gate?" When I arrived and left the property last time, there was an armed guard posted at the entrance. There isn't another soul in sight now.

Something is wrong! the intuitive voice screams at me. My hand, which has been wrapped around the leather leash attached to the dog sitting tensely on the seat next to me, tightens.

Mathis's eyes meet mine in the rearview mirror. "The boss called a bunch of people off their regular posts today to help with whatever is happening at the hotel and nightclub."

That doesn't make any sense. With Tiernan and Bogdan still strung up in the basement here, Emeric wouldn't risk removing security away from the property. Not when Niall and Koslov have no doubt been searching the state for their kids for the past three days. Bogdan is also crafty. His chance of trying to escape on his own is too high for Emeric to not have guards posted at every possible point. No matter how dire the situation is in the city, Emeric is too damn smart to leave this property without guards.

The alarm bells that had only been making vague warning noises in the back of my head during the drive are now blaring like tornado sirens.

Refusing to shy away from Mathis's stare, I look at him in the mirror and nod. "Oh, okay. That makes sense." *Keep playing dumb, Rio, and let them underestimate you.*

The road, which has turned into dark gray gravel that crunches beneath the tires, is the only sound that fills the inside of the car as we slowly make our way toward the cabin on the backside of the land.

It's not until the sharp roofline of the black A-frame "cabin" comes into view does Mathis speak again. "Emeric will do whatever it takes to protect his family."

My eyebrows draw together. "I know he will. That's what he's doing right now. Protecting his family." The erratically pounding organ in my chest warms at the knowledge that I'm now Emeric's family.

For a tense couple of seconds, Mathis flicks his attention between the mirror and the road in front of him. "I have a son. Did you know that?"

"No, I didn't." Aside from the limited information I learned about Anneli, I don't know anything personal about any of Emeric's employees, but I think this was done on purpose.

"Most don't since I've always tried my damnedest to keep him away from the world I've chosen to work in," he explains. "His name is Soren and he's almost six. His mother died during childbirth, and until I brought Anneli home, I was the only family he had."

I shift uneasily in my seat as a new wave of dread falls over my shoulders. The weight is nearly unbearable. "I'm sorry to hear about his mother," I tell him after clearing my throat. "And I'm glad Anneli could become a part of his life, but you don't exactly strike me as the type of man who wants to bond over family trauma. I don't understand why you're telling me about this now, Mathis."

He pulls to a stop in front of the silent and still-looking house. The second he puts the car in park, I have my seat belt undone. Both of them follow suit in the front seat.

With a weary sigh, he scrubs his hand over his tense face. "I'm telling you this, Mrs. Banes, because I'm also a man who will do whatever it takes to keep his family safe."

The words are barely out of his mouth before the sound of a gun cocking fills the inside of the SUV. It doesn't come from Mathis's hand, but from Anneli. In her perfectly manicured hand is a small revolver that is pointed directly at my chest.

A guttural and downright chilling warning snarl rips out of the Doberman's chest when he, too, sees the weapon. My whole body lurches when Anneli redirects the weapon at Cerberus.

"No!" I shout, trying my best to block the animal with my body.

Mathis turns in the front seat. "He wasn't supposed to be here! I gave you so many chances to keep him away, but you didn't listen. Your damn dog could have been far away at the container yard, but you threw a tantrum like a goddamn child when I tried to send him there, and you didn't listen when I told you to leave him at home today. If you can't rein him in, I will kill him. I won't have a choice. There's too much on the line."

He doesn't want Cerberus here because he's against killing an animal. He doesn't want him here because he knows the highly trained dog is a threat to him and whatever his endgame is here.

"Cerberus, halt." *Stop.* I keep myself positioned slightly in front of him just in case. My focus remains locked on the woman with the gun—the woman I thought could be my friend one day—while I ask the man beside her, "What are you doing?"

"I'm protecting my family."

"They took Soren six days ago," Anneli's accented voice breaks. "He's innocent in all of this. Just a child. We couldn't let anything happen to him."

The heartbroken and terror-riddled look on her face is an expression only a mother can wear.

405

Aside from Nova, Emeric doesn't bring his employees up in casual conversation. Emeric runs a tight ship, and I will be admittedly impressed if they've managed to keep this clearly very involved relationship a secret from him all this time.

"Who took him?"

The grave laugh that comes from Mathis is full of pain. "Who do you think?" he asks once he's done laughing. "If I didn't help them, they were going to kill my son. I couldn't allow that to happen, so I've done as they've asked."

What happened to Camden suddenly isn't such a mystery anymore. We theorized there could be a double agent working within the organization, but I don't think any of us saw it being one of Emeric's higher-ranking guys. "You killed Camden, didn't you?"

Guilt blazes across his sullen face like a strike of lightning. "I liked that kid. He was smart and had a lot of potential, but Cam didn't stand a chance against me. He never saw it coming."

"That's because he trusted you!" I yell.

"I didn't have a choice!" Mathis matches my hostile octave. "They have my fucking kid, and I will do anything to get him back safely. Even if it means delivering my boss's wife on a silver platter."

"What—" Whatever else I was going to say shrivels up on my tongue when two menacing figures exit the front door of the cabin as if they own the fucking place. "W-what did you do?"

"Whatever was asked of me," Mathis answers solemnly but his reply sounds distant and vague.

Standing on the porch looking a little tired and rough around the edges are Bogdan and my brother. They're both still wearing the same clothes from the fundraiser days ago. In tandem, matching smiles grow on their mouths when they find me staring through the windshield. Not taking his focus off me, Bogdan extends the hand not currently holding a curved knife through the front door. He pulls out a terrified-looking little boy with dark blond hair and a tear-stained red face.

An additional man I don't recognize follows the boy out onto the wooden porch. My guess is he's one of Koslov's men and he's the one who delivered the poor child to Bogdan and Tiernan.

In the front seat, Anneli's gasp is violent enough to rattle bones. "Soren…"

"You let them out of the basement?" I question.

Mathis's hard eyes land on mine. "Whatever they asked of me," he repeats. "Please get out of the car, Mrs. Banes."

I stay where I'm sitting, spine painfully straight as the inky thickness of realization settles in my core. "What's happening back in the city, is it just a distraction to get me here?"

"I don't know their plans." Mathis's stiff shoulders rise once. "I just did what I was told, but if I had to guess, they knew the only way they were getting their hands on you was if the boss was called away, and, honestly, they just really want to kill Banes. I think this was more of a 'two birds, one stone' situation."

"Were you ever loyal to him? To us?" I can't help but ask.

Another flash of guilt darts across his features. "I was, but my loyalty to my son will always come first."

"You have to understand." Anneli's voice is a hoarse scratch.

I look between the two scared parental figures and incline my head. "I do, but I'll warn you. Wherever you're planning on going and hiding after this, you better get there fast, because the second Emeric finds out what you've done he's going to hunt you like you're nothing more than bleeding, wounded prey."

They at least have the intelligence to look terrified at the thought of being tracked down by Emeric. *Good.*

Anneli might as well have pulled the trigger with the way Mathis's next sentence slices through my chest.

"Only if he's alive." He doesn't wait for a response. Turning in his seat, he exits the SUV and seconds later, the chilly outside air whips around me as he opens my door for me. "Get out, let's get this over with." Mathis stiffens when Cerberus follows me out and lands near his feet. "You better keep that dog in check. If you sic him on any of us before I get my kid back, I'll put a bullet between his eyes."

I lift my chin and narrow my eyes at this. "I lied before. If that happens, Emeric won't be the only one hunting you down. I'll be right there with him."

The muscle in his jaw jumps when he grabs my arm, and he drags me around the car to greet the demon twins. I drop his leash, but Cerberus refuses to give me any kind of space. With each step I make, he keeps his muscular body pressed tightly to my leg.

With a predator's gleam, Bogdan's grin grows and his eyes twinkle when I come into view. "What did I tell you, Rionach? I was always going to get you back." The Russian psychopath waves his hand toward Emeric's man at my side. "Did he tell you how he's been helping us for days? Killed his own man and everything."

"Stop talking," Mathis snaps. "We had a deal. I brought you the girl. Give us back our boy."

Standing between Bogdan's and Tiernan's legs, Soren whimpers, his big light brown eyes full of tears. "Daddy..."

"It's okay, sweetheart," Anneli soothes from her place beside the passenger door of the black SUV. "We're here. We'll be leaving shortly."

My brother hasn't pulled his attention away from me since

408

I walked up. His stare, which seemed dazed and unfocused, is locked onto my face. His thin lips move as if he's mumbling words, but from where I stand, I can't make out a single word he says. In his left hand he holds a gun. In a rhythmic pattern, he taps it against his thigh. The unhinged and crazed energy I'd felt on him last time seems to have worsened over the past couple of days. I'm not sure how long they were stuck in that cellar before Mathis helped orchestrate their escape, but I can imagine any amount of time spent in those conditions is going to have a lasting effect.

"Where are the guards that were here watching the property?" I question, turning to Bogdan. The energy coming off him reeks of bloodlust. The frenzied expression in his eyes dares me to look away. Like all the women before me, he craves to see me cower and I have no intention of giving him what he wants, so I meet his gaze with a blandness I know will drive him mad.

As if he's proud to show me what he's done, Bogdan waves the knife in his hand with a flourish toward the tree line on the left side of the house. "We took a page out of Banes's book." My stomach bubbles with a mixture of horror and anger when I find three men, stripped completely naked, hanging from the lower branches of the trees. The front of their bare bodies is painted red from where their throats were cut. "With Mathis's clear direction and assistance with the security feeds, a team of my father's men were able to arrive early this morning and apprehend Banes's guards before freeing us. After I'd recuperated some of my strength, I got to work on the guards. What do you think? Will Banes approve of my rendition?"

That's how they'd managed to do this. While Emeric and his men in the city were busy dealing with whatever happened in Queens early this morning, Mathis was secretly instructing Koslov's men to this property. Nova was right, it was all a distraction.

"Stop talking!" Mathis repeats with a furious yell. "Let my kid go. *Now.*"

Bogdan shoots Mathis a taunting grin before he slowly lowers himself in a squat in front of Soren. "What do you say, kiddo? Are you ready to go back to your daddy?"

"Yes please," Soren's broken, snot-filled cry makes my heart hurt. He never should have gotten caught up in this. It isn't fair to him.

Turning the blade in his palm so he won't slice the poor child's face, Koslov mockingly wipes away one of Soren's fat tears. "Do you love your daddy?"

"Yes," the boy sobs, his head bouncing in a jerky nod.

Koslov cuts us all a brief look before he tells Soren, "Tell your daddy how much you love him."

Soren's confused and terrified, but he does as he's told. Big, red-rimmed eyes turn to Mathis as he croaks, "I love you, Daddy."

The last syllable hasn't fully formed on Soren's tongue when the piercing gunshot rings out through the space and surrounding trees. The deafening sound is followed closely by a shrill, heartbreaking female scream and the hollow thud of a body hitting the gravel ground next to me. I'm so stunned, I'm only vaguely aware of the spray of warm blood across the left side of my face.

Anneli and Soren's combined cries turn into dull, distant noises when I look down at Mathis's unmoving body. Blood from the gunshot in his forehead pools around his dark hair in the fine gray gravel.

My world, which was momentarily moving in slow motion as if we were underwater, snaps back into crystal-clear focus and normal speed at the same time I turn my head to look at Bogdan. While he squatted in front of the boy, he pulled a gun out of his waistband without any of us noticing.

That very gun is now pointed at Emeric's housekeeper.

"Ann—" The rest of her name is ripped away and silenced when a second gunshot splits through the air. The stunningly beautiful woman falls to the ground in front of the SUV with a matching hole in her forehead.

With a shit-eating grin plastered across his fucked-up face, Bogdan takes a step off the porch. The confidence in which he moves makes me see red. He's pleased with himself and the lives he's just stolen.

He takes one more step in my direction and then all hell breaks loose.

For a single second, Bogdan's attention is pulled away from me when the sound of another gun goes off behind him. Koslov's goon crumples to the ground in screaming agony from the wound that's ripped a hole through his gut. Tiernan stands over the Russian with the gun still pointed at him.

Why the hell did Tiernan just shoot that man? Aren't they on the same team?

The single second of distraction is all Cerberus needs.

Without being told, the dog launches himself at Bogdan with so much power, he takes the impressively built psychopath to the ground. The gun that he had used on Mathis and Anneli skids across the gravel driveway as Cerberus's teeth sink into the unblemished side of Koslov's face. His screams of pain join the symphony of Cerberus's vicious snarls.

My heart leaps into my throat when a sharp, pained whine interrupts the brutal sounds. In his left hand, Bogdan's curved blade is now red. The attack dog is forced to let up just enough that Bogdan begins to wiggle free. As he does this, he lifts the blade up again, but Cerberus, who's unwilling to back down, clamps his powerful jaw down on Bogdan's wrist with such force, I can hear bones snap from where I stand yards away. The dog violently shakes his head,

411

tearing skin and muscle until the knife also clatters to the ground.

Koslov's screams of pain and terror increase when my dog returns his attention to the Russian's already bloody and mangled face. And then his throat. The screams quickly shift into choked, gargled noises, and Bogdan's attempts to push the animal away turn weaker.

A child's terrified cries pulls my gaze away from the carnage in front of me. Soren, who's remained curled up on the porch with Tiernan and the unknown dying Koslov employee, is trying to make himself as small as possible by curling his body into a tight ball. His blond head is tucked between his knees and his little hands try to block out the horrific sounds by covering his ears.

Tiernan pays the kid no mind, his focus solely on the Russian being mauled in front of him, but that doesn't mean he's not a danger to the child. He's now just as unpredictable as Koslov is.

I don't think about it. I just start running for the little boy. His screams break my heart when my arms wrap around his small body and lift him off the now bloodstained decking.

"It's okay, I've got you." He's so inconsolable at this point, I don't think he's hearing a word I'm saying, but that doesn't stop me from repeating myself. "You're okay, Soren. I promise."

I promise... This might end up being a big fat lie because I have no idea if more of Koslov's men will be showing up here soon, or what the plan was for after they got me here. From the fleeting look of confusion I saw on Bogdan's face when Tiernan's gun went off, I don't think killing the Koslov soldier was part of their previously agreed upon arrangement. And most importantly, I have no idea if my husband is going to come and save me because I don't know if he's even alive right now. I've been trying and failing to keep the images of him being crushed by concrete rubble at bay since Mathis first told me The Daria exploded. If I allow myself to succumb to those excruciating thoughts, I won't be able to focus on what I need to do now.

I can't truthfully promise Soren everything will be okay, but I will go down fighting making sure nothing else happens to this kid. That's a promise I can make to myself.

With Soren tucked against my chest the best I can, I turn away from where Tiernan still hovers near the slowly dying Russian man and start to go back down the three simple wooden steps of the porch. The toe of my right boot just barely touches the planks of the last step when something hard cracks against the back of my skull.

The blow instantly steals my balance, and I'm falling forward before I have a chance to piece together what's just happened.

I try my best to angle myself so I don't land directly atop the weeping boy in my arms.

The impact of the unforgiving hard ground against my left shoulder and side joins the litany of pain radiating from the back of my head. My vision goes in and out of focus as I fight to reorient myself with my surroundings and current predicament.

Out of the corner of my eye, Tiernan is prowling down the steps. His mouth is moving again as if he's having a full-blown conversation, but he still doesn't make a sound.

"*Soren*," I gasp, my head is still spinning, and nausea has started to twist in my stomach. With how hard Tiernan hit me, I wouldn't be surprised if I reached back and found my scalp bleeding. With a pained groan, I roll onto my stomach so I can watch the kid crawl away on his hands and knees. Big, tear-filled brown eyes look over his shoulder at me and his bottom lip trembles with hysterical sobs. "Run. You have to run and hide, okay?" He gives me zero sign he's understanding what I'm saying. "Soren, run! Right now!" My raised and slightly panicked voice is what finally has him stumbling to his feet.

He nearly trips over his feet again when his small legs carry him past his father's body. No child should be forced to see their parents like this. It's not fair. I think he's still wailing, but the ringing now in my ears blocks any other sound. My vision tilts as I watch him run in the direction of the thick tree line on the opposite side of the driveway from where Emeric's dead men hang.

"Cerberus!" I holler, my own voice sounding miles away to my ears. "Cerberus, *halt!*" The Doberman reluctantly lifts his head from where he's had his jaw clamped down on Bogdan's throat and stares expectantly at me. "*Pass auf!*" *Guard.* The muscles in my arm shake as I lift my hand to point at where the little boy is running. "*Pass auf!*" He doesn't want to leave me. I can see it in the way his pointed ears waver and he takes a half step toward where I lie. "No! Not me. Him. *Pass auf,* Cerberus!"

With a low whine, he finally does what I asked.

The relief I feel knowing my dog will watch over the innocent boy is fleeting.

Tiernan's stalking frame casts a shadow when he comes to a stop at my feet. He stares down at me with an unblinking gaze for a long moment before he lifts his head and arm. Gun raised, he settles his aim on Soren's back.

"No!" I scream, my boot slamming into his shin at the same time. My brother stumbles forward and lands on both knees. If it weren't for the gun now being pointed in my direction, I might have enjoyed his scream of pain that comes out of him when he's forced to catch his balance with his still healing stump.

"Get up," Tiernan sneers at me, his pale and exhausted face turning a familiar shade of red. Ungracefully, he pulls himself back to his feet. When I don't follow suit, he waves the gun impatiently a foot away from my face. "I said, get the fuck up!"

Trembling, I rise from the ground, my dizzy head and uneasy stomach intensifying as I stand before him. "Tiernan..."

"It isn't how this was supposed to happen!" he roars, lunging at me at a speed my concussed brain has trouble following. His right arm loops around my neck at the same time there's a bite of hard metal against my temple. "Everything was ruined!"

Unceremoniously, he drags me back up the porch steps and into the A-frame cabin. Underneath my stumbling feet, the debris of the once pristine decor and furniture crunch. From the looks of it, while they were waiting for me to arrive, they spent their time destroying the inside of Emeric's once immaculately decorated home. The couch has deep slashes through the cushions and back of it and the stuffing is scattered across the once white rug. What looks to be red wine is spilled all over the carpet now. The wall of windows that overlook the trees at the back of the house are shattered and the shards of glass are everywhere.

"He kept us tied up down here for two days," my brother says when we reach the open door of the basement. "Did you know that? Did you know how he left us to rot?"

"I—"

I miss the first step when he forces us down the dimly lit stairwell. My hand flails for something to grasp so I don't go tumbling and crack my head on the concrete floors below. It's Tiernan's arm tightening around my throat and bringing me tighter to his sweaty chest that keeps me upright. It's slow, clumsy work getting us down all the steps, and once we reach the bottom, he lets me go with an unforgiving shove.

I stumble forward but catch myself on one of the many

stacks of wooden crates full of liquor. The open bottle of Irish whiskey that had been left on top teeters off and crashes to the hard floors. Pieces of glass decorate the floor at my feet and whiskey splashes up and splatters the exposed skin of my shins.

Breathing heavily, I turn and look at my big brother—a man I hardly recognize anymore. "Yes, I knew he had you guys down here," I admit. "Emeric showed me the live footage."

"*Don't!*" Tiernan, who's positioned himself directly in front of the wood and iron staircase, takes a single angry step forward. "I don't want to hear his fucking name come out of your mouth one more time. You don't belong to him. You're not his. Don't speak his name again!" He scratches the side of his head with the barrel of his gun, his brown eyes darting chaotically all over my body.

"He's my husband—"

A bullet takes a chunk out of the stone floor two feet in front of me. I drop to my haunches and cover my head with my arms as my body braces for him to shoot again.

"No, he's not!" Tiernan's roar doesn't even sound like him. It's full of turmoil and wild animal-like anger. Something in his mind is well and truly cracked. "He stole you!"

I peek at him from behind my arm. He's pacing now, the gun still rhythmically scratching his sweaty temple.

"He stole me from Koslov, I know." Warily, I stand to my full height again as I watch his every movement. With every pass he makes in front of the staircase, he moves farther and farther away. If I time it right, this could give me an opening to dart up the stairs while his back is turned.

He aggressively whips around. "Not from them! From *me*! You were never going to marry Bogdan. I was going to make sure of it. I told you once that Dad was making a mistake, and I was going to fix it." The confusion I feel must be written across my face and is as obvious as a glowing neon sign that says *What the actual fuck?* because he explains, "Don't you get it, Rionach? We were never meant to marry anyone else. We were created for each other. By preserving our bloodline and making it strong again, we're going to save our family. It's destiny."

Oh... oh fuck no.

There's about twenty pounds of crazy in a five-pound bag staring at me like I'm the solution to all his very obvious problems.

This is so much worse than I thought it was. Between violently losing a hand and then being strung up naked in a cold cellar like a slab of meat, his weakening grasp on reality made sense. That's what I was blaming his deteriorating mental state on, but what he's saying now isn't a new development or a result of the trauma he's experienced lately.

He's been having these corrupt thoughts for much longer. I mean, hell, he basically told me his whole plan over a month ago when he came to my room and warned me about marrying outside of our bloodline. His change in attitude toward me when I went through puberty is also now glaringly obvious too. All the random excuses to touch me and the way he watched me when I entered a room. This whole time he wanted...

I swallow the bile creeping up the back of my throat. "I'm your sister."

"I know." He nods over his shoulder at me as he continues his pacing. "It's perfect. Our children will be pure, and they'll grow strong, just like our empire will once again when we rectify all the wrongs that have been made over the decades. Because of our union, our bloodline will return to its rightful glory."

"Our c-children?" My immediate instinct is to argue with him and his immoral plans, but there's no point. When someone is this far gone and this deep in their delusion, they're

417

not going to see reason. My brother has been in this for so long, there's no pulling him out.

"Once Dad's done dealing with *him*, and he gets here, we'll deal with Igor together. He'll understand why I went against the alliance. He has to understand, and he'll help make this right," Tiernan mumbles the last sentence like he's saying it for himself. "After we take care of that, we'll take you to the doctor. You've been whoring yourself out to *him* for over a month. We have to make sure you're not... infested with his offspring. Once that's taken care of, we'll be married like we were always destined to be."

Dad and Igor are possibly headed here, and they have no idea that Tiernan's gone off the deep end. If it wasn't already dire that I get out of this basement and far away from this cabin before, it sure as hell is now. All hell is going to break loose when they learn what's happened, and I don't want to be in the same zip code when Igor finds his mauled son. Emeric's stories have told me what he's capable of and that scares the shit out of me.

Tiernan passes the bottom of the staircase again with his head down and his lips moving again with more silent conversation.

I don't hesitate, I just run. This might be my only opening.

My right foot hits the bottom step at the same time Tiernan's hand wraps around the long strands of my hair and he rips me unforgivingly backward by it. The air is knocked out of my lungs and my body screams in agony when I land on the glass-covered concrete floor.

I'm fighting for my next breath when Tiernan's bulky body straddles my hips and a menacing smirk I've never seen before distorts his face. I thought I knew fear, that I was more familiar with the emotion than I ought to be, but nothing has scared me more than his hand going to the buckle of his beige pants.

"Tiernan, no!" I beg, my body fighting like hell beneath his unforgiving weight. I find it hard to be relieved the gun is nowhere to be seen when I'm trapped under him because being shot is almost preferable to what he's currently trying to do. "I'm your sister!"

"Shh..." The sound is anything but soothing to my ears. "It's okay. You'll be my wife soon enough." Vomit threatens to come up when he moves on from the zipper of his pants to his shirt. Grabbing the back of the short-sleeved collared shirt, he rips it over his head and reveals the pasty white skin of his torso. "A husband is allowed to lie with his wife, Rionach. In fact, I believe it's encouraged."

My fingers claw and fight off his hand when he reaches for the fabric of my dress. He doesn't flinch or even seem to notice that I've drawn blood. He simply keeps true to his mission and pulls at the fabric until my navy-blue lace panties are exposed to him.

The growl of approval that rumbles in his chest at the sight of them has ice-like fingers of dread crawling across my skin. My body tries in vain to twist away but he manages to drag one of his stubby thick fingers across the fabric over the seam of my most intimate place.

The scream that rips from my throat is deafening to my own ears.

"I have to get you nice and wet," he says, sounding completely at ease with what he's doing. Like what he's doing is perfectly acceptable. "I don't want it to hurt when I fuck you, Rionach, but if you don't stay still and let me touch you, I won't be able to get you ready to take me."

My legs try to kick and thrash beneath him, but he's so goddamn heavy and I've never felt weaker—more vulnerable— in my entire life. Tears are pouring out of my eyes in rivulets and my vision is nearly completely blurry because of them. I'm oddly grateful for the tears because they make Tiernan's foreboding figure and the disturbingly peaceful expression on his face nothing more than watery smears.

This can't be happening. This can't be happening. This can't be happening.

My left hand shoves and tries to block his prodding, aggressive fingers while my right hand searches for something—anything—nearby that could help me get him off me. Maybe when he dropped the gun to grab my hair, it landed somewhere close enough I could grab it?

Pain slices across my fingertips when they run through the glass shards above my head.

Glass.

The broken bottle.

With newfound determination, my hand swipes through the pieces of glass. I'm numb to the pain of cuts slicing into my palm and fingers as I do. I just wish I was numb to the sensation of Tiernan's finger forcing itself inside of me.

I throw everything I have into my thrashing and fighting. This time I'm incapable of hearing it, but I know without any doubt that I'm screaming because my throat burns. My eyes squeeze tight. It's like my mind is unconsciously trying to protect me from physically seeing what is about to happen.

My body fights me when I force them open once again.

I need to see this part.

My vision, momentarily void of tears, is in crystal-clear clarity when I meet the sinister gaze of my brother as the severed top of the Irish whiskey bottle in my bloody fingers sinks into his jugular.

Tiernan's bulky body lurches on top of mine and a pained and startled gasp escapes his thin lips. The way he stares down at me, it's like he doesn't understand why I've done what I just did. It's a look of utter betrayal.

"Rio—" My name is cut off by a choking cough. Blood spray across his mouth and onto my face. "Why..."

Why? Did he really just ask that?

I'd laugh but my body has gone deathly still and silent. Numb. This might be shock, but I can't be sure.

"Because I'm your sister." My fingers wrap around the neck of the broken bottle and rip it free of his flesh. Vibrant blood sprays from his severed artery and paints my face and chest red. "And you're a monster! A fucking monster!"

Then I stab him again.

And again.

THIRTY-NINE
EMERIC

THE SOUND of her screams when I nearly topple out of my SUV almost have me falling to my knees on the gravel driveway. We broke every traffic law known to man getting here, and I felt like a little piece of my already black soul wilted and died with every agonizing minute that passed.

I just needed to get to her.

That's all I knew when I discovered she'd been taken to the cabin, and that's still all I know now as I sprint toward the open front door. I'm so focused on the gut-wrenching sounds of her terrified screams that I barely register that the guard kneeling over the mangled body of Bogdan announces that the Russian psychopath is still breathing. *Good.* I have plans for him and he doesn't get to die on me yet. I promised his father that he'd get to say goodbye to his son too, and I'm a man of my word.

If her screams weren't currently wreaking havoc on my insides, I might be able to feel a sliver of relief knowing she had the foresight to bring Cerberus with her, but right now, I'm incapable of feeling anything but sickening dread.

Ignoring the disaster that's become of my sanctuary away

from the city, I sprint through the house. I reach the hallway leading to the basement door as her cries go quiet and another piece of my very being withers away.

No!

Due to the frenzied speed in which I fly down the wood staircase, it's beyond my knowledge how I make it down without eating shit.

The relief I was hoping to obtain once I had her in my sights doesn't come when I find her on the concrete floor. No, my terror only grows until it steals my very ability to fucking breathe.

Pinned beneath her slumped-over, half-naked and exsanguinated brother, is my hysterical wife. I don't know how many years it will take for the visual currently being seared into my brain to not cause pain, but I know it won't be anytime soon.

Tiernan, pale and unmoving, traps Rionach to the ground with his dead weight. In her blood-soaked hand is a dagger-like neck of a broken liquor bottle. From the open gashes on Tiernan's mutilated jugular and torso, she's plunged her makeshift weapon into him numerous times and she shows no signs of stopping. Weakly, she raises the glass to stab it into his side again.

"You're a monster," she chokes out, but her breathless words are barely audible from where I stand. "*A monster*. I'm your little sister. Why would you do this... why would you do this to me?"

The tip of the green glass barely penetrates Tiernan's flesh this time.

She doesn't have anything left. Her brother took everything out of her.

"Princess," I call to her and silently beg that she's hearing me. "I'm here, baby. I'm here."

Taking Tiernan under his arms, I lift the dense weight of

his lifeless body from Rionach and drag him across the room away from her. The only thing that stops me from absolutely losing my shit is the fact that his dick is still tucked into his pants. She stopped him before he could get that far.

Freed from his grasp, she doesn't move, and she's in the same position when I return to her side.

In the puddle of her brother's blood, I fall to my knees beside her. The way her dark floral-print dress is hiked up around her waist and her lace panties are askew have my vision momentarily turning red. The guilt eats away at me because I wasn't here. I promised I would protect her and keep her safe, but I wasn't here when she needed me.

All because of fucking Igor and Niall and the trap they'd orchestrated for me in the city. They'd laid the bait and like a dumbass, I'd almost walked directly into it. If it weren't for the helping hand I'd received from an unexpected source, I wouldn't be here for her now.

Tiernan's death by Rionach's hand was brutal and bloody, but I'm pissed he's already gone. I wanted to make him suffer for longer than he got. I wanted to draw it out for days until he begged to be released, and more importantly, I wanted both Niall and Tiernan to watch each other die.

I take her blood-splattered face between my hands and peer down at her. Those precious gem-like eyes stare back but they're unfocused. Unseeing.

"Baby, please talk to me," my plea is nothing more than a broken whisper. I feel broken seeing her in this state. Something irreparable is cracking inside of my chest as we speak. "Are you hurt? There's too much blood, princess, I can't tell if any of it is yours. You have to tell me if you're hurt."

Almost trancelike, Rionach's hand lets go of the broken glass and reaches for me. My heart stutters beneath my sternum when she trails a featherlight touch down the side of my face. She transfers sticky blood onto temple and cheekbone, but I don't give a fuck. The only thing I care about is that she's here and she's *breathing*.

I don't pray because I'm almost positive if there is a god, he had forsaken me a long time ago for my vast and colorful sins, but when I learned she'd been removed from our home and brought here to them, I prayed I would get to her in time.

I prayed, I pleaded, and I bargained.

"You're alive." her bottom lip, also splattered in blood, wobbles.

And then she breaks.

Before my very eyes, my strong, living, breathing, wildfire of a wife crumples in front of me. Her body heaves and violently shakes as tears pour from her beautiful eyes. The sound that comes out of her, a heartbreaking wail, nearly tears me in half and permanently engraves itself in my mind. For twenty years, my nightmares have consisted almost exclusively of Igor Koslov and the hellhole he kept me in, but I already know her wail will be accompanying the demons from my past in my dreams.

I take hold of her in a grasp that is nowhere near gentle enough for my liking. The desperation I feel to have her pressed to my chest, to have her heartbeat pound against mine, overrides my desire to be tender with her.

In the next breath, I have her off the ground and in my lap. Her legs and arms snake around my torso and neck like vises as she buries her tear-soaked face in my shoulder. The combination of her sobs and the adrenaline shooting through her veins has her entire body uncontrollably trembling.

All I can do is hold her tightly and breathe her in.

"I'm here, princess," I murmur into her ear after pressing my lips to her wild hair. "I'm here and I've got you. Nothing else is going to happen to you. *Ever.* I can fucking promise you that, Rionach. You're safe."

Her only acknowledgment that she's heard what I've said is her arms tightening around me and her face burrowing deeper.

"You're safe and you're mine. You have been since I saw you standing on the roof during New Year's Eve." I've been waiting to tell her the truth, and I can't think of a better time than now to do it. When it can possibly help pull her back from the darkness she's been forcibly thrust into. "Do you have any idea how beautiful you looked surrounded by all those fireworks? Seeing you up there, so free—so alive—it did something to me. It *changed* me. I've never wanted something or someone more than when I saw you. I'm a selfish bastard, I know, but I can't bring myself to regret making you mine. I've never believed in something as trivial as fate, but, princess, you are the other half of my twisted soul."

The unyielding hold she has on my neck loosens as she pulls back. Tears still fill her eyes and leave streaks through the blood staining her cheeks, but her sobs have slowly started to settle. For the first time since I've found her, the bleary expression in her green gaze is clear. She's here with me and she's hearing what I'm saying. Thank fuck.

"I knew I craved you that night on the roof. I knew I wanted you when you walked down the aisle to me. And I knew I needed you when I told you about the ghosts from my past that still haunt me, and without hesitation, you told me you'd help keep them at bay." As gently as I can, I pull the strands of her dark red hair out of the dried blood on her face and tuck them behind her ears. "I need you in a way I've never needed another person, Rionach. I'm unable and unwilling to go through this life without you because you've broken and altered me in ways that can't be undone. What happened today will never happen again—it can't happen again—because I

427

don't think I will survive it. I won't survive it because on top of everything else, you've done the impossible and managed to make me fall in love with you."

More tears form in her eyes but this time they're for a different reason. Wordlessly, she threads her fingers through my hair and drops her forehead against mine. She holds me to her as if she's trying to commit the sensation to memory. Peace settles over me like a warm balm to my shredded, dark soul.

"Say it again," she whispers as her nose skims down mine.

I hold her fiercely against me so she understands the gravity and the truth of what I'm telling her. "I love you, Rionach Banes."

Her breath catches in her throat. "No one has ever told me that."

My mother wasn't around for long, but she made sure that I heard her tell me she loved me every single day. This additional reminder of how Rionach's parents failed her only makes my hatred and bloodlust for them grow deeper. "I'll tell you every day, princess.'

Fingers still in my hair, she pulls my face to hers and presses her mouth to mine. It's a messy and desperate kind of kiss, but it's exactly what both of us need. She clings to me and opens her mouth obediently when my tongue trails along the seam of her perfect plump lips. I lick into her mouth and savor the taste of her.

Within a minute, she breathlessly pulls and removes the black jacket that had already been halfway off her shoulders. Past the point of caring, she discards it behind her in the puddle of crimson red. Her thin fingers taking hold of the fabric of her dress next have my fingers locking around her wrists and stopping her.

"Rio—"

"Please," she pleads. "I need to feel your touch instead of his. His hands... I can still feel them on me. Please, Emeric, touch me and wash him away."

How could I possibly deny her this? Or *anything*? She has me so wrapped around her little finger that I would bring her the moon if she asked.

With her hands free once more, she pulls the floral dress over the top of her head and tosses it on top of her jacket. She rises up onto her knees to remove her panties, and I shake my head. I've never felt particularly bad for destroying her lacy undergarments but with this pair, I truly couldn't give a single shit as I rip the thin material at her hips. After Tiernan forcibly tried to remove this thong from her body, I had no intentions of allowing her to keep it. Destroying it now ensures this.

With her body free of clothing, her red-stained fingers grip the material of my white dress shirt and pops each of the buttons with one unforgiving yank. Her warm hands are on my chest within seconds. They trace soft lines until she reaches the trail of hair below my navel.

Rionach wastes no time attacking the zipper and button of my slacks and taking my stiffening cock out. Her deft fingers stroke me until I'm throbbing and the slit at the head has a pearl of precum forming. Green eyes that are still red around the edges lock with mine as she swipes the droplet up with her thumb before sinking the digit into her mouth.

The way she hums in contentment almost has me grabbing her hips and bringing her down onto my pulsating length. It goes against my nature to do so, but Rionach is in complete control here. She's calling the shots and this one time, I'm her willing servant. She can use me any way she needs to if it helps eliminate some of the tangible tendrils of fear still circulating within her.

Taking hold of the thick base of my cock, she rises back onto her knees and runs the weeping crown through her slick pussy lips. Her movements are slow and border on torturous, but still, I continue to grant her full control. I'm unable to stop the heady groan that slips through my lips when she presses the head of my dick against her warm, beckoning entrance.

Fingers digging into the soft flesh of her hips, I drop my forehead against her bare shoulder and fight the urge to thrust upward to meet her halfway as she slowly starts to sink down. The tight and quivering muscles of her pussy envelop me and welcome me inside inch by glorious inch until she is fully seated on my shaft.

Taking hold of my face, she forces me to look at her again. Her pale skin is streaked with her brother's blood and her eyes are swollen from crying, but she's still the most beautiful thing I've seen.

"I need to see your face," she says softly. "I need to see your face so I know that it's you fucking me."

Inky black and violent wrath surges within me. "It'll only ever be me fucking you, princess. No one else. Do you hear what I'm saying? You are mine and mine alone. Your body, heart, and soul belong to me, just as mine belong to you. As long as I'm breathing, no one else will ever touch you or this pussy again, and even in death, I will find a way to escape the underworld and eviscerate the poor sap who dares to try and touch what is mine."

Excruciatingly slowly, she lifts almost completely up, leaving only the overly sensitive and pulsing crown buried inside. Her lips part in a silent gasp when she rocks her hips down and welcomes all of me back into her wet heat.

"I hear what you're saying," she answers just mere millimeters from my lips. "I hear you and I feel you." Against my mouth, she quickly adds, "Only you," before she kisses me again.

On the blood-soaked concrete floor of my cellar, my wife rides my cock until my touch is the only one she remembers.

FORTY
EMERIC

"Igor knew I'd personally go to The Daria and that's why
there weren't any bombs left at Tartarus," I tell her, as my soap-
covered hands glide over her smooth skin and wash away the
evidence of what she was forced to do today. The water around
the shower drain has only just started to run clear after many
long minutes of scrubbing. I don't want to make her stay here in
the cabin any longer than necessary, but I knew we needed to
get the mixture of Mathis's and Tiernan's blood off of her. The
moment I have her dried and in clean clothes, I'm taking her
back to the city. Once I'm done dealing with Niall and the
Koslovs, I don't plan to let her out of my sight for a downright
obscene amount of time. "That's the problem when dealing
with someone who knows you on a personal level. Igor knew
what that hotel represented, and he used it against me. His
plan of luring me away from you and into a building rigged to
blow nearly worked because of the sentiment I still have
toward that hotel."

Rionach pushes her soaked hair back from her face. Water

droplets stick in her dark eyelashes, and they fall when she blinks up at me. "Is it really gone? The hotel?"

"It's gone," I sigh. "They put enough explosives in the basement that we're lucky the neighboring buildings didn't also come down."

I'm beyond grateful and fucking lucky that I have placed people with power in my back pocket because stopping the nosey government agencies from sniffing around this shitstorm without their help would be almost impossible. On top of their assistance, many of the chits I've collected over the years are going to have to be called in to make sure this is reported as a gas main explosion and nothing more. The cost of protecting my business and my interests will always be worth every penny. It's a price I will gladly play ten times over.

My left hand covers hers when she places her palm over my heartbeat. The pristine pink polish that had decorated her nails this morning when I left her in what I believed to be safe hands is now chipped and cracked. Along with the vast array of bruises already developing on her pale skin, her ruined nails are just more proof of how hard she fought today.

I'm so proud of her, but I will use every resource at my disposal to ensure she's never put in a position where she has to fight like that again. I failed her once already by trusting her with Mathis, and that is a mistake I won't make twice.

"What are you going to do?" she asks. The pronounced circles beneath her still red-rimmed eyes are growing darker by the second. I want nothing more than to crawl into bed with her, but we can't rest. Not yet, anyway. There's still something we need to deal with before either of us can get the sleep we desperately need. It's already been well over twenty-four hours since I've slept myself. "Will you rebuild?"

"Yes." The fingers of my right hand trail over the purple marks forming on her side and hip. Before we'd untangled ourselves from each other and left the basement, she told me what had happened here. Her hold on me only tightened more the longer she talked about what Mathis and Anneli had done for Soren, and then what happen with Bogdan and Tiernan. The only reason I'd been able to remain relatively calm during this is because her naked body wrapped around mine kept me grounded. "We'll rebuild and we'll find a way to honor and compensate the families of the ones who didn't get out of the building in time."

The warning I'd received about the hotel had saved my life along with the team of men who'd accompanied me there, but it also gave me the ability to order an immediate evacuation. If I hadn't gotten that text message from my secret ally, over five hundred lives would have been lost in the blast instead of a dozen.

It doesn't surprise me Igor Koslov, and subsequently Niall Moran, were willing to eliminate that many innocent lives just for a chance at ending my existence. Their desperation and ugly greed are making them act impulsively, and that kind of mentality can only lead to casualties.

"I want to help," she doesn't hesitate to offer. "The work at Tartarus can wait for a while because this is important. I want to help rebuild your mother's hotel."

"It was never actually her hotel," I correct, my hand tightening around hers.

She waves me off. "It was hers in every way that counted, and I want to make sure we preserve the memory of her. She was your mom and she loved you. We'll make sure The Daria is returned to its former glory."

A crushing weight of an emotion I can't quite place crashes into me and all I can do against it is wrap Rionach tightly up in my arms. I press her now clean body against mine and hold on for dear fucking life.

She clings to me just as fiercely and for several quiet moments, this is how we stay. Wrapped up in each other, standing beneath the warm spray of water from the waterfall showerhead above us.

The moment comes to a bittersweet end when she whispers against my sternum, "Is my dad dead too?"

Too.

This never should have happened. Her hands should have been able to remain clean.

"No," I answer, my chin resting atop the crown of her head. "Niall isn't dead yet. Both fathers are in my custody in the basement of Tartarus, and Bogdan is being delivered there as we speak."

It was a text I received that consisted of only a single word, but it's a message I will always be eternally grateful for because it saved my men from losing their lives and it ensured that I was able to return home to her.

Trap.

He risked everything by sending me that one syllable and because of it, I'm forever in his debt.

It was after we had retreated to the fleet of armored SUVs and started heading across town to meet Nova and his team at the club that I received a second message. This one was equally as important and the key to putting this war between our families to bed at last. We'd been circling each other long enough, and I was and *still* am fucking tired of playing these goddamn games.

The Irish Wife -B

If it still hadn't been clear who was behind these messages, the emoji of a four-leaf clover at the end of the second text made it glaringly obvious. The men riding in the car with me had all stared when I had started to laugh. The symmetry of this all starting with his help and ending with it was hysterical to me because with one text, the final nail in the coffin of Niall Moran's legacy was hammered in place. And by one of his most trusted men, no less.

The location had proven correct when both Nova and I, along with our teams of trained men, descended upon the decaying Irish pub and found both Niall and Igor prematurely toasting to their victory against me. The way the chubby Irish man's face paled and the reality of his demise flashed in his eyes made the beast residing within me purr.

Igor, snide and smug till the bitter end, had just smirked at me once he was restrained, and asked, "Where's that whore of yours, Banes?"

My fist connecting with his face—repeatedly—had silenced him, but that seed he'd planted had taken root.

She doesn't know, but the night I removed her IUD, I'd also implanted something in her. A tracker. The night I couldn't find her at Holloway's fundraiser turned the whispering impulse I'd originally had about putting a chip in her neck into a dire need. I was never going to be caught in a situation where I didn't know her location again. It was a nonnegotiable fact.

Because of Igor's parting words, seeing the red dot on the tracking app lead to the cabin did little to settle me. Between that and Mathis's sudden radio silence, I knew it in my bones something was very wrong. It wasn't until I carried her out of the cellar that I felt like I could finally take a fucking breath.

Rionach stiffens in my arms. "Bogdan is still alive?"

"Barely." Cerberus did a number on that fucker's face. I've seen ground hamburger look better than that mangled mess. "I called in the good doctor to keep him breathing."

Her chin presses against my chest as she stares wide-eyed up at me. "Why would you do that?"

"He doesn't get to die yet. Not until I've had my time with him. With *all* of them." I wipe the drops the water collected beneath her eyes with my thumbs. She could be bothered by what I'm saying and shy away from my touch, and I wouldn't fault her. I'm all but admitting I'm going to tear the man she believes is her father into teeny-tiny pieces, after all, but Rionach doesn't flinch. Doesn't balk. She's so fucking strong and she's accepted this needs to be done. "Twice now, they've attempted to take you from me. The only way any of them will be granted the sweet mercy of death is by my hand. I will accept nothing less."

Wiping Igor Koslov from the face of this earth has been a long time coming. It should have happened two decades ago.

Green flames flare in her eyes. "Make it hurt."

"I promise, princess."

─────

WITH CERBERUS STANDING guard over her and Yates positioned at my locked office door, I left my sleeping wife on the black leather sofa in my office before I made my way to the concrete room in the club's basement. In the back seat of the SUV, Rionach had passed out with her head in my lap on our drive here. I want to take her home and crawl into bed beside her, but taking care of this is far more important.

The life I want to provide for Rionach can't happen while these men are still breathing. The threat they pose to her, and our future family, can't stand any longer.

The tarp scrapes across the clean concrete floors as I drag my gift to Niall through the metal door Nova holds open for me.

The effects that today have had on my friend and second-in-command are written clearly across his stone-like face. Another man he put hundreds of hours into personally training died today. Mathis betrayed us, and then he was killed. The loss of losing Camden still weighs heavily on the big man's tattooed shoulders, but to learn that the young soldier was slain by Mathis... that blow is going to take time to recover from. Just like I had, Nova put his life and trust in Mathis's hands many times, and to learn he didn't trust us enough in return to come to us about what was happening with Soren is a tough pill to swallow for Nova.

My wife reminded both Nova and me before we left the cabin that Mathis and Anneli did what they thought they had to in order to protect their family.

Now that I personally know the kind of desperation that infects you when someone you love is taken, I can't bring myself to completely fault the pair for their actions. But they didn't have to die. Their deaths could have been avoided if they'd only told me the truth because I would have told them that Bogdan was never going to let them walk away. Making them beg for their child and then killing them in front of Soren fed his psychopathic soul. He got off on their anguish and fear.

The boy, who Nova had found in the woods being guarded by Cerberus, is understandably traumatized by what's happened. We've tried to get him to speak, but so far, the kid refuses to make a peep. Due to his friendship with Mathis, Nova has spent the most time with Soren out of all of us. This connection has resulted in Soren imprinting on my second-in-command and clinging to him like he's his safety blanket. It was a struggled to get Soren to release his hold on Nova's tattooed neck so he could join me here now. And I can tell by the look in the tattooed beast of a man's face that he wants to get back to the little boy.

When all is said and done, I have no doubt who will end up taking Soren in. I just wonder if Nova's figured it out yet himself.

Nova gives me a nod of solidarity before pulling the metal door closed and locking me in the room with them.

Let the games begin.

I know the precise second Niall sees what my gift is when his muffled, inconsolable wails fill the soundproof room.

With a dramatic flourish of my hand, I gesture at the bloodied and very still body of his son atop the blue tarp. "Did I or did I not tell you both you'd get to see your sons again?" I ask the two gagged men who are strapped down naked on rolling steel tables. The black straps across their chests and legs keep them firmly in place and right where I need them. To the left of Igor is Bogdan in a similar state. The only difference is the collection of bloodstained bandages covering his unrecognizable face and throat, and the IV in his arm. It would seem Doc went all out to follow my orders to keep the Russian breathing. Good. "I always follow through with my promises."

I nudge Tiernan's head with the toe of my shoe until it lolls to the right. Milky, lifeless eyes now stare in the direction of his pathetic, weepy father.

Stepping over the speed bump that is technically my brother-in-law, I pass through Igor's and Niall's tables. My knuckles tap rhythmically against the shiny metal surface of both as I pass to stand at Niall's head. Leaning over him, terrified and tear-filled eyes peer up at me. Fear-induced adrenaline makes his body quake like he's a fucking Chihuahua. He's downright pitiful.

Niall wanted to be at the top of the food chain, but he never had what it takes to sit upon my throne. He would have been eaten alive.

"I do believe I made you a promise at your shitty bar, Moran," I tell him, the corners of my lips already tugging as a familiar thrill begins to hum in my bloodstream. "I told you

440

what would happen if your family moved against mine. *Again.* Do you remember this?"

He doesn't offer me any form of answer.

My tongue clucks disapprovingly. "Perhaps you don't. You were nursing your sorrows that night in a bottle of whiskey. Let me remind you. I told you that before I killed you I would take you apart bit by bit. Is this starting to ring a bell in your meat-loaf of a brain yet?"

Niall's eyes squeeze closed and force more bitch-baby tears to stream down the sides of his ruddy face.

"I promised you that your god wouldn't recognize you by the time you go to heaven's gates." I mockingly cross myself before leaving him and going to stand above Igor. "Just like your son, you taught me the art of flaying flesh off bodies. While your spawn was out butchering random women for sport, I was perfecting my craft with hopes that you'd one day be the one under my blade." A delightful mixture of hatred and rage settles on Igor's face as he glares up at me. "During all those years I spent as your student, did you ever think I'd end up using your teachings against you? I know my father never saw it coming. He thought you'd managed to beat me into submission, but as it turns out, all you did was create a much bigger problem. Do you think as he choked to death on his blood, he realized his mistake?"

Unsurprisingly, Igor doesn't offer me any kind of response.

I take the wicked sharp switchblade from my pocket. The swishing sound of it opening bounces off the stone walls.

"Slicing away every inch of skin from a person's body is a tedious task. It takes precision and patience. As we both know, I'm not historically a patient man, but for this—for you—I will make an exception." To really drive my point home, I drag the tip of the blade over his heart. My pressure isn't hard enough that real damage is caused. Only a whisper-thin line is sliced into his skin. "Most don't survive being skinned alive. The pain causes the body to go into shock and the heart just gives out. The ones who do survive, they inevitably die of hypothermia. See, without your skin, your body loses its ability to keep heat in and you freeze to death."

I leave the head of his table and begin to slowly prowl between all three. Bogdan is so close to death as it is, I don't know if he's comprehending what I'm saying. His head turns ever so slightly in my direction as he tracks the sound of me moving around the room. He only had one good eye to begin with and after Cerberus's attack, I have no idea if either eyeball is still intact. The white bandages Doc placed conceal whatever remains, not that it really matters at this point whether or not he can see me coming. We both know I'll be his executioner.

"What do you say, Niall and Igor?" I jovially ask the set of fathers as I push the sleeves of my shirt farther up my forearms. I have other plans for Bogdan Koslov but forcing him to listen to his father be flayed alive seems like a decadent amuse-bouche for his own death. "Do you think you'll live long enough to freeze to death? I sure hope you both do because I would just hate to see our time together cut so short." Blade twisting between my fingers, I come to a stop at the end of Igor's bed. "Who wants to go first?"

FORTY-ONE
RIONACH

One Week Later

THE WIND HOWLS through the private airstrip and whips my loose hair around my face and shoulders. It's offensively early and the morning sky has just started to come alive with colors as the sun crests. I could be home, cuddled up in our bed, but I needed to be here for this. Emeric tried to get me to stay. I wouldn't hear it.

I need to see this through.

The door of the private plane opens and a moment later, a familiar broad figure appears at the doorway. He descends the stairs and stalks across the tarmac alone. The armed security I know he brought with him is nowhere to be found. I'm not sure if he's doing this as a show of good faith or if he stupidly believes my husband isn't a threat to him anymore because they happened to part ways last time on relatively civil terms.

Emeric's warm hand envelops my much colder one and he gives me a reassuring squeeze. *Everything is going to be okay.*

This past week, things have been better. Calm. After

sleeping for over five hours on the couch in Emeric's office at Tartarus, I waited another five for him to emerge from the basement. He was wired with a chaotic energy I've never seen in him before, and he was covered in blood. One day I might ask him how he ended their lives, but I haven't yet. Maybe when the shock of what happened with Tiernan lessens, I'll find the courage to ask. The amount of blood that was painted on my husband tells me it was brutal, and that's all I need to know. Right now, I'm content not having all the gory details.

What I do know is the peace of mind of knowing they're no longer out there posing a threat to us has been priceless. While there has been peace, there has also been grief. I haven't been mourning the lives of my father and Tiernan. They don't deserve that kind of energy and mental space from me, but the neglected little girl who still resides within me is mourning the loss of how things could have been. In another life, I could have been born into a family that loved and valued me, and the notion of that idealistic life is something worth grieving for. The little girl mourns that things will never change or get better. She's sad that this is what it came down to, and this is how her family was undone.

I might not have been born into a loving family, but I can build one and that gives me hope for the future. A future I will share with *him*.

Emeric leads me forward to greet the new arrival.

"Tadhg."

"Emeric."

We're using first names, that's a good sign.

My grandfather stands before us, looking as stoic as ever in his three-piece tweed suit. Despite the seven-hour flight from Dublin, there isn't a single wrinkle in the fabric. He could be angry and upset for the reason he was called back to the States so soon, but he appears to be completely neutral.

444

With his hands held casually behind him, Tadhg shifts his focus to me, and his observant eyes linger on the fading dark circles around my eyes. On top of the concussion that I got from Tiernan hitting the back of my head, I also got a matching pair of black eyes. They appeared about twelve hours after the whole ordeal.

"Rionach, I'm relieved to see that you're well."

I wish I could easily believe he means this, but my experience with my bloodline makes me tentative to accept his kind words.

"She almost wasn't, thanks to your cockroach of a grandson." The venom that laces Emeric's voice has chills of awareness running down my spine.

My grandfather shifts uneasily on his feet. "Yes, both your grandmother and I were appalled to hear what had transpired between you two. Tiernan's behavior is something we would never condone," he tells me with what looks to be genuine sympathy on his face. "How his depraved behavior went unnoticed for so long is beyond me."

"It wasn't unnoticed," I calmly argue. "It was purposely ignored because Tiernan was the golden child and my parents held him up on an untouchable pedestal. They told him over and over again how special he was, and how the world was his for the taking. He could do no wrong. It shouldn't shock anyone that he would take that literally."

To my utter surprise, my grandfather nods his head in agreement. "You're right. His upbringing set him up for failure."

At a loss for words, all I can do is stare at the man before me.

"*Failure*," Emeric repeats slowly like he's trying it out on his tongue. "Is that what we're calling almost raping your own sister these days? A *failure*?" He makes a tsking sound as he shakes his head. "No. That wasn't a fucking failure. Tiernan is lucky my wife took care of the problem before I had a chance to get my hands on him, because I would have slowly and methodically taken him apart, and then made him eat the pieces."

All of us standing here know he means every word he's saying.

Tadhg clears his throat. "An understandable punishment. I would have reacted the same way if someone tried to force themselves upon my wife."

"Glad we're in agreement," Emeric tells him, contempt still infused in his tone. "Let's move on to why you're here so we can get on with our day. You have a long flight back to Ireland, and Rionach and I have better things to do than chitchatting on a tarmac."

My grandfather inclines his head. "Agreed."

Emeric turns toward the three SUVs parked by the gate of the airfield and makes a quick motion with his free hand. Yates, who's become Emeric's go-to guard this past week, pushes off the back door he'd been casually leaning against so he can open it. He waits a moment for the person inside to emerge.

Looking more disheveled than I've ever seen her, my mother, Imogen, climbs out of the black vehicle. Her familiar red hair is knotted and tousled on one side of her head, and the cream sweater is buttoned wrong in the front and askew. Normally, she can walk in a pair of heels like she was born wearing them, but now, as she's led toward us by Yates, she moves like a newborn calf learning to walk.

At my grandfather's displeased inhale, Emeric passes him a bored look. "Given her current appearance I can see how you'd think we're the cause of it, but I can assure you, your daughter has been perfectly safe while in our custody. The only person to blame for that hot mess is her. As you can imagine, she hasn't exactly been handling the loss of her spouse and titty-baby well. She doesn't look it, but fuck, that woman has some pipes on her. She screamed for nearly six hours straight. We finally had to sedate her just so my men could get some peace and quiet."

"What reaction did you expect from her after you told her Niall was tortured to death and her child was killed? Your men then kept her sequestered within her bedroom for days on end like a prisoner," my grandfather snaps, showing the first hint of agitation since arriving.

"Tadhg, before you get your knickers in a twist, I would like to remind you that allowing you to take your daughter home is an act of kindness from me. She was more than happy to sell her daughter to the Koslovs if it meant her social status increased and she got an extra couple million in her pocket. That act alone makes it well within my right to keep her. Just ask my brother's mother-in-law. My brother had her enslaved to my empire for her crimes against her daughter. I would have no problem doing the same to Imogen, but like I said, I decided to be kind. So instead of staring at me with that irritating look on your face, perhaps you should be thanking me."

My grandfather schools his expression and tightly says, "Thank you for allowing me to bring my daughter home. It will clearly be what is best for her."

"You're so very welcome," Emeric replies, the satisfaction he's feeling clear in his tone.

I step closer to Emeric's side, and my hand tightens around his when my mother is delivered to our little group. Sensing my discomfort, my husband releases my hand so he can wrap his arm around me instead. I'm not scared of Imogen or anything like that, but there's a lot of water under that bridge now and I don't know how to navigate it.

Tadhg wraps his daughter into a tight hug that she doesn't

return and places a kiss to her messy hair before asking Yates, "Would you deliver her to the jet. I will join her in just a moment."

Not willing to take an order from an outsider, Yates looks at Emeric for confirmation and once he has it, he takes my mother by her upper arm and tries to steer her away.

She allows him to lead her a foot away before her head whips violently around and her callous blue eyes pierce into mine. "This is all your fault. You ruined everything. We were on our way back to greatness, and you couldn't play your fucking part. Now look at us. There's nothing left. They're dead and it's your fault, you selfish brat."

"Imogen!" It was rare that I ever heard my grandfather raise his voice during our few-and-far-between visits but hearing him roar her name reminds me why he's been in charge in the UK for as long as he has. Tadhg Kelly has and always will be a force to be reckoned with. "Your family acted foolishly and were met with appropriate consequences. None of this is Rionach's fault. Now shut your bloody mouth and get on the fucking plane!"

The already lackluster color drains from my mother's face as she looks away and allows Yates to escort her to the waiting plane.

It'd be easy to think she said those things because of her declining mental state, but I know that isn't the case. She wasn't just lashing out. She was showing what's always been behind the poised housewife mask she's worn. Her mask has cracked over the years and I've experienced the vitriol that's leaked out, but it's never been like this.

Pop waits until she's halfway there to turn back to us, and says, "I apologize for my daughter. She's—"

"Don't apologize or make a shitty excuse for her behavior," Emeric interrupts. "Just make sure it's clear to your daughter that if she returns to my city, I won't have any kindness left in me."

With an exhausted sigh, Tadhg slightly inclines his head. "It never should have come to this, Banes. Niall was a small, imprudent man who thought he deserved everything. A trait he evidently passed on to his son. I know it was for the sake of your bride that you kept giving them chances, but they were never going to stop. We all knew it. I tried my best to warn them what would happen if they kept at it. They refused to listen." He looks between both Emeric and me. "For what it is worth, I am abundantly sorry for the hardships they've caused, and, Rionach, no woman should ever be put in the position that you were. It was unfair. Your upbringing was unfair."

My throat is suddenly tight because I've waited years to hear someone tell me this—for someone to acknowledge how I was treated. His apology is nice, but it's not going to heal the wounds I've amassed through the years.

"You're right," I say. "It was unfair." Emeric's arm tightens around me like a calming cocoon. "Despite their best efforts, I now know what it's like to be loved by someone unconditionally and how I should be treated. I know I didn't deserve how they treated me."

Being with Emeric, even with all his faults, has made it that much clearer just how emotionally neglected I was. He loves me and all the twisted pieces of my soul. Emeric isn't with me because he has something to gain from it. If anything, making me his wife came with costs. Men died and The Daria is in ruins because he made me his. He did all of it because he wanted me. Just me.

"It isn't worth much, I know, but I am pleased to know you are happy, Rionach," my grandfather says. "And safe. Emeric Banes is a lot of things, yes, but he will keep you safe."

"I shouldn't have had to protect her from her own family,"

Emeric snaps before pressing his lips to my temple and leading me back a step. "Come on, princess. It's time to go. There's somewhere I want to take you."

I grant my grandfather a half smile and a small wave as I allow Emeric to guild me back to the waiting fleet of black cars.

"Princess," Tadhg repeats loudly, forcing us to stop and turn around. "You call her princess," he muses.

"Is that funny to you, Kelly?"

"It is," he admits. "Do you know what Rionach means, Banes?" Taking Emeric's silence as an answer, he continues, "It means queenly."

———

LOOKING over the roof's ledge, I tell Emeric, "When you said you wanted to bring me somewhere, I didn't think you meant here."

Large hands rest on my hips from behind. "This is where it all started. This is where I saw you—*really* saw you—for the first time," he says close to my ear. "You stood right here on this ledge. I thought you were going to jump at first, and something in my chest cracked at the idea of snuffing out your flame, but then you raised your arms and smiled up at the sky. That's when I knew you were mine."

"Just like that?"

"Yes." The warmth of his chest presses against my back as he pulls me closer to him.

Last week in the cabin's cellar, when he first admitted our interaction in the hotel lobby that same night wasn't our first encounter like I'd thought, I'd been too emotionally wrecked to ask any questions. Or even wrap my head around it.

And then he went and told me he loved me for the first time. After that, I definitely didn't have the mental real estate to ponder the truth of how our story started. Now that we've both had time to decompress and settle, I want to know everything.

"You didn't marry me as payment for their debt, then?" I ask, already knowing the answer, but I still want to hear him say it out loud.

"Your family stealing from me handed you to me on a silver platter. I had already been working on a plan to claim you, but then your brother raided my warehouse, and it was just too perfect to pass up. I was going to punish your family and I was going to take you as my wife. Our wedding gave me the opportunity to do both." He runs his nose down the side of my face. "When you stormed down that church aisle, your eyes blazing with anger, I knew I'd made the right choice. You were magnificent, and there won't be a day I'm not thankful to have that image of you ingrained in my brain. Just like the visual of you standing on this very wall is."

He'd orchestrated the whole thing. Emeric knew what he wanted—me—and he used my brother stealing from him to his advantage. I've said it before, but we really are just a bunch of puppets and he's the one pulling our strings.

Hearing him confirm I've always meant more to him than a token he acquired as payment has the invisible wall I'd placed between us shattering at our feet. It was the safeguard I'd built around my heart when I believed falling in love with him would only end in disaster. I believed one day he would realize he made a rash decision driven by revenge and spite and decide he wanted nothing to do with me.

I now know that isn't the case because he loves me.

Emeric Banes, the monster, the devil, the cruel king, loves *me*.

How many people are lucky enough to say that?

He chose me, and in return, I will choose him. Every day.

"What made you follow me up here that night?"

He sighs. "I watched how you moved around the room trying your best to blend in with the walls. To make yourself small. I knew with one look at you that you were pretending to be someone you weren't, and I wanted to know why. I wanted to know the version of you that you were trying so hard to hide." His deft fingers collect my hair and brush it over my right shoulder. "When I found you up here, I got a glimpse of the woman you could be. I saw the life—the potential—that could thrive, if only given the chance. Most importantly, I found a kindred soul to match my jagged one."

I once told him we fit together like a fucked-up puzzle—that we fit together. What took me many weeks to figure out, he learned in mere minutes.

"How did you know I was meant to be yours so fast?"

"When I looked at you, it was like I'd found my reason to breathe."

His lips press to my temple before he releases me and moves to stand at my side. Confused, I watch him remove the black wool coat. Just like I'd done with my heels on New Year's Eve, he discards it in the gravel beneath our feet.

With a devious smirk that makes butterflies erupt in my lower stomach and heat spread in my veins, Emeric pulls himself up onto the roof's brick parapet wall. "Come on, princess, a little danger is good for the soul. It reminds us that we're alive."

Grinning like a lovestruck fool, I accept the hand he extends. With well-practiced skill, I join him on the ledge. The mid-morning sun shining down on us is a little different than the celebratory fireworks that were here the last time I stood on this roof, but the view is no less stunning. In fact, it's better because I'm no longer standing up here experiencing the rush of adrenaline alone.

I'm no longer alone in this life because I don't have to hide who I am anymore. The mask that has smothered me for so many years has been burned to ashes, and now I can just *be*. And it's all thanks to him.

The man so many people fear, the man who stole me and set me free.

My husband.

Pressing the side of my body against his, I lift up on my tippy-toes and softly kiss his stubbly cheek. "I love you too," I whisper against his skin. "Thank you for stealing me and making me your wife."

He stares back at me and for the first time since I've known him, the violent storm in his gray eyes has calmed.

While I've found freedom in him, Emeric has found peace in me.

EPILOGUE 1
RIONACH

Three Months Later

"You're doing so fucking good, baby." The combination of his praise and his fingers trailing down the vertebra of my arched spine has goosebumps dancing across my heated flesh. "I'm so proud of you. Just a little bit more, you can do it."

Instantly, a mewl of disagreement leaks from my parted lips. I've never felt fuller in my entire life. "I can't. It's too much."

His palm slides down my back again, only to smack my ass. In my current state, my cheek resting on the smooth buttery soft sheets and my ass raised in the air, I'm in prime position for a spanking. A fact he's been taking full advantage of since he flipped me over after he was done making me see stars with his skilled tongue. I've said it once, and I'll say it again, my favorite way to wake up is with my husband's face between my thighs.

"Shh... yes, you can," Emeric insists. "Let me help you."

Reaching between our sweaty bodies, he presses the familiar U-shaped vibrator harder against my clit. The delightful wave of increased pleasure instantly has my muscles relaxing, something he wastes no time exploiting. The simultaneous sensations of ecstasy stemming from my pussy and the intoxicating bite of pain of his fat cock trying to enter me in a place no other man has ever been has my fingers digging into the sheets.

"Oh, fuck," I groan.

"That's it. Just like that," Emeric encourages, his hand continuing to apply pressure to the toy between my legs. "Push back as I push in. You're so close to taking all of me. Fuck, princess. Do you have any idea how sexy it is to watch my cock sink into your ass?"

We've been working toward this for many weeks with various-sized plugs. It's been a process I've found quite enjoyable. Especially when Emeric would insert one before we left the house and have me wear it all day. There's just something deliciously erotic about sitting in a meeting with a team of architects and engineers as we go over the rebuild of The Daria with a plug in my ass. It's a dirty little secret that makes me soaking wet every single time. Emeric is fully aware what kind of affect this has on me and has loved reaping his reward on the conference room table the second everyone leaves.

I had naïvely believed if I could take the last rather large plug up my ass, that I could take my husband without much difficulty. I was wrong. It's never been an unknown fact that Emeric has been more than blessed in the big-dick department, but the way he's stretching the tight ring of muscle now makes him feel twice as big.

The only reason I'm not tapping out is because of the waves of pleasure that accompany the pain of being pushed to my body's limit.

"Relax and let me in, baby," he commands gently.

From my eyebrows to my curled toes, I force my muscles to

ease up and Emeric presses his hips forward at the same time. The sensation of him being fully seated, deep inside of me, nearly has me rearing up. His calming palm pressing to the middle of my back keeps me in his desired position.

My breathing has turned into rapid pants that escape my parted lips. He doesn't move and allows me time to adjust to his invasion.

"You're such a good girl," he praises as he bends down to press his lips to the ridges of my spine once. Twice. Three times. He never stops manipulating the toy. It vibrates against my swollen clit and that deep, allusive place inside my pussy. My body is torn between the two vying sensations happening. Part of me wants to pull my hips away from his intrusion and press harder to the pink silicon vibrator, and the other part wants to thrust backward into him because it somehow still craves more. "Look at you. You're taking every inch of my cock."

"Oh my God," my whimper comes out partially muffled because of the way I now have my face buried in the sheets beneath me. "*Emeric.*"

"I fucking love when you say my name like you're pleading with your god," he growls. "Are you ready for me to move?"

"Yes. *Please.*"

"I'll never get tired of you begging for my cock."

"Stop fucking talking and—"

Every thought inside of my brain abandons me along with my ability to breathe properly when he pulls back, only to tunnel deep back inside a second later. I squirm beneath him from the fullness in my ass and the vibrations at my pussy. It's simultaneously too much and not enough, and all I can do is take it. Take everything he gives me.

He keeps this up, his thrusts alternating between deep and shallow, and agonizing slow and breath-stealing fast. It could be minutes or it could be seconds later—my ability to comprehend time is no longer intact as I'm overcome with the way he plays my body—when the telltale signs of an orgasm barreling toward me swirls in my lower stomach.

"Your ass is going to look so good with cum leaking out of it," Emeric tells me between clenched teeth before I feel something warm drip where his dick is buried inside of me. Spit. He just spit on my asshole. Which is something I arguably shouldn't find hot, but I do. I really fucking do.

"I'm so close," I pant, my fingers tearing and pulling at the fabric beneath my overheated body. "Please make me come."

He's repeatedly told me he will give me anything I want. All I have to do is open my mouth and ask for it. Now is no different. The tempo in which he rocks the vibrator against me and his thrusts have colors erupting behind my tightly closed eyes.

The simmering hum of my impending release morphs into something intense and uncontrollable. It crashes into me without much warning. Waves upon waves of ecstasy overtake me. Muscles locking, my body shakes beneath his. I think I scream, but the blood pounding in my eardrums has left me deaf. His grip tightens on me to the point it almost hurts and a moment later, I'm filled with the warm rush of his cum.

My quivering knees give up and I fall flat against the mattress. Emeric, careful to not crush me, pulls out of my ass and removes the toy. My breath hitches as he does, the raw nerves down there making every feeling more intense.

I'm nothing but pliable rubber bones when he turns me on my side and lies with his chest pressed to my back. We stay like that, both of us fighting to slow our breathing and heartbeats, for a long moment. The pads of his fingertips trace designs across my heated flesh until goosebumps are dancing beneath his touch. He travels down my left arm and when he reaches my painted fingernails, he captures my hand in his. His thumb immediately begins to twist the emerald-cut diamond that now resides there. It's a habit he's acquired since slipping the ring on my finger while I slept months ago. The hopeful look in Emeric's gaze when I'd woken up to the impressive diamond weighing down my limb silenced any argument I had about its impractical size. He'd taken the time to select this ring for me himself, and I wasn't about to squash that just because I was worried about blinding the astronauts in space. They have goggles and shit, they'll be fine.

With our hands clasped together, he brings them to rest on my lower stomach—another habit he's fallen into as of late—and each time he does it, butterflies erupt in my chest and my heart squeezes.

"How's my baby?" he asks, his breath tickling the shell of my ear.

I'm incapable of fighting the grin that overtakes my face. "I'm good."

His chuckle only makes the muscle in my chest constrict tighter. "Oh, I know you are, princess, but how's my other baby?"

My palm presses over the nearly nonexistent bump that is starting to form—to the place where our baby is growing.

Three weeks after the whole ordeal with my family and the Koslovs, Emeric got his wish and put his baby inside of me. He'd figured it out before I did and when he'd ordered Doc to come draw my blood to make sure, I thought he was being ridiculous. I'd been blaming my fatigue on the lingering emotional side effects of what had happened at the cabin, and I'd waved off my erratic period on the fact Emeric had removed my IUD and you can spot for weeks after that happens. As it turns out, I was very wrong.

After Doc confirmed the pregnancy, the way Emeric stared

459

at my flat stomach in awe and wonderment had tears bursting from my eyes. They weren't caused by sadness or anger, but of elation. I was happier in a way I hadn't anticipated, and every day that's passed since then, my joy has only grown.

Emeric Banes made me a wife and now he's going to make me a mom.

"They're loved," I tell my husband. "And cherished."

"Just as you."

Images of our baby growing up in a household where they're happy and they know they're wanted flood my mind. They will never have the traditional white picket fence upbringing, but what does that matter when I know without a shadow of a doubt they will be healthy and safe? They will be surrounded by people who care about them, and they will thrive because of it.

Before I have time to put up the mental barricade, the reoccurring thought I've been having since we first found out creeps into my brain. Emeric notices the second my face falls.

"What's wrong?"

I wave him off. "Nothing, I think I'm just being hormonal. It's silly."

Emeric rolls me onto my back so he can hover above me and look into my eyes. "Anything that can force you to make this heartbreaking face isn't silly, princess. Tell me."

My face cuddles into the hand he cups around my jaw and cheek. "Sometimes I mourn that our baby won't have grandparents, which is ridiculous, I know, because we wouldn't allow my parents to be in the same zip code of our child if they were still here, and your father... Daria would have been an amazing grandmother, and I guess I'm grieving for them that they'll never get to experience the love of a grandparent. See, I told you. It's silly."

I try to look away, but he doesn't allow me to. For a long,

heavy moment, he examines my face before looking deep into my eyes. "Did you know it's genetically impossible for a parent with brown eyes and a parent with blue eyes to have a baby with green eyes?"

I frown at him as my mind struggles to make sense of what he's telling me. "My parents had brown and blue eyes."

Emeric traces a slow circle around my left orbital bone. "For Imogen to have a child with eyes like yours, she would have had to be impregnated by someone with green or blue eyes." He does the same to my right orbital bone and then stops moving altogether. "You know who has green eyes?"

Dumbfounded, all I can do is shake my head.

"He's the same man who first warned me about the agreement Niall and Igor had made regarding your marriage to Bogdan, and he's the same man who sent me a warning text the day The Daria exploded," he reveals. My heart, which had just calmed down to a normal rhythm after having him fuck me in the ass for the first time, begins to pound again. "Brayden has green eyes."

"Are you trying to tell me—"

"Brayden Kennedy is your father."

EPILOGUE 2

EMERIC

Seven Months Later

"No, I'm not dealing with that tonight," I say into the phone I hold between my shoulder and chin. "The Turks have been itching for me to put my foot in one of their asses for months with how they've been shorting our shipments and talking to our competitors. If I go to the shipping yard to address this problem, I'm going to end up wearing someone's guts and that is not how I want to return home to my sleep-deprived wife, Nova. As it is, it's already two hours past when I told her I'd be home."

The Viking has the fucking balls to laugh at me. "I never thought I'd see the day the great Emeric Banes allowed himself to be bossed around and by a lady, no less."

Scowling, I take the key out of my pocket so I can open the door to my office here at Tartarus. There's a file I need for my meeting tomorrow with the legal team at Banes Corporation that I left on my desk. I just need to grab it real quick, and then I'll be able to head straight home to Rionach and Bellamy.

My wife gave me the greatest gift of my life when she fearlessly brought our daughter, Bellamy Aria Banes, into this word a couple weeks ago. Watching Rionach become a mother to our baby has only made my obsession and love for her grow fiercer, and my protective streak turn downright unbearable. Rionach thought I was overzealous with her safety before. That all looks like child's play now that we have Bellamy. I've rarely met a line I wasn't willing to across, but for my wife and child, I will joyfully skip over every moral line before I set it on fire if it means I keep my family safe. I understand even less now how Imogen was able to neglect her daughter like she did. Looking at my daughter is like looking at my beating heart outside of my chest. There's only one other person alive who will protect my girls like I would, and that is why I hired Brayden the week after we found out she was pregnant. Brayden protects and loves them like I do because they're his blood too.

Rionach's relationship with her birth father was slow growing at first. It took her a while to wrap her head around the fact Niall was never her real dad. They met for coffee and took walks around the park, and as they did, she got to know him as more than just her bodyguard. They both got to know each other as father and daughter. There has always been a bond between the pair and over the months as they've grown into their new dynamic, that bond has only grown stronger. I would never tell another soul, but the first time Rionach called Brayden Dad, his green eyes shone with unshed tears. I'm happy he's here because my wife deserves to have people who love her in her life.

"That lady just gave me a baby. She can ask for anything she damn well pleases," I snap as I turn the key in the lock. "Rionach is more important. The Turks can wait until tomorrow."

Nova releases a tired-sounding sigh in my ear. "That's probably for the best. Soren has therapy early in the morning before his tutor comes."

My assumption had been correct. Nova did end up taking Soren in after the events at the cabin. With a few strings pulled, the paperwork for Nova to officially adopt the boy were accepted a few months ago.

"He still hasn't said a word?"

"No, not one," Nova admits. "The therapists all say it's from his PTSD. People react to trauma in different ways. I saw this kind of thing all the time when I was in the service. Soren will get there one day. Until then, we just have to be patient with him."

"You're good for him," I say, pushing open the heavy wooden door. "Have a good night with your kid, Nova. I'll see you tomorrow."

"You do the same. Night, boss."

The line goes dead as I step into the dark office. My hand runs along the wall to flip the light switch, but my fingers never find it. A figure materializes from the shadows to my left near the bookcase there. I turn to face the threat head-on, but it's already too late. Their powerful body collides with mine. My arm lifts to block their fist aimed at my head, but I'm a millisecond too slow to block the one at my ribs.

Air knocked out of my lungs, I have no choice but to bend over and wheeze. My attacker takes advantage of this. One moment I'm standing on my own two feet and the next, I'm on my back and there's a gun pressed to my forehead.

His face is still concealed by the shadows and the dark hoodie he wears over his head. It's not until he leans closer that I make out the features of his face.

His very fucking familiar face. He's aged, but I would still recognize him anywhere. It doesn't matter how many years have passed.

"Ledger?"

"Hello, baby brother."

Golden Wings &
PRETTY THINGS

KAYLEIGH KING

GOLDEN WINGS & PRETTY THINGS

Chapter 1: Indie

July

"Watch out!" is the only warning I get before ice-cold water splashes across my skin, stunning me out of the relaxed state I'd found myself in. The group erupts into laughter and cheers as I fly up into a sitting position on the large inflatable dock just in time to watch Callan's head resurface.

His perfectly straight teeth flash when he finds me gaping at him in shock. "Did I get you?"

This causes even more laughter from our friends, who either lie on the dock with me or float on smaller, colorful rafts all around us. Callan is the only one fully submerged in the frigid water. It may be July, but Lake Washington never gets much above sixty-five degrees.

I look down at my now waterlogged yellow bikini and back at my boyfriend. "Maybe just a little bit." It takes effort to keep my face pulled in a scowl, a smile and laugh fighting to the surface.

Callan sees right through it though. "Only a little bit?" His muscular arms, tan from spending our summer on the lake, glide with ease through the water. He stops just feet in front of me, his dark-blue eyes searching me over. "Show me where I missed. I'm going to need to get there too," he taunts, his lips pulling into a smug smirk.

It's refreshing to see Callan like this. He's been so serious lately. I've tried asking him about it, but he's been cagey and vague with his answers. The desire to push him on it is strong, but when people pry me for information, it makes me want to punch them in the nose. So, I've tried my best to be patient.

He'll tell me when he's ready. Or at least I hope he will.

It's always been a toss-up with Callan. Since the beginning, it's felt like he's been holding back.

His hand wraps around my ankle, and with a harsh pull, he yanks me dangerously close to the edge. My nails dig into the surface to try and prevent him from pulling me farther. I have a feeling it's in vain though. My legs now dangle in the chilly water, making goose bumps dance across my skin.

"How about a quick dip, Indie?" Callan takes my other ankle in his grasp too. "Just so we can get all the places I missed."

"Don't you dare," I warn, my smile still threatening to escape no matter how much I don't want to get back in the lake. It took thirty minutes of lying in the sun to finally warm myself up after my brisk swim out here. Shore isn't far, forty feet at most, but it feels a lot farther when your muscles seize up from the icy water.

"Wouldn't dream of it. I promise." Callan lifts my foot out of the lake, bringing it to his mouth. He presses a kiss to the arch, his eyes locked with mine while he does.

It's a sweet moment he completely ruins by breaking his promise.

There's barely enough time for me to release a startled yelp before I'm fully submerged. The abrupt change in temperature is a shock to the system. My body stiffens and my chest aches.

It's only a few seconds I'm under, but it feels like minutes.

Not once do Callan's hands leave my body as he pulls me up and I surface, making a screeching sound. *"Holy shit!"* I shriek once I've sucked in a breath.

My boyfriend's laugh fills my ears while I shove the hair that's stuck to my forehead back. "Look how fast you get wet for me," he muses.

His hands flex on my hips and a shiver of anticipation shoots through me. It's been too long since we've slept together, and I miss being touched. In addition to his new evasive demeanor, he's been coming over less and less. When he does, he doesn't spend the night.

Since summer break started, he hasn't invited me over to his place on campus either. Before, there were times I spent two weeks there, not once returning to my own apartment. When we first got together almost six months ago, it was all heat. Didn't matter where we were, Callan's hands were on me, but now, I feel like I have to *work* to get him to show interest in me. And I'm starting to grow tired.

The red flags are basically glowing neon signs at this point.

I'm wary, but still pleased by his change in attitude now. I don't even care that our friends are five feet away from us, possibly eavesdropping.

"Mmmhmm," I agree, looping my arms around his neck, bringing our faces closer. "You got me wet, now what are you going to do about it?"

Callan's eyes flick to my lips, but where I should see desire reflected in them, all I find is contemplation.

Fuck this.

No longer waiting for him to make a move, I close the distance myself and test the waters.

I remember the first time Callan Banes kissed me. He literally swept me off my feet because he stole my ability to stand with a simple kiss. It was the epitome of making a girl weak in the knees. At the time, I thought that kiss was going to be my last first kiss.

Our kiss now confirms that I may have been wrong that night. Ever since then, I've been chasing that feeling like an addict chasing their first high. And now I'm starting to wonder if it's even worth it.

People sometimes describe kisses like a dance. There's passion and an elegant rhythm. The choreography should be exciting to perform. It feels taxing and boring now. Almost like it's a chore.

"Callan!" Hansen hollers from the dock I'd been yanked from, making Callan pull away. "Get your ass up here. I need a partner. Zadie and Lark think they have a chance against me in beer pong."

"Oh! I don't *think* anything," Zadie shouts back at Hansen from the hot-pink raft she sits on. "I *know*. I saw how you threw the ball last week at practice. We have this in the bag." Her hand points at the floating beer pong table, the various bracelets she wears chime every time she moves. "I'll bet you two hundred dollars right now that us *girls* can kick your ass six ways from Sunday."

Zadie Hill looks like a sweet little pixie, but she can verbally destroy the strongest of men. It's one of my favorite things to witness.

"Hey!" Hansen shouts at her. "Don't be a bitch."

"I'm not a bitch, I'm a fucking lady," Zadie hurls the ball in her lap at him. He catches it with ease, causing a scowl to form. "Stop talking and let's play."

472

Callan laughs, his handsome face pulling into a huge smile. "You're on, Hill." His quick kiss on my cheek feels like a dismissal as he pushes away from me without a second thought.

I stay there treading water, watching him swim away, not really sure what I'm waiting for him to do. Come back? Ask me to join? Just...*something*.

It's Lark, the stunning, soft-spoken blonde with the kind smile that yells over to me. Not my boyfriend. "Indie! Come on!" She motions to me with her hand. "We can take turns."

I think over her offer for all of two seconds before I shake my head at her. "No, it's okay," I lie. "You guys go ahead. I need to go inside and see if my mom called me back."

Not a complete lie. I have an event this weekend and need to make sure that everything is still okay on her end. When I told Mom my wish to participate in this competition, she dragged her feet on giving me her blessing. I'm counting down the days till I no longer need her permission.

For three years, I've squirreled away every loose piece of change and dollar bill I don't need to live so I can finally buy Jupiter from her. It's ridiculous that I would have to do such a thing when my dad gave me his beloved stallion as a gift when I was thirteen. The horse is rightfully mine, but when Dad died, my mom put her name on Jupiter's paperwork.

As long as she's the rightful owner of him, I need her permission for every event we participate in. It's just another way for her to keep me under her controlling thumb. Her new boyfriend isn't helping matters either.

Turning from my friends, I begin to swim back to the shore. I get no more than ten feet away when my name is called again.

This time it's Callan.

Treading water again, I look at the man I'm growing tired of wasting time on.

"I think my dad is working with that damn eagle again

today," he warns from his place on the floating dock. His hand shields his eyes from the high afternoon sun as he squints at me. "It's never done anything, but I don't trust it. Just be careful."

"Oh," I nod once. "Okay."

With that, Callan turns his back on me. Confirming what I already know in my heart and making the disappointment I feel grow.

I don't chase after boys, but our story is the oldest one in the book. A popular upperclassman takes interest in the wide-eyed freshman. She's shy but loves that he takes her everywhere, showing her off. He introduces her to everyone like he's truly proud to have her at his side. She believes his whispered sweet nothings and false promises. She becomes swept up in him and thrives off the heat between them.

But what happens when it turns stone cold, and the sweet nothings become lies?

You discover it was all smoke and mirrors, and you're left clinging to something that never existed in the first place.

Chapter 2: Astor

Jealousy.

It's a peculiar emotion to experience when you're a man who's never wanted for anything. Yet I find that unbecoming shade of green working its way through my system more frequently as of late. It appears during the smallest moments, like now, watching the eagle soar up ahead.

I envy the bird of prey's freedom and ability to fly away from it all. His liberty is fleeting, but every second is priceless to him. I crave those own seconds for myself.

With a low whistle, I call the bird back to me. It's taken years and endless patience to get to this point, but he doesn't hesitate even a moment before swooping back toward the ground. The piece of rabbit leg I have in the leather pouch at my side keeps him coming back.

It's his reward.

Protected by a thick leather glove, he lands gracefully on my arm. He makes a low squawking sound, his yellow, ever-observant eyes looking for the treat he knows he's owed.

"Good boy," I praise, stroking a hand down his brown feathers before reattaching the leash to the leather straps around his ankles. It took us a long time to get here, but the contact no longer makes him uneasy. It wasn't an easy road, and I will forever carry scars on my hands and forearms as reminders of our progress.

The outcome has been more than worth it.

Taking his reward from me, he holds the piece of meat in his talons and eats happily as I carry him to the enclosure on the left side of the property. It's built in a dome shape, tight-knit black netting covering the whole structure. It's large enough the bird will never feel cooped up, and in the middle is a raised wooden building—almost like a small tree house—where he can escape the Washington rains.

Releasing the tied leash from his foot, I free him, lingering only a moment to watch him fly to a perch. His head nods once, as if he's bidding me farewell as I close the keypad-protected door behind me and head back toward my house.

The sound of boisterous laughter and yelling comes from the lake below, reminding me that I'll have another day of college kids in and out of my house. Early in the summer, I made the mistake of allowing Callan to have a few friends over. He has a house on campus he rents with a friend, but they wanted to swim in the lake my house sits on.

Had I known it was going to turn into a weekly event

throughout the entire break, I would have rethought my original answer.

Especially had I known he would always bring *her* here.

I've never been one to deny myself what I want, but she is the exception. I've been forced to restrain my cravings for months—something that doesn't come naturally but it is required of me.

It would have been better had she never been put in my sights, but now that I know she exists, I can't seem to escape her.

Now is no different.

I enter through the tall glass backdoors of my home to find the main source of my growing jealousy standing in my kitchen.

The small triangles of her bikini cover little, revealing her sun-kissed skin. She doesn't hear me enter and her attention remains locked on the phone in her hand.

Even though I know I shouldn't, I take this moment to observe the girl who's unintentionally captured my attention.

She stands on a dish towel in an attempt to not get water on my hardwood floors, but it's not working. Small puddles are forming at her feet. A steady drip comes from her dark hair that doesn't quite reach her shoulders. I watch as a drop falls down her chest. My eyes follow the bead as it travels down her body, stopping only when it disappears into the waistband of her bright-yellow bottoms.

The unwelcome desire I feel for the girl rears its ugly head. My teeth clench in anger knowing that, without even trying, she's crawled under my skin. I'm even more infuriated by the fact I've allowed someone so unattainable to do so.

It's one thing to be jealous of another man, it's another thing entirely to be jealous of your own son.

And when I look at Indie Riverton, I'm uncontrollably

envious that my son found her first and I'm angry he doesn't fully appreciate the prize he's obtained.

A siren whose song I must ignore.

She's a pretty thing that I'm aching to play with.

A toy that isn't mine to break.

Burying the ill-advised stirrings she causes, I focus on the resentment knowing I can't have her, and I clear my throat harshly.

Her amber eyes drift from the screen and noticeably widen when she finds me standing here. "Mr. Banes," she gasps. "I didn't see you there."

I shift forward a foot, hands behind my back. "You're dripping water on my floors."

She blinks slowly at me as if she's not understanding my remark. Finally, it clicks, and she quickly says, "*Crap.* I'm so sorry. I needed to check my phone, and I forgot to bring my towel up with me." Keeping her feet planted on the small towel, she reaches for the other dish towel that's folded neatly on the marble countertop. "I'll clean it up," she promises.

Before I can say another word, she squats down and wipes at the puddles on the hardwood. With each one she cleans, another appears from the water still escaping her drenched hair.

Shaking my head, I spin on my heels and head toward the laundry room where I know the housekeeper left a pile of fresh towels.

I return to find her on her hands and knees, a sight that makes my hands flex. Stepping closer, I dangle the towel off my fingertip in front of her face.

Indie's chin lifts, our eyes locking. The prettiest blush I've ever seen spreads across her face as her thin fingers wrap around the offering. "Thank you," she whispers with a sheepish smile.

I don't offer any reply or extend my hand to help her stand. I merely watch the way she nibbles on her bottom lip. It's a nervous tic I've seen her do many times. She does it when she's waiting for Callan to look at her or even acknowledge her. Her big doe-like eyes stare at him, silently pleading for him to remember that she's there, but he never does.

I've never been one to interfere with my son's personal life, and in truth, he's never responded well to hand-holding. He needs to make these mistakes so he can learn from them. He'll realize too late that he's fucked up. Though, I'm not convinced his retreat from her hasn't been methodically planned.

"Why are you in here?" I ask. "Shouldn't you be down there with the rest of them?" *With my son.*

Returning to her feet, Indie uses the towel to ring out the moisture from her hair. "I needed a break from the sun." She tells a lie better than most, but the falsehood is written in her amber eyes when she speaks. "And I've been waiting for my mom to get back to me all day about a show jumping event I have this Sunday. She's out of town with her boyfriend, so getting a hold of her has been tricky."

Another thing I've noticed is she also rambles when she's nervous. It shouldn't please me as much as it does that I've caused such a reaction from her. It's not the reaction I desire, but then again, I shouldn't be craving a single thing from her.

"You turned down the spot on our equestrian team along with the scholarship that came with it, did you not?" It was an abuse of my power to look into her school records, but along with my jealousy, my curiosity was also piqued. "Why would you opt for a merit-based scholarship that covers less when you could have received a full ride?"

My question takes Indie by surprise. Her mouth opens and closes a couple of times before she finally finds her words. "I always forget you're the university president and know all this stuff about everyone."

"Not everyone."

Her mouth tilts in a playful smile. "So, I'm pretty special then, huh?"

"No." My correction comes with a terse edge, instantly killing her smile. "When my son is dating a fellow student, I tend to take an interest. I'm not fond of having strangers in my home to begin with, and Callan's judgment when it comes to the girls he brings home has been less than ideal."

After his senior year of high school, it went downhill fast and that is partially why I'm shocked he picked someone like Indie.

At the mention of dating Callan, Indie's face falls further, and her hands tighten around the white towel she's still holding. "*Right,* obviously." She nods. "That makes sense."

"Does mentioning my son's past conquests upset you?"

"Upset me? Not at all." Indie makes a scoffing noise before she can help it. It appears it comes as a surprise to even her by the way she covers her mouth. "I... I just mean, I know everyone has a past, and Callan is no different." She attempts to recover, but the damage has been done.

Silence falls between us when I don't offer a reply. Instead, I try to uncover the secrets she keeps guarded behind her pretty face.

She breaks it by answering my earlier question. "I'm good at what I do because of the horse I ride. We're a team, and if I can't compete with him, there's no point in me competing at all. My mom wouldn't allow me to bring him here to Seattle, and without her blessing, my hands were tied. I took the next best option the school offered me, which was the merit scholarship."

"I suppose that makes sense. It takes a long time to establish a bond with an animal, and once they're formed, they're not easily replaced."

Indie glances toward the backyard where I'd just been with the eagle. "I can't begin to imagine the kind of time it took you to bond with him. The patience alone to train an animal like him must have been intense. *How* exactly does one train a golden eagle?"

With her standing this close, I can't help my eyes from wandering across her tanned skin or my lungs from inhaling her. The sunscreen she wears smells of coconut and there's a light trail of freckles on her nose from spending her summer days lounging in my backyard.

"Training something is easy once you know what motivates them, Indie," I begin, my tone sounding darker than I intend it to, but her nearness is destroying my resolve.

Indie picks up on it and her teeth stop their nibbling on her bottom lip. Her eyes lock with mine and her breath shudders as the air suddenly shifts between us. She's looked at me before, but it's as if this is the first time she's truly allowing herself to *see* me.

"For the eagle, it's the promise of food. As long as I continue to reward him, he'll come when I call. Humans are just as easy. They want money, power, or sex. Once you know which they desire, you can have them eating out of your hand just like the eagle does mine."

She stares up at me with her lips parted and chest rising faster than before. My own heart thuds against my chest and my mind fills with the filthy things I would do to her if she were my plaything.

Indie swallows hard, her throat bobbing. "Which one do you crave?" she boldly asks.

My hand reaches out and I push the wet strand of hair that sticks to her blushing cheek behind her ear. "I don't crave just one, I want all of them," I pause, my hand lingering longer on her skin than it should. "And I'll accept nothing less."

I'm already playing with fire and toeing the line that's been drawn in the sand.

To hell with it.

There are a million reasons to keep my distance, the biggest ones being Indie is Callan's girlfriend and a student at my university, but that doesn't stop me. *Can't* stop me.

Shifting forward another step, I bow my head. I'm not sure if she's even aware that she reacts and moves closer. Her chin tilts up toward me, further bridging the space between us. She's shorter than me by many inches, but we're close enough that I can feel her shaky breath across my chin.

"You would be just as easy," I tell her darkly, eyes cutting to her pink lips. "Once I figured out which reward you craved, I could make you just as obedient. Just like him, you'll come when I call." Even to me, I'm not sure if this is a threat or a promise. Maybe it's a mixture of both. "Just something to keep in mind." Searching for the resolve I originally entered the room with, I harden myself once more. "Please do bring a towel with you next time, Indie. I would hate to see you ruin my floors."

It's best for the both of us that I turn and leave before she can respond.

REVIEWS

Thank you for reading ***Black Wings & Stolen Things***! I hope you love Emeric and Rionach as much as I do, and that I checked off all your kinky boxes!

I would be forever grateful if you considered leaving a review on Amazon, Goodreads, and/or Bookbub. Reivews help fellow readers find and discover new books just like this one!

If you make a post on Instagram or Tiktok, be sure to tag me so I can see it!

-kk

ACKNOWLEDGMENTS

First and foremost I have to thank my **readers** for sticking around and waiting while I was getting my life together. Thank you for being patient with me between these past two releases. I know there was a big gap, and you'll never know how much I appreciate you waiting for me.

Jess & Tegan: Thank you for ~~forcing me~~ telling me to write this book before all my other ideas and for holding my hand through it. Thank you for telling me my words are pretty when I didn't believe it myself.

Greer: You will always be my number one and my voice of reason when need it.

To my Betas: Thank you for taking the time to read my unpolished work and for helping me make it pretty. Also, thank you for dealing with my bullshit timeline. I know you all have lives and are busy, so thank you for making the time to read.

Rumi: Girl... thank you so fucking much for taking me on as a client. Working with you has been amazing. Remember when I told you this book was going to be 60k words? Lmfao, sorry I lied.

ABOUT THE AUTHOR

USA Today Bestselling author Kayleigh King is a writer of contemporary and paranormal romance. She creates love stories that will stick with you, almost like they're haunting you.

She's a Diet Coke and cold brew addict, sharing music is her love language, and she seriously lacks a filter. Anything she thinks, she usually says. And if she doesn't say it, her facial expressions will say it for her. Currently residing in Denver Colorado, you'll never find her on a snowboard since she avoids the snow like the plague.

Want to chat about books, music, or life in general? Make sure you join her Facebook reader group and follow her on Instagram. Her DMs are always open to her readers.

ALSO BY KAYLEIGH KING

Fractured Rhymes

Golden Wings & Pretty Things

Black Wings & Stolen Things

Butterflies & Vicious Lies

The Crimson Crown Duet

Bloody Kingdom

Midnight Queen

The White Wolf Prophecy Series

Wolf Bound

Soul Bound

Shadow Bound

Fire Bound

Standalone Books

Catching Lightning

Printed in Poland
by Amazon Fulfillment
Poland Sp. z o.o., Wrocław

35747784R00285